OTHER BOOKS AND AUDIO BOOKS
BY GALE SEARS:

Autumn Sky

Until the Dawn

a novel

GALE SEARS

Covenant Communications, Inc.

Covenant

Cover art:

  Our Legacy © Al Rounds. For print information call 801-278-6789 or visit us at www.alrounds.com.

Cover design copyrighted 2006 by Covenant Communications, Inc.

Published by Covenant Communications, Inc.
American Fork, Utah

Printed in Canada
First Printing: May 2006

12 11 10 09 08 07 06   10 9 8 7 6 5 4 3 2 1

ISBN 1-59811-074-8

To my mom,
who always believed in me

ACKNOWLEDGEMENTS

To Teri Boldt—the first reader. Also to Roxann Glassey, Cindi Meier, Nancy Tullis, and Chris Bond—wonderful readers and friends. To Annette Capener for going more than a year misspelled. To Rondi Mann for insights into Brussels. To Dawn Bates for keeping me sane and in shape. To Chandler for taking up the slack. To Shauna Chymboryk for editing perseverance above and beyond the call of duty. To Angela Eschler, my enigmatic and supportive editor. And to Larry Zuckerman for his insightful book on Belgium during the Great War. Finally to Shauna Humphreys for her patience in answering all my questions, her editorial insight, and for sharing genuine excitement over that first acceptance. I will miss her, but wish her happiness in her new life.

Chapter One

"I think the gold's buried over here!" Elias Erickson yelled, holding his shovel high then plunging it into the soil at his feet.

Nephi looked across the lush pastureland to where his dark-haired brother stood digging in earnest. He shook his head in disgust, hefted his pickax, and trudged across the field. The hot July sun burned onto his face. It had to be a hundred degrees, but his body felt cold. Maybe the shame of what they were doing was making him sick. This was their grandfather's property, and they had no right to be tearing apart his field in search of supposed treasure.

"Hey! Hold on a minute," Nephi cajoled as he came to his brother's side. "Do you really think there's treasure buried here?"

Elias grunted as he shoved the blade into the ground with his boot. "Why would he make up such a story? If he says he brought gold from Denmark and buried it here in his pasture, who are we to call him a liar?"

"Elias, he told us that story when we were youngsters, along with the story of the troll queen and the two-headed dog. He told us lots of stories."

"Yeah, well, this one I believe," Elias said, wiping sweat from his face. "So get busy."

Nephi didn't move. "It's not right."

Elias glared at him. "Don't be getting righteous on me, little brother! You're the one who went gallivanting off to California and brought back a wife to support. Do you expect our mother to take care of you two forever?"

Nephi's face flushed with shame, and his grip tightened on the handle of the pickax. Why was Elias treating him with such contempt? They had always been close, sons of the second wife, united against the world. Nephi bit back the angry words that knotted in his chest. After all, Elias was right. He had made a mess of his life. *Just dig and forget about everything else.* He swung the pickax high and let it fall at the edge of the hole Elias had started. A large chunk of ground fell away, and Nephi saw a glint of metal tumble down the edge of the dark earth. He dropped to his knees and grabbed for it, but Elias was faster. His fingers closed around the treasure, and with a whoop he brought it up out of the dirt.

"There now, brother!" Elias said, jumping up and waving his clenched fist in Nephi's face. "We'd better think twice about troll queens and two-headed dogs, wouldn't you say?"

Nephi shaded his eyes from the sun and watched as Elias opened his fingers to reveal the coin. The brown eyes hardened, and the smile was smothered by a scowl.

"What? What is it?" Nephi asked.

"We've been digging all morning for this?" Elias growled.

"What is it?" Nephi asked again.

"Nothing but junk," Elias answered bitterly, throwing the piece back into the hole. "I'm done for the day," he added through clenched teeth. "I'm going in for dinner."

Nephi didn't answer him or even turn in his direction, for his attention was riveted on the silver object half buried in the mud at the bottom of the hole, the delicate ivy embossing clotted with dirt. His heart grieved, for he knew this piece of jewelry. It had been his mother's picture locket, and he'd given it to his wife before they were married—given it to her on her birthday to ease some of her sorrow. "Alaina, why would you throw this away?" Nephi whispered, closing his mind against an answer. He felt an ache in his throat as he reached down to pick up the trinket. Gently he brushed away the bits of soil and opened the clasp. Unwillingly his eyes took in the two pictures he had drawn for her, now stained and smeared with muddy water. His mind backed away again from the possibility that by discarding the locket his wife was discarding him. He knew the pictures of the apple tree and of Samuel Lund, Alaina's father, could be redrawn, but he could not draw love from a woman who saw him only as a friend. He stood. No. It didn't make sense for her to throw away the locket. He knew she cherished the gift—cherished the memories the drawings brought of a father and a home so recently taken from her. Hadn't she said she would keep it forever? Hadn't he seen her undo the clasp and look lovingly at the pictures many times a day?

"Nephi?"

He stiffened at the sound of her voice, but he could not answer her.

"Nephi?"

Her voice reached through the darkness, and he opened his eyes. He found his face dangerously near to the potbellied stove used to heat their small, rented cabin. He sat back instinctively, pulling a quilt around him. He took a deep breath of cold air and tried to clear his thinking.

Alaina giggled. "Are you all right?"

"It's freezing," he said in a muddled voice.

"You need to build up the fire," she answered simply.

"Where are we?"

"Nephi Erickson, are you awake?" Alaina asked in a stronger voice.

He sat for a moment staring at her through the morning dimness. "Are we still in Lake Tahoe?"

"We are," she answered slowly. "This is our last day here."

He sat quietly, noting the regret in her voice. It was a feeling he mirrored, as the short time they'd spent in the beauty and peace of this high mountain retreat had sheltered them from the sorrow left behind and the challenge in front of them. In the afternoon they would catch the number 3 train out of Tahoe City into Truckee, where they would pick up Alaina's prize filly from Mr. Gray's boarding stable. They would then secure passage on the evening train to Reno, then on to Utah and his home. Home. Nephi knew the dream of his brother Elias and the castaway locket was prompted by his fear and reluctance to return to Salt Lake City. He would have loved to stay at the farm in California, but that was not an option.

Pale light filtered through the cabin windows, and Nephi could see that Alaina was looking at him with a wondering expression. "I . . .

must have been dreaming," he said sheepishly, ruffling his hair and yawning.

Alaina sat up Indian style with two quilts wrapped around her. "I figured as much, the way you were gibbering in your sleep."

Nephi focused on her. "What did I say?"

"I couldn't tell you," she said, smiling. "It was just a lot of mumbling."

"Oh," he answered, relieved.

"How about wood for the fire?" she said, poking one finger towards the wood box.

"Oh! Sorry," Nephi answered. He reached over, grabbed a log, and used it to open the latch on the metal door. He then threw the piece of pine onto the hot coals. As he blew on the embers to start a flame, he tried to wipe away the unsettling images of his dream.

"I thought I was the dreamer," Alaina said, edging nearer to the stove. "Do you want to tell me what yours was about?"

Nephi shook his head. "No. I mean, no . . . no. It was nothing important." Nonetheless, he checked for the locket and was relieved to find it resting against the bodice of her nightdress. *It was only a silly dream,* he reassured himself. "All right, I'm getting up," he announced, giving his wife time to turn her face to the wall. He stood, stripping off his old shirt and reaching for a clean one hanging from a peg near the stovepipe. "All right, I'm dressed," he said, pulling on his boots. "I'll wait for you down by the lake."

Alaina nodded as he shrugged on his coat and moved into the clear-skied morning. It had become a ritual for them, sitting quietly together on the log bench overlooking the lake, then going into Mrs. Lawson's kitchen and wolfing down a huge breakfast. Alaina sighed as she stood to dress. She positioned herself as close to the little stove as possible and quickly put on her clothes. Once boots, coat, and wool scarf were in place, she took a moment to look at the pictures in her locket. She smiled at the likeness of her father. She missed him terribly. This morning, however, as she looked at the perfect picture, she found the usual stab of loneliness blunted by images of Nephi yawning and ruffling his hair. She shifted her gaze to the skillfully drawn apple tree—this image always made her think of her sweet sister Eleanor and their times together tromping through the orchards. But this morning she remembered Nephi helping her to pick the last of the apples and send them off to market. He was a good man who had married her to save the farm, only to find that her mother had sold the property out from under them. Alaina shook her head and pulled on her mittens. She wouldn't think of her mother, now transplanted to Aunt Ida's home in San Francisco—taking with her Kathryn and dear Eleanor. How she missed Eleanor. *Enough of that.* If she allowed her mind to gnaw on past injustices and loneliness, she and Nephi's final day of adventuring would be spoiled by bitter feelings. She opened the cabin door and stepped out into the snow-clad wonderland. One final image of her mother's elegant face flickered through her mind before being replaced by blue sky and the pungent smell of pine. Alaina breathed deeply and marched off through the snow to find her husband.

Chapter Two

The Victorian house at 238 Beacon Street, San Francisco, had been through fire, flood, and earthquake; it had welcomed joy and sheltered grief; but now within its stately walls there were harsh words and strife, and as in most of life's conflicts, the weight of blame fell on the shoulders of the lower class.

Kerri McKee threw down her maid's cap in the servants' hall and kicked the coal bucket. "Daft woman! The nerve of her to think she has the authority to sack me!"

"Hush, Kerri, they'll hear you upstairs."

The unrepentant girl turned to glare at her coworker and friend. "Don't be shushing me now, Ina Bell Latham, for I'll have none of it. I've put up with that mad woman for a month, and my voice can fly up there like a croaking raven."

"We have all put up with her."

"Aye, but 'twas me she gave notice, not you." Kerri's Scottish brogue came heavy with the temper, and Ina Bell whimpered as she heard purposeful footsteps echoing down the hallway.

"Now see what you've done?" Ina Bell hissed at her friend, but Miss McKee did not answer. She stood stiff and defiant, daring anyone to knock her down, but Ina Bell watched the fury drain from her face, leaving her peaked.

Mr. Palmer, the head butler, stood silently at the door of the servants' hall fixing each girl with a disdainful stare that neither would meet. "Miss Latham," he said finally, "return to your polishing. Miss McKee, you will accompany me to the parlor." He turned and began walking down the hall towards the back staircase, but Kerri McKee did not follow.

Ina Bell choked. "Are you mad? Get going!" Doubt flickered across Kerri's face, but she held her place. "I mean it, Kerri; do you want to lose your position?" Mr. Palmer's footfalls were becoming fainter. "There's nowhere else for you to go!"

Kerri's feet began to move. She came up quickly and quietly behind Mr. Palmer, who had stopped at the bottom of the stairs, his shiny boot pausing on the first rise. "I see that wiser heads have prevailed. You must thank Miss Latham. Had you not followed, Miss McKee, I would have had no choice but to throw you out into the street." He continued his march, and Kerri followed. She was filled with so much anger and humiliation that her head hurt, and she tripped several times. She felt like kicking everything in sight or screaming, but, when they reached the landing, she clenched her jaw and straightened her cap.

Oriental rugs softened their footsteps as they proceeded towards the parlor, and Kerri glared at the intricate parquet flooring on either side of the rugs. How often had she been down on her hands and knees polishing that wood? A growl came into her throat, and Mr. Palmer stopped abruptly. He turned to her with narrowed eyes.

"That will be enough of that," he said, marking each syllable in sotto voce, "unless you wish to abandon your post here."

Kerri's stomach flipped, and she shook her head.

"Very well then." Mr. Palmer opened the door to the parlor and led her inside.

Mrs. Westfield, mistress of the house, sat on the green velvet sofa trying to look calm and stern, but not succeeding. She held a large lace handkerchief, which she kept absentmindedly wrapping around her fingers. As Mr. Palmer approached, she sat straighter and cupped her hands in her lap, which indeed made her look more imposing, but Kerri observed a twitch at the corner of her mouth, and she knew that even in her stiff, black mourning dress and rows of expensive pearls, Mrs. Westfield was a doe frightened out of cover.

Mr. Palmer nodded his head. "Miss McKee, madam."

Kerri curtsied.

Mrs. Westfield took a breath and began speaking. Her voice was thin and girlish. It was an acceptable voice for speaking of the arrangement of flowers or the proper polishing of the silver, but carried no authority whatsoever when it came to reprimands. Out of the corner of her eye Kerri saw Mr. Palmer purse his lips, and she had to force herself not to smile.

"Miss McKee, you . . . you have greatly upset my sister. She says you were trying to steal her dressing gown. That she woke to find you sneaking out of her room with her dressing gown. I will not tolerate thievery in this house. Your father and mother, God rest their souls, were good, honest workers, and I shudder to think of their feelings. Mr. Westfield and I kept you on . . ."

Kerri held her temper. "Excuse me, ma'am. I was not tryin' to steal anything. I have never taken so much as a sewing pin that didn't belong to me."

Mrs. Westfield's eyes widened. "My sister says you had the dressing gown in your hand."

"Yes, ma'am. I went in to make up the room, but found Mrs. Lund still asleep. I was quietly on my way out when I noticed the dressing gown. It had a tea stain on the front, and I was takin' it down to be laundered."

"Well . . ." Mrs. Westfield rose and moved to the fireplace. "Well, that is quite a story."

"And true as sunrise. You can check the gown yourself."

"My sister also said you raised your voice to her."

Kerri hesitated. "Only after she sacked me. I was trying to get her to see reason."

Mrs. Westfield looked as though she might faint. "You . . . you have no right to . . ." She paced the room. "I have never heard of such . . . my sister is a guest in this house, and she has every right to reprimand you or give you notice."

The parlor door opened, and Mrs. Westfield's niece entered.

"This is not a good time, Eleanor!" her aunt snapped.

"I'm sorry to bother you, Aunt Ida, but I've just had a talk with Mother."

Mrs. Westfield waved her handkerchief at Kerri. "Yes, but I have this situation to take care of."

"I know, and I think I may be able to help." Eleanor offered Kerri a genuine smile of reassurance.

Kerri liked this girl. At fifteen, Miss Lund was only a few years her junior, but she seemed older. Perhaps it was the way she cared for her mother, or her independent spirit. She wasn't a grand-looking girl, but she more than made up for that in kindness and wit.

"Miss McKee has offended your mother," Aunt Ida said petulantly.

"I'm sure she didn't mean to," Eleanor replied, bringing her mother's dressing gown from behind her back to exhibit the obvious tea stain. Eleanor waited for her aunt to speak.

"Well, yes . . . I see . . . I see that." She ran her hand over her pearls. "Still, it does not give a servant the right to raise their voice to their betters."

Kerri saw Miss Lund's grip tighten around the dressing gown, and a look of pity wash her face.

"Yes, I am sure that is most upsetting to you, Auntie," Eleanor soothed, stepping closer to her aunt and lowering her voice. "But I'm also sure that Miss McKee was not trying to be rude. I think she was simply doing her job, and when mother accused her, she was trying to explain." Mrs. Westfield twisted her handkerchief, finding it difficult to reply. Eleanor gently took her aunt's hand. "We know that mother's mind does not always grasp the reality of a situation, and I think allowances should be made."

Mrs. Westfield's eyes flickered to Miss McKee and Mr. Palmer, hoping Eleanor's words had not been overheard. Her sister Elizabeth had lost her husband only a few months after Mrs. Westfield's sweet Cedrick had died, but, unlike her own handling of grief, her sister's mind seemed to have strayed from reason and propriety. Such family secrets were certainly not to be discussed in front of the staff—secrets that would most assuredly be fodder for gossip understair.

Eleanor let go of her aunt's hand and stepped back. "You don't want to let Miss McKee go, do you?"

Her aunt's eyes blinked several times. "Well . . . no, of course not. Her father and mother were with us for fifteen years. Miss McKee grew from a child understair."

Eleanor smiled. "Then it's settled."

"But," Mrs. Westfield pressed, "she must apologize to my sister. I insist. Oh, yes. I insist on that."

Eleanor turned to look at Kerri, who lowered her head contritely.

"Yes, ma'am, of course. I truly didn't mean to offend anyone."

Smart girl, Eleanor thought, moving to Kerri and handing her the dressing gown. "If you will see that this is cleaned then, Miss McKee?"

"Certainly, miss."

"And thank you for keeping such careful watch of my mother's things." She gave Kerri a wink, which made the servant girl smile.

Mr. Palmer had had enough. "Come, Miss McKee, there's work to be done."

"Yes, sir."

He paused before leaving. "Is there anything you need, madam?"

"Yes, Palmer, please have Cook send dinner to my room. I will be indisposed for the rest of the day."

"Yes, madam." He left the parlor with Miss McKee following him.

Eleanor felt sorry for her aunt. The woman hated conflict and did not have the mental prowess to run the entire house. Her husband, Cedrick, had been the one to supervise everything, with Ida serving as his simple, fluttery companion. Cedrick had died the end of June, leaving his little wife in a state of grief and dismay. Having her widowed sister and two nieces move in six months later was surely pushing her fragile sensibilities to their limit.

Eleanor looked kindly on her auntie's face, and saw pale reflections of her mother's striking features. Aunt Ida did not have mother's stiff carriage, nor had she been blessed with the beautiful chestnut hair. Ida's light brown hair was flecked with gray, and she wore it pulled up on top of her head in a mass of curls and twists, only adding to the picture of innocent inability.

Mrs. Westfield picked up her shawl from the back of the sofa and tucked her handkerchief into the pocket of her dress. "So, that's done with then."

"Yes, Auntie."

"And your mother won't be angry with me?"

"No, ma'am. I'll explain everything to her." Eleanor smiled. "It is your home, Aunt Ida."

"Well, yes . . . yes, that's true. It is my home." She handed the shawl to Eleanor, who laid it across her aunt's shoulders. "I'll be going to my room now."

"Yes, ma'am."

"Oh, and please see that Kathryn does not make too much noise."

"She's out with her nanny at the moment, but when Miss Clawson brings her in, I'll tell them."

"Thank you, Eleanor." Mrs. Westfield waited at the door for her niece to open it, passing out into the front foyer in a rustle of stiff taffeta.

Eleanor watched her aunt ascend the stairs, then turned back into the parlor and closed the doors. Normally the doors stood open so visitors would see the lavishly appointed parlor as soon as they entered, but Eleanor wanted solitude. She looked around at the extravagant surroundings and shook her head. Even after a month she found the room suffocating. It was beautiful, to be sure, but she did not care for the heavy orange and green brocade draperies, or the muted gold wallpaper covered with orange birds, or the carpeting festooned with green vines. She longed for the plain white walls and pine-planked flooring of their farmhouse in the Sierra foothills.

Eleanor moved quickly to the window, pushing back the lace underlay and looking out into the formal courtyard. It wasn't her meadowland or fruit trees, but at least there were growing things. Even in January there were growing things. Tears came to her eyes, and she pressed her hand against the glass to distract herself from sorrow. She felt ashamed of her self-pity, knowing that if *she* was mourning the loss of the farm, her older sister's heart was breaking. For years, Alaina had been their father's favored helper in the groves, joyously content with hard work and harvest. Eleanor didn't mind hard work, but her fulfillment lay in books and scholarship. At sixteen, her brother, James, cared more for animals than apples, and her little sister, Kathryn, cared only that her needs were met. With their father's death, their lives had been torn apart, and Eleanor wondered if there would ever be a chance of mending them. She sat on the window bench and laid her head against the glass. Noisy automobiles passed on the street, and Eleanor longed for the quiet of the farm; she longed for her father, Samuel, with his tender ways and ready humor; she longed for her sister Alaina. How strange their lives had become. Eleanor closed her eyes and thought about her sister's wedding at the Methodist church in Sutter Creek—Pastor Wilton pronouncing the words that would forever change Alaina's life; their farmhand, Nephi Erickson, holding the hand of his bride and looking as though he'd been given the world; their schoolteacher, Miss Johnson, watching Alaina with pride; their sweet neighbor, Mr. Robinson, in tears; and his son Daniel . . .

Eleanor stood abruptly, wiping the moisture from her cheeks and stamping her foot. *What a goose, Eleanor Lund! There is no time for melancholy.* She straightened the lace curtain and turned to leave. Just as she reached the doors, someone knocked from the other side. Eleanor opened the doors to a wide-eyed servant girl.

Ina Bell Latham held up her polishing basket as if in explanation. "Oh! Oh, I'm sorry, miss! I thought everyone had gone out," she sputtered. With reddened face, the young girl curtsied and backed away.

"Wait, Miss Latham, it's all right. I didn't mean to startle you. I'm just leaving, so the room is empty," Eleanor said.

"Yes. Thank you, miss." Ina Bell curtsied again and hurried into the parlor.

Eleanor hesitated and then followed her. "Miss Latham."

Ina Bell turned quickly. "Yes, miss?"

"Could I ask you for something?"

"Yes, miss, of course."

"Could we talk?"

"I beg your pardon, miss?"

"Talk. Could we sit down and talk? You seem to be about my sister's age, and I . . . how old are you?"

"Seventeen, miss."

Eleanor sat down on the sofa. "My brother, James, turns seventeen in March."

Ina Bell stared at her. "Actually, Miss Lund, I don't think it's allowed."

"Excuse me?"

The young maid looked nervously at the open parlor doors. "I don't think we're allowed to talk. Besides, I have my work to do."

Eleanor brightened. "I could help you!"

A touch of panic imprinted itself onto Ina Bell's face. "Oh, no! If Mr. Palmer saw such goings-on I'd be sacked for sure."

Eleanor sat back dejectedly. "Sorry."

Ina Bell took out the rags and polishing bottle, watching the dark-haired girl carefully. "But, I suppose I could go on with my cleaning, and it would only be proper if I answered your questions. Do you think there's harm in that?"

The light came back into Eleanor's face. "No harm at all!"

Ina Bell smiled and went about her work.

Eleanor slipped off her shoes and tucked her feet up under herself. The maid raised her eyebrows, but did not comment. She reminded herself that Miss Lund had been brought up on a farm, where the rules of decorum were probably quite different. Then again, Eleanor's mother was Mrs. Westfield's sister, and *their* proper upbringing had been strictly enforced. She knew that etiquette must have been passed down to the Lund children because Kathryn, the youngest child, though quite churlish, did know her manners.

Eleanor looked up at her with a sly smile. "This is very improper, isn't it?" she said, seeming to read the servant girl's thoughts. "I know Mother would give me a severe scolding if she found me sitting like this."

Ina Bell smiled at the note of defiance in her voice. "Actually, miss, that's how I sit on my bed at the end of a long day."

"Really? It is comfortable, isn't it?"

"It is, miss."

"Miss Latham, would you please call me Eleanor?"

Ina Bell hesitated. "I will, miss, but only when there's no one else to hear."

"Fair enough. And may I call you Ina Bell?"

"Yes, miss. Of course."

"I've wanted to talk to you and Miss McKee for ever so long, but didn't want to get you into trouble. You're always so busy," she said, and Ina Bell smiled. "I envy you, you know," Eleanor continued. "I miss work. During the harvest, we'd work twelve to fourteen hours every day."

"Didn't you go to school?"

"Oh yes, of course. In September and October I'd work after school—drying fruit, harvesting the garden, or canning. Then there was the cooking and cleaning and mending." Eleanor's thoughts drifted off to another place and time, and Ina Bell looked at her with deeper insight.

"I would love all that work outdoors," Miss Latham said, running her cloth over the marble-topped coffee table. "All that fresh air and sunshine sounds like heaven."

Eleanor laughed. "Actually, mucking out the chicken coop when its thirty degrees is more like the other place."

Ina Bell grimaced. "I guess every occupation has its bad points."

Eleanor nodded. "Have you been a servant all your life?"

"Well, since I was the age for it."

"And you've always lived here?"

Ina Bell picked up a bronze figurine to dust. "At Westfield House?" She shook her head. "No. I've only been here two years. I came up when I was your age."

"Came up? Came up from where?"

"Los Angeles. Mr. Knight sent me from his service to work for his daughter. My mother and father are still at the mansion there."

"Grandfather's mansion?"

"Yes, miss."

"You lived with my grandfather?"

Ina Bell smiled.

"What?" Eleanor asked, trying to figure out what had amused the girl.

"It just seems funny to hear Mr. Knight called Grandfather."

"Yes. I suppose so. What is he like?" Eleanor asked leaning forward.

"Excuse me, miss?"

"My grandfather. Tell me about him."

"Oh, I couldn't do that, Miss Eleanor. It wouldn't be proper." She dusted the mantel. "You've never met him?"

"No. Never. I've seen a few photographs. He and Grandmother always look so distant and elegant."

"They are very high in society, that's for sure. The Knight house has seen dinners for fifty people many times, with the mayor and governor attending."

Eleanor was staggered. "Fifty? Fifty people? Where do they all sit?"

Ina Bell laughed. "At the table in the grand hall."

Eleanor thought of the small table in their kitchen at the farm, and found it hard to imagine a room, let alone a table, that could hold fifty people.

"Did your mother never tell you how she was raised?" Ina Bell asked.

Eleanor shook her head. "Not much. Seems when she married my father, she left her old life behind."

"Or it left her," Ina Bell said, carefully setting down the glass parrot she'd been cleaning. "Sorry, Miss Eleanor, I was speaking out of turn."

"No, Ina Bell, you're probably right. I do think my grandparents disowned my mother for marrying so far beneath her station."

"I think it's romantic. Your father must have been quite wonderful."

Eleanor nodded, holding on tightly to her emotions. "He was a good man."

"That's the highest praise a man should hope to hear," Ina Bell replied, wiping off the crystal candlesticks. "Mr. Westfield was that type of man. Very wealthy and cultured, but always caring about others."

"Eleanor?"

"Mother! I . . ." Eleanor stood quickly, kicking one of her shoes across the room. She didn't see where it landed, as her eyes were fixed on her mother standing at the door.

Mrs. Lund's face was sullen with disapproval. "Were you conversing with a servant?"

" I . . . I was, yes. I wanted to know more about Uncle Cedrick."

Mrs. Lund stood taller. She had dressed herself in a burgundy and cream day dress, but had forgotten her shoes and stockings, and her hair was just as it had been when she'd risen that morning. "We do not glean information from the servants, Eleanor. If you wish to know about Uncle Cedrick, then ask your aunt."

"Yes, ma'am." Eleanor went to retrieve her other shoe, casting an apologetic look at Ina Bell. The girl returned a slight smile and went on cleaning.

Eleanor sighed as she leaned down to pick up her shoe. The midmorning sun flickered through the lace curtains, offering the hope of warmer days to come. The San Francisco cold was another thing Eleanor had a hard time accepting—the chill January wind blowing in off the ocean cut through to the bone. She shivered and chided herself for pessimism, forcing herself to think of all the different and grand things she was experiencing with city life. Indoor plumbing and electric lights were marvels of the city and the new century. As it often did, her mind jumped to her sister Alaina, and she wondered if she had such conveniences in her home in Salt Lake City.

Eleanor was anxious for information, as she'd had only one letter from her sister, sent from Reno, Nevada.

Dear Elly,

When the train stopped in Truckee, Nephi surprised me with a side trip to Lake Tahoe. It is the most beautiful place I have ever seen. He is a good man, and I care for him, but we are friends and nothing more. Tomorrow we leave for Reno, and then on to Utah. I'm scared and I miss you. I miss everything. How is James doing at Mr. Regosi's ranch? Are the horses well? When do you leave for San Francisco? It snowed last night. It is beautiful but freezing! My hands are stiff with the cold.

I love you. Stay strong.
Laina

P.S. Please inform Miss Johnson of my whereabouts and thank her for her kindness to me. Hug Joanna and tell her that Miss Titus is well.

Eleanor smiled to think of Joanna Wilton's parting gift to Alaina. The beautiful little horse was a perfect symbol of the girls' long friendship, and Alaina had vowed never to part with the filly, even if it meant transporting her seven hundred miles to a strange new place.

Eleanor's thoughts came back to the parlor, as she realized her mother had been talking and she had not been listening.

". . . to find the brown trunk."

"Which brown trunk?" Eleanor asked, attempting to cover her inattention.

"The one with the books. I just said that."

"Oh, of course!" Eleanor said brightly. "I found that trunk several days ago. It's in my room. Would you like to go see it?" She leaned over and put on her shoe. "I was just coming up, Mother, to see if you wanted breakfast. You could have breakfast and look for your book."

A frown crossed Elizabeth Lund's face as if her daughter's cheery reply had driven other thoughts from her mind. She pressed her fingertips to her mouth and looked down at the floor.

Eleanor moved quickly and took her mother's arm. "Why don't we go to your room and have Palmer send up some toast and tea?"

"Yes, I would like toast," her mother answered.

Eleanor led her to the stairs. "And I'll do your hair."

Ina Bell watched them for a moment, and then went earnestly back to work. She greatly missed her own parents, but contented herself with the knowledge that they loved her and were proud of her work and sacrifice. She crossed herself and said a prayer for Eleanor and her mother, and for her friend Kerri who had lost both her parents in the great earthquake of '06. Ina Bell sighed and shook her head. *The world is full of sorrow, true enough.*

At that moment Kerri McKee struggled into the parlor hauling a heavy coal bucket. "Leave it to Mr. Palmer to give me Mr. Randall's work as punishment," she growled, moving to the fireplace and dumping the load into the coal bin. "Was that the Dragon I seen being taken upstairs?"

"Kerri! Don't call her that."

"Well, 'tis true, isn't it?" Kerri sniffed.

"Mrs. Lund has had a hard time of it," Ina Bell defended.

"Wot? Lost her husband? So's the mistress, and ya don't see her goin' off. Seems ta me it's her daughter Eleanor's got the worst of it . . . her two oldest daughters, anyway."

"Kerri, you really must mind your place."

"Now, that little one, she gets a bit of pampering, don't she?" Kerri went on without pause. "Wonder if her ma would have sold the farm out from under *her?*"

Ina Bell almost dropped the mantel clock she was holding. "Hush now! We're not supposed to talk about that."

"Poor girl goes and marries the farmhand so she can keep the farm, and her mum sells it anyway, just because the groom doesn't suit her fancy. Just because he's a Mormon lad."

Ina Bell set the clock down and crossed herself.

"Don't ya be prayin' for me, Miss Latham, just cause I'm speakin' the truth. Far better you should pray for Eleanor's sister."

Ina Bell threw her cloth into the basket. "I was praying for both of you, you heathen girl."

Kerri started to laugh, then checked herself when she heard Mr. Palmer's approaching footsteps. The two girls picked up their burdens and headed out of the parlor, passing Mr. Palmer in the hallway, their heads bowed with the humility appropriate to their station.

"All finished then?" he asked them.

Kerri hesitated. "Yes, sir. Clean as a whistle."

Mr. Palmer frowned. "We'll see. You two go now and help in the scullery."

Kerri looked indignant, and Ina Bell knew what was coming. "Yes, sir," she said quickly, cutting off her friend's reply. "We'll be more than glad to help in the scullery."

Kerri gave Ina Bell a secret look of mock disgust as they kept moving down the hallway at a measured pace, controlling the urge to run.

Mr. Palmer inspected the parlor, wiped the brass door handles, and went about his work.

Chapter Three

"Kaiser Wilhelm the Second, emperor of Germany; President Woodrow Wilson, president of the United States; Emperor Franz Josef, emperor of Austria-Hungary; King George the Fifth, king of England . . ."

"Miss Johnson?" A voice interrupted the teacher's fluid recitation.

Philomene Johnson turned from writing on the blackboard to smile at the student who had spoken. "Yes, Mary, did you have a question?" she asked sincerely. Unlike many educators, Philomene Johnson encouraged and enjoyed independent thinking and eager inquiry, and had for the twenty years she'd been teaching.

Her thirteen-year-old charge hesitated, reconsidering the merit of her question. Miss Johnson stood calmly waiting, while Martin Flynn turned to make a face at his classmate. Mary ignored him.

"I just wanted to know why we have to memorize all the heads of different countries."

Martin sniggered, but Mary forged ahead. "I mean, I understand knowing President Wilson and King George, but why all the others?"

Martin made a grotesque face, which indicated he thought she was dumb.

"It's a very good question," Miss Johnson said, laying down her chalk and moving towards Martin's desk. "Mr. Flynn, would you like to answer Miss Carrillo's insightful question?"

Martin turned quickly in his seat, the mocking look on his face dropping away.

"I . . . I don't know, Miss Johnson."

"Hmm. Perhaps it would be prudent, Mr. Flynn, to spend your time and energy thinking of your own insightful questions." She smiled at him, and he smiled back.

"Yes, Miss Johnson."

Philomene raised her eyes to the rest of the class. "I have just one word to say to Miss Carrillo's question. *Electricity.*"

The students waited for more, but Miss Johnson picked up her chalk and turned back to the blackboard. "Czar Nicholas the Second, emperor of the Russian Empire."

"Miss Johnson?"

"Yes, Mr. Flynn?"

"You just said *electricity.* What's that gotta do with what Mary asked about?"

Miss Johnson turned to him, ignoring his rough grammar. "What do you think, Mr. Flynn?"

Martin sat very still; only his eyes betrayed the turmoil going on inside his head. Finally he took a deep breath and ventured, "Because all those leaders got electricity?"

The class laughed, but Miss Johnson nodded. "Yes. They do have electricity. You're on the right track, Mr. Flynn. Now, where does your mind go from there?"

"They got telephones?"

"Right, they *have* telephones."

"And telegraphs."

Hands were shooting up around the classroom. Miss Johnson smiled. "Exactly. And what else?"

"Lots of modern things!" someone called out.

"Please wait to be called on, Mr. Trenton, but yes, you're right. Exactly right. We live in an age of modern marvels, Mr. Trenton." Miss Johnson looked down at another marvel as the introverted D'Amatto girl raised her hand, a feat she had not accomplished all year. "Yes, Miss D'Amatto?"

"Automobiles and aeroplanes."

"Indeed. When I was your age we could not have imagined such things." Another hand was waving. "Yes, Miss McMahon?"

"Steamships."

"Yes. The world is shrinking, students. Invention has drawn the neighbors of the world close. So, this is my question. Do we sit over here on this side of the ocean and pretend the troubles of the European countries have nothing to do with us?"

Martin raised his hand. "What troubles, Miss Johnson?"

Philomene paused. "Old hatreds and bitter envies," she said slowly. "It just needs something to fan the smoldering embers, and I'm afraid the fire will erupt."

"You mean war, don't you?" Mary Carrillo asked, her eyes wide with apprehension.

"But that wouldn't have nothin' to do with us. It'd be their war," Martin insisted.

"Ah, some in this country would agree with you, Mr. Flynn."

"But you don't?" Mr. Trenton asked without raising his hand.

Miss Johnson was not only a good teacher, but also wise. She knew the sensibilities of her students had been stretched far enough with these ponderous issues, and it was time to reassure them.

"The world has much to do with struggle and chaos, but it is also filled with goodness and wonder. Somehow we will find a way." She watched the pinched brows and tight mouths relax. "And now I think we should pursue the fascinating subject raised by Miss D'Amatto. Automobiles and airplanes."

"I fly sometimes in my dreams!" William Trenton blurted out. The class laughed, and William's freckled face blushed red.

"I also fly, Mr. Trenton," Miss Johnson said simply. "I am a glorious red hawk, and I soar just over the treetops, my bright eyes watching— ever watching." She moved towards Miss McMahon, her fingers curled like talons. "And I am always ready to swoop down on . . ."

"Rabbits!" someone called out.

"Squirrels!"

Miss Johnson turned quickly and latched onto Mr. Trenton's shoulder with her mock talons. "No! Students who do not turn in their homework." William jumped and the class laughed. Philomene Johnson laughed with them and patted William tenderly. "Of course, I never catch any of you as you are model students who never forget an assignment."

The bell rang, signaling the end of school. The students arranged their belongings on their desks and sat quietly, waiting for dismissal.

Miss Johnson walked to the front of the class. "Today's quote is from Shakespeare. 'This above all: to thine own self be true, and it must follow, as the night the day, thou canst not then be false to any man.' The interpretation?"

"Don't be a liar!" William blurted out.

"Your hand, Mr. Trenton."

William raised his hand, and the class laughed. Miss Johnson turned to the blackboard to cover her amusement. "Thank you for another remarkable day, students. Class dismissed."

As she walked home in the winter twilight, Miss Johnson smiled at the glory of her life. Hers was not the world of husband and children, but she had lives enough to fill her soul with gratitude: Miss Carrillo, Mr. Flynn, and Mr. Trenton. She chuckled to herself when thinking of Mr. Trenton. How could so much energy be bottled up in one slight boy? Though she had to require discipline in her classroom, she loved how William's exuberance was forever unraveling his decorum. Her thoughts drifted to former students in her catalogue of tender feelings, and she saw before her the Lund children, each so different in their expectations and abilities. She wondered how they were doing. She saw James periodically when he came into Sutter Creek for supplies for the Regosi ranch, but the girls were scattered like milkweed floss, and though she checked the post daily, there had, as yet, been no word. Was Eleanor allowed to pursue an education there in the narrow, structured world of San Francisco's elite? Was Kathryn's character being glutted with opulence and attention? And what of dear Alaina? Her strength and peace had always come from working the land with her father, and now Samuel Lund was gone and Alaina was married.

Philomene smiled again as she thought of Nephi Erickson, the young Mormon man who had come to work on the Lund farm, and who had been Alaina's refuge in the end. The two had married with only friendship to bind their commitment, and though it was a strong tie, Philomene wondered if it could endure such a different place and culture. She said a little prayer for Mr. and Mrs. Erickson in Salt Lake City, and Eleanor and Kathryn in San Francisco. She shifted her book bag, and included a thought for Elizabeth Lund. "May she find some peace," Philomene said out loud.

"Good afternoon, Miss Johnson," Elijah Greggs said as he stepped out of the post office. "We're closed up for the day, but there was a letter for you, so I brought it out." He reached into his coat pocket and drew out an envelope. "Come from San Francisco, or that's where it was stamped."

Philomene took the letter and smiled at the town's tall, genial postmaster. "Thank you, Mr. Greggs." She turned to go.

"I expect it's from Mrs. Lund," the postmaster said as he hurriedly locked the door and made to follow Philomene.

"Perhaps, Mr. Greggs, or it may be from Eleanor Lund. She would be the one to keep up correspondence."

Mr. Greggs shrugged into his coat. "She was one of your scholars, if I remember right."

"She was indeed."

"Too bad about that whole situation. Samuel Lund was one of the best farmers around these parts, and a good man."

"A very good man," Philomene responded, sticking the letter into her pocket and hefting her book bag.

"I could carry that for you, Miss Johnson."

Philomene smiled. "No thank you, Mr. Greggs. It's part of my daily exercise. Prepares me for my summer adventure."

"Off for Europe again?"

"I am."

"And where to this time?"

"I've decided on Belgium. I have a great-aunt who lives there, and she's invited me to stay for several months."

"Sounds interesting. Probably what makes you such a fine teacher, Miss Johnson, all that traveling you do."

"It's kind of you to say so, Mr. Greggs," she answered, surprised by the compliment.

"Plain truth," he said, tipping his hat and stopping in front of the café. "I don't suppose you'd care for some supper?"

Philomene stopped abruptly and stared at him. They were the two confirmed unmarried folks in Sutter Creek and had always been content with admiring each other's independent natures. They were neighbors and nothing more. "That's very nice of you, Mr. Greggs, but I have much to occupy my evening."

He tipped his hat again and gave her an unembarrassed smile. "Of course. Perhaps some other time."

At that moment Markus Salter came up behind them, hesitating as he tried to figure out how to get by without intruding. "Uh, excuse me, Miss Johnson."

"Oh, Markus! How are you?"

"Fine, ma'am."

"And your new job at the electricity station?"

"Wonderful, ma'am. Couldn't be better. Hello, Mr. Greggs."

"Hello, Markus. Going in for supper?"

"Yes, sir."

"Well, let me buy, and you can tell me all about your new job, and we can talk about starting up that baseball club in the spring."

Markus's face brightened at the prospect of a free meal and conversation. "Really, sir? Oh, that would be fine."

Philomene chuckled at her former student's obvious enthusiasm.

Mr. Greggs tipped his hat again. "Good evening, Miss Johnson."

Mr. Salter followed suit. "Good evening, ma'am."

"Good night, you two. I understand the lamb shank is very good."

Mr. Greggs opened the café door and ushered Markus inside. "We may have to give it a try."

The door closed, and Philomene Johnson started off for home. She thought of the precious little cottage waiting for her in the evening shadows, a treasure willed to her when her parents died. She thought of the plum and birch trees, and of her climbing roses that would fill the world with beauty come spring. She felt an ache in her heart as she thought of her mother's plum jelly and her father's wisdom and ready humor. How she missed them. A starling's melody glimmered through the air, and Philomene stopped, looking east towards the Methodist church. The sun dropped out of sight in the west, turning the horizon a soft rose and signaling the time of day when hearth and home beckoned. Miss Johnson turned from the prospect and headed towards the church instead, knowing that some promises were to be honored above personal comfort.

She approached the quiet cemetery with reverence, delighting when she came upon a group of winter birds dining on crusts of bread. Most likely Pastor Wilton's daughter, Joanna, had been the Samaritan, and Philomene thought of the school days when Joanna

Wilton and Alaina Lund had been inseparable friends. It was strange how only seven months earlier she had seen the two young women at the Fourth of July celebration enjoying the parade and baseball game, unaware of how the future would bend the paths of their lives to separation.

Miss Johnson tried not to disturb the little congregation of birds as she lit one of the churchyard lanterns, and moved off among the graceful statuary and stone markers. Vivid images jumped into her mind as she passed by names of people, often marked by titles deserved or otherwise. Didn't everyone in town know that Patrick Rice was a crook, that Lorna McGill had a bitter tongue, and that Mitt Jenkins was a firebrand? Philomene found it interesting that the sentiments on the headstones said only *Rest in peace, Beloved mother,* or *Waiting for the resurrection,* and she wondered if shallow earthly labels were shed in the presence of the Lord's all-knowing judgment.

She reached her destination under the leafless oak, and sat down on the squat stone wall. She ran her hand over the granite headstone, admiring its unadorned simplicity—so much like the life of the man. She set the lantern close and reached into her pocket. "Hello, my friend Samuel. I have come to share something with you."

As the sky turned lavender and the trees became dark silhouettes, Miss Johnson opened Eleanor Lund's letter and began reading.

Chapter Four

Three hours, and the horse would not yield. The quivering flanks showed the strain of the contest, but the stallion's look was mad with defiance.

James Lund rubbed the muscles in his lower back and gave the cinnamon horse an equally determined look of engagement. "I refuse to put him down, Mr. Regosi. He's a magnificent animal."

The seasoned rancher stood outside the paddock clucking like a mother hen. "Yeah. Yeah. But I think he gotta go. I think he rile up all the other horses."

James climbed onto the fence and sat down on the top rail. "Well, he does do that."

The stallion bolted at them, turning just before slamming into the fence.

"Hey! Stop that, you monster!" Mr. Regosi yelled. James watched the old man's weathered face with interest. He saw frustration but also admiration as Mr. Regosi shook his head and reached out his hands to the marauding animal. "You want to be sent down?" he asked in a worried voice. "You want to be shoe leather?" The horse tossed its head.

"No, I not think so. So let this nice young man take care of you. He teach you some manners."

The horse snorted.

"I don't think he believes you," James said, laughing.

"We see at the end of the day," Mr. Regosi answered, slapping the tethering rope against his thigh. "Now, I go see what Mrs. Regosi fix for supper. You need some food. You grow six inches just the month you been here."

James lowered his head contritely. "Can I help it if your wife is the best cook in California?"

Mr. Regosi laughed openly. "I gonna tell her what you said, and she's gonna give you an extra piece of applesauce cake." He handed James the rope and headed for the house, chuckling to himself.

James watched him with great affection. The man was seventy years old, five feet eight, and tough as an old pair of boots. James was fifty-four years younger and four inches taller, but he knew he didn't stand a chance in a wrestling match with the man. Emilio Regosi had survived some of the bloodiest battles of the Civil War, serving with the Fourth Cavalry Regiment out of New York State. At eighteen, he'd smuggled supplies past enemy lines, pulled mules and horses out of mud pits, and lost two fingers on his right hand to frostbite during the winter expedition to Liberty Mills. The stories of his life, told at the supper table, amazed and terrified James, who would have had a hard time believing the stories if Mr. Regosi weren't a humble man of absolute honesty.

James brought his attention back to the horse, amused at its stoic demeanor. He took off his gloves, reached into the pocket of his coat, and brought out an apple. He held it out to the haughty animal, not really expecting the horse to shorten the distance between them.

"Stubborn," he said, throwing the apple to the horse.

The horse shied sideways, then moved over to sniff at the offering.

"Go on, it's not poison."

The stallion picked up the apple warily and tossed his head while he ate. When he was done, he stood quietly watching James and, after several minutes of mutual assessment, the stallion moved forward.

"Ah, you liked that," James said in a low, soothing voice, reaching into his pocket for another apple. The horse's ears flicked.

"You gotta come closer for this one." He held out the temptation, and the horse whinnied, holding its ground. "Nope, I'm not throwing this one. If you want it, you have to come get it." He watched the horse intently, every movement telling him something. "Come on."

The big animal lowered its head slightly and moved forward. It shied several times, and James spoke softly. "Come on. Come see that I'm not such a bad fellow." The horse came closer. James slowly reached out his hand, and the offering was accepted. The stallion moved back several paces to eat, but the gap had narrowed, and James was satisfied.

He looked across the yard to the small farmhouse, feeling a sense of pride and contentment. He was lucky Mr. Regosi had taken him in and given him work—work he loved. Where else would he have gone once Mother had sold the farm?

He thought about his home only two miles east, and felt, as always, that unwanted ache in his chest. He missed the meadow, and the big barn, and his father. James looked down at his hands and saw the hands of Samuel Lund, knowing that as he grew taller, his lanky body more and more resembled that of his sire.

He slapped the rope on the side of the fence, swung his legs over the rail, and jumped down. He tried not to think of Mr. Blackhurst, the new owner of the farm, or of his family's final scenes of leaving. His mother had insisted on abandoning most of the furnishings and farm equipment, choosing to take only a few personal possessions. The animals were also left to the new owner, except for the horses. It was such good fortune that he'd been hired on at Mr. Regosi's ranch, as horses were the commodity and Emilio Regosi the best horse handler in six counties. Moccasin, Friar Tuck, and Titus would live out their lives well worked and well cared for. Alaina had insisted these treasured animals not be sold to strangers, and James remembered the relief on her face when he announced he would be able to care for them.

He felt cheated that he and his older sister were just beginning to understand each other when their world fell apart. He hadn't heard from her in the two months she'd been gone, and he wondered if she and Nephi were settled in Salt Lake City and how Miss Titus was doing. His sister Eleanor had shared one letter about their trip out, but now Eleanor was in San Francisco and there'd been no other news. It was silly, but he wanted to hear their chattering voices again.

Mr. Regosi came out onto the front porch and rang the bell for supper. He waved enthusiastically at James, motioning him to hurry. "Oh, you should see this table! A king should eat so good."

James's stomach grumbled, and he set aside thoughts of things he couldn't control and went into the warmth of the kitchen and the smell of herb bread and ravioli.

* * *

The city was noisy and crowded and cold. Alaina Erickson kicked at a pile of dirty snow on the sidewalk, her heart returning to a ridge of dark pines frosted white against a bright blue sky. She wrenched her mind from the image of the farm in California, and looked east down Second South Street, where she saw dingy, brown buildings, automobiles, and people in dark clothing.

Salt Lake City, with its ninety-five thousand inhabitants, was the largest city Alaina had ever seen. The only other city she knew was Jackson, the seat of Amador County, California, and that was really a town in comparison. Boasting a population of three thousand, Jackson had five major streets, a movie theater, two newspapers, a telegraph and telephone office, and only six buildings that stood taller than two stories. Alaina had been to San Francisco once when she was a child, but since all of her time was spent in the house on Beacon Street, she remembered little. Eleanor was cooped up in that house now, and she knew that her sister, like herself, was longing for open fields and peacefulness. She missed Eleanor so much that she found it painful to think of her too often. Memories of Eleanor were memories of home.

Alaina kicked at the snow again, jumping as a trolley bell clanged nearby. She was intimidated by the bustle of this Mormon enclave with its electric trolley cars and automobiles. When Nephi had first talked about his home, he'd talked about mountains and canyons and trees. She sighed and looked up to the snow-covered peaks.

"Good afternoon, Mrs. Erickson," came a voice behind her.

She turned to see Nephi's older brother, Elias, approaching. He was taller than Nephi, favoring his father's height and looks, though his darker coloring and wavy brown hair were definitely inherited from the Keel side of the family. Elias always made her feel inferior, and even though she had never met Nephi's father, she imagined he and Elias shared the same aloof personality.

Following behind Elias was his wife, Sarah, who was the exact opposite of her husband's look and manner. She had a thin mouth and apologetic hazel eyes that stood out predominantly in her small face. Her features lacked softness because the retiring young woman insisted on wearing her ash brown hair pulled back into a braid.

"So, he's left you standing on the street corner," Elias said, smirking.

Alaina smiled and ignored him. "Hello, Sarah. Did you find the blanket you wanted?"

Sarah's eyes flickered up to Alaina's face then back down to her shoes. "We did," she said, holding out a paper-wrapped package. "Thank you for asking."

Elias took out his watch. "So, where is that hay-headed brother of mine?"

A spark of anger snapped into Alaina's eyes, but she looked away and bit back her first reply. "It's probably just taking longer at the interview," she answered in a steady voice.

Sarah looked over at her, and Alaina saw a slight smile catch the corner of her mouth before she covered it with her hand.

"Well, we'll go get the truck," Elias said, moving off. "Hopefully we won't have to wait."

Sarah followed. "I hope Nephi got the job," she whispered to Alaina as she passed by.

"Thanks, Sarah. Me too."

The last two months had been difficult for Nephi, having to live in his mother's house after being out on his own, not having a job other than helping with chores around the three-acre farm, and then, of course, having to deal with their relationship, or lack of one. Alaina kicked the snow pile, attempting to dislodge the guilt that tightened in her stomach whenever she thought of their marriage.

He only married me out of pity because I begged him to help me save the farm, and now look at the mess we're in.

She shook her head and looked up again to the mountains. It was the end of January, and storm clouds gathered around the peaks; a douse of snow was expected, which meant another day indoors in the small house. Alaina chided herself for ingratitude.

A trolley rattled by, and Alaina's thoughts returned to her train ride from California—of leaving beautiful Lake Tahoe and descending into the desolation of the Nevada desert near Reno. She hated leaving Lake Tahoe, as the three days spent there had been a postponement of worrisome prospects ahead, and a solace from past wounds.

Mrs. Lawson, owner of the cabin retreat where she and Nephi had stayed, took a liking to the "youngsters," and let them use her little boat to row along the shoreline, and her fishing poles to fish off the dock. She taught Alaina how to cook spaetzle and German meatballs while Nephi shoveled snow, chopped firewood, and made repairs on several of the cabins. The newlyweds would get up early, have a big breakfast of fried mush, bacon, and tinned fruit, and then journey off on snowshoes to explore. On one of these outings they found the imposing Tahoe Tavern lodge. The four-story edifice with its gabled roof and striking tower was closed down and boarded for the winter, but nestled in the snow and surrounded by ancient pines, it was an enchanting thing of wonder. The two unassuming admirers spent most of the clement day peeking through slits in the shutters, catching glimpses of massive beams, electric chandeliers, and covered furniture. They tromped around the extensive grounds, imagining they were wealthy patrons having tea and cakes on the wide veranda.

Often Alaina would catch Nephi lost in thought and knew he was using the distraction of the mountain splendor to escape thinking of their future life together. On rare occasions he would talk a little about his life in Salt Lake City: of his mother, Eleanor Patience Keel Erickson; of his older brother, Elias; and of his sister, Evelyn, who was born prior to Elias but had died at seven months. He bragged a little about his mother's skill as a dressmaker, and apologized that the home in which they would be living was small and sat on only three acres. He remained silent on the subject of his father, and of his parent's estrangement, but in truth, Alaina didn't want clarification. The crystal blue of the lake and the towering granite peaks swept away melancholy contemplations, and a good snowball fight always brought them into the glee of the moment.

A trolley bell sounded, and Alaina looked furtively down the street in search of Nephi. She shook her head as memories of the final part of their train journey east began to creep into her thoughts. The terrain from Reno to Ogden was bland, and the weather was dismal. Furthermore, with every mile that brought him closer to home, Nephi became increasingly agitated. Finally, a hundred miles out of Ogden, he sat down across from her, put his hands on his knees and looked her straight in the face. "My father's name is Alma Erickson, and he has . . . had two wives." He watched her face carefully. "Eunice Drake Erickson is his first wife and they have six children, and my mother is—was—his second wife."

Alaina hardly heard the rest of his words as he recited the names and ages of his half brothers and sisters. Finally, she held up her hand and he stopped talking. "Why didn't you tell me any of this before?"

He looked down at his hands. "Why would I?"

It was not the answer she had expected. "You didn't think it was important to tell me your father had two wives?"

"No."

She didn't know what to say to that.

Nephi took her hand. "I never thought we'd be coming back here." He cleared the emotion from his voice. "I thought we'd be living on the farm—that my past wouldn't have any part of . . ."

She pulled her hand away. "Why didn't you tell me after the farm was sold and your mother offered to have us live with her in Salt Lake City?"

"Would it have made any difference?"

Alaina didn't answer. *Would it have made a difference? Where else did we have to go?* She didn't know the answer.

"Mother no longer lives in the big house. They haven't lived together since the year I was born. She has her own home on the outskirts of the city." Alaina had tried to think of more questions, tried to formulate what this meant to her, but her mind was stuck on the very idea of a man having two wives in this modern world. It seemed like a custom for biblical days or Arab lands, and it was frightening to think she was going to a place where she would meet and live with people who had embraced such archaic practices.

Nephi told her about his family's hardware business, about his argument with Eunice Drake Erickson, the first wife, an argument that had ended in bitter feelings and Nephi throwing a wrench through the hardware store window. Eunice had made hard remarks about his mother that had angered Nephi beyond restraint. He told of his estrangement from his father, who had refused to admit culpability or regret. Nephi's tone altered markedly when he spoke about his mother and how she made her own money as a seamstress. His devotion to her was evident.

Eleanor Patience Erickson. Alaina smiled, returning to the present, and pulling her scarf up over her ears. She loved to recall the first time she saw Mother Erickson's kindly face through the train window. She and Nephi had changed trains one last time in Ogden and, after moving luggage and transferring Miss Titus, Alaina felt so weary that she found it hard to breathe. She had sat with her head against the window, tears seeping out of the corners of her eyes. Nephi had moved close, murmuring comfort and patting her hand, but the look on his face was one of desolation. As the train pulled into the station in Salt Lake City, Alaina and Nephi had both turned their faces to the window. There was a small crowd of people on the platform, but Nephi found his mother immediately.

"Look! Look! There she is! The one with the flag."

Alaina saw a short, round woman in a black coat, eagerly searching every window in the train and waving a handmade California State flag. Alaina had burst into tears and loved her from that moment.

"Alaina!" Nephi's excited voice cut into her mental drifting, and she looked down the street to watch him approach. He crossed the wide street at a run, dodging carriages and automobiles. The driver of a shiny red Pierce Roadster braked forcefully and yelled an unfriendly name at him. Nephi merely smiled more broadly and tipped his hat to the man.

Suddenly her husband was beside her, grabbing her in an energetic hug and lifting her a few inches off the ground. She let out a yelp of surprise. Nephi had never been this forward with her, and she found it hard to catch her breath. He set her down, and she smiled at him and patted his arm.

"I got the job!" He hugged her again and she laughed. "I got the job!"

"I can tell," she said, stepping back and straightening her hat.

They both laughed, and Nephi took her hand. "Yep, an official worker on the Utah State Capitol! I'm only a hod tender, but it pays two dollars a day! Isn't that great?"

"That's very good. I'm proud of you."

He went to hug her again when an auto horn sounded, and Nephi turned abruptly to wave his hat at the approaching black truck. It was the company truck with "Erickson's Hardware Since 1885" painted on the side door.

Nephi jumped into the street before Elias could pull the truck to the curb and ran around to the driver's side. "I got the job! What do you think of that?"

Elias stepped from the vehicle. "I think that's great," he answered, smiling at Nephi's enthusiasm and shaking his hand, "but it took you long enough. What'd you have to do, wrestle everybody in the place before they'd hire you?"

Nephi smiled good-naturedly. "No such thing. The construction boss was interested about my time in California, and then Mr. Stewart, the big boss, came out of his office, and I got to shake his hand."

Elias laughed and thumped his brother on the shoulder. "Would you like to drive up by the site before we head home?"

Nephi grinned. "I'd love it!"

"Congratulations, Nephi!" Sarah called out to him.

"Thanks, Sarah," he answered, running around to the other side of the truck and opening the door for Alaina. "I'll just hop in the back," he said, helping Alaina arrange the packages at her feet.

"We can make room," she argued.

"No, it's fine."

"But it's freezing out there!"

Nephi shut the door, giving her a foolish grin.

Elias winked at her. "Don't worry, Mrs. Erickson. We come from tough pioneer stock." He put the truck in gear and pulled out onto the street, turning abruptly so they were heading north on Main Street towards the temple block.

"Elias Erickson!" Sarah squealed. "Slow down!"

Alaina's stomach had lurched at the maneuver, but she liked it. She sat back against the seat, hiding her smile and marveling that she was riding in an automobile. She'd been in the truck a half a dozen times now, but it still amazed her. In fact, she was amazed by many of the feats of engineering and craftsmanship that had come with the turning of the century: the transcontinental railroad, concrete streets, trolley cars, electricity, buildings twenty stories tall. As they neared Temple Square, Alaina leaned forward so she could see the temple clearly through the front window. Miss Johnson had shown her students pictures of cathedrals in Italy and France, but here was a splendid structure in her own backyard. She loved the surrounding gardens and the Tabernacle with its sweeping dome, but it was the temple that lifted the eye to heaven. She often stood staring up at the spires wondering how those struggling pioneer people could build such a glorious edifice and, even more perplexing, why.

Elias turned right on South Temple, then left onto State Street, enjoying how his wife gasped and clutched his arm at each maneuver. He pulled the truck close to the barriers surrounding the capitol construction site and turned off the engine.

"Well, does anyone want a closer . . . ?"

Nephi drummed on the roof. "Come on, let's get a closer look!" he said, jumping out of the truck and moving to the perimeter fence.

Elias opened his door. "I guess we're going for a closer look." He went to open Alaina's door and help the ladies out. "Mrs. Erickson, Sister Erickson, watch your skirts, it's muddy out here."

Alaina knew she was being oversensitive, but she always felt that when Elias called her *Mrs.* Erickson, there was a note of disapproval in his voice. As soon as they met Nephi at the fence, he pointed to the scaffolding around the first level of the rotunda. "See that man up there? That's gonna be me come Monday."

"It's so huge," Sarah ventured.

"And that's just the skeleton. Wait till the dome's finished."

Elias snorted. "You talk like you've worked on it from the beginning."

Alaina butted in. "How long until it's finished?"

"At least another year," Nephi answered, looking at the structure with awe. "It's hard to think that Great-Grandfather Erickson came here in a wagon." He turned to look down over the city. "And now look at us."

"The fulfillment of Joseph Smith's vision," Elias added, looking directly at Alaina. "Our ancestors were part of that grand revelation on gathering."

Alaina smiled an uncomfortable smile and looked back at the capitol building. She wondered at the pride the men took in their great-grandfather's story, as she'd found it distressing from the first telling.

The Jens Erickson family had joined the Mormon Church in Denmark in 1839 and had come to America a year later. Well, some had come. Lars Erickson, Nephi's grandfather, was nine years old and frail at the time, so it was decided that he and his mother, Hansine, would stay in Denmark for a few years while Jens and their two older children would go ahead and establish a place. In 1842, the three finally settled in Nauvoo, Illinois.

In Denmark, young Lars worked diligently to build his strength so he and his mother could quickly join the rest of the family. His youthful innocence kept him from realizing that his mother's fervor for the gospel was waning. Now, instead of conviction and encouragement in her letters to America, Hansine Erickson's sentiments became appeals for Jens to abandon his errant faith and return home. Jens did not return, but moved on with the Saints to Salt Lake City, hoping that someday Hansine would find her testimony and her way to him. It was not to be. In fact, it would be ten years before his youngest son would save sufficient funds to make the journey to Utah with his new bride.

Alaina found it sad that the religious faith that should have tied the family closer together was the means of its demise. She was also bewildered by what she saw as callous choices. A harsh wind blew down from the canyon, prompting her and Sarah to pull their scarves more tightly around their necks.

"Come on, little brother," Elias said, putting his arm around his wife. "Let's get ourselves home before we freeze."

The ride out to Mother Erickson's on Twelfth East and Fourteenth South was slow and bumpy, as the concrete roads ended only a few blocks out of the downtown area. Jens Erickson, Nephi's great-grandfather, had bought a hundred and fifty acres southeast of the city proper when he first came to the valley. When the shrewd, venerable patriarch became unable to work his trade, he had the land parceled into lots for homes and small farms as the city grew. Elias and Sarah lived in a wonderful little cottage just two blocks south of Mother Erickson, and Nephi had his eye on buying an eight-acre piece that sat five blocks east. Finding a job made that prospect more reasonable, and Alaina was sure it was one of the reasons he was so pleased. She turned in her seat to look out at her husband, cold but in high spirits in the back of the truck. He saw her look and waved. He was a good man and he was trying hard to provide for them, willing even to be a hod tender, whatever that was. She smiled at him.

"There's Mother Erickson out on the porch," Sarah said as they neared the modest wooden house. Elias shifted to a lower gear, and the truck began to slow. Eleanor Patience Erickson, whom her friends all knew by her middle name, waved her apron skirt as Nephi jumped from the back of the truck and ran to the house.

"I got the job at the capitol, Mom!"

The stout little woman clapped her hands, then took her big son in her arms and gave him a squeeze.

Nephi returned quickly to open Alaina's door and help her with the packages. Alaina was anxious to show Mother Erickson what a good purchase she'd made on tinned meat and bar soap. She'd also spent some of her money on three yards of navy blue broadcloth, a dress shirt for Nephi, a new coverlet, and a currycomb for Miss Titus.

Elias rolled down his window, and his mother came over to pat his arm. "Hello, son. Thanks for taking the youngsters into town. Hello, Miss Sarah. How are you today?"

"Fine, thank you," Sarah said, beaming.

"Did you find that baby blanket you wanted?"

"I did, Mother Erickson. Thank you for asking."

Patience Erickson turned her attention to Alaina. "Looks like you bought out the store, Miss Alaina."

Alaina smiled. "I did, and at a very good price."

Mother Erickson chuckled. "Good girl. I may just have to give you a prize for being such a wise steward." She reached into the pocket of her apron and brought out a white envelope.

Alaina drew in her breath. "Is that . . . ?"

Mother Erickson nodded. "A letter from San Francisco," she answered, laughing as she watched light dance onto Alaina's face.

Alaina moved to her. "I don't have hands," she moaned, shifting the packages back and forth.

Nephi followed. "Here, give me those."

Alaina gratefully piled the lot into his arms and took the letter. "Thank you." She turned to Elias and Sarah. "Thank you for the ride," she said and was gone, racing into the solitude of the house and the solace of news from her sister.

Mother Erickson watched her with tenderness, then spoke to Elias and Sarah. "We'll see you two Sunday?"

"Yes, ma'am," Elias said, smiling. "Are we still having corned beef?"

"Unless I changed the menu and forgot to tell myself," Mother Erickson answered.

Elias put the truck into gear and waved as they started off. Nephi and his mother watched the vehicle until it turned onto the street to their cottage, then Patience thumped her son on the back and looked at him with a big smile.

"Proud of you, Nephi."

"Thanks."

"How'd Alaina take the news?"

"She was glad for me. Seemed so, anyway." He shifted the packages in his arms. "I gave her a hug, and she didn't seem to mind."

"Well, that's good," Mother Erickson said simply. "Poor little cherub's got some broken wings, and that's a fact." She took one of the packages from her son and headed for the house. "I think I'll make that little angel an angel food cake. Isn't that a dandy idea?"

Nephi followed her. "And what about the working man?"

Mother Erickson paused with her hand on the doorknob. "Chicken and dumplings."

Nephi laughed as they moved into the house, shutting the door on the first flakes of snow.

Chapter Five

Kathryn's shrill scream echoed down the hallway as Eleanor fell out of bed. She scrambled around on the floor, completely disoriented, feeling the floor shaking under her hands. Kathryn screamed again, and Eleanor heard footsteps pounding down the hall and glass breaking. Her door flew open and her mother rushed into the room, jumping onto the bed and scattering pillows onto the floor.

"Eleanor! Eleanor!" she screamed hoarsely. "Where are you?"

Eleanor reached up and grabbed her mother's ankle. Elizabeth Lund yelled and kicked out. "Mother, it's me!" Eleanor said fiercely. "It's me!" She tried to stand, but the floor was moving under her and she jolted sideways. She grabbed the coverlet and dragged herself onto the bed. "Where's Kathryn?" she asked, looking at her mother's terrified face. "Did you see Kathryn?" More glass was breaking, and Eleanor realized that Elizabeth Lund was too lost in her own fear to be concerned with her youngest child. Eleanor jumped off the bed, making her way to the door and into the corridor. She smashed into Kerri McKee who took her by the shoulders.

"Are ya all right, miss?"

Eleanor nodded, noting the look of determination on Kerri's face.

"Where's your mother?"

Eleanor pointed to her room.

"Is she all right?"

"Yes."

"And your sister?"

"I don't know."

Immediately Kerri moved off to Kathryn's room with Eleanor lurching after her. They reached the room together. A picture fell off the wall, and they heard crying from farther down the hallway. Both girls turned to peer into the gloomy expanse and saw a huddled form on the floor. The shaking was beginning to subside, making it easier for the rescuers to reach the sobbing victim.

Kerri squatted beside Kathryn, checking quickly for blood in the dim light. The shaking stopped, and the house swayed slightly. "Miss Kathryn, are ya hurt?" Kathryn didn't answer. Kerri lifted her chin. "Are ya hurt, miss?"

Eleanor kneeled down on Kathryn's other side. "Kathryn? Stop crying and open your eyes."

The door at the end of the hall flew open, and Mrs. Westfield stood there trembling. "Who's there? Who's there? Is everyone all right?"

Kerri rose quickly and went to her. "Yes, ma'am. I think so."

"Who's on the floor?"

"It's Miss Kathryn, ma'am. She may have got a bump on her head."

Mrs. Westfield was rooted to her spot, but called out in a taut voice, "Eleanor, is that you with your little sister?"

"Yes, Aunt Ida."

"How is she?"

"I don't know. She won't stop crying."

Mrs. Westfield gave Kerri's arm a little shove. "Miss McKee, go to her and make her stop crying. My nerves cannot take that sound."

"Yes, ma'am. I'll see what I can do."

Kerri reached Kathryn's side just as Mr. Palmer came to the top of the stairs. He moved quickly down the hall, barely glancing at the girls as he passed them, and stopping only when he reached Mrs. Westfield.

"Are you injured, madam?"

"No. No, Palmer, I'm not. What time is it?"

"Near six, madam."

Mrs. Westfield looked at a glass lamp smashed on the floor. "Is there much damage?"

"I can't say as yet, madam, but I don't believe so. The quake was moderate."

Mrs. Westfield's eyes narrowed as she looked back down the hallway. "Oh, for heaven's sake, make her stop that racket."

Mr. Palmer walked quickly back to Kathryn, moving Kerri out of the way. He kneeled down next to the hysterical little girl. Removing a small glass vial from his pocket, he opened it and waved it under Kathryn's nose. She snorted and gasped several times, swatting at the butler's hand and kicking at him, but the crying stopped.

Mr. Palmer recapped the vial and put it back into his pocket. "That's better now, Miss Kathryn. Nothing to fear. The quake is over and you're as safe as can be."

Kathryn's face puckered and her mouth opened as though she would cry again. "Should I get out the salts again, miss?" Mr. Palmer asked in a soothing voice.

Kathryn's mouth snapped shut, and her lips trembled, but she did not cry. She pushed herself away from him and closer to Eleanor, opening her eyes and glaring at the servant as if he were some evil creature.

Elizabeth Lund came out of Eleanor's bedroom carrying a pillow over her head. "Where's Kathryn?"

Kathryn began whimpering and stood up. "I'm here, Mommy. I'm right here."

Mrs. Lund dropped the pillow and moved to her. "Are you hurt?"

"My head hurts," Kathryn answered. "I think something hit my head. I was in my room all by myself, and nobody came to help me." This last she said with an accusatory look at the group of people on the floor.

Mr. Palmer stood slowly, ignoring the child's yammering. He helped Eleanor to stand as Kerri got to her feet. "I'll send for the doctor immediately, Mrs. Lund, if you think your daughter requires attention."

Kathryn pressed herself against her mother, terrified that a doctor's ministrations would turn out to be worse than what she'd already suffered. "It's just a bump," she said petulantly. "I don't need a doctor for a bump."

Mr. Palmer ignored her. "Mrs. Lund?"

Elizabeth hesitated. "No. No, Palmer. I'll look after her myself."

Mr. Palmer nodded. "Very well, madam." He turned to Kerri. "We will serve breakfast to everyone in their rooms this morning, Miss McKee." He turned to Mrs. Westfield. "If that is all right with you, madam?"

"Yes, Palmer, whatever you think best."

Eleanor noticed for the first time that Mr. Palmer was the only one of the group not in nightclothes. In fact, his black coat and pants were pressed, his shirt collar in place, and his hair neatly brushed. She wondered what sort of upbringing a lad had to have to attain such an assured proficiency.

"Are you well, Miss Eleanor?" Palmer asked.

"Excuse me?" she said, coming out of her stupor.

Mr. Palmer held her by the elbow. "Do you need the salts?"

"The salts?"

He set her in one of the untoppled hallway chairs. "You seem on the verge of fainting, miss."

"Do I?" Eleanor was amused. "Really? I've never fainted in my life. How interesting. One time on the farm my brother James ran over a pig with the wagon and I threw up, but I didn't faint."

Mr. Palmer squeezed her hand tightly.

"Ow!"

"Sorry, Miss Eleanor, but that was necessary."

Eleanor's thoughts cleared, and she realized her heart was racing and her body was trembling. "What a goose!" she said loudly, holding back a laugh.

"Not at all," Mr. Palmer answered, releasing her hand. "You've had a shock."

"Actually, I've had a shake," Eleanor replied, giggling.

"Miss McKee, get the ladies back into their beds, and I will send up some strong tea," Mr. Palmer said calmly. "And mind the broken glass."

"Yes, sir."

Kathryn clung to her mother. "I'm going with you! I'm going with you!"

"All right!" Mrs. Lund snapped, prying Kathryn's hands off her clothing. "Just stop grabbing at me." She took Kathryn by the wrist and went to her bedroom.

Mrs. Westfield hesitated before retreating into her chamber. "Palmer, please let me know as soon as possible what things have been damaged."

"And people, Palmer," Eleanor quipped, "what *people* have been damaged."

Kerri raised Eleanor out of the chair and led her into her bedroom, shushing her gently. She shut the door behind them and moved Eleanor to the bed. "Careful of the broken glass, miss," she instructed, maneuvering Eleanor around the remnants of the lamp, and getting her into bed. "Surely, Miss Eleanor," she said chuckling, "you do win the prize."

Eleanor sat back against the pillows and tried to control the thoughts banging around in her head. "Do I?"

"You don't think so?" Kerri questioned, raising her eyebrows. She righted the fallen side table, then pulled the coverlet over Eleanor's legs. "Speaking your mind like that to your aunt?"

Eleanor groaned, then took a deep breath. "My mind isn't working too well right now."

"Land of Perdition! I can't imagine why not," Kerri answered with an amused smile.

Eleanor closed her eyes. "I just wish my heart would slow down."

"It will. Give it time." Kerri moved to the window and pulled back the heavy outer drape.

A cold light filtered in through the lace covering, and Eleanor drew the coverlet closer. "I know this is probably a silly question," she said tentatively, "but is the house in danger of falling down?"

Kerri turned to look her square in the face. "It's not a silly question at all." She moved to the bed. "You've never been through a quake before, so ya don't know what may happen." Kerri plumped Eleanor's pillow. "That quake wasn't very big, and I'm thinkin' it was pretty far away, so we only caught the fringe."

Eleanor swallowed and nodded. "How can you be so calm about it?" Her thoughts were still jumping around in her head. "I mean, didn't your parents die in an earthquake?" Kerri stood very still. "I'm sorry, Kerri! That was a stupid thing to ask. I told you my brain's not working right."

"It's all right, miss. I've fairly come to terms with it," Kerri answered, picking up the vanity tray and replacing it on the table. "'Twas eight years ago this month, April 18, 1906." She stood still for a moment, caught up in a thought. "I was your sister Kathryn's age. Ten." She smiled and picked up the ivory-handled hairbrush. "Ten years old, and all boney arms and elbows. Law, but I was a sight."

"And your parents worked here?" Eleanor inquired, desiring the soothing voice to continue.

"Yes, miss. Fifteen years at that time."

"But, but how did they . . . I mean, this house wasn't destroyed."

"No, miss. Sure it wasn't. But me mother wasn't here at the time."

"She wasn't?"

Kerri shook her head, retrieving two tortoise-shell hair combs from the rug. "No, she was down at the Southern Pacific Company Hospital fighting off the consumption."

Eleanor flinched. She had studied pulmonary tuberculosis, and it was nearly always fatal.

"Mr. Westfield found her a place in that hospital because his bank had dealings with the Southern P."

Eleanor didn't understand the note of pride in her voice. "Was it a good hospital?"

"Oh, 'twas a grand place. Me father took me down there one day, corner of Fourteenth and Mission." Eleanor could tell that Kerri was walking those streets again, and she wondered at the girl's calm demeanor. "We couldn't go in because of the quarantine, but Da arranged it so she was at the window, and we got to wave to her. She would have gone to the county hospital if it wasn't for Mr. Westfield." There were tears in Kerri's eyes as she straightened the coverlet. "I do think she was gettin' on, but then the quake hit and . . . well, you know."

Eleanor nodded. They had studied the devastating quake in Miss Johnson's class, and she felt again the anguished knot that had sat in her stomach for days after the discussion, as she pondered the death and destruction.

"Fire Chief Sullivan himself tried to pull me mother out of the rubble, but she was already gone. Then the fire swept through, and more walls came down. That hero of a man was injured terrible tryin' to get the wounded out. He died later."

"And your father?" Eleanor whispered.

"He was mad with fright that morning. He took the master's auto and drove into the wreckage. He got caught in the fire. Died before he knew me mother was gone."

Eleanor felt tears on her face. "I'm so sorry, Kerri."

Kerri came to her and took her hand. "Oh, not to fret, miss. As I said, I've come to terms with it, and I get along fine. You know what it's like to lose someone."

"You were very brave this morning," Eleanor said quickly, changing the subject.

"You weren't so bad yourself," Kerri answered lightly, deflecting the praise. "Rushin' into the hall like that when you didn't know a thing about what was goin' on."

Eleanor laughed and let go of Kerri's hand. "Well, that was it, wasn't it? Ignorance, not bravery." The two laughed and Eleanor felt the tightness in her chest relax.

There was a knock on the door, and Ina Bell Latham entered, carrying a tray of tea items. She gave Kerri a reprimanding look as she brought the tray to Eleanor's bedside.

"Good morning, Miss Eleanor," she said with a curtsy. "Are you doing all right?"

"Better now, Ina Bell, thank you."

Ina Bell set the tray on the bed table, and poured Eleanor tea from a small, flowered teapot. "Mr. Palmer had it made up extra strong," she said, handing Eleanor a cup. "And," she said, giving Kerri a frown and a nod of the head, "he wants you downstairs right away."

Eleanor noticed the exchange and came to Kerri's defense. "I'm afraid that was my fault, Ina Bell. I . . . I didn't want to be left alone right away."

Ina Bell's face softened. "Oh, of course not, miss. I understand." There was an uncomfortable pause. "Well . . . are you doing better now? Because there's much for Kerri and me to do down in the kitchen, what with breakfast, and more tea to bring up."

Eleanor sat up straighter in bed. "Yes, yes, of course. You two go on. I'm fine. I'll be fine. I'm sorry to have kept her so long."

"Oh, not to worry, miss," Ina Bell said hurriedly. "Mr. Palmer's sure to understand."

The two girls curtsied and left the room.

Eleanor envied them their "much to do." There was a nagging disquiet in her head and hands, which she knew had nothing and everything to do with her life in San Francisco. She sat back against the damask pillow, sipping the hot tea, and thinking about mucking out the chicken coop. To her current sensibilities, even that seemed a joyful occupation.

* * *

In the afternoon the staff was busy cleaning, Mother and Aunt Ida were playing canasta, and Kathryn was working on her stitch book under the strict eye of Miss Clawson, the nanny. Though it was a chilly day, even for April, Eleanor put on her coat and scarf and decided on an outing. Her aunt refused to let her go alone and sent the under butler with her as an escort. He was thrilled. Bib Randall had only been with the family two years, but had proven himself a reliable asset. He was well over six feet tall, with rounded shoulders and a bright, boyish face. Eleanor noticed that despite very crooked teeth he was perpetually smiling, and though his feet and hands were large, she always found his gate assured and his manner graceful.

Clouds were moving in off the ocean, and a periodic cold wind blew in their faces and tugged at their hats. April was proving a char-latan—offering bright blue skies and warmth one day, fog and sleet the next. The two adventurers tromped on without complaint or discouragement, walking eight blocks to catch the trolley, and giving sighs of relief only when they were settled.

"Are you well, Miss Eleanor?" Bib asked, readjusting the cap on his head.

"Yes, Mr. Randall, thank you. It feels good to be out and active." She watched as he put his hands into the pockets of his well-worn cloth coat. "And you? Are you warm enough?" she asked in return.

He smiled that winning smile. "Couldn't be better, Miss Eleanor. And, I agree, it's a joy to be outdoors." He took a piece of candy out of his pocket and offered it to her. "Molasses peppermint chew?" he asked, holding out his hand.

Eleanor grinned at the eager look on his face. "Yes, thank you," she said, taking the candy. "I love these. I'd never tasted them before coming here."

"Well, at least there's one good thing about San Francisco," Bib said, unwrapping a sweet for himself. He kept talking energetically as if he were talking about the weather or the menu for supper, not a very personal subject. "I mean, you don't really want to be here, do you? So it must be hard."

Eleanor only nodded and looked out the window. They were heading into the downtown area, and the number of buildings and businesses and cars always made her a bit lightheaded. They passed the hook and ladder company, the post office, Mrs. Brunelli's boarding house, and sundry small shops with inviting display windows: a bake shop filled with bread and pastry, a men's haberdashery, and the Marseilles clock company. Eleanor looked hard to see if she could discern whether the quake had done any major damage to the beautiful clocks, but all seemed well. When they approached a lovely five-story building on the corner of Post and Mason, Bib tapped his finger on the window to get her attention.

"See that? That's the Men's Olympic Club."

Eleanor nodded, admiring the structure fronted in yellow pressed brick and finished in Corinthian-style marble work.

"I used to escort Mr. Westfield there every Thursday night," Bib said proudly. "He'd play handball and exercise in the swimming tank." The building slid behind them, and Bib turned to take one last look. "They even have a steam room and a rifle range."

"A rifle range?" Eleanor asked, incredulous. "Inside a building?"

Bib laughed. "Yep. It's a wonder of a place. I plan on being an instructor there someday."

Now Eleanor was completely taken aback. "You do?"

Bib laughed again. "Don't look so shocked."

"Oh! Oh, no . . . it's . . . it's just that, sorry, I mean . . . what kind of instructor?" she asked finally, feeling her face redden with embarrassment.

"Swimming," Bib answered, being a gentleman and not mentioning her change of color. "I almost qualified for the Olympic team two years ago. Sweden. Wouldn't that have been great?"

"What happened?"

Bib shrugged. "Didn't make the time. I might have met Jim Thorpe—greatest athlete in the world." He adjusted his hat again. "Sorry, I'm talking too much."

"Not at all," Eleanor countered, "it's fascinating. Where did you learn to swim?"

"Ocean. My dad taught me."

"But wasn't it cold?"

"Yep. I didn't mind."

"Was he a lifeguard?" Eleanor asked, fascinated by the odd story.

Bib smiled. "No. Actually, he was a preacher of sorts. Taught me swimming and baptized me in the same ocean. He was the one who gave me my name."

"Bib?"

"Well, Bib's the short version. Full name's Bible Old Testament Randall."

Eleanor was stunned. She tried to hide her shocked expression quickly, but Bib had caught its meaning. "Sorry," Eleanor stammered, "it's just that . . ."

Bib laughed loudly and slapped his knee. "Don't worry, Miss Eleanor. Everyone thinks it's a crackpot name. You swim?"

"Pardon?" Eleanor asked, trying to clear her brain. "Swim? Me? No." She quickly changed the subject. "So, you don't want to go on to be a butler?"

Bib smiled broadly. "Now could you see me as Mr. Palmer?"

She shook her head. "No. You don't frown enough." They laughed together, and he handed her another candy. "You think you might try for the Olympics again?" she asked earnestly.

"Naw, that's past. I'm twenty-two, so I'd better start getting serious about my life."

Eleanor nodded. "I'd imagine being a swim instructor would be a good life."

"For a while," Bib answered, nodding his head, "but I plan to work my way up to club manager."

Eleanor was impressed. An under butler, setting his sights to be the head of an important business was brave and ambitious.

"And what do you want to be, Miss Eleanor?"

She turned to look at him straight on. Only Father and Philomene Johnson had ever been interested in her academic achievements, and it felt odd to be asked such a question by a stranger. She cleared her throat. "I . . . I suppose a teacher." She hesitated. "Actually, a nurse."

"You'd be very good at either one," Bib said, nodding. "Understair, we all talk about how smart you are."

"You do?" She felt her face warm. "Well, it's just a farfetched dream."

"Ah, don't give up on dreams, Miss Eleanor," he said, pulling the bell cord for their stop.

"But didn't you give up your dream to be in the Olympics?" she pressed, as they stood to exit the trolley.

Bib jumped deftly from the train and held out his hand to her. "Well, sometimes your dreams have to change a little. My new and sensible dream is to be an instructor at the Men's Olympic Club."

Eleanor took his hand and jumped down. She admired his temperate demeanor—it made him seem like a big brother you could go to with problems, and she found comfort in that revelation.

"So, the library, was it?" Bib interjected.

"Yes," Eleanor answered, moving to the sidewalk.

"That's pretty boring, Miss Lund. If I may say so."

"Is it? Where would you go?" she questioned, intrigued by his bluntness.

Bib smiled at the gaiety playing on her face. "Well, I'd probably go down to the wharf and watch the boats bring in the day's catch: fish, crabs, lobsters." He expected the look on her face to change to disgust, but he was surprised.

"Lobsters? I'd love that!" she answered eagerly, putting on her gloves and looking around. "Which way is the wharf?"

Bib gave her a quizzical look. "Are you sure?"

"Of course! What an interesting letter that will be to Alaina and Miss Johnson!"

"All right, then," Bib said, heading down the hill. "But you have to promise not to let Mrs. Westfield know we changed our plans."

As Eleanor hurried to keep up with Bib Randall's long-legged gait, she crossed her heart and pretended to poke herself in the eye. Why would she tell her auntie about a marvelous adventure that would only upset her fragile sensibilities? Eleanor raced along, feeling as if she may have found her first happy memory of San Francisco.

Chapter Six

"Brussels? Is that where you're gonna go, Miss Johnson?" William Trenton scoffed. "As in brussels sprouts?"

Philomene Johnson smiled at her student's slight witticism. "Yes, Mr. Trenton, Brussels, Belgium, it is." She readjusted her sun hat and reached for a pair of newly sharpened shears. She had never left the trimming of her roses till this late in spring, and she was determined to spend her entire Saturday dedicated to their beautification.

The April air was soft, and filled with the scent of grass and blossoms and plowed field. Philomene's honeysuckle vine was overtaking the side-yard trellis, and it would need a reprimand before the day was through.

"So, what's so great about Brussels that you wanna go there?" William pestered, picking up a pair of trimmers and absently nipping off a flower bud. "Oops! Sorry, Miss Johnson."

"If you wish to help me, William, please direct your energies to dead vegetation only."

William's eyebrows lifted. "Really? I can help?"

"Only if you're not derelict from duties at home."

"Huh?"

"Did you get your chores done?"

"Oh, yes, ma'am. Bright and early. I slopped the hogs, filled the wood bin, and cleared brush from the side quarter acre. Mom's gonna make the garden bigger this year."

Miss Johnson looked surprised. "Bigger? Your mother grows the biggest garden in the county, maybe even the state."

William smiled proudly. "Well, she says us kids gobble up too much of her produce, so she's gotta grow more to sell."

Philomene shook her head as she thought about Ernestine Trenton: five feet tall in her stocking feet, and ninety-eight pounds of pure grit. She was raising seven children on her own after losing her husband, Joe, to a mine cave-in.

"So?"

Miss Johnson came back from her mental wanderings to find William staring at her. She busied herself with her Yellow Dynasty roses. "I suppose the question still concerns my plans to go to Belgium?"

"Yes, ma'am."

"I have a great-aunt who lives in Brussels, and she has invited me to stay for the summer."

"But what will you do over there?"

Philomene smiled. "Museums, art galleries, hikes, excursions, learn to cook their food, improve my French."

William hacked away at a large stalk of tough rosewood. "Sounds boring. You could do most of that stuff here. Well . . . some of it."

Philomene began to dispute his remarks, then she stopped, grasping the true meaning of her young charge's dissension to her plans. They snipped together in silence for a time, minding their work and its outcome.

"Have you been thinking about the troubles in Europe, William?"

He yanked the disconnected branch free and threw it into the trash heap. "No. Well, yes. I mean, I guess so. My oldest brother, Joseph . . . you know him."

Miss Johnson nodded. "Yes, of course."

"Anyway, he says it's a powder keg over there. That don't sound good."

"No, it doesn't," Philomene answered calmly, "but luckily the powder keg does not sit in Belgium."

"It don't?"

"Doesn't."

"Sorry. It doesn't?"

"No." She kept on trimming, watching William's demeanor lose some of its combativeness.

"But, it still could be dangerous." He scowled.

She removed her hat and fanned her face. "True enough. But, one cannot go through life afraid, Mr. Trenton. I would never get on that ship in New York if fear ruled my spirit."

"You afraid of boats?"

"Boats are fine, William. It's the expanse of ocean that worries me. Thousands of miles of swirling, endless ocean."

William chuckled. "Heck, it's just water."

Miss Johnson raised her eyebrows. "Thousands of feet deep."

"Then why do you go?"

"Avarice."

"Ava what?"

"Avarice. It means I'm greedy."

William looked over to his teacher's small cottage. "You?"

"Oh, not for money, William, but for knowledge and experience, and my travel satisfies both. I suppose I will continue as long as my health and inheritance hold out."

William snorted. "Still sounds boring to me."

Miss Johnson chuckled. "Then you and I shall be at loggerheads over this subject, Mr. Trenton."

He closed one eye and looked at her sideways. "Does that mean we're gonna disagree?"

She smiled and trimmed out an overgrown branch. "Exactly so, Mr. Trenton, but I appreciate your concern."

She glanced up from her work to see James Lund riding past on a high-stepping, cinnamon-colored stallion. She admired Emilio Regosi doubly for his husbandry of such magnificent horseflesh, and for seeing in Mr. Lund the innate ability to handle the creatures. She removed her garden gloves and stepped to her gate. "Mr. Lund!" she called. Her low, mellow voice carried well, and James checked the horse and turned to look in her direction. She smiled and waved him over.

"Good afternoon, Miss Johnson," James said as he neared. "Beautiful day for outside adventures."

Philomene grinned. "What a nice thing to call yard work, Mr. Lund. How are you doing?"

"Fine, ma'am."

"Getting on at Mr. Regosi's?"

"Yes, ma'am. He and his wife treat me very well."

"I'm glad to hear it," Miss Johnson replied sincerely. "And you must be a great help to them."

"I hope so, ma'am."

The cinnamon horse tossed its head and stamped.

"Whoa, Solomon," James said in a warm voice.

"That horse is a beauty!" William called out, coming to stand beside Miss Johnson.

"I think so too," James answered, smiling.

Miss Johnson moved William forward. "James Lund, this is William Trenton. I think you went to school with his brother Joseph."

"Yes, ma'am, I did. Good to meet you, William. You're a fine judge of horses."

William's freckled face blushed rose, but he didn't step back. "I mean to get me a horse someday. I couldn't afford nothing like that horse, but just some old plug would do. Of course, if I could get me an Appaloosa, now that would be the ticket. Ain't nothin' prettier."

James chuckled at William's enthusiasm, while Miss Johnson raised her eyebrows at his atrocious grammar and use of slang.

"I been saving since I was six," William boasted.

"Good for you," James praised. "If you can get out to the Regosi ranch someday, I'll let you ride a beautiful little Appaloosa I own."

William's eyes widened. "Really? I could, really? You ain't just pullin' my leg?"

Solomon snorted and tossed his head.

"Yes, I agree, Mr. Solomon!" Philomene Johnson said in a shocked tone. "Such language! And from such a bright boy!"

William gulped back his next words and smiled sheepishly. "Sorry, Miss Johnson. My mom says when I get talking too fast all the proper English just flies out of my brain."

Philomene laid her hands on the boy's shoulders and smiled. "Good thing school will keep you close by where I can keep an eye on you for a few more years."

"Yes, ma'am. But I sure hope you're not trying to make a silk purse out of a sow's ear," William said earnestly. He handed Miss Johnson the trimmers. "Well, I'd better be gettin' back home before my mom wallops me."

Philomene gasped. "William Trenton! Your mother is kindness itself!"

William's grin broadened. "Yes, ma'am, that's a fact. She probably won't wallop me, but she might take away my supper."

Miss Johnson nodded. "Which would be punishment indeed."

"Yes, ma'am." William pushed open the gate and stood facing the big chestnut stallion. "Hey, Solomon," he said softly, scratching the white star on the stallion's forehead. William smiled as the horse's ears flicked. "You sure are beautiful, and I promise to speak better English next time I see you." Solomon whinnied, and William laughed. "This is one smart horse!" He backed away down the street. "Nice to have met you, Mr. Lund."

"You too, William. Keep saving your money."

"I will, sir!" William took one last look at Solomon, then turned and ran for home.

James shook his head. "What a strange thing."

"The lively Mr. Trenton?"

"No," James said, staring after William. "To be called sir, and Mr. Lund. Land sakes! I'm only a few years older than he is." "Four years older," Miss Johnson corrected, "and sitting atop a very big horse."

James chuckled. "Yes, ma'am. I see your point."

"I'm glad you're doing well, James. I wish your sisters were doing better. I received letters from both back in March, and they seemed bored and fretful."

"Yes, ma'am. That's just the feeling I get. Eleanor wrote me the first of April and said she wanted to attend school, but Mother refused."

Philomene slapped her gloves on the fence. "What a waste. I hope at least she's keeping up with her reading."

"I think so," James answered. "My Uncle Cedrick kept a large library, from what Mother told us."

Philomene noted the tensing of James's voice whenever he mentioned his mother, and wondered at the depth of resentment he carried.

James leaned over and patted Solomon's neck. "I heard from Alaina about a week ago. Seems she's helping Nephi's mother in her sewing work, and Nephi is working on the crew that's building the Utah State Capitol."

"Yes. She mentioned that to me also." Philomene slapped her gloves on the fence again. "This must be a hard time for her, being spring. I'm sure she's thinking about all the trees in bloom and the farm coming back to life." James shifted in his saddle. "Have you heard word on how things are going up there?"

James shook his head. "No, ma'am. And I don't much care."

Philomene noted the pain that washed across his face. "I understand, James, of course, but I do think you may want to keep an eye on things."

"Ma'am?"

"As painful as it may be, I think both your sisters are going to want to know how the land is being cared for, and you're the only one to know."

James sat still for a moment, staring at the reins in his hands. He blew out a breath of air and looked at her. "I guess you're right, Miss Johnson. I'll head up in a week or two and check."

Miss Johnson nodded.

"Well, I've got supplies to pick up at the mercantile for Mr. Regosi, so I'd better be going." James tipped his hat and managed a slight smile. "If you're writing my sisters, could you send along a hello from me?"

"Wouldn't you like to do that yourself?"

"Heck, Miss Johnson, you remember my penmanship from school."

Philomene grinned. "Ah, yes. I do. I'll be glad to include word from you to your sisters."

James chuckled. "Thanks. Just tell them I like my work, and Mrs. Regosi feeds me well, and . . ." he hesitated, patting Solomon's neck, "and that I hope they're doing fine, and that I . . ." He looked away down the street. "Well, I guess that's all."

Philomene felt an ache in her throat. "I'll tell them, James."

James nodded and turned Solomon toward town. The observant teacher noticed how beautifully rider and horse melded, and was glad at least one of the Lund children was realizing his calling. She moved out onto the sidewalk and followed her former student's retreat, willing him strength and peace.

"Give my regards to Emilio and Rosa!" she called, stopping at the edge of her fence.

"Yes, ma'am," James answered, waving.

He looks so much like his father. Philomene Johnson's thoughts jumped to William Trenton—another young man who had lost his father well before the proper time. She shook her head at the vagaries of life. Uninvited trials descended upon man without prejudice—their duration, depth, and purpose comprehended only by the God of Job—and the only thing that man could choose in the struggle was victory or defeat. Philomene sighed. It surely was a puzzle over which mankind had grappled since Adam's emergence from the garden.

Birdsong filtered into her philosophy, and the educator put on her gloves and went back to her rosebushes.

Chapter Seven

She was home. The green meadow was filled with white and blue lupine and yellow buttercup. The apple trees stood in blossom on the hillside, and the last of the storm clouds moved away towards the Sierras. The crisp air was filled with the smell of leaf and soil, and she breathed deeply, taking off her blue straw hat so the sun could light on her face. Her hand held tightly to the fence rail as she watched Titus toss his head at the little filly, which bucked and kicked her way around the paddock.

The young man at Alaina's side laughed out loud. "Full of spirit, that one."

Alaina nodded, fanning her face with her hat. "Good bloodline."

The young man's green eyes lit up with amusement. "Interesting how much of ourselves gets passed down."

Alaina reached into her pocket for carrots to offer the sweet little horse, but her fingers struck a hard surface. She frowned at the unexpected object and lifted it out of her pocket. She stared at the book in her hand, wondering how it came to be there and where she'd seen it before. She ran her fingers along the green cover, absently opening the book and flipping through the blank pages. *Blank pages? Who would give me a book with blank pages?* Her head began to hurt as she tried to resurrect a memory of what the object meant to her.

The young man leaned across the fence and started humming. She wanted to tell him to stop because the sound confused her and made it difficult to concentrate on the book. She wanted to tell him, but her mind was focused on the blank pages. She had to remember something about these pages.

A harsh wind came down from the mountains, flipping the fragile paper with distain. Alaina tried to close the book, but she was frozen in place and could only watch as the pages turned yellow and crumbled in her hands. The wind blew the scraps across the dirt, and Alaina thought she saw fragments of a fine penmanship scrawled on some of the pieces. Her heart lurched after the broken expressions, and she felt pain press against her chest. She willed herself to move, to chase after the bits of yellow parchment, but a hand grabbed her wrist and held her back. She flung herself around, angry at the restraint, only to find herself staring into the somber face of the young man. She tried to yank her arm free, but his grip did not yield. Frantically she watched as the last of the papers blew away across the meadow. She kept trying to pull free, but to no avail. She was furious with his callous indifference. The band of pain around her chest released in an angry torrent of tears. She gave her captor an anguished look of desperation, but he had his head bowed and would not look at her.

Alaina came awake with a shudder to find that she was sitting up, her back pressed against the posts of her iron bedstead, her sobbing loud in the quiet night. *Stupid dreams. Will they never give me any peace?* She gulped air, trying to calm the horrid sound she was making.

A knock came at her door.

She put her hand over her mouth, humiliated that she had disrupted Mother Erickson's untroubled sleep.

A second knock.

"I'm . . . I'm all right," she choked. The door opened. "Truly. I'm sorry I bothered you, Mother Erickson."

"Alaina?"

Nephi's low voice made her gasp.

He stepped into the room. "I didn't mean to frighten you."

She whimpered at the tenderness of his voice as all the pain and fear came back to overwhelm her. Since their arrival in Salt Lake City she had kept tight control on any maudlin show of weakness, but that control was an illusion, an illusion unmasked by the quiet concern of her husband's voice.

Alaina grabbed a pillow and pressed it to her face to cover the tears and the shame. She was tired of being a burden, of not being able to put the past behind her and get on with her life. She heard the door close and felt desolation at being left alone.

Suddenly Nephi was beside her, his voice whispering in her ear, "May I hold you?"

She was embarrassed, but could think of nothing she wanted more than the comfort of his arms around her. She nodded and moved over to make room. He slipped into the bed beside her, wrapping her in his arms and smoothing the damp hair away from her face. Alaina buried her head in his neck and wept.

"It's all right," Nephi reassured her, rubbing her arm and pulling her close. "We'll figure it out. Somehow we'll figure it out."

Her fingers plucked at a button at the neck of his long johns. "I'm sorry. Sorry I'm not a good wife to you."

He wiped the tears from her cheek. "You are a good wife."

"No, I'm not." The words came through clenched teeth and were filled with bitterness. "I'm not."

He patted her arm. "We'll figure it out."

It wrenched her heart to hear his words of comfort when she offered him nothing but uninvolved conversation and a reason to be working ten hours a day. She knew she should be concerned with his life, but her heart was full of loss and resentment, which left no room for him.

"Did you have one of your bad dreams?" he asked.

The low timbre of his voice was soothing, and Alaina felt the knot of pain in her chest release. Her father used to hold her when she was hurt or frightened, his low voice blocking out the nightmare scenes and reassuring her that things would be better in the morning.

"You're in your bed, Fancy. Outside are the meadow and the big white moon."

"Father?"

"Yes, little miss?"

"Is the moon smiling?"

"Grinning that silly grin."

"And there aren't any big black birds in the apple trees?"

"Is that what you dreamed?"

"Yes, sir. Eating up all the fruit."

"Don't you fret. There are no big black birds in our precious trees, only starlings and chickadees, and they're just eating up bugs. Ah, look at that big yawn. Are you sleepy now?"

"Yes, sir."

"Would you like me to go, or stay for a while?"

Father's voice faded.

"Stay. Please stay for a while."

Nephi's arms tightened around her, and she realized she had said the last words out loud. She did not regret the misunderstanding.

"You can sleep if you'd like," Nephi said, adjusting his head lower on the pillow.

"I'd rather talk, if that's all right?"

He rubbed her arm. "Of course."

She wanted to talk to him, but the words were jumbled in her head, and she felt foolish. In the brightness of day she and her husband spoke only of household things, of chores, of Nephi's work on the capitol building. What could she say to him now in the intimacy of night with their bodies pressed so close?

Alaina swallowed and tried to clear her thoughts. "I did have a bad dream. It was about my father's journal." She had mentioned Father's journal to Nephi a few times, but only in passing. As she herself had only read one entry, there wasn't much to share. She sat up, reached under the pillow, and brought out the green book. She lay back down in the curve of Nephi's arm, holding the keepsake close and trying to recall the distressing images that had disrupted her sleep.

"I dreamed his book was falling apart—all the pages just crumbling to pieces. At first the pages were blank, and then there was writing, but the pages were scattered and I couldn't read any of it." She shuddered, and Nephi gave her a slight squeeze.

"Are you afraid that his book might get lost or something?"

"I . . . I don't know. Maybe."

"But, you'd still have the words in your head."

She took a deep breath. "No. No, I wouldn't. I've never read it. I've only read the one thing about me being able to run the farm."

Nephi hesitated. "You've never read it?"

Alaina pressed the book closer. "No, because they're his thoughts and feelings—his secret dreams. It wouldn't be right for me to read those things."

Nephi was quiet for a long time, and then he said slowly, "Your father loved you, Alaina. I think he'd like to share those things with you."

She forced control into her voice. "Do you truly think that?"

"I do. You miss him, and I think his words would be a comfort to you."

Serenity flooded her body as she considered reading her father's words. It *would* be a comfort to her. It would be like having him back for a time. She was grateful for Nephi's sensitive assessment, and determined that she wanted to share the experience with him.

"Would you read them to me?" she asked.

"What?"

"My father's words. Would you read them to me? It might be like he was talking to me . . . to us. I know how he cared for you."

Nephi took her hand. "I don't read very well, but I'd be glad to try."

"Good. Every night before bed we'll read some," she answered innocently. Alaina felt a sudden change in Nephi's breathing as the air seemed to catch in his chest. "Are you all right?" she asked.

He was silent for a time, and she sensed he was trying to calm his emotions before answering her.

"What do you mean by 'every night before bed'?" he asked slowly.

Suddenly Alaina realized the implication of her request, and heat rose into her face. What did she mean? Did she want him with her every night? Was she willing to try and be a wife? Surely he didn't think of her that way. They had been married five months and had shared only slight physical contact. She thought of the times Nephi would lightly touch her hand to get her attention or hold her arm when helping her in and out of the truck. She knew well the feeling of his warm hand on her back as he guided her around obstacles. She would take his arm when they walked downtown together, and he would place his hand over hers. There were pats on the arm and brief hugs, but all these exchanges were courtesy or protection or friendship.

Doubts about her plain face and awkwardness crowded out the good feelings of moments before, and she felt sick. *He only married me out of pity, and now he thinks I'm asking him for more—begging him for tenderness and intimacy.*

Nephi waited—willing himself not to talk, willing himself to allow her whatever time she needed to decide their relationship.

"I . . . I . . ." Alaina stammered. "I just want you to read Father's journal to me. I want to share that with you, but . . . but if you'd rather not, I'll understand."

Nephi felt a sting of disappointment. Not that he wanted anything more from her than an indication that she was becoming more comfortable with him—that perhaps stronger feelings for him were emerging because she'd let him hold her and share her bed. *No,* he reminded himself, *she doesn't feel that way about me. She cares for me, but she doesn't love me.*

He wanted to tell her how hard it would be to come to her room every night, to sit near and be intimately connected to her by Samuel's words. He wanted to tell her no, but then he thought of the night she stood before him in her nightgown and her father's work boots, asking him to marry her, and he remembered the silent promise he'd made to try and minimize the pain in her life.

She sat up. "Really, Nephi, if you'd rather not . . ."

He sat up beside her and put his hand on her back. "Of course I want to. I would love to read Samuel's words." He felt her body relax, and was glad that at least she would accept his companionship.

Morning light was edging its way into the room, pushing back the fragile separation of night. Alaina thought of her unwashed face and her bushy hair. She was frantic that he would see her like this, and wanted to hide under the covers or make a dash for the water closet. Whether he sensed her discomfort or was also reluctant to see her in such a state, she felt him move away from her to the edge of the bed.

"Well, it's about time for milking," he stated.

Alaina peeked at him through a slit in her hair. She could see the muscles in his back through the fabric of his long johns, and she blushed and turned away as he stood up.

"Mind if I borrow this quilt?" he asked sheepishly. "I wouldn't want Mother to catch me in my night clothes."

Alaina panicked anew. Mother Erickson! Mother Erickson could be in the kitchen already. What would she think if she saw Nephi coming out of her bedroom? Alaina put the pillow back over her face. She'd probably think it was much more normal for a married couple than the sideshow she'd been seeing for the past five months.

Alaina groaned.

Nephi turned to her. "Are you all right?"

"Fine," she mumbled through the pillow. "I'll be fine."

"What did you say?"

She turned her head to the side. "Fine. I'll be fine."

He paused. "I'll see you at breakfast then," he said quietly, moving out of the room and shutting the door behind him.

She didn't know if it was nerves or tiredness, but for some reason she found the last two minutes very funny, and she broke into a fit of giggles. She remembered one time when she and Eleanor were little girls and had gone into a fit of giggles at church. Mother had sent them out to sit in the wagon until the service was over, where the liberated twosome had a marvelous time playing games and eating bits of food from the picnic lunch—dried apple rounds and fruitcake.

Alaina lifted her face to the window. *Apple rounds.* Not long ago she and Eleanor had spent a day slicing apple rounds for drying. That was the same day Kathryn said she knew for a fact that her oldest sister would never be married.

Alaina threw the pillow against the bedpost and got up to dress for the day. She picked up her hairbrush and saw the simple wedding band on her finger. *Well, I fooled you, Miss Kathryn, didn't I? It may not be much of a marriage, but it is a marriage nonetheless.*

Chapter Eight

"That's a lovely piece of toast!" Mother Erickson said, smiling.

Alaina looked at the piece of bread she was holding over the opening in the wood stove, and realized it was on the verge of becoming charcoal. She snatched the tongs back. "Oh! Oh, I'm sorry, Mother Erickson."

"It's fine, you little muffin. We'll just scrape off some of the black into the slop bucket. No harm. I think you're just tired. You look a little tired."

"Yes, ma'am. I didn't sleep well last night."

"Well, back in you get! Go lie down. I can handle breakfast."

"Oh no, ma'am. I'm just fine." Alaina sliced another piece of bread and watched carefully as she held it over the fire.

"You are quite a woman, Alaina Lund Erickson."

Alaina was always surprised by Mother Erickson's straight talk, and this direct evaluation embarrassed her. She stared more intently at the bread she was toasting, hoping her mother-in-law would be distracted into other topics.

"Even with all your grief, you come in, you do your part—never complaining. That's a mighty strength of character. Yes, it is." Mother Erickson came to the stove and poured the egg mixture she'd been beating into the large cast-iron fry pan, stirring it immediately so the eggs wouldn't brown.

Alaina breathed in the heavenly smell and tried to deflect the praise. "Everybody has something hard to deal with," she answered, placing the perfectly done piece of toast on the serving platter. She had matured enough to know that everyone's life held misery and loss. She shuddered as she thought about Sarah losing two babies not long after their births, of Nephi's estrangement from his father, of Mother Erickson's difficult childhood. Eleanor Patience Erickson had lost her mother at eight and her father at thirteen. She was taken in by a neighbor family and was taught dressmaking as a means of paying her way.

Alaina sighed and shook her head. "No one has a life free from care."

Mother Erickson patted her arm. "True enough, but some mules cause their own grief, don't ya think?"

Alaina chuckled. "Yes, ma'am."

"And some folks mewl and whine over the smallest burden, while others, whose backs are bent over with the weight of unasked-for trials, trudge along saying, 'Oh no, I'm doing fine. I'll be fine. Don't worry about me.'"

Alaina laughed at her mother-in-law's comical antics.

"The secret," Mother Erickson said kindly, "is to not trudge along alone until the burdens smash you flat." She dumped the pan of eggs onto the platter and held the ceramic dish out for Alaina's final piece of toast.

Alaina's countenance changed to contemplation as she looked into Mother Erickson's round face. "Yes, ma'am."

"Good girl. Now go call your husband to breakfast."

Alaina nodded. As she went to the back porch to call Nephi, she found herself smiling. If any other person had tried to give her advice on how to deal with her pain, Alaina was sure her pride and temper would have thrown their offerings into the slop bucket, but with Mother Erickson, Alaina understood that love was her only motivation.

Alaina opened the squeaky screen door and saw Nephi at the entrance to the barn. He looked up and waved.

The sky was brilliant blue, and though there was morning frost on the grass, Alaina knew that would be gone with the first touch of sunlight. "Breakfast!" she called loudly.

"Yes, ma'am," he called back. "Thank you!"

He had just turned Miss Titus out into the pasture, and Alaina smiled as she watched the beautiful little filly race across the yard to pester the milk cow. Alaina turned reluctantly from the vision of the day to help with final preparations in the kitchen. She passed by Nephi's winter coat hanging in the back porch, absently taking one of the sleeves and pressing it to her face. She breathed in the smell of him, feeling a sense of peace come over her. She stepped back. What was she doing? She looked down at the sleeve in her hand and thought of apple and pear trees, of Pine Grove and Sutter Creek, of Philomene Johnson and Joanna Wilton, of Titus and Friar Tuck, of her dear sister Eleanor. She pressed the sleeve to her eyes trying to block out the cherished images of home. It did not do to dwell on things beyond her reach. Impulsively she wrapped her arms around the coat and breathed deeply. This smell was Utah grass and winter snow and the brown cow in the pasture. This smell was here and now, of Nephi with his sandy hair and astonishingly blue eyes. She thought of last night and his warm arms holding her close, causing the nightmare to retreat. Alaina stepped back, rearranging the coat on the hook and smoothing out any wrinkles. She brushed wisps of hair away from her face and calmed her breathing before heading off to the kitchen. She had been so intent on her thoughts and feelings that she hadn't noticed Nephi coming to the back porch door, hadn't seen his face as he watched her actions with a mingled sense of wonder and desire, hadn't heard him whisper her name when she'd moved away to the kitchen.

* * *

"Only two helpings of eggs? You normally have at least three," Mother Erickson said with a bemused grin. She attempted to put eggs and toast on her son's plate, but he flatly refused.

"I'm not that hungry this morning."

"Pshaw," she snorted. "You've never stepped out of this house with that scrawny a breakfast."

Alaina laughed. "It was probably my burned toast that put him off."

"Your burned toast was wonderful," he said with a mischievous grin. "From now on that's the way I want my toast."

Alaina laughed and put a forkful of egg into her mouth, glancing over at Nephi then averting her eyes to her plate.

He finished the last of his toast and leaned back contentedly. "Ah, best toast in three counties."

Alaina rolled her eyes. "Oh, for heaven's sake, go to work."

Nephi stood and reached for his lunch pail. "Ever dutiful, I'm off." He hesitated. "There's only one problem."

"What's that?" Alaina asked curtly.

"I can't go until Elias stops by to pick me up."

"Well, go wait on the porch," Alaina said with a dismissive wave of her hand.

Mother Erickson watched the two carefully. Something was different. Their usual demeanor with each other was polite and a bit stiff, but this morning each seemed more willing to let their guard down—to be playful. She said a little prayer of hope. She loved them both and wanted them to find peace in their union.

"Good-bye, Mother," Nephi said, bending to kiss her on the forehead. "She's making me wait on the porch."

"Serves you right," Mother Erickson said sternly. "That will teach you to tease." They shared a look, and Nephi smiled.

"Have a good day," he said to Alaina. "I'm going now to freeze on the front porch."

"I thought you came from tough pioneer stock," she countered.

Mother Erickson hooted with delight. "She has you there, son!"

Nephi grinned.

All three heard the hardware truck pull up in front of the house, and Nephi headed for the door with Mother and Alaina following. Elias parked the truck and opened his door to get out. Normally he just gave a wave and drove off as soon as Nephi was in the vehicle, but today it was clear his intention was to talk to his mother.

It was chilly in the shadow of the porch, and Alaina pulled her shawl close as she watched Elias approach.

"Morning," Elias said as he reached them.

"Morning, son."

"Sarah's not feeling well this morning, Mother, and wonders if you could tend to Grandfather Erickson?"

"Of course, be glad to. Anything we can do for Miss Sarah?"

Elias shook his head. "I think she just needs rest."

"Quite a job, making a baby," Mother Erickson stated.

Alaina blushed at the pronouncement and found a string to tug on her apron pocket.

"Alaina and I will take some soup over to her later this afternoon," Mother Erickson assured him.

Alaina glanced up to find Elias looking at her, and it made her uncomfortable.

"I'm sure your soup would be welcomed," Elias answered, looking back and smiling at his mother. He slapped Nephi on the shoulder. "We'd better be going, little brother. Good day, Mrs. Erickson," he said, tipping his cap.

Nephi turned to smile at Alaina. "See you at supper."

"Have a good day," she answered, aware that Elias was watching them.

The two women waved as the truck pulled away, then Patience Erickson turned abruptly and moved back into the house. "Off we go, angel, much to do today."

Alaina smiled at her mother-in-law's pluck and energy as she followed her inside. The woman was a tireless worker: along with her successful sewing business there was always cleaning, baking, mending, taking care of civic responsibilities, gardening, and attending to Church duties. Mother Erickson taught the wee ones in the Children's Primary Association and had a flock of little lambs that Alaina adored. Alaina didn't attend Sunday services with the family, for she'd found them restrictive and excessive the very first time she'd tried. The different meetings took up the whole day, and Alaina found that a burden, but she did love going with Mother Erickson every Wednesday afternoon to sit in the chapel and watch the innocents file into the room with their arms folded. She also liked to hear their sweet voices lifted in song, or to laugh with them when they asked funny questions during the lesson.

"Your hands won't work if your head is not behind them," Mother Erickson chuckled as she patted Alaina on the arm.

Embarrassed for daydreaming, Alaina pulled her mind to the present and went to work. Indeed, the next hour was a flurry of activity as breakfast was cleared, kitchen scrubbed, stove banked, eggs gathered, Miss Titus attended to, and ingredients gathered for soup. It was decided they'd cook the soup at Grandfather Erickson's house; then they could leave him a portion and take the rest to Sarah.

Alaina had only been to Grandfather Erickson's home a few times since coming to Salt Lake, and had never really had the chance to talk to him. In truth, she was intimidated by his gruff look and large stature, and though she knew from past experience with her father's friend, Fredrick Robinson, that size was no indication of a person's temperament, Grandfather Erickson's stoic demeanor made him seem unapproachable. Born in Denmark in the 1830s, he had not chosen fishing or farming as a trade, but fur trapping and boat building. Hiking the backwoods and felling and hauling trees was just the rough work needed to build his body and stamina, and even though he was in his eighties he was still a formidable force. Alaina had to remind herself that he was also an artisan whose way with wood was remarkable. The houses he had built in the Salt Lake Valley had the reputation of being the best, and the wood carvings he did as a hobby were prized treasures of anyone lucky enough to possess one. Alaina guessed that Nephi's artistic talent came to him from his grandfather, and she wondered what other qualities they might have in common. She also knew that Grandfather was generous, as several in the family were fortunate to have inherited one of the homes constructed by the burly Dane. Many of the homes were built on parcels of land he'd inherited from his father, beautiful tracts nestled in the high foothills of the Wasatch Mountains.

The first house Lars Erickson built for himself and his wife, Caroline, was the cottage now occupied by Elias and Sarah. The second, larger house nearer to town was taken over by Nephi's father, his first wife Eunice, and their children, leaving the eighty-year-old patriarch to finish out his days in the house he built for Caroline in her declining years. He was sixty-three years old when he began the labor of love, which stood only six blocks northeast of Mother Erickson's. The house enchanted Alaina, for it looked like something out of a fairy tale. It was set back from the road and encircled by shade and fruit trees. The shingles on the roof were rounded and stained different shades of brown; the fireplace chimney and the house's foundation up to the bottom of the first-floor windows were round river rock; and the quaint porch, which surrounded the house on two sides, had supporting columns carved with woodland animals, ferns, and flowers. Mother Erickson said that Caroline would sit for hours on the porch and watch her husband carve. The oval window in the front door was filled with a beautiful stained glass of purple irises. Purple iris was Caroline's favorite flower, and every home they owned had them somewhere on the property.

The home Mother Erickson occupied had been built for Lars's son Peter. Peter and his family lived in the home only two years before being sent by Brigham Young to Manti to help settle the area. When Nephi told her Uncle Peter's story, Alaina thought it foolish for a man to uproot his family and move them to a wilderness just because another man gave the edict. She had never voiced her opinion about the subject, but filed it away with the other things she found odd about her husband's faith.

Alaina pulled her mind to the present, glancing out the window to the north yard where Caroline's enchanting purple flowers would be blooming in a month or so. She finished packing the sewing basket with darning that would keep her hands busy for hours, and a blouse Mother Erickson wanted to finish for a customer. When Eleanor Erickson said "much to do," she meant it.

The six-block walk to Grandfather Erickson's was a delight. The sun's warmth had dried the grass of dew and taken the chill out of the morning air, and though their burdens were many, they were nothing the two women couldn't manage for the brief jaunt. They turned onto the pathway from the road, and Alaina felt the cool of the shadowed walk. She caught sight of the cottage through the trees and smiled. She knew it was a silly fantasy, but she thought she heard the house whisper hello and welcome them as they drew near.

Mother Erickson hesitated on the path. "Hear that?"

Alaina jumped. *Had Mother Erickson heard the house's welcome too?* Alaina listened and heard someone playing the piano. She nodded. "Piano."

"He must be feeling better today," her mother-in-law said, continuing on toward the front steps. "I haven't heard him play in almost a year."

Alaina caught up. "He plays piano?"

"Beautiful piano and violin. Plays by ear." She knocked loudly on the front door, hesitated a moment, then opened it. "Father Erickson? It's Patience."

The playing stopped. "Come in. Come in, Patience."

She entered the house with Alaina right behind her, walking to the back room where they found Lars Erickson seated in a chair facing the well-worn upright piano. He was obviously surprised to see the two Erickson women.

"Vere is Sarah?" he questioned.

"Not feeling well," Mother Erickson answered, shifting her bags. "We're going to get you settled and make some soup."

Though Mother Erickson was talking, Lars kept his attention on Alaina. She looked around the room, unwilling to meet his scrutiny. She felt vulnerable and plain. Her wandering gaze finally fell on the piano, and she quickly checked her expression as she saw Grandfather Erickson's gnarled and deformed hands, the swollen knuckles, the fingers bent at unnatural angles. Why hadn't she noticed this on prior visits? She thought back and realized that he'd always been sitting in his chair with a plaid woolen blanket over his lap and his hands beneath. Her other visits had been in the winter, and she well understood the misery of winter cold on sore, aching joints.

"I loved that song you were playing," Alaina ventured. She was surprised at the steadiness of her voice.

Mother Erickson gave her an approving look. "I'm going to take these things to the kitchen." She nodded to Alaina and moved off with the bags.

Alaina inched closer to the piano, setting down the sewing basket. "'Praise to the Lord.' My father used to sing that song."

"Hymn."

Alaina stepped back. "Yes, sir. A beautiful hymn. Would you play it for me?"

Grandfather Erickson took his hands from the keys and laid them in his lap. "Not so good."

She sat down in a chair at the side of the piano so she was facing him. "I thought it was wonderful. It made me think of my father." She wondered how she was being so brave. Usually she was ill at ease and shy around strangers.

"Your father was a Lutheran man to know dis hymn?"

"Well, he started out Presbyterian, then became Methodist when he married my mother, then joined . . . your church after Nephi gave him a Book of Mormon."

Grandfather Erickson chuckled. "Ya. Nephi tell me the story. I like to have met your father. He vas searching yust like me."

Alaina was so taken aback by Grandfather Erickson's unexpected affability that she forgot to respond. The big Dane laid his hands back onto the keys and plunked out a few notes.

"I von time made a piano."

Alaina stared at him to see if he was teasing her. "Really?"

"Vell, I carve the outside. Vas for my mother, before I leave Denmark." He played a few notes, then started again the hymn he'd been playing when the women arrived.

Alaina sat motionless, her mind imagining the lush countryside of Denmark and a young man with strong hands and straight fingers carving memories into the wood of his mother's piano—a keepsake for a mother he would never see again. Visions of apple trees in bloom and her father's singing pushed their way into the music, and she felt an ache in her throat. She laid her hand on Grandfather Erickson's arm. "Stop." She looked up, aghast at what she'd just done. "I'm sorry," she stammered, "it was beautiful. It's just that . . ."

"I understand," he answered, sliding his fingers off the keys. "You miss your papa."

She nodded.

"Come. You take me back to my chair."

She nodded again and helped him to stand.

"You are very strong voman," he complimented as they moved towards the front room.

"And you're a mountain," she said with genuine admiration.

Grandfather Erickson laughed deep and loud, causing Patience to rush from the kitchen, carrots clenched in her fist, a look of concern on her face. "Are you all right?"

"Yah. Not to vorry, Patience. She make me laugh." He put his gnarled hand on the top of Alaina's head, and they continued their trek.

Mother Erickson wondered at the camaraderie of the twosome. She knew that her father-in-law had been observing Alaina on their last few visits, evaluating the caliber of the young woman who had married his grandson. She also knew the venerated patriarch was an astute judge of character, and the ease with which he incorporated his granddaughter-in-law into his normally austere company indicated a favorable impression. Patience was glad. She could empathize with the loneliness and separation Alaina was feeling and knew that any warmth offered would help ease that isolation. She sighed and looked down at the carrots in her hand, which were dripping water all over the floor. "Oh, my goodness!" she chirped, rushing back into the kitchen.

Alaina held tightly to Grandfather Erickson's arm as he maneuvered himself into his chair. "I can get around by myself," he said gruffly, "but, nicer to have company." A slight smile touched the corners of his mouth, and Alaina chided herself for ever thinking of the man with trepidation.

"Now, you have vork?" he asked, looking at her sternly.

"Mending," she answered.

"Vell, go get it, den you sit dere on the divan and keep me company. And don't look unhappy. Mending is pretty good job."

Alaina raised her eyebrows. "Really? I hate mending," she growled as she went to get the sewing basket.

Grandfather Erickson chuckled. "And laundry?"

"Well, that's not as bad as mending," she said, coming to sit down.

"And cooking?"

"I don't mind cooking, but I'm not very good at it."

"Better at picking apples."

She caught her breath. "Yes," she said slowly. "I'm very good at that."

"And pruning?

"Pruning?" She was sure he already knew the answer to his own question, but decided to humor him. *What is he up to?* "Yes, sir. I know how to prune fruit trees."

"I have fruit trees."

"Yes, I've seen them."

"Pretty bad shape," he said with a solemn shake of his head.

"Well, they haven't been tended for a while."

"You can do dat for me?"

"Take care of your trees?"

"Yah. Get dem in shape."

Alaina's emotions jumped. There were only a dozen or so trees—nothing like the hundreds that covered the hillsides of her home, but it still would be a joyful enterprise.

"I would love to take care of your trees!" she answered, delight radiating into her face.

Lars Erickson nodded. "Yah, goot. You come venever you vant. I have tools in de shed."

Alaina stared at the weathered face. "Thank you."

"No, it's for me," he answered, shaking his head. "I vant aeblekage. Apple cake."

Alaina smiled, pulling one of Nephi's work shirts out of the basket and rummaging in the case for the appropriate-size buttons. As she threaded her needle she watched Grandfather Erickson's eyelids droop and his head loll against the pillowed back of his chair. She tried to see him as a young man, imposing Nephi's youthful features over the mask of age. She stitched and pictured Lars Erickson on a rugged coastal shore building a boat and singing a Danish song, his rumbling bass voice carried out to sea by an aggressive wind. She imagined his first faltering attempts to talk to an attractive young woman who would later become his treasured companion. She thought of the young man sharing the message of the religion his family had found years before, of reading with her the words of a new Bible, of leaving the green beauty of their homeland to travel to a place of struggle and desolation. *Why? Why would they do such a thing?*

She looked up to find Grandfather Erickson watching her. "Are you all right?" she asked softly. "Can I get you anything?"

"I'm fine," he said, looking out the window to the blue sky now flecked with clouds. His sight drifted to the stained glass window in the front door. "You remind me a little bit of my Caroline." Alaina didn't answer. "She vas fine voman. Strong voman. But her heart failed her. You know dis?" Alaina nodded. He was silent for a long time, and Alaina wondered if he were drifting back to sleep. Finally he spoke. "May I ask you question?"

Alaina looked up. "Of course."

"I vant to ask vy you married my grandson."

Alaina's hand jerked, and she nearly poked herself with the needle. *Well, that was blunt.* She blinked several times thinking that at any moment he would issue an apology, say it was none of his business, but the big man just sat there waiting for a reply. She closed her mouth and swallowed. How was she supposed to answer that question? She shook her head to clear her thoughts, and still he waited, his blue eyes penetrating. Was he going to reprimand her callous use of his grandson? Alaina was confused. She had thought he liked her. Hadn't he just asked her to care for his fruit trees? Yet his uncomfortable question hung in the air, and he obviously expected an answer.

"I . . ." she began weakly. "I wanted to save our farm. I had to be married to hold the deed, and . . ." How could she possibly admit that no one else would have her? "And Nephi loved the farm too, so I thought . . ." What had she thought? "I thought that . . ."

"You tink dat you grow to love each other?"

Alaina found herself clenching the material in her hand, feeling heat rise into her face. "No," she replied squarely. "No. I never expected that. I thought we'd work the farm as friends." She realized how cold that sounded as soon as the words left her mouth, so she was not surprised to see Grandfather Erickson's brow furrow in response. "I . . . I" she stammered on foolishly, "I never expected that Nephi could . . . that he would . . . love me." She looked down at her hands, unable to meet the big man's gaze.

"Stakkels lille spruv," the patriarch interrupted in Danish. "Man kan ikke se skogen for trærne."

Alaina looked up. "What does that mean?" she asked, a note of irritation in her voice.

"It means, little sparrow, dat you cannot see da forest because of all da trees," he answered.

"And what does that mean?" she asked again, trying to control the emotion that had clamped itself around her throat.

Grandfather Erickson leaned forward, looking at her with eyes of tenderness. "It means you cannot see dat my grandson loves you already."

Chapter Nine

"A plain face, but the dark hair is lovely," Mrs. Colin Fitzpatrick said briskly, smiling at Eleanor across her teacup, and then turning her face to Mrs. Westfield.

Aunt Ida's head bobbed up and down in agreement as she offered Mrs. Fitzpatrick another scone. "She tends to dress unadorned," Aunt Ida added, "but I think that is all right for the young girls."

"As long as she does not go back to that country clothing," Mrs. Fitzpatrick stated with obvious distaste.

Eleanor stiffened but said nothing. She had become accustomed to the women in her aunt's circle of acquaintances speaking their minds without compunction, at least when speaking of or to their lessers, and Eleanor was certainly aware that she was less than Mrs. Colin Fitzpatrick: wife of the bank president of the Pacific Bank, chairwoman of the Civic League, and heir to the Derbon fortune.

Eleanor smiled behind her teacup. *Well, perhaps I'm less in money and status, but certainly not less in kindness and intelligence.* Eleanor chided herself for thinking ill of an elder and attempted a more level evaluation. There was no denying that Mrs. Fitzpatrick was an elegant woman in face, dress, and manner. She wore a gray silk suit edged in white; a collection of teardrop crystal necklaces, and an impressive folded hat draped with soft, gray ostrich feathers. Eleanor was mesmerized at how the feathers fluttered each time Mrs. Fitzpatrick moved her head. She drew her eyes away from the hat and thought of her father. Perhaps he sat in this very chair in this very drawing room, meeting her mother for the first time. She doubted that Uncle Cedrick had spoken down to her father or disparaged his simple dress and manner. In fact, Aunt Ida had divulged that Cedrick had been quite taken with Samuel Lund, and Samuel's green eyes and honesty had charmed her sister Elizabeth. *Had Father told any of his humorous stories? Had Mother laughed?*

Eleanor fidgeted in her straight-backed chair. Perhaps Mother married the simple country farm boy to escape the restrictive furniture and stiff clothing of her upbringing. She looked over at Bib Randall standing elegantly by the buffet cart in his formal serving uniform, black tie, and white gloves. She recognized the vacant stare that all the servants adopted when serving—a look that indicated they were unable to hear a word of conversation going on five feet from where they stood. She always found the deception funny.

"Did you want more tea, Eleanor?" Aunt Ida asked in a slightly reprimanding tone.

Eleanor jumped. "Ah, yes, Aunt Ida. More tea would be lovely."

Mrs. Westfield raised her hand. "Mr. Randall, more tea for Miss Lund."

Bib Randall picked up the teapot and gracefully poured more tea for the young woman, concealing any show of friendship.

"Ruth, would you care for more tea?" Aunt Ida asked her companion.

"Oh, no thank you, Ida," Mrs. Fitzpatrick said, dismissing the servant with a flick of her hand. "I am meeting with Genevieve Allen on the Barbary Coast situation."

Eleanor was surprised by the startled look on her aunt's face and became immediately interested in the conversation. "Excuse my asking, Mrs. Fitzpatrick, but what is the Barbary Coast situation?"

Aunt Ida tutted. "Never mind. Just never you mind. It is none of your concern."

"Oh, for heaven's sake, Ida, some of the girls down there are her age. You can't keep her forever from the world."

Mrs. Westfield opened her mouth as though to argue, then picked up her napkin and pressed it to her lips. Eleanor, on seeing that her aunt's protest had been silenced, looked back to Mrs. Fitzpatrick with expectation.

Mrs. Fitzpatrick addressed her directly. "Many groups interested in civic betterment have been trying to help the women in the red light district find other means of employment."

Eleanor brightened. "Oh yes! I've read about that."

Aunt Ida's teaspoon clattered onto her saucer. "You've what?"

"Read about it. *The Chronicle* had a related article about the California Red Light Abatement Act."

"Read about it?" Aunt Ida interrupted, her normally rosy cheeks scarlet. "Read about it? Where did you get a newspaper?"

Out of the corner of her eye Eleanor saw Bib Randall shift his weight and cover a cough with a gloved hand. This breech of conduct went unnoticed by the two older women, who were both looking intently at Eleanor—Aunt Ida's face a mask of mortification.

Mrs. Fitzpatrick, on the other hand, seemed amused by Eleanor's mature grasp of reality. "The Barbary Coast is the red light district where women of the YWCA and California Civic League are centering their efforts of redemption."

Eleanor nodded. "Do many accept the help?" she asked sincerely.

Aunt Ida spluttered, but Mrs. Fitzpatrick ignored her. "It is an astute question, Miss Lund, and the answer is no. Although we have many businesses willing to give employment to those competent to fill positions, many of the women choose to stay in the district."

Eleanor nodded again.

"You don't find that remarkable?" Mrs. Fitzpatrick questioned, anxious to hear Eleanor's response.

"No," Eleanor said simply. "They probably make more money."

Aunt Ida had had enough. "Eleanor Lund! How do you presume to talk about such subjects?"

"She's right, Ida, even if they choose to sell food or drinks in the district, the women do indeed make more money," Mrs. Fitzpatrick stated, looking at Eleanor with a curious admiration.

"I would go after the men that frequent the place," Eleanor said bluntly.

Aunt Ida looked on the verge of collapse. "Well . . . well, I never! I must say Ruth, I truly do not think it conversation for afternoon tea, not for one so young."

"Auntie, I'll be sixteen in August," Eleanor stated.

Aunt Ida fluttered her fingers at her. "That's two months. And two months are two months."

Eleanor ignored her and turned to Mrs. Fitzpatrick with a new respect. "I would love to help. I'm sure there's so much to be done."

"Absolutely not!" Aunt Ida said sharply, her fragile voice taking on a note of hysteria.

Mrs. Fitzpatrick smiled. "Your aunt is right, Eleanor. The work there is for older women—women with toughened sensibilities." Eleanor started to protest, but Mrs. Fitzpatrick held up a gloved hand. "However, I am involved in other projects that could use your intelligence and energy, if you are interested."

"I'm very interested," Eleanor said, amazed at Mrs. Fitzpatrick's altered treatment.

Ruth Fitzpatrick turned to her friend. "If it meets with your approval, Ida, I will call on your niece after her birthday to discuss the options."

Ida was in such a state of shock that she merely nodded.

"And now I must be on my way," Mrs. Fitzpatrick announced.

Bib Randall came forward immediately to pull out her chair. He then stepped to the back of Mrs. Westfield's chair and did the same. Eleanor shoved back her own chair and stood before he could reach her, which merited a look of chagrin from her already-flustered aunt.

"I must say I'm surprised to find so capable a mind coming from your country background," Mrs. Fitzpatrick said, a hint of superiority in her voice.

"Actually, I had a remarkable education," Eleanor defended. "One teacher, Miss Philomene Johnson, was especially brilliant."

Mrs. Fitzpatrick raised her eyebrows. "Well, it's good to know that California is attempting to keep up somewhat with the eastern states." She moved to the door, which Mr. Randall opened smoothly, allowing the women to pour into the entry foyer.

Mr. Palmer stood at the front door, placing his hand on the doorknob as the women approached. He handed Mrs. Fitzpatrick her sun umbrella and nodded.

"Thank you, Palmer. It's always nice to see you."

"A pleasure, Mrs. Fitzpatrick. And how is Mr. Fitzpatrick?"

"Doing well, Palmer, thank you." She held out her hand to Ida and Eleanor in turn. "Thank you for tea, Ida, and your donation to the temperance league. And you, Miss Lund, I will be scouting out a place for you, so be prepared." Mrs. Fitzpatrick moved onto the front landing where she was met by her driver and escorted down the stairs and to her automobile.

Eleanor went to the window to watch her departure. She had seen Mrs. Fitzpatrick come and go from the house on many occasions, but this was the first time she'd been invited to share her company. How different now her views of the woman. Yes, Mrs. Fitzpatrick had money, servants, and prestige, but she was far from frivolous or wasteful of her position. She used her status to effect change and to help people. Eleanor smiled at the prospect of participating in some great work set out by Mrs. Fitzpatrick.

"Come away from the window!" Aunt Ida snapped. "It is not seemly."

Eleanor sighed and turned back into the foyer.

"I will be going to my room for a rest before supper, Eleanor," her aunt said melodramatically. "Please entertain yourself in any quiet manner."

"Yes, Aunt Ida."

"And Palmer, I believe Cook is serving roasted chicken for supper. Please remind her that the last one was dry. She must be diligent with the basting."

"Yes, ma'am."

Aunt Ida turned to the stairs, and Mr. Palmer left for the kitchen, leaving Eleanor alone to ponder how to occupy herself on another boring afternoon. Stitchery? Playing cards with Mother? She straightened the floral arrangement on the foyer's center table. She could always hide herself away in Uncle Cedrick's well-stocked library, but she didn't feel like reading today—even a medical book she'd found on the human anatomy did not entice her. Perhaps she could sneak out of the house and go on an outing.

"Psst!"

What was that?

"Psst. Miss Eleanor, over here."

Eleanor turned to see Miss McKee peeking out from behind the drawing room door and beckoning to her. She checked her surroundings, then slipped quickly into the room. As soon as she was inside she saw Ina Bell and Bib clearing the tea items from the table.

"Hello, Miss Lund," Ina Bell said with a curtsy, picking up the plate of scones and placing it on a large serving tray.

"So, did your aunt survive?" Bib asked, clearing the teapot from the buffet cart.

"What do you mean?" Eleanor asked, looking around at the three. She could see that each was suppressing laughter.

"Did you actually talk to Mrs. Fitzpatrick about the Barbary Coast?" Ina Bell asked, a look of wonder on her face.

"I did, yes," Eleanor answered, grinning.

"I'm findin' it strange that Mrs. Westfield didn't faint dead away," Kerri said, stopping her work to stare at Eleanor.

"I thought I was going to have to run for Mr. Palmer and the salts," Bib stated, a gleam in his eyes. "You should have seen the look on the mistress's face!"

They were all laughing now.

"Well, Mrs. Fitzpatrick didn't think it was an inappropriate topic," Eleanor said.

"Aye, but Mrs. Fitzpatrick is Mrs. Fitzpatrick now, isn't she?" Kerri answered. "The woman's taken on votes for women, political graft, and the demon rum."

Eleanor was shocked. "She has?"

"She has indeed. Don't ya be fooled by her graceful manner and elegant dress; she's a badger when it comes to causes."

Eleanor shook her head. "How did she and my aunt ever become friends?"

"Their husbands were both presidents of banks, so they were," Kerri said, picking up the table linens and folding each piece. "Mrs. Fitzpatrick knows she can never get Mrs. Westfield to actually help with any of the work, but that makes her generous with donations. Helps soothe her conscience, I'm thinkin'."

"Kerri McKee! Mind your tongue!" Ina Bell scolded.

"Oh, it's just us here," Kerri said, giving her friend a haughty look.

"And Mrs. Westfield's niece," Ina Bell reminded.

"What? Eleanor Lund? Why she's practically one of us now, isn't she?"

Bib laughed. "Truly spoken, Miss McKee. Truly spoken."

Eleanor felt a rush of gratitude to be included in their circle of friendship.

"And are you really going to help?" Ina Bell asked.

Eleanor nodded. "I am. Well, not with the Barbary Coast situation, but with something. I hope something difficult and useful."

"That will be good for you," Bib said, giving Eleanor a little wink. "I believe your ability is wasted on stitchery, and I'm sure even reading can get boring after a time."

Miss McKee gave Eleanor a supporting look. "Me da used to say, 'twas a shame to plant an oak seed in a flower pot."

Ina Bell burst out laughing.

"Now don't you be laughing at me da, Ina Bell Latham!"

"I'm not! I'm not!" Ina Bell said, trying to control herself. "It's just that he came up with the funniest sayings." Kerri looked at her with narrowed eyes, and Ina Bell quickly picked up the serving tray and headed for the door. "I didn't mean that in a bad way," she said, rushing out, the fragile china teacups rattling as she ran.

Kerri picked up the linens and followed. "Let's see how steady you are on the stairs with those things."

Eleanor and Bib listened as Ina Bell's laughter and squeals faded down the hall, then Bib turned to Eleanor, a big grin on his face. "Never a dull moment with those two."

"I wish it were never a dull moment," Eleanor replied, moving over to help him clear the last of the tea items. "I'm about to go mad with nothing to do." She picked up a lemon slice off the tray and threw it down again. "How will I stand it the next two months until Mrs. Fitzpatrick gives me an occupation? I'm used to work and learning, not idleness and social engagements." She was pacing the room now, and Bib smiled at her. "I mean, even Kathryn is kept busy with outings and schooling, and all the little brat does is complain about it." She imitated Kathryn's petulant tone. "'Miss Clawson makes me do numbers and I hate numbers, and tomorrow we're going to the museum and I hate the museum. I just want to be lazy at home, and look beautiful, and bother my sister.'"

Bib laughed.

Eleanor stopped her pacing. "Oh, I'm so sorry. I'm being awful, aren't I?"

Bib shook his head. "Not at all. I'd imagine this is a terrible life for you."

She was surprised by his directness. "Yes, it is." She started pacing again. "I shouldn't complain. I'm sure things aren't easy for my sister Alaina either, but at least she does sewing and helps around the house, and trains Miss Titus, and milks the cow."

"A charmed life, indeed," Bib said, laughing.

"Don't you tease me, Bib Randall," Eleanor scolded. "And from what Miss Johnson writes, my brother James is doing well on the Regosi's ranch. He gets to do something he loves." She kicked at the leg of the buffet cart. "Oh, I'm just being a screeching scullery maid. Actually, right now, I think I'd enjoy being a screeching scullery maid."

The drawing room door opened and Mr. Palmer entered. Eleanor saw Bib stoop immediately to pick up the serving tray—the look on his face one of efficient detachment.

"Everything tidy, Mr. Randall?" Mr. Palmer asked, surveying the room.

"Yes, Mr. Palmer. Just so."

"Good." The head butler turned his attention to Eleanor. "The post has just arrived, Miss Lund, and there are two letters for you."

"Two?"

"Yes, miss." He held out the silver tray on which the envelopes rested, and she took them eagerly.

"Thank you, Palmer. Thank you very much."

"You are welcome, miss." He turned to leave. "I will hold the door for you, Mr. Randall."

"Thank you, sir." Bib moved out of the room, ignoring Eleanor as though she was a complete stranger. She might have been offended had she not known it was part of the strategy to keep any hint of friendship from Mr. Palmer's scrutiny. Ina Bell and Kerri followed the same line of conduct.

As soon as the door was closed, Eleanor went to the large over-stuffed chair to read her letters. One was from Miss Johnson and the other . . . she looked more closely at the script to see that she had read correctly. The penmanship was atrocious, adding credence to her guess that the letter was from her brother, James. She was delighted. She ripped off the end of the envelope and pulled out the letter. It was one page with writing on only one side, but she didn't care; in the six months they'd been separated this was his first letter.

May 30, 1914

Dear Eleanor,

You are probably surprised to get a letter from me. Don't get used to it because it probably won't happen much. News about me will likely come through Miss Johnson, as my handwriting is bad. I just wanted to let you know I've been up to the farm and every-thing seems fine. 'Course it's our work that I was looking at, but I just wanted you to know that the fences haven't fallen down, and the barn is still standing. I didn't see any of the Blackhurst people, but I didn't go close as the farm doesn't belong to us anymore and it would be trespassing.

How are you?
I'm doing fine at the ranch and the horses are well.

James

Eleanor smiled at his brevity, running her finger over the scrawled letters and trying to imagine her brother sitting at some small writing desk penning the precious words onto borrowed stationery. She felt a twist of loneliness and berated the fact that she and James had never talked much. Of course, they were such different people that ease of fellowship was never likely.

She slipped the letter back into the envelope and set it aside. She picked up Miss Johnson's letter, anticipating pages of elegant script and wondrous news. She brought her legs up under herself and ripped open the envelope.

June 2, 1914

My dear Eleanor,

I sit staring at my travel trunk packed and ready for sailing, feeling as I always do—the pull between staying and leaving, the lust for adventure and experience at odds with the tranquility of hearth and home.

School year 1913–14 is complete, and I saw the usual variety of scholarship. Overall, I am pleased with the advancement, and close my grade book with satisfaction.

I have enlisted the service of one of my students, a Mr. William Trenton, to care for my garden the months I am away. He assures me he will be vigilant, yet I worry that my asters and sweet peas will scatter themselves to the four corners, while my roses languish and my hollyhocks topple. It's silly, I know, to worry about flowers, and I shudder to think the angst I'd feel if I had a dog.

Mr. Greggs has offered to come in the morning and escort myself and my luggage to the train station. I know as the train skirts across the top of Utah I will desire to stop and see Alaina and Nephi, but there is not opportunity. Her last letter indicated that she is still trying to "fit in," but neighbors and Church members are standoffish, and even certain family members, whom she does not name, carry an air of coldness toward her. She has yet to meet Nephi's father or Eunice Erickson, the first wife. She adores her mother-in-law, Patience Erickson, who seems to be a woman of warmth and wisdom. She is also fond of Nephi's grandfather, who has asked her to care for his fruit trees. He sounds to me like a man of compassion. She says little of herself and Nephi other than that he is working hard on the capitol building and they are reading your father's journal together.

Eleanor looked up from the pale lavender stationery and closed her eyes. *Father's journal.* Alaina's last letters to her had not mentioned this, and she wondered what had prompted her sister to finally read their father's words. Since its discovery, after Father's death, Alaina had kept the book like a sacred relic. Eleanor smiled. *Well, I've kept his Book of Mormon much the same,* she admitted to herself, *but at least I read it occasionally.*

She found her place in the letter and continued.

My thoughts turn now to you, Miss Eleanor. Are you still captivated by your uncle's library, or has the enchantment worn thin?

Learning without application proves to be a boat without oars in the middle of an expansive lake.

Be of good cheer, Miss Eleanor. Someday your intelligence will be put to good use.

Assuring myself that I will arrive safely, I will write to you from Belgium.

I remain your friend.

Philomene Johnson

Eleanor's eyes lingered on the lines penned to her . . . *someday your intelligence will be put to good use.* Eleanor rose from her seat, stretched her back, and put Miss Johnson's letter into its envelope. She hoped that statement would prove true, as it galled her to waste her days and abilities. She did not think grandly of herself, only confident that work was a better master of her time. Looking out the window into the flower garden, she thought of Mrs. Fitzpatrick and her promise to find her occupation when she reached sixteen. In years gone by, Eleanor had always wanted spring to linger, but now she wished for the days to fly along until the eleventh of August, and her coming of age.

 Chapter Ten

James stood staring at the house. Weeds grew up around the front steps, and a scattering of apple crates and tools from the toolbox decorated the side yard. The rose-of-Sharon bush, which had once graced the front porch, was missing, exposing a broken pane of glass in the grimy windows.

James had had a walk in the orchard where the apple trees boasted of a bountiful harvest, and he wondered if their offerings would be gathered or fall to the ground to rot. He tied Friar Tuck to the hitching post and looked around in disgust. This was his second trip out to the farm, and he intended this time to meet the hired caretaker.

Mr. Blackhurst, a clever and resourceful man who always had his eyes open for a business venture, had snapped up the Lund farm at its rock-bottom price, never actually intending to work the land, but to use it only as an investment. He had hired a man to look after things until he could find a buyer who would give him an appreciable increase on his purchase. James wondered how Mr. Blackhurst would feel if he saw the deplorable state of things.

Since working at the Regosi ranch, James had come to realize the value and satisfaction of work done well, and he was saddened by the chaos that was slowly taking over his father's competent industry. On his first visit he'd only seen the property from a distance, so of course all seemed well, but when he'd met up with Daniel Chart in Sutter Creek one day, Daniel told him about going out to the farm to meet the new neighbors and finding the wretched state of things. James looked again at the house and shook his head. He had previously written to both his sisters that the farm seemed well tended—now he would have to send another letter with different news.

James heard a voice at a distance and turned to see a man emerging from the barn, releasing a sow and her piglets into a side paddock. The man did not take notice of James, who was walking towards him now with intent. Just before Mr. Blackhurst's hire stepped into the barn, James called to him. The man turned abruptly, shading his eyes and frowning in James's direction. He did not move or change expression as James came up to him.

"What can I do for ya?" the man growled, his voice low and husky, his rheumy eyes unwelcoming.

James took stock of the man's weathered face and stooped shoulders. His once-burly frame had slumped with the years, but his overlarge hands still held strength. The man's gray hair was scraggly around his face, and from the corner of his mouth drooped a hand-rolled cigarette. He took a long pull from it, allowing the smoke to seep out through his nose.

James extended his hand, but the man did not take it. "I'm James Lund."

The man's eyes showed recognition of the name. "Folks used to own this place?"

"Yes, sir."

The man took another pull on the cigarette. "What'd ya want?"

"Thought I'd take a look around."

"What for? Ain't none of your business now," the man sneered.

James bristled at this surly response, but held his temper. "Just wondering if Mr. Blackhurst has found a buyer."

"That ain't none of your business neither."

James put his foot on the second rail of the fence and jumped over, landing in the paddock only a few feet from the obstinate man. The sow snorted while the piglets squealed with fright, taking off in every direction.

"Listen, mister," James said in his strong baritone voice, "I'm not trying to make trouble, but if you can't be civil and give me a bit of information, I may just have to send a telegraph to Mr. Blackhurst and tell him what a lousy job you're doing taking care of his property."

The man's jaw clenched and his eyes narrowed, but he did not move. James stood his ground, hoping the old man wouldn't choose a fistfight over talk.

"Clayborn," the man growled.

"What?" James asked, puzzled by the odd response.

"Name's Clayborn," he said again, throwing the cigarette butt to the ground and grinding it with his boot, "and I ain't gotta tell ya nothin', but I'm gonna be civil," he emphasized the word, "and tell ya that a man's comin' first of next week to take a look at the place."

"Too bad Mr. Blackhurst isn't going to get top dollar on his investment," James said, looking the man square in the face.

Mr. Clayborn cussed under his breath and clenched his fists. "I'm watching everything just fine."

"The house?" James questioned.

"I ain't gotta take care of that—only the livestock," Mr. Clayborn snapped.

"Well, there's a scythe in the shed that'd bring down those weeds, and vinegar to wash the windows."

The man looked at him as if he were mad. "I ain't washin' no windows."

"Mr. Blackhurst would get a better price for things. Might just give you a bonus for your trouble," James answered.

"Shouldn't make no never mind to you. It ain't your place anymore."

James felt a pang of loss, which made him want to punch Mr. Clayborn in the face. He measured his response. "It does matter. Our family lived here a long time, and I'd like to see things looked after."

The man snorted. "Well, I hate to disappoint ya, but that ain't what I been hired to do. Keep the livestock alive. That's the long and short of it." He kicked out at one of the piglets that was rooting around near his foot, and it squealed off to its mother. "Now I think it's time you git, 'cause I ain't feelin' very civil no more."

James knew he might as well be talking to a fence post. He shook his head and turned to jump back over the corral fence.

When Mr. Clayborn realized James wasn't going to put up a fight, he followed after him, leaning on the rails and throwing out threats with a newfound bravado. "And don't be comin' out here again or I might have to let my shotgun do the talkin', and it ain't civil at all, no it ain't."

James swung himself up on Friar Tuck and turned the horse's head toward the main gate. Suddenly Tuck squealed and bucked sideways, and James wheeled around to see Mr. Clayborn aiming a second rock in their direction. James gave Tuck a command, and the big horse pelted towards the fence directly where the grimy hired man was standing—his smug expression changing to astonishment at the unexpected assault. Just as they reached the fence, James pulled Tuck to the side, grabbing Mr. Clayborn's still raised arm and yanking him over. The startled man lost his balance and ended up on his backside.

"You're lucky I don't have a shotgun, mister!" James yelled at him. "Or Mr. Blackhurst just might be having to hire on a new man to look after this farm."

Mr. Clayborn looked shaken, and James figured the fight had been taken out of him. He was in no mood to stay around and hear any more threats from this pitiful excuse for a man. Anyone who would maliciously harm an animal was mean and low, and James loathed his presence. He turned Friar Tuck towards the Carson Track, and the horse took off at a gallop, seemingly as eager to be away as his rider.

After ten minutes of fast riding they were up and over Morris Hill, and James slowed their pace. He pulled Tuck to a stop at a small creek to see if any damage was done and to let the horse drink. It was plenty hot for mid-June, and James felt the scorcher of a summer coming on. He ran his hand along Tuck's left side, and, finding no mark, moved to his backside. He saw it immediately—there on the fetlock just above the left rear hoof was a smear of red. It didn't seem to be a deep cut, but the sharp rock had obviously been thrown hard to cause such damage. There was dirt mixed with the clotted blood, and James took out his neckerchief, dipped it in the cool water of the creek, and bent down to wash the wound clean.

"Hey, hey now," he spoke in a soothing voice, running his hand gently over the leg. "Let's take a look at this, let's take a look."

Tuck moved over slightly then stood still as James took care of the injury. He cleaned off all the dirt till he could see the actual damage, a small gash oozing blood. James gritted his teeth and thought about going back and giving Mr. Clayborn a proper punishment for such devilry. The cut would heal fine, but James hated to see any animal in pain. The gentle horse flinched as he bound the wound with the neckerchief, and James ran his hand reassuringly over Tuck's thigh.

"There you go, Mr. Tuck. You're gonna be fine." He stood. "Sure wish that scum had been standing closer so you could have given him a good kick." Tuck snorted and James smiled. "Yep, a well-placed kick would have served him right."

James picked up the reins and patted Tuck's shoulder. "How about if I just walk along with you for a little while?" He set off at a good pace, watching for a sinking of the horse's hindquarters or a nodding of the head which would indicate lameness. James's competence with animals told him that Tuck was fit, yet he was anxious for Mr. Regosi's experienced assessment. As he walked, James's mind drifted back to the white farmhouse and the neglected fruit trees. He thought of all the times he'd been sullen about any work assigned him on the farm, any work that didn't deal with the horses, and he regretted his reluctance to labor beside his father in the orchard. Now his father was dead and the apples left without a caretaker. His mind pulled up images of his older sister, Alaina, climbing the ladders to pick fruit, her face flushed with a healthy glow, her expression bright. His regret deepened. Why had he been so mean to her when she'd tried to save the farm? Now he understood what a devastating loss it had been for her.

He growled deeply. *Maybe it would be better if we all just forgot about the farm and got on with our lives.* He found himself thinking about the day in Sutter Creek when Miss Johnson had suggested he look in on the farm and keep his sisters aware of what was happening. He didn't know now if it had been such a good idea. Suddenly he laughed as he thought about how Miss Johnson would have reacted to Mr. Clayborn's ill manners and coarse language—what would have happened had she been with him to confront the ruffian. If the resolute educator had had her umbrella, the brute of a man would have been righteously thrashed like the money changers in the temple.

James moved Tuck out onto the Carson Track, and held him to the side of the road as a logging wagon passed. James admired the team of eight that pulled the huge rig, and called a greeting to the handlers. They were bringing logs from the high Sierras, and as they passed, James breathed in the clean scent of pine sap. The day was fair with wispy clouds floating their way east on a light breeze, the hills still green from the abundant spring rain, a scattering of wildflowers holding on against the ever-warming sun.

Alaina, Eleanor, and Miss Johnson were all in cities surrounded by buildings and automobiles and strange cultures, and he envied none of them. If he were magic he'd wish them back at his side. He well knew that Miss Johnson would return mid-August from her ill-advised adventuring in Europe, but he feared Eleanor and Alaina might never return to Eden, and it made him sad. Every year Miss Johnson imparted a favorite saying to her students—something about looking down and seeing mud or looking up and seeing stars. For Eleanor and Alaina, James was sure it was mud and only mud.

Chapter Eleven

"After this we can either venture to the Musée de la Tapisserie, or go have a peek at Manneken Pis."

Philomene Johnson forced her gaze away from the lacework turrets of the Brussels town hall, and looked over at her great-aunt. She blinked several times to clear the wonder from her eyes, and her aunt laughed. "That is becoming a familiar expression for you, dear niece," she commented, "but I must admit it was also my expression when I first saw the Grand' Place ten years ago."

Philomene shook her head. "This is like no market square I've ever seen, Auntie. It is absolutely breathtaking." She looked again to the town hall on her left, the ornate and magical guild houses in front of her, and the king's house on her right. She turned in a slow circle with her arms outstretched, feeling young and alive. "The city of Brussels is exquisite."

"And wait for a few weeks for the celebration of Ommegang," her aunt said, smiling, "when this entire center area," she moved her hand gracefully to indicate the pavement of cobblestones, "will be covered with a carpet of flowers."

Philomene wrapped her arms around her aunt and gave her a squeeze.

"Careful now, don't break me," her aunt cautioned. "Be respectful of the white hair."

But Philomene only laughed. "You, Aunt Hannah, are the sturdiest woman I know."

"For my ancient years," her aunt replied. "Now stay here. I'm going to buy us some chocolates."

She turned and moved off across the square towards the beautifully decorated chocolatier. Philomene watched her go, admiring her statuesque build and straight carriage. Over the years, Hannah Johnson Finn had served as a role model for Philomene, sending letters of adventure and accomplishment, and encouraging her great-niece to embrace books and daily physical exercise. Philomene's grandfather, Seth Johnson, had been the oldest of twelve children, and Aunt Hannah had been the youngest, so there was only an eight-year span between Philomene's father and his aunt.

Philomene's father, Abel Johnson, loved to tell stories of his childhood in Baltimore, and how Hannah often tried to boss him around because she was "his aunt and his elder and he had to do what she said." In reality the two spent many happy hours using their vivid imaginations to conjure knights, ladies, dragons, piracy on the high seas, and mountain climbing in Tibet. Father admitted that he'd cried for days when his branch of the family moved from Maryland to California, leaving behind hearth, home, and dear Aunt Hannah.

The separation had come because Philomene's grandfather had caught "gold fever" and was pompously sure he'd strike it rich in California, which, after a few false starts, he did. So, Philomene's father grew to be an educated man and a merchant "way out west," while Aunt Hannah remained on the family estate, becoming a debutante and marrying an American diplomat with whom she traveled the world. Her husband, Sir William Conner Finn, had died in 1909 while serving in Brussels as a foreign attaché, and Aunt Hannah, then 68, had made up her mind to spend her remaining years in their stately apartments on the rue de la Montagne.

Philomene refocused her mind on the striking town hall, and studied the hundreds of small statues rimming the entire façade of the structure. She pinched herself. *Yes, Miss Johnson, you are actually standing in this remarkable place.* She shaded her eyes and looked up at the elaborately decorated roofs of the Guild Halls, then back down to her guidebook. It seemed that instead of numbered addresses, each hall was known by a name. "The Mountain of Thabor, The Rose, The Golden Tree," she mumbled to herself. "If you look to the top floors of The Horn or House of the Sailors, you will see it resembles the rear end of a ship." She looked up at the imposing structure, putting her guidebook in her pocket and raising her Kodak Brownie camera to take a picture.

She was so intent on picture-taking that she was not aware of her aunt's returning until she heard her voice quite near. She was speaking to someone, and Philomene looked over quickly so as not to appear rude. She wondered if they'd heard her mumbling to herself like a mad woman.

"Ah, here she is, just where I left her," her aunt announced, as though Philomene was some deposited parcel. "My dear," she said, taking Philomene's arm, "I have run into a friend of mine, and I so want you to meet her. Philomene, this is my dear friend Edith Cavell. Edith, my great-niece Miss Philomene Johnson."

Philomene extended her hand and the woman took it. Her grip was strong and sure. Philomene noted that they were both about the same height, but she judged Miss Cavell to be a few years older. She was a handsome woman who Philomene could see did not indulge in gratuitous expressions. Her face was placid and her deportment reserved. She also observed that Miss Cavell was not prone to frivolous hairstyles or fashion; her light brown hair was brushed back from her face and fixed in a bun at the nape of her neck. She wore a navy blue skirt, a white blouse with wide blue stripes, and a yellow flounce tie. Simple, sturdy walking shoes and a basic blue hat finished the ensemble.

Aunt Hannah continued with the introductions. "Edith is the angel nurse who cared for my Conner when he was in hospital. She is from Britain, and a more gifted caretaker I have yet to see. She actually trains nurses at the L'École d'Infirmière Dimplonier." Miss Cavell gave her friend an indulgent smile, while Aunt Hannah turned to her niece. "I have already told her much about your life as a teacher in Sutter Creek, Philomene, and she is impressed by your scholarship."

Edith nodded. "It's very nice to meet you, Miss Johnson. Your aunt has been looking forward to your visit for months."

"A pleasure to meet you also, Miss Cavell. Do you live permanently in Brussels?"

"I do. I first came in 1890 when I was governess for the François family. In 1895 I went home to Swardeston for a time to care for my ill father."

Aunt Hannah handed around chocolates. "It was then she trained to be a nurse, returning here in—1906 was it, Edith?"

"1907."

"1907. And I thank my lucky stars for it."

"Bonjour, Mademoiselle Cavell."

Edith turned to wave at a group of nuns passing through the square. "Bonjour, Sœur Renan. De bonne grâce."

Philomene was charmed by Miss Cavell's flawless French, knowing that her own attempts were passable but somewhat stilted. She consoled herself with reminders that her two companions had had years to immerse themselves in the sounds and flavor of the language, while she practiced occasionally in the privacy of her garden.

Aunt Hannah chuckled. "I find it interesting how they accept you now, Edith."

"What do you mean?" Philomene asked, watching as the nuns moved off down one of the side streets.

"When Dr. Depage first came up with his idea for Edith to train nurses along the lines of Florence Nightingale, he stirred up quite a hornet's nest, didn't he, my friend?"

A smile touched the corners of Edith's mouth. "I'm afraid he did."

"Why?" Philomene questioned.

"Until then the nuns had been responsible for the care of the sick," Edith answered.

Aunt Hannah scoffed. "And no matter how kind and well-intentioned, they had no training for the work. Thank heavens the infirmary was well established by the time my Conner needed looking after."

"So—unhappy nuns. That was the hornet's nest?"

Aunt Hannah chuckled, and Edith smiled again. "Well, that and the resistance from the majority of the people in the city."

"In the country, you mean," Hannah added.

Philomene was puzzled. "They didn't want nurses?"

Aunt Hannah handed her another chocolate. "Most still held to the idea that it was a disgrace for women to work—that women of good birth and education lost their place in society by earning their own living."

Philomene shook her head, thinking about her former student Alaina Lund and the difficult time she'd faced in wanting to run the family apple farm after her father's passing. "I take it something changed their minds," she asserted, turning to her aunt.

Aunt Hannah smiled slyly. "*Someone.* Someone, my dear. And no one less than the queen of the Belgians herself! Elisabeth had broken her arm and sent to the school for a trained nurse to care for her."

Philomene narrowed her eyes. "Are you making that up?"

"I am not! Gardez la foi! Keep faith, dear niece! The queen of the Belgians herself. When word got out, the status of Miss Cavell and her school was assured."

"Well, the school anyway," Edith said quietly.

"You are much too modest, Edith," Aunt Hannah answered, shaking her head and turning to Philomene. "Now she provides nurses for three hospitals plus communal schools and kindergartens all over the country. Indeed, I account Miss Cavell one of the most gifted women I know—nurse, administrator, teacher . . . and, besides all that, she paints and plays a wonderful game of tennis."

Philomene brightened. "Tennis? I would love to learn to play tennis."

Edith smiled. "Perhaps when I return from Britain I can teach you."

Aunt Hannah shaded her eyes. "Going to visit your mother?"

"Yes. With father gone she gets lonely for me. I'll only be gone a month, then back to Brussels again and work, work, work."

Aunt Hannah chuckled. "Do you need me to look after Don and Jack?"

Edith shook her head. "Dr. Depage said he would take them to the country with him."

"Where they will have the time of their lives chasing pigs and chickens."

"Indeed."

Aunt Hannah looked at Philomene's quizzical expression. "Don and Jack are Edith's lovely mongrels."

Philomene nodded. "Of course. I thought as much."

"So, Miss Cavell," Aunt Hannah continued enthusiastically, "can you spare an hour or two from your busy schedule to join us in les adventures? Be our compagne de voyage? You could tell Philomene all the legends surrounding Manneken Pis."

Edith laughed out loud. "I might have known that would be one of your first visits, Hannah Finn." She turned to Philomene. "Your aunt is a scallywag, Miss Johnson, so be careful of her influence. Manneken Pis may be the most famous statue in Belgium, but please don't expect anything like your Statue of Liberty. Our little boy statue has been famous for hundreds of years, and no one really knows why."

Aunt Hannah chuckled. "Don't give it away, Edith. Let her see for herself. So, can you join us?"

Edith took out her pocket watch to check the time. "I do have an hour or so before my next lecture. I would love to join you."

"Grand!" Aunt Hannah answered. "Friends, chocolates, and an afternoon with Manneken Pis! What could be better?" She turned, taking Philomene by the arm, guiding her down the Rue Violette, with Edith on her other side.

Philomene Johnson was captivated by the enchantment of the day, and she gloried in the yellow sunlight on the brown cobbles, the sound of children's voices pouring out an open door, and the light scent of her aunt's expensive French perfume. She knew that many people in Sutter Creek thought it eccentric for her to spend summers traveling to far-off places. Even her trip to the Grand Canyon raised eyebrows, let alone the host of other remarkable sites she'd visited over the years: Washington DC, Italy, England, and now Belgium. Those disinclined to explore thought it a waste of her inheritance to trot around the globe gazing at statues and paintings and landscapes. But surely they'd change their minds if they could once experience the thrill of standing within a five-hundred-year-old Gothic cathedral and breathing in the musty smell of history.

She took the proffered chocolate from her aunt and popped it into her mouth. In the Grand' Place she had gone from woman to young woman. Now the taste of the luscious sweet transformed her from young woman to child. She looked over at her dear aunt Hannah, unable to find sufficient words to express her feelings about the day.

Huh! Let the few narrow-minded souls of Sutter Creek criticize the way I use my money, she thought. She knew her life was richer for the exposure to a hundred new sights, sounds, and smells, and that her students would hopefully benefit from the knowledge she brought home to them. Philomene took the guidebook out of her pocket to look up the Musée de la Tapisserie. Perhaps they could visit there later in the afternoon. She wondered what she would eat for the noon meal—perhaps rabbit casserole or pheasant braised with endive. She smiled as she thought back to William Trenton's joke about brussels sprouts. Perhaps she would have brussels sprouts in his honor.

She tripped on a prominent cobble, and her guidebook went sliding across the street. "Ma foi!" she gasped, struggling to stay standing. "Qu'est-ce que je suis une bête!"

"Don't be embarrassed," Miss Cavell laughed, running to retrieve the book. "It is the performance of many a visitor—so much to look at all at once. And I admire how you exclaimed in French."

"Yes, indeed," her aunt chuckled. "Your accent was marvelous. We must scare you into using French more often." She straightened Philomene's hat. "Are you all right, dear niece?" she solicited.

"Yes, ma'am."

"No broken toes or sprained ankles?"

"No, ma'am."

"Fantastic! Then on we go to see our scandalous little statue."

Her aunt started off at such a pace that Philomene had to hurry to keep up. For some reason she thought about her aunt as a young girl and her father as a child—the happy times they must have had together. Perhaps her father was looking down from heaven and sharing in their marvelous adventure. The thought made her smile, and she hoped her imagining was true, as she knew he would love every minute.

Chapter Twelve

They sat in the warm kitchen, Nephi reading Samuel Lund's words in a pleasing, low voice, Alaina sitting with her elbows on the table, her cheek resting in her hand. The outside summer air brooded at the screen door, ruffled now and again by the cooler evening breeze that worried the leaves of the honey locust tree. It was nearing the end of June, and Alaina found it interesting how the dry heat of the day dropped with the setting of the sun. High desert, Nephi had explained to her, and though she didn't understand the reasoning she loved the result.

She watched her husband's face as the light from the gas lamp flickered on his tanned skin and illuminated his blue eyes. She watched his lips moving, and her mind jumped back to the words Grandfather Erickson had said to her months before, that Nephi loved her. *Loved me?* That was impossible. The hopeful patriarch had mistaken his grandson's compassion for stronger feelings—feelings Alaina was sure did not exist. The pronouncement by Grandfather had caused some sleepless nights and awkward moments, as over the ensuing weeks she found herself watching her husband more closely as he did chores or talked with his mother. He was more often in her thoughts, and, most unsettling—in her dreams. She knew she was making a fool of herself, and it embarrassed her. Was she growing attached to a man who saw her only as a charity case—at best a friend? *My grandson loves you already.* Alaina dismissed the idea as absurd. She sighed and rubbed her eyes.

"Alaina?"

Nephi's inquiry jolted her from the daydream, and she sat up straighter in her chair. "What? I . . . was I . . ."

He closed the journal. "Sorry. My voice was putting you to sleep."

She put her hand on his. "Oh, no, not at all. My mind was just going back to the farm. Please keep reading. Just start back a little ways."

He opened the book again with a grin. "What's the last thing you remember?"

Alaina bit her lip. "Ah . . . ah, something about parts for the threshing machine." Nephi flipped back several pages, and Alaina made a funny face. "Sorry."

"It's not your fault. Threshing machines aren't very interesting." He found a spot to begin. *"Should finish the repair tomorrow, then into town on Thursday to meet with Dr. McIntyre about Elizabeth's illness."*

Alaina flinched at her mother's name, and Nephi noticed.

"Are you all right?"

"Yes," she said, undoing her braid. "No, not really. I don't like to hear my mother's name. That's terrible isn't it?"

"No." Nephi sat back in his chair and watched as her hair cascaded onto her shoulders. He swallowed hard and looked down at the book. "She's the cause of a lot of sorrow."

"Yes, but Father would be upset to know that I was still angry with her." Alaina stood abruptly. A rush of cold emotion had dropped into her chest, and she hid the symptoms by moving to the sideboard and uncovering the apple cake. "Would you like a piece?" she asked, not turning to look at him.

He knew the duplicity of her action and answered kindly, "I'd love a piece, thank you."

She shoved a small bite of cake into her mouth to stop the tears while she cut him a slice. When would these waves of grief and anger go away? They happened less and less often, but they still caught her unawares. She got a plate out of the cupboard and slapped the slice of cake on it. "He loved her," she said flatly. "I don't know why, but he did."

"What was her illness?" Nephi asked, changing the subject.

Alaina hesitated. "I'm . . . I'm not sure." She blushed. "It might have been when she was carrying Eleanor. I guess she was very sick with all of us." She secured a fork and set the cake in front of him. "I'd rather not talk about her."

Nephi ate his cake silently as Alaina picked up her father's journal, randomly opening it to a page, and reading. *"February 8, 1913. I have decided to stop being stubborn and take my good wife's advice. Come spring, I will hire on a farmhand to help in the orchard. The fatigue that always comes at the end of the harvest season is still with me, and my dear Lizzie keeps reminding me that we are not as young as we once were. I suppose I could require more of James, and I know Alaina will still be of great help, but . . ."* The words caught in her throat.

Nephi put his hand on her arm. "Should I finish?"

She nodded, and he took the book from her. He found the place where she'd left off. *"But it is time for my girl to learn the tasks of being a wife and mother."* Nephi's voice grew soft and husky. "We can read something else. Go back to the other entry."

"No. I want to hear it."

He took a breath. *"It won't be long before she leaves us to make a home of her own, and Lizzie assures me that there are not many men like me who will be patient while their wives learn cooking and sewing and cleaning. I'm afraid it will prove a challenge, for I know our daughter's heart lives in the orchard. It may be a problem for me also as I so enjoy her company, but Lizzie is right, my poor health tells me I need another strong pair of hands to help me run the farm."*

Alaina's face was frozen in pain.

"Alaina, I . . ."

"Did you know? Did you know he was sick?"

Nephi shook his head. "Tired, but no, not sick like that . . . he never let on."

"Of course he wouldn't," she said in a whisper. "Of course he wouldn't." She rubbed her forehead with her fingertips. "And all those months I was angry with you . . . so angry and jealous for you taking my place in the orchard when you were actually saving my father's life."

Nephi put down the book. "Alaina, don't."

"I'm sorry, Nephi. I am not a good wife to you, and you've been so patient and understanding . . ."

He moved his chair closer and put his hand on her arm.

She jumped up immediately at his touch. "Don't! Please don't be nice to me! I . . ." she paced the room, "I can't stand it that you're so nice to me." Nephi's face was ashen. "You've done so much for me, and I'm nothing but selfish and mean. I'm trying, but . . . but the only time I feel like I have a soul is when I'm tending Grandfather Erickson's fruit trees. And . . . and he said you loved me, so I've been trying, trying not to be so selfish, trying to show you how grateful I am that you married me."

"What did you say?"

Alaina stopped pacing and stared at him. What had she said? "I don't . . . don't know," she stammered. "How grateful I am that you married me?"

He was giving her an odd look. "No, about what Grandfather Erickson said."

A panic gripped her throat. What had she said? She could not think, and speaking was impossible.

"He told you that I loved you?"

She put her head down, unable to face him.

Nephi stood. "Alaina, look at me."

She could not bring herself to obey his request. How could she look into those eyes as he explained his grandfather's mistake?

"When did he tell you this?"

"Months ago," she whimpered. *How awkward and embarrassing.* She stepped back, not lifting her head. She must seem hideous to him, and it broke her heart, for she realized that he had become dear to her, realized that her heart had found a place for him.

"I'm sorry my grandfather told you that," he said slowly.

Alaina nodded, knowing that would be his answer—feeling his rejection knot in her stomach.

"It makes it difficult for you to think of me only as a friend."

"I know," she answered weakly, her voice sounding like a child.

He stepped toward her and she stepped back, painfully aware of her plainness and her pitiful circumstance.

"I've tried to hide it over these months together because I knew you didn't have feelings for me . . . might never have those kind of feelings for me, but . . ." He hesitated, and she looked up into his face. "What Grandfather Erickson told you was plain truth. I do love you."

Alaina looked into his eyes and saw only tenderness and affirmation. "You do?"

"I have loved you for a long time."

"But, how?" she questioned, not believing the words she was hearing.

He smiled. "How?"

She grasped her precious locket. "I thought when we were married we were just friends."

He cleared his throat. "We were friends, but for me . . . it was more."

"You've loved me through all the months when I've been distant and sad?"

"You've had a right to be sad."

"No," she said abruptly. "No. You deserved better."

"Alaina, you told me your feelings from the beginning, that you cared for me but didn't love me, and I accept . . ."

A moan came up from her chest, and she pushed past him to the back porch door.

"Alaina, I'm sorry!" he called after her, but she was out the door into the chill night air.

The edge of a bright, full moon was pushing itself over the mountain peak, casting shimmery light onto the pasture as she stumbled away from the house. *He isn't telling me the truth. Can he really love me?* She stopped walking. The look in his eyes and the sincerity in his voice confirmed his words. *He loves me.* She shivered as a breeze blew strands of hair into her face. She heard the back porch door close and Nephi's footsteps coming towards her. She shivered again. *What will I say to him? He thinks I don't love him, but I do.* She turned to face him as he came the last ten feet, holding out his coat to her.

"Thought you might need this."

Unspeaking, Alaina held out her arms and he slipped the coat onto her. She turned back to him, her dark eyes full of embarrassment.

A painful longing welled up in Nephi's chest. He remembered the night back on the farm in California when she'd stood before him in her well-worn coat and her father's work boots, asking him to marry her. He had prayed many prayers since his acceptance those many months ago that somehow she might come to love him. What could he say to make things right?

"Nephi, I need to tell you something."

Her voice brought his mind from wandering. She looked like a young girl standing there in his overlarge coat, wisps of dark hair playing about her face, but her voice was strong and full of determination, and he tried to steel himself against the grim pronouncement he knew was coming.

"I love you too."

"What?"

His voice was loud in the quiet dark, and it made her smile. "I love you." She saw his face momentarily bathed in moonlight and wonder. *Does he believe me?* He was standing like a statue, and Alaina was fearful he was weighing the sincerity of her pronouncement. She bumbled on. "I . . . I know I haven't shown you the kind of affection you deserve, Nephi, but . . ." Suddenly she was caught up in his arms, and she closed her eyes in delight. She couldn't stop herself from laughing. Nephi laughed with her as he kissed her face and ears and neck.

"Bless Grandfather Erickson for his good Danish honesty!" he said happily, stopping his caresses and looking her square in the face. "I was hoping and praying for this!"

She stepped back, but he held on to the lapels of her coat. "Praying for it?" she teased. "Oh, then I didn't have a chance, did I?" She was finding it hard to catch her breath.

He chuckled. "No, I guess not."

They stood looking at each other, grinning—then Alaina moved to him, threw her arms around his neck, and kissed him on the mouth. He held onto her coat and kept her near. She had never kissed anyone before, so she didn't know if she was doing it right, but it felt wonderful and Nephi didn't seem to mind.

They heard Miss Titus whinny, and the two started laughing again.

Alaina stepped back. "She's probably chastising me for being so forward," she said with an embarrassed smile.

"Or congratulating us for finally being honest," Nephi answered.

Alaina nodded, and took a deep breath. "Nephi?"

He noted the serious tenor of her voice. "Yes?"

"I don't want to sleep alone ever again."

He ran his fingers through her hair as he worked to control his emotions. He nodded, then leaned in and kissed the corner of her mouth as he'd done on their wedding day.

* * *

The truck horn was honking and Nephi didn't care. He stood in the doorway of the kitchen with his wife in his arms and contentment in his soul that surpassed anything he'd ever felt.

Mother Erickson stood at the kitchen sink with her back to the couple, washing breakfast dishes, smiling, and pretending not to hear the whispered silliness going on between the two.

"He's honking again!" Alaina giggled. "You'd better get going." She broke out of his embrace and then latched onto his belt as though she'd never let him go.

"Well, I guess I'll just have to take you with me," he said playfully, dragging her along as he moved towards the front door.

"Wait! You didn't pack me a lunch," she protested.

He stopped. "You're right. Besides, I don't want you around all those other men." He kissed her mouth.

"You could always stay home," she answered, a mischievous look in her eyes.

He groaned. "Don't tempt me."

The truck horn honked three more times.

Alaina giggled. "Oh, my. Elias is getting impatient."

"Let him wait until Christmas," Nephi said, pulling her close to him.

Alaina tried to be serious as Nephi went to kiss her neck. "No, really. You'd better go. You're very late."

"Booting me out, are you?"

She turned him around and pushed against his back. "I'd keep you with me every second, but we both have work to do."

"What are you doing today?" he asked, moving to the front door under his wife's insistence.

"I told you—working at Grandfather Erickson's."

Nephi opened the door and stepped out onto the front porch. "Ah, Grandfather Erickson! Honest, kind Grandfather Erickson!"

Alaina shushed him.

Elias had the windows of the truck rolled down, and he called out as soon as he saw them come out onto the porch. "Hurry up, little brother! We're going to be late!" He was surprised when Nephi, instead of bounding down the front steps to the truck, turned back to Alaina and took her in his arms. He strained to hear what they were saying, but it was only mumbling.

"I want to stay with you," Nephi confided, nuzzling her neck.

"Stop that now!" she scolded. "What is Elias going to think?"

"Hmm . . . maybe that I love you."

She stopped trying to push him away and smiled. "I love you too, but we don't need to make a spectacle of ourselves on the front porch."

"You're right," he answered, backing away from her respectfully. "It's just that I can't stand the thought of being six inches away from you."

Alaina blushed at his heartfelt pronouncement, amazed that this handsome young man could have such feelings for her.

"Nephi!" Elias yelled.

Nephi gave Alaina one last kiss and ran for the truck. He yanked open the door and hopped in.

Elias ground the truck into gear and took off. "What was that all about?" he asked, a critical edge to his voice.

"Love," Nephi answered.

"Love?" Elias questioned, not wanting to accept the implication of his younger brother's euphoric behavior.

Nephi leaned out the window and waved at his wife who was still standing on the porch steps. "Yep, love," Nephi answered with a sigh. He was far too happy to notice the scowl on Elias's face or his tightened grip on the truck's steering wheel.

Chapter Thirteen

Bib Randall put one hand on top of his bowler hat and ran—in his other hand he held the *San Francisco Chronicle* newspaper dated June 29, 1914. The newsie who had sold him the copy had been calling out the headline in a louder-than-usual voice—a voice that Bib could hear for blocks: "Archduke Franz Ferdinand and Princess Sophia Shot by Mad Assassin! Member of Radical Serbian Group Cuts Down Royal Couple!"

A crowd of men was standing by the newsboys and their stacks of papers, talking in heightened voices.

"Gavrilo Princip . . . is that who shot them?" an older, white-haired man asked, trying to read without his glasses.

"Seems so," another answered. "Some eighteen-year-old Serbian student."

A portly gentleman in a navy serge suit broke in. "Can't tell me he wasn't just a puppet in the hands of Serbian intelligence."

"Oh, Father, you see spies around every corner," a younger version of the man answered.

"The world is becoming a very dangerous place, John, and you're a fool if you don't acknowledge it."

"Heir to the throne," someone mumbled. "Left behind children, two boys and a little girl. Rotten shame. Poor little orphans."

Bib had stood there with the crowd, stunned at the tragedy and implications.

"That area's a powder keg ready to blow," a young man stated, snapping the paper in disgust. "Why Austria-Hungry had to annex Bosnia from Turkey is anybody's guess."

"Franz Ferdinand and Wife Shot Dead in Bosnia!" the newsie yelled, and more people gathered.

"Well, well, well, and I tell you the heir apparent was not going to put up with those radical protests," the white-haired man snorted.

"Most likely what got him killed," the young man answered.

"Cowardly to kill the princess," the portly gentleman grumbled. "Her poor children. First orphans of the war."

"War? What war?" someone shouted.

"Do you think it will lead to that?" Bib asked.

There were murmurs around the group, but no one seemed willing to speculate where the horrific incident would lead.

Bib Randall had never liked the holy wrath and destruction his father preached to his cowering congregation, but gravitated instead to the scriptures of healing and hope offered by Jesus during His sojourn and ministry. Now there was a knot in Bib's stomach like a Sunday sermon, and he was running in the glorious morning sunshine to cleanse his heart from the hatred of the world; he was running to get back to the house on Beacon Street to share the news with someone.

Mr. Palmer would turn the sad event into a philosophical diatribe on man's basic quest for dominance. Ina Bell would listen halfheartedly as she went about her chores, figuring that the faraway incident had no effect on whether the floors were scrubbed or the carpets beaten. And Kerri, who did not like aristocracy in any form, would probably quote her da and say something like, "Well, the high have further to fall, Mr. Randall."

Bib knew instinctively that it was Eleanor Lund to whom he was rushing. Even at her young age her mind was lucid and would grasp the horror and meaning of the assassination. He needed to unburden his mind of confusion, and his soul of grief, and Eleanor Lund could help. He passed a honeysuckle bush and breathed in the sweet fragrance, trying to reassure himself that goodness would prevail.

* * *

William Trenton saw the chestnut Appaloosa horse from three blocks away and ran in its direction. The animal was tied to a post in front of Simpson's hardware store, and William was sure that if he could just get to the creature and rub his hand along its neck it would be a magic omen that he was surely going to own such a horse someday. He took little notice of the group of men standing outside the store talking intently; grown-up talk held no interest for him, especially when his heart's desire stood before his eyes. He slowed as he neared the front of the store, creeping up beside the horse and murmuring words of admiration and friendship. He ran his hand over the spotted rump and thrilled as the horse turned its head to look at him.

"Hey. Hey, girl," he said, moving to the mare's shoulder. "Ain't you pretty? Ain't you about the prettiest thing I ever seen?" He knew Miss Johnson would skin him for such bad language, but he was too excited to correct himself. He stooped and looked under the mare's neck to see if the owner of the horse had taken note of his forwardness. He saw Mr. Greggs, the postmaster; Pastor Wilton; big Mr. Robinson; his stepson Daniel (who was a darn good baseball player); and James Lund. William's mind jumped. *Of course! This here's Mr. Lund's prize Appaloosa.* He was sure Mr. Lund wouldn't mind him paying his horse some attention, but then again, he hadn't asked permission and felt a bit guilty—especially in the presence of the minister. But, since no one in the knot of fellowship had turned, or even glanced over at him, William kept up his ministrations to the magic Appaloosa, while keeping one ear on what the men were saying.

"Local conflict," the postmaster said, "nothing but a local conflict."

"You think other countries won't step in?" the pastor questioned. "Perfect opportunity to grab up some land and power."

"That's what I think," Daniel Chart said, taking off his hat and pushing his dark hair away from his face. "Seems like somebody over there is always itching for a fight."

Mr. Robinson growled. "Awful to kill a woman. Bad enough to kill that duke fellow, but his wife? Awful."

William looked up to see James Lund shake his head. "Why can't people just get along?"

The pastor stood a little taller. "Revelation 19:15. 'And out of his mouth goeth a sharp sword, that with it he should smite the nations: and he shall rule them with a rod of iron.'"

"Doesn't seem to have done a whole heck of a lot of good over the generations, Pastor," the postmaster replied. "Seems like most rulers of nations think they're the big powers. No god to rule over them."

"So it is, Mr. Greggs. So it is," Pastor Wilton acknowledged.

"What about Miss Johnson?" James Lund asked suddenly. "Is she in any danger?"

William's head snapped up at the mention of Miss Johnson, and he moved closer to the group.

"I should think not," Mr. Greggs answered, his voice taut with emotion. "As I said before, it's just a local conflict. Belgium has nothing to do with it."

"Hmm. I hope you're right, Elijah," Mr. Robinson said, clamping a large hand onto his son's shoulder. "It's bad enough when men are put in jeopardy." He growled and shook his head. "It goes against nature to harm a woman. Against nature."

James looked over and saw William Trenton standing with his hands clenched and his face drained of color. He moved to him. "Hello, William! Come to visit my beautiful Appaloosa?"

But William would not be deterred from his panic. "It's the spark, isn't it?" The other men of the group looked over at the anxious boy. "Miss Johnson told us about a fire that could start over in Europe. This is it, isn't it? My brother says it's a powder keg—a powder keg, and Miss Johnson is over there!"

The Appaloosa whinnied and stamped.

Mr. Robinson moved to William and kneeled down in front of him. "Now, now, son. Take it easy. Like Mr. Greggs said, it's just a small local problem, so don't worry. Miss Johnson is a very smart woman. She'll keep herself safe—you can bet on it. Right, James?"

William looked up at James, who nodded.

Fredrick Robinson stood and patted the lad on the back. "Now, I bet if you asked him, Mr. Lund would let you ride that magnificent horse." The expression on William's face changed immediately, and Mr. Robinson laughed.

"Really?" he questioned, looking intently at James.

"Of course," James answered. "Her name's Moccasin, and I'm sure she would be pleased to carry such an admirer."

The men parted company, leaving William to a brighter prospect.

"Where are you headed, Mr. Trenton?" James asked, waving good-bye to Daniel and his father.

"I was on my way to tend Miss Johnson's garden."

"Then up you get!" James said, untying Moccasin from the post. "You can ride there in style."

William sucked in his breath and pulled himself onto the saddle.

James handed him the reins and nodded. "She's got a tender mouth, so she responds easy. Be gentle."

"Oh, yes sir."

"Ride around for a while if you'd like. I have a few things to get at the hardware store, then I'll meet you at Miss Johnson's."

"Really, Mr. Lund?" William spluttered. "Oh, thanks! Thanks, sir!"

James moved into the hardware store chuckling to himself as William turned the Appaloosa with a slight tug on the rein. The horse responded immediately, and William felt his heart swell in his chest. He tried to worry about Miss Johnson and troubles in a country far away, but he was a boy on top of an Appaloosa horse, and the summer sun was shining.

* * *

Philomene sat at an outdoor table on the Rue des Bouchers, waiting for the garçon to bring her pastry and refill her coffee. She felt foolish in her new French hat. It was emerald green felt with two large silk-ribbon feathers jutting off on the side. It was the most outlandish piece of clothing she'd ever owned, but her aunt had insisted she have it, even paying for the extravagance so her niece could not refuse.

"Your clothes are stylish, Philomene," Aunt Hannah had stated, "but they lack a certain flair of excitement."

"I am too old for flair and excitement," the unpretentious school-teacher had protested.

"Nonsense!" her dear aunt had returned, giving her a worried look. "You must have excitement until the day you are carted away."

"Auntie!"

"No, I mean it. Now go sit outside that café and charm the public while I make a few visits. I will meet you midmorning."

So, here she sat, reading her guidebook and trying to look comfortable. She looked up just in time to catch the eye of a young man flying by on a bicycle. He smiled rakishly and tipped his hat.

Philomene felt color come into her cheeks, and she reprimanded herself. *Oh, for heaven's sake! You are some years past forty, Philomene Johnson. This silly hat is making you feel giddy.* She brought out her camera and took a few pictures of people in the square.

The garçon arrived with her pastry. "Merci beaucoup," she said. "Il fait beau."

"Ah non, madame," he said solemnly. "Il ne fait pas beau. Est-ce que vous n'avez pas entendu les nouvelles?"

He was speaking so quickly that she understood little except something about news. "News?" she asked in English.

The man changed to broken English. "There is murder, c'est grave. Franz Ferdinand and his femme."

"Murdered?"

"Oui, madame." He turned to his other customers.

Philomene looked around the square and noticed for the first time the small knots of people conversing and gesturing. She caught snatches of *madman* and *Sophia* and *Bosnia*. She looked over and saw a young man intently reading the headlines of *Le Soir.* Where had she been for the last several hours since the newspapers had been dispersed? *Caught up in shopping and embarrassment over my new green hat.* She chided herself.

"Philomene! Philomene!" She saw her aunt striding across the square, a look of devastation on her face. "Have you heard? Have you heard, my dear?"

"Just now," Philomene answered, standing and taking her aunt's arm, "but I don't know if I understand. Archduke Ferdinand of Austria-Hungry has been murdered?"

"Yes, assassinated. He and Sophia." Tears welled up in her aunt's eyes. "I met them. I met them, you know. Here in Belgium at a dinner." Philomene put her arm around her aunt's waist. "He was stern and quite cold, but she . . . oh, she was a lovely woman."

Philomene threw some coins onto the table, picking up her bag and holding her aunt close. Hannah was weeping openly now, and in public. It was a thing Philomene thought never to see.

"She and I spoke for quite some time . . . mostly about her children . . . oh, her dear little children." Mrs. William Conner Finn had lost all sense of decorum, and several people looked over with pity at the weeping woman. "The newspaper says the duke called out to her after they were shot. He said 'Sophie, dear Sophie, don't die! Stay alive for our children.'" Her voice was frayed with anguish. "Oh, Philomene, what will become of her dear little children?"

"Come, Auntie, let's get you home."

As Philomene hailed a carriage, she was thinking, oddly enough, not of Sophia or her children, but of Ferdinand's uncle, Franz Josef. The man was powerful—emperor of Austria and king of Hungary. The ruler was in his eighties and had already suffered the suicide of his son Rudolf, the execution of his brother, and the assassination of his wife. *The curse of the Hapsburgs,* Philomene reflected. How would he endure this latest blow—the assassination of his nephew and heir? She saw the broken monarch wandering the glittering halls of the palace, yelling at the worried servants to keep away, and dropping to the floor the medals and ribboned tributes of his station. She pulled her mind from the poignant scene to staunch the flood of emotion. She must keep her feelings in check—keep her wits about her. A carriage approached and she stood straighter to greet it.

Her auntie had worried about Sophia's orphaned children and what would become of the innocent darlings, but as Philomene stepped into the carriage and settled her distraught aunt, she wondered what would become of them all.

* * *

"Well, look what's coming to town!" Nephi announced. "August seventh."

"What?" Alaina asked. She turned from the stove to look, but Nephi held the newspaper from her. "Ah, ah. Watch what you're doing. Don't burn my oats."

"I thought you liked your breakfast burned."

"Just toast."

"Oh, I see." She smiled and went back to stirring. "It's yesterday's paper, anyway. I may have already read it."

"No, you haven't. You never read the paper. Now, I want you to guess."

"Guess what?"

"What's coming to town August seventh."

"Nephi," she said in a slightly scolding tone.

"Come on," he implored. "At least try."

"The president of the United States."

He scoffed. "I said what, not who."

"A rodeo?"

"Nope."

"A moving picture show?"

"Nope."

"The circus."

"That's it!"

"A circus?"

"You guessed it, you smart girl! And not just any circus. The Barnum and Bailey circus. The greatest show on earth!"

"I take it you like the circus," she said, coming around to spoon oats into his dish.

"Don't you?" he asked, incredulous at her calm tone.

"I don't know. I've never been to one."

"What?"

"I'm just an uncultured country girl, remember?"

"Well, we definitely have to go then!"

She laughed at his exuberance. "It's over a month away."

"But we have to prepare. Read that." He shoved the paper to her, and she read the ad out loud as he spooned butter and brown sugar onto his oats.

Alaina cleared her throat and read dramatically, "The Greatest Show on Earth! Barnum and Bailey Circus! August seventh. Main and Eighth South. Thirty-five hundred costumes! Three hundred and fifty musical instrumentalists! Three hundred dancing and singing girls!"

Nephi raised his eyebrows and she slapped his arm. "Eat your breakfast. The Wizard Prince of Arabia! One hundred and ten dens of the world's rarest and costliest beasts. Eleanor would find that interesting," she said, dropping the paper down. Nephi gave her an impatient wave to continue. "And, last but not least . . ." She paused for effect, "Forty famously funny clowns!"

"See!" Nephi said, laughing. "What country girl wouldn't like that?"

"But, it's fifty cents a ticket," she answered, thinking of his meager salary.

"We can manage that." He leaned over and kissed her. "We'll become dull and boring if all we do is work." He was about to kiss her again when Mother Erickson walked into the kitchen with Elias.

"Hey!" Nephi said, sitting back in his chair. "You're early."

"Elias has brought over today's paper," Mother Erickson said softly.

The atmosphere in the room turned to ice.

"What is it?" Nephi asked, reaching for the offered paper. "What's wrong? Is it President Wilson?"

Elias shook his head. "No. The assassination of a royal over in Europe."

"What?" Nephi said sharply. He spread the paper out onto the table.

Alaina stood abruptly. "I . . . I have to check on Miss Titus. She needs her morning exercise." She shoved her chair aside and moved towards the back door.

Nephi called after her. "But don't you want to know what's happened?"

"No," she answered tersely. "No." She stepped out into the summer sunlight and ran for the barn.

Chapter Fourteen

Eleanor paced from the green velvet settee to the bay window. She had been waiting over two hours for Mrs. Colin Fitzpatrick to arrive, but because of the thick morning fog it was likely the visit would be postponed or canceled. She continued her pacing, wrapping her shawl tightly around her shoulders. It was July, and yet the fog made everything chill and dreary. *Stupid fog!* Eleanor thought spitefully. Like so many other things in her life, it conspired to keep her trapped and isolated. She felt like she was inside an alabaster box with the lid tightly closed and no chance for escape. She had hoped that Mrs. Fitzpatrick might prove to be the one to free her, but Mrs. Fitzpatrick was stopped by the fog, and Eleanor could do nothing but lament her fate.

When Mr. Palmer had brought the note from Aunt Ida's friend indicating that an earlier-than-August meeting was imperative and that she would be calling the next day, Eleanor's hopes had soared. It could only mean that Mrs. Fitzpatrick had found some suitable occupation for her that needed immediate tending.

Eleanor stopped at the bay window, glaring out at the gray day and wishing for Mrs. Fitzpatrick's shiny black automobile to appear through the mist.

"Psst."

Eleanor turned to see Kerri McKee at the parlor door, smiling brightly and motioning her to come closer. "Pardon me, Miss Eleanor, but if you're not engaged at the moment we have work for you in the kitchen."

Eleanor giggled as she moved closer. "Work? Really?"

Kerri crossed her heart. "As I'm a true and faithful Catholic girl."

"Below stair?" Eleanor asked, and Kerri nodded. "But what about Mr. Palmer?"

"Day off. Once a month. Gone to visit his sister in the Mission District."

"And my aunt?"

"Takin' a bit of a nap before dinner, and yer mum's in with Kathryn and Miss Clawson."

Eleanor glanced out the window. "I don't suppose Mrs. Fitzpatrick will be coming in this fog."

"She'd have to be daft, and she's not that," Kerri answered. "So, come along then, there's work to be done, and no time for idle hands." The dark-haired girl turned toward the back stairs, and Eleanor followed dutifully. "Ah, there's another surprise I've got for you," Kerri added.

"What?" Eleanor asked, catching up.

"Never you mind. You'll see when we get below stair."

As the girls filed down the narrow staircase Eleanor felt her spirits lift. The warmth and smells from the kitchen came to greet her, and she felt at home with the unadorned white walls and functional linoleum floors. She heard voices and laughter coming from the servants' hall, which melted away much of her melancholy. She heard and recognized Ina Bell's soft lilt and Bib's rumbling bass, but there were other voices unfamiliar to her ear, and she knew that unexpected visitors must be Kerri's other surprise. They moved into the servants' hall, and Eleanor was greeted warmly by her friends.

Kerri cleared her throat. "Miss Eleanor Lund," she said in her proper voice, "may I have the pleasure in presentin' Mr. Albert Glassey and his daughter, Roxann."

The two strangers had risen when the girls entered the room, and now Mr. Glassey, a short man with a round ruddy, face, nodded in her direction, and Roxann, a beauty of a girl just a few years younger than Eleanor, curtsied.

"Mr. Glassey and Miss Roxann, may I introduce Miss Eleanor Lund sometimes of upstairs, but much more comfortable below."

"Kerri McKee!" Ina Bell said sharply. "Really!"

"Ah, keep yer cap on," Kerri chided. "See, everybody else is laughin' about it."

Ina Bell just shook her head and rolled her eyes at her friend's inappropriate behavior, returning to her darning with intent.

"Now," Kerri continued, "Mr. Glassey is our favorite butcher . . ."

"Our only butcher," Bib broke in.

"Our only favorite butcher, and he knows between a flank and a shank, I'll tell ya that," Kerri said with pride.

Eleanor smiled at Mr. Glassey, who was bobbing his head shyly at the compliment.

"Another interestin' thing about these two is that they're members of that Mormon Church your father joined."

A thrill went through Eleanor from the top of her head to her toes, and she fixed Mr. Glassey with a look of delight. "Is that true, Mr. Glassey?"

"It is, miss, yes. My father came on to San Francisco with Captain Sam Brannon."

Eleanor had no idea who that was, but as Mr. Glassey seemed pretty proud of the association, she responded with interest, "And are there many Mormons in San Francisco, Mr. Glassey?"

"Oh, yes, miss. We have a hundred or so members. Mission head-quarters is down on McAllister. President Robinson's the mission president. San Fran used to be mission headquarters for all of California till the big quake in '06, then everybody got nervous and moved it to Los Angeles." Roxann reached over and gently laid her hand on her father's arm. He jumped slightly and chuckled. "Oh, my! There's my little weather vane, letting me know when I'm spouting off too much. Just what her mother used to do before she passed on. Rest her soul."

"So you've been a member all your life, Mr. Glassey?" Eleanor asked.

"Well, I was sort of on again off again for a time, to tell the truth. I had a little trouble with the drink, don't ya know. But when my Roxann here was healed of the influenza by the elders, well, I changed my ways. Yes I did. Haven't had a drop in four years." Eleanor smiled at the guileless banter, and Mr. Glassey grinned back. "You're not a member then?"

Eleanor shook her head. "I know it's true, Mr. Glassey, but I won't be joining until I'm no longer under my mother's . . . until I'm of

age." The kind-faced man nodded, and Eleanor discerned his understanding. "I'd love to attend church with your congregation though, if
that would be all right?"

Mr. Glassey's head bobbed energetically. "Of course, Miss Lund.
We'd be pleased to have you attend. Pleased."

"Will your aunt and your mother be lettin' you do that, miss?"
Kerri asked. "Meanin' no disrespect."

Eleanor hadn't thought about that problem. She shrugged. "I
don't know. I have a feeling Mother will object."

"I have a feelin' you're right," Kerri agreed. "But, as my da used to
say, 'Let's not go swimming till we see if the water's warm.'"

Ina Bell rolled her eyes—an act that luckily Kerri did not see.

Kerri turned to Eleanor and put her hands on her hips. "So, Miss
Eleanor, I bring ya down to work and here ya stand chattin' away like
a fishwife to her sister."

Ina Bell's head jerked up. "Kerri McKee! Are you mad? She can't
work!"

"Of course she can," Kerri said stubbornly. "Even though she's a
thin slip of a girl—look how strong she is. She could probably do my
work and your work together."

"That isn't the point!" Ina Bell returned. "She is Mrs. Westfield's
niece."

"So?"

"So, she doesn't have to work."

"I know she doesn't have to work, but maybe she wants to work,"
Kerri said with a sniff.

"I do, Ina Bell," Eleanor said quickly. "I really do want to work."

"See," Kerri said making a face at her friend. "You make it seem
like I'm twistin' her arm." She turned to Eleanor. "So, would you like
to darn, separate the cream, or read to all of us?"

"Reading? Is that really one of the jobs?"

"'Tis," Kerri answered.

"Well, I'd read," Eleanor said, "but I do that all the time . . . so, I
think I'll separate the cream."

"Ah. Then that's the contraption," Kerri said, pointing to a
machine that stood in the corner of the kitchen. "The dreaded cream
separator."

"And you'll show me how it works?"

"Gladly," Kerri nodded. She turned to Bib. "And will you be favoring us with your reading then, Mr. Randall?"

"I'd love to!" Bib answered, moving to a small bookcase and retrieving several books. "So, we have *Julius the Street Boy* by Horatio Alger, *The Son of Monte Cristo* by Dumas, or *Spark the Wonder Dog.*"

"I'm for *Spark the Wonder Dog,*" Kerri said, taking Eleanor over for instruction on the separator.

"Me too," Ina Bell said.

"I like any kind of reading," Mr. Glassey offered meekly, and Roxann nodded.

"*Wonder Dog* it is then," Bib answered, sliding the other books back onto the shelf.

The next hour passed pleasantly as Bib read and Eleanor worked along with Kerri and Ina Bell. Mrs. Todd, the cook, moved unobtrusively back and forth from stove to larder to table, and just as Eleanor's shoulders and elbow were stiffening from the turning of the separator's handle, the competent chef gently shooed everyone out so she could make final preparations for the noon meal.

Cook was a woman of contrast—heavyset and stern looking, but in actuality terribly shy and self-conscious. She rarely looked people in the eye and never raised her voice to anyone, even when one of the girls spilled her famous sauce on the serving tray. She stood quietly at the back door now, ushering out Roxann and Mr. Glassey, and when she turned back into the room, Eleanor noticed she was holding a small, white package.

"Aye, what's that now, Mrs. Todd?" Kerri asked, moving to her and sneaking a peek inside the bag. Mrs. Todd blushed red and chuckled. "Ah, look here," Kerri said, pulling a sugar cone out of the bag. "Mr. Glassey's brought you a sugar cone now, has he? I think he's sweet on you, Mabel."

Mrs. Todd tried to protest and snatch back the cone, but her giggles rendered her helpless. Just as Kerri was about to continue with the teasing, a bell clanged on the calling board. Ina Bell shot out of her seat, and Bib rose and put on his jacket.

"Not to worry, Ina Bell. It is Mr. Randall at the ready!" he said with a wink.

Kerri laughed, and Ina Bell sat down, patting her chest to calm herself.

"Miss Lund," Bib said in an official tone, "I believe you should follow me." He led the way out of the servants' hall, calling back over his shoulder. "Mrs. Todd, you may expect one more for dinner."

"Very good, Mr. Randall," came the reply.

"Thanks for your help, Miss Lund," Kerri yelled to her.

Eleanor heard a *shhh* from Ina Bell, and she smiled. "It was my pleasure!" Eleanor yelled back. She smoothed her hair and checked to make sure there were no spatterings of milk on her dress. As they moved down the upper hallway, Eleanor hesitated for a moment to look out through the parlor windows. She marveled at how the fog had lifted in her hour of occupation. She was thrilled to see the trees and houses across the street, and even more excited to see the silhouette of a woman in a large hat through the etched glass of the front door. Eleanor's heart jumped to think that Mrs. Fitzpatrick might have braved the weather to seek her out.

"If you will wait in the parlor, Miss Lund," Bib said officiously, "I will see who is calling."

"Yes, Mr. Palmer," Eleanor teased, giving him a playful shove.

He smiled as he righted himself, straightening his coat and moving gracefully to the door.

Eleanor walked into the parlor trying to decide where she should stand to receive guests. She planted herself by the fireplace mantel, listening to the muffled voices coming from the entry foyer. There seemed to be two women's voices, and Eleanor was suddenly anxious that she would have to meet a stranger.

The parlor door opened, and Mr. Randall stepped in. "Mrs. Colin Fitzpatrick and Mrs. Antonia," he announced.

"Thank you, Mr. Randall," Eleanor answered, trying to sound older and proper.

Mrs. Fitzpatrick and Mrs. Antonia came into the parlor and went directly to Eleanor. Mrs. Antonia was a tall, elegant woman with dark brown hair and golden brown eyes. Her skin was pale ivory and flawless. She looked like someone who should be riding around in carriages and attending the theater. Eleanor felt rustic in her presence.

"Should I waken Mrs. Westfield and set two more for dinner?" Bib asked pointedly to Mrs. Fitzpatrick.

"Oh, no. No thank you, Mr. Randall. Our time is limited. Mrs. Antonia and I have much catching up to do this afternoon because of the reprehensible fog."

"Very good, madam." Bib bowed and backed out of the room, giving Eleanor an encouraging nod.

Mrs. Fitzpatrick finished removing her gloves and turned to Eleanor. "Miss Lund, may I introduce Mrs. Antonia—a good friend and a tireless worker for the poor and downtrodden."

"How do you do, Mrs. Antonia?" Eleanor said with a nod.

"How do you do, Miss Lund?" Mrs. Antonia answered, looking intently at Eleanor.

"Won't you sit down?" Eleanor asked, motioning to the brocaded armchairs.

"Thank you, yes," Mrs. Fitzpatrick answered, sitting, "but only for a moment, then we're off." She looked into Eleanor's face. "Now I know it is only July, Miss Lund, and I promised your aunt that I would wait until your sixteenth birthday, but when Gladys came to me with her new project, I thought of you immediately."

Eleanor felt a rush of importance when Mrs. Fitzpatrick spoke of her, and she wondered at the position she would be filling. Mrs. Antonia seemed like an intelligent and capable woman, and she felt awed that Mrs. Fitzpatrick thought her worthy to be paired with such a leader.

Mrs. Fitzpatrick turned to her friend. "Gladys, would you like to explain?"

Mrs. Antonia nodded. "Are you familiar with foot binding, Miss Lund?"

Eleanor stared at her blankly. "Food binding? I'm afraid not, Mrs. Antonia."

"Well, it's an ancient Chinese custom where a little girl's small toes are broken." Eleanor stiffened. "Then the mother of this four- or five-year-old takes long, narrow bandages and binds her feet tightly so that the feet will not grow. The bandages are retightened every day for two years."

Eleanor was horrified at such a practice, yet she wondered why Mrs. Antonia was telling her about it.

"In 1911," Mrs. Antonia went on, "the new Chinese government forbade the practice of foot binding for all its women, but sadly it still takes place."

"In China?" Eleanor questioned, trying to formulate the significance to her.

"Actually, right here in San Francisco," Mrs. Fitzpatrick interjected. "Mrs. Antonia has made the Civic League aware that foot binding is still being performed on young girls in Chinatown."

Is this the project that's been chosen for me? Eleanor wondered. During the month since Mrs. Fitzpatrick had indicated that her help would be welcomed, Eleanor had pondered in what bit of the vineyard she would be serving. Never in a thousand years did she guess her toil would come in this odd and obscure part of the field. Eleanor reprimanded herself. *Does it really matter where I help?* She looked up to see Mrs. Antonia staring at her.

"Sorry, Mrs. Antonia. I was just trying to imagine how painful that would be."

Mrs. Fitzpatrick and Mrs. Antonia shared a look. "I told you she was a bright one, Gladys."

"You did indeed, Ruth," Mrs. Antonia said. She turned back to look at Eleanor. "Painful, Miss Lund? We cannot even imagine. Skin on the foot dies, so often there is infection, gangrene, or blood poisoning. And the smell . . . well, it's . . ." She stopped, noticing the look of revulsion on Eleanor's face. She smoothed her skirt. "The Civic League has commissioned myself and one other woman to go into Chinatown and take care of this problem."

"And how does one do that?" Eleanor asked.

"Education, Miss Lund. Education. We will observe first and report our findings to a physician. Hopefully we can put an end to such a barbaric custom."

"Why would they do such a thing?" Eleanor asked.

Mrs. Antonia pulled a beautiful, silk embroidered shoe from her purse. It was three or four inches long. "So they can fit their foot into this."

"But that's a child's shoe," Eleanor said in disbelief.

"No, this is called a lotus shoe, and it is meant to fit a full-grown woman."

Eleanor felt sick. "I don't understand."

"None of us can," Mrs. Fitzpatrick said fiercely. "Small feet. More pleasing to the eye. It used to be Chinese men wouldn't marry a woman unless she had small feet."

"But . . . but wouldn't the woman be crippled?" Eleanor asked, her voice thick with indignation

"Often," Mrs. Antonia answered, putting the shoe away and looking her straight in the face. "So, do you wish to help me, Miss Lund?"

Eleanor looked back into Mrs. Antonia's fixed gaze. "Of course, I will help. I must help."

"Good woman!" Mrs. Fitzpatrick said, rising. "Gladys and I will work out the details, and I will inform your aunt." She took Eleanor by the hand. "We are glad to have you with us, Eleanor."

For a long while after the women's departure, Eleanor sat alone in the parlor looking out the bay window and thinking about the vagaries of life. For hundreds of years—actually almost a thousand— women in China had been suffering in silence the tyranny of a mean- ingless and harmful tradition. Millions of women unknown to her. How many other cruel indignities were being suffered because of ignorance or domination? In that moment her life's aspiration settled into her soul. She would learn nursing and travel to the darkest regions of the world to bring people the light of education and healing. God had given her life purpose, and she would honor Him with commitment.

Bib came in to announce that the afternoon meal was prepared, inviting her to follow him to the dining room. She followed him mechanically, her head full of frightful images and her heart full of compassion. Bib seated her at the table and within a few moments Aunt Ida, Mother, and Kathryn came in. Eleanor was trying to ignore them, but Kathryn was chattering on about a new dress her nanny was making her, and Aunt Ida was commenting that the poached salmon looked a bit dry.

Eleanor cleared her throat. "Excuse me. Did you know there are young girls in Chinatown who are having their feet mutilated so they can fit into three-inch shoes?"

The room went deathly quiet.

Aunt Ida's face was frozen in shock, and Kathryn frowned at being interrupted. Mother looked imperious, and, surprisingly, was the first to speak. "You are an odd child, Eleanor. What in the world would possess you to talk about such a thing?"

Eleanor had lost her train of thought. She was upset that her mother would call her odd. She had been about to tell them of Mrs. Fitzpatrick's visit and her call to assist Mrs. Antonia in the noble work of helping these young innocents. But, against Mother's disdain, her confidence failed, and she felt foolish and unsure.

"What a hayhead," Kathryn scoffed, refusing the piece of salmon offered by the servant girl, and babbling on again about her new summer dress.

Eleanor listened for a time to the clink of silverware on the china plates, then rose quietly and left the room.

 Chapter Fifteen

"Strike two!" the umpire called, and Alaina worked to stifle a smile. She knew it was terrible, but she hoped Elias would strike out. He and Nephi both played on the Union team, but Elias was the captain and the hardest hitter. And now his teammates were rooting for him to hit the winning run. Alaina crossed her fingers for another strike.

Over the months that she and Nephi had been in Salt Lake City, Elias had only spoken a dozen sentences to her, and most of those felt like condescension or criticism. She had never spoken to Nephi's father and had only ever seen him at a distance, but Elias was very like him in facial feature, and she imagined in temperament, too. She wondered how Nephi's brother could claim to believe in a purer form of Christianity yet mock its gentle teachings by his actions.

"Oh, I hope he hits this next one," Sarah said quietly. "He's not very happy when the team loses."

Alaina straightened her back. "Come on, Elias! Whack it out of the park!" she yelled.

Sarah jumped and started giggling. "Alaina, that was so loud!"

"Well, they can't hear you if you whisper," Mother Erickson said, patting Sarah's hand. "Come on, Elias! Whack it out of the park!"

Alaina laughed as she watched Elias grimace at the unladylike antics of his mother and sister-in-law. Alaina wondered if he thought her a bad influence. Maybe he would forbid Sarah to associate with her anymore, fearing that she might corrupt his wife's saintly personality.

Sarah slipped her arm through Alaina's and laid her head on her shoulder.

Too late, Alaina thought. *We are fast friends already.*

The pitcher was ready to throw the next ball, and a palpable tension ran through the crowd. Elias's face was taut with concentration, and Sarah sat up covering her eyes with her hands. The next second there was a loud crack, and a cheer exploded from the crowd. Sarah's hands flew from her eyes, and she started clapping.

Elias's two-base line drive sent a runner home and won Union the game—nine to eight. It was only an exhibition game against the team from the University of Utah, but the fans reacted as though it were for a national championship. Elias's teammates ran onto the field to greet their champion as he sauntered back to the dugout. Alaina watched as Nephi shook his brother's hand and pounded him on the back. She recalled the first time she'd seen Nephi play baseball; it was at the Fourth of July celebration in Sutter Creek, and people were amazed by the Mormon boy's ability to play the game. His powerful hitting and command at first base helped Sutter Creek win against Amador and had gained Nephi at least tacit acceptance by town members. Watching these Mormon men in their uniforms and ball caps, she wondered if the wily Mormon prophet, Brigham Young, had calculated to bring the game to Utah for the exact purpose of making his peculiar people seem more normal to national sensibilities.

She shook her head as other pictures of that Fourth of July inched their way into her memory: pictures of her and Father riding into town together, of dropping potatoes at Granny Pitman's, and of Titus trying to eat her straw hat . . . she shook her head again. What odd, unwelcome recollections. She worked hard to block out the image of Father's tired face—a ghostly tiredness that foreshadowed the heart problems that would cheat him of life a few months later. Alaina felt the familiar anguish pour into her stomach. She looked up. The noise of the crowd was dying down, and people were rising from their seats and moving to the exits. She stood quickly, looking for Sarah and Mother Erickson. They were moving to the end of the row where they turned, carefully maneuvering the bleacher steps to the ground. She watched as Elias left the group of well-wishers to help Sarah down from the steps. He was solicitous with his wife who, though small, was showing her six months of pregnancy.

"Wonderful game!" Sarah said, beaming up at her husband.

He put his arm around her. "Are you well? That's a long time for you to be sitting."

She smiled at him. "Oh, I stood up every time the crowd did. I'm fine, really."

"That's my girl."

Alaina saw him tug his wife's braid and kiss her forehead. Then, as he looked over to watch his sister-in-law's approach, Alaina saw his eyes harden and the expression on his face change from warmth to critical evaluation.

"Where's Nephi?" Sarah asked, also noticing Alaina drawing closer.

"He's taken Ernie Anastasio over to the locker room to see the team doctor. He's sprained his ankle or something. Nephi will probably change before he comes back."

Mother Erickson broke away from the group of women with whom she'd been conversing and walked over to her family. "Great hit, Elias! I was sure that ball was gonna hit the back fence!"

Elias chuckled. "Well, I had to do something to stop your cheering."

Sarah fanned herself with her handbag.

"Here now," Elias said quickly, "we need to get you out of this sun."

"I'll take her over to the truck," Mother Erickson said. "You go on and change." She took Sarah's arm.

"Yes, ma'am. Thank you," Elias responded. "Get her some lemonade or something."

"Good idea," Mother Erickson said, turning toward the concession stand. "Coming, Alaina?"

"I think I'll wait here for Nephi," she answered.

"Hmm . . . guess she prefers her husband's company to ours," Mother Erickson said to Sarah.

Alaina blushed.

"As it should be," Sarah responded happily.

The two women went off together, while Elias turned his back on his sister-in-law and walked away towards the locker room. Although it was a rude action, Alaina was actually glad they did not have to be alone together. Suddenly Elias stopped and turned back, walking to her in long strides. She tried to present a calm face, but her stomach was aching and her palms were sweaty. *Maybe he's just coming back to thank me for cheering for him.*

"Mrs. Erickson," he said, stopping only a foot in front of her and speaking in a low rumble. "May I ask you a question?"

Her stomach twisted. "Only if you call me Alaina," she answered, trying to sound cavalier.

He ignored her attempt to lighten the mood. "Have you ever read any of the Book of Mormon?"

"I . . ." She was completely stunned by this question. "I . . . what do you mean?"

"It's a simple question. I take it Nephi's given you a Book of Mormon to read."

"No, Elias," she said, trying to control her rising temper, "he hasn't."

"No?" He seemed surprised by this answer. "But there are copies about my mother's house, aren't there?"

"Yes."

"And you've never picked one up to read it?"

He was backing her into a corner, and she didn't like it. "No. I have not found it necessary."

Elias was still speaking low, but his words were like knives. "Not necessary? It is a book fundamental to your husband's faith, and you have not considered it necessary to show him the least degree of respect by reading it?"

A knot of anger and humiliation was aching in her throat, preventing her from speaking, preventing her from defending herself.

"You have been husband and wife for nine months now. Nine months. My brother gave up his chance for eternal exaltation to help you, and this is your thanks?" The look on Elias's face was frightening, and Alaina stepped back, but her brother-in-law pursued her. "When you first arrived here, I knew you weren't truly husband and wife. I could tell he meant nothing to you, and I kept hoping he would tire of your selfishness and send you back to California." Alaina fought desperately to speak back, but emotion had overwhelmed all of her senses except her hearing. Elias, knowing he held the upper hand, continued to pour his indignation into her ears. "And now it seems, judging from my brother's behavior, you have shared his bed and he is stuck with you."

These last words were so wrenching and inappropriate that they unloosed her tongue. "How dare you!" she hissed, aware that several people turned to look in their direction. She knew they were too far away to hear the conversation, but the looks on her face and Elias's did not indicate a pleasant exchange.

Elias was not intimidated by her anger. "You have no idea what he's given up for you, do you? You don't know because you haven't taken one moment to find out anything about our faith."

"Why would I do that," she spit out, "when your faith makes you mean and superior?" She knew that wasn't true of Nephi, or Mother Erickson, or Sarah, but her temper had taken over her tongue, and all she wanted to do was fight back and stop Elias from talking. It was obvious that Elias had held these bitter feelings for her from the beginning, though he'd masked them in charlatan civility. Elias saw her as a cankerous thorn in the side of his family—a thorn he obviously felt compelled to remove.

"My brother is a good man, and he deserves better," Elias pronounced, his dark eyes locking on hers, a malicious sneer twisting his mouth. "You can't even honor your own father by finding out why he converted to our faith."

Before she knew what was happening, her hand made sharp contact with the side of Elias's face. He stepped back, glaring at her, then turned his face ever so slightly. "But whosoever shall smite thee on thy right cheek, turn to him the other also."

Alaina's face burned with shame, but her indignation prevented her from offering even the slightest indication of regret. Elias looked at her as though she had just confirmed the unworthiness of her person.

"Alaina!" Nephi's cheerful voice came from the direction of the team building. For the moment Elias's frame was blocking Nephi's view of her, but Alaina knew that was temporary. Shame and anger washed over her, and she turned and ran for a stand of trees on the west side of the ball field. She hated Elias Erickson. With her newfound intimacy with Nephi had come a feeling of belonging and a semblance of family. Nephi's unfettered love had offered her a small cache of warmth and happiness to trust, and now Elias had taken that away. She felt spite snake its way into her soul, and she vowed never to read the Book of Mormon or study a religion that had such people in it.

She heard Nephi calling after her, but her only thought was to make it to the seclusion of the trees. She reached the edge of the shade, doubling over in pain, and vomited the contents of her stomach.

Chapter Sixteen

"Come down. Come down, little sparrow." Grandfather Erickson stood at the base of one of his apple trees entreating Alaina with tender words to give up her perch and come down to him. She had been sitting in the tree for several hours, and his worry had finally brought him out of the house to discover the cause of her exile. All he knew was that she'd shown up hours earlier, secured the tools from the shed, and headed out to the trees.

Alaina had come to Grandfather Erickson's small grove on the pretense of tending to the apples, but hiding from her husband and blunting her sadness were the true motivations. When she was young, sitting in the apple trees had brought consolation and refuge, and she longed for that serenity now. Perhaps in that calm she could figure out the disorder that was her life. When Nephi had caught up with her at the ball field, she had lied about her behavior, saying she wasn't feeling well. Actually, that had been a partial truth; she just never explained the reason for her illness.

Alaina looked down into the rugged, worn face of Grandfather Erickson and saw tears glistening in his eyes. "I'm sorry," she said in a whisper. "I'll come down." She maneuvered her way to the lower branches and jumped deftly to the ground.

He said nothing, removing a leaf from her hair and patting her back.

"I . . ." she began timidly.

"Is all right," he interrupted. "You can keep your story if you like. Come, you valk me back to the house. Is hot out here."

Humiliation clouded her look. "I'm sorry. It was my silliness that brought you out."

"Not silly. Some troubles need a good climb into a tree." Alaina laughed in spite of her sorrow. "I vood climb dere myself if I could." He laid his gnarled hand on her shoulder, and they started for the house. They didn't talk as the afternoon heat mocked their advancement.

"Whew!" Lars Erickson breathed out, scowling at the cloudless sky. "Dis is vere de devil comes to play. Is never hot in Denmark."

Alaina stepped into the shade of a giant pine and stopped. "Should I run to the house and get you some water?"

"Nah, I don't vant you running anyvere in dis heat," he answered, shaking his head. "Ven ve get to house, you grab a bucket and give us a soaking."

"Don't tempt me!" she said grinning at him.

"You tink I'm teasing?"

Alaina laughed as they started again. "Come now, what's a little heat to a tough pioneer?"

"Yah, is true. But I vas only tventy-two ven I came across dis big country. Yah, tventy-two—Nephi's age. I'm old man now, and I vant lemonade."

"I'll make some as soon as we get to the house," Alaina said eagerly. The family would never forgive her if she let the venerated patriarch of the family get heat stroke. She remembered a time on their farm in California when her dear sister Eleanor had brought her lemonade when she was suffering a heat headache. *Don't think about home*, Alaina warned herself. She knew if she let her thoughts linger too long on the white house, the apple trees, or the face of her sister, melancholy would settle even deeper into her heart. Her thoughts jumped to Nephi working away at the capitol-building site. Often he would come home exhausted from the day's toil, especially now with the summer heat. Of course, this thought did nothing to comfort her, and she growled at its intrusion.

Grandfather Erickson chuckled. "Yah. Dat's vat ve do ven tings are bad; ve growl at dem—ve growl and kick."

Alaina started giggling and crying at the same time, and Grandfather Erickson patted her shoulder. She growled at herself again and wiped the tears angrily from her cheeks. "I would have been a terrible pioneer," she said through gritted teeth. "I probably would have complained every step of the way. Actually, I wouldn't have come. Why would I walk all that way for something I didn't believe?" She swiped more tears away. "Why would I leave my home and go off to some barren desolation to live with people who didn't care for me?"

Grandfather Erickson stopped again in the shade of another tree. "Vat happened, little sparrow? Who made you feel so bad? Did Nephi say something?"

"No." She bent over, putting her hands on her knees. "No. He is always kind to me."

Grandfather watched her carefully. "Are you sick?"

"A little," she said, straightening. "It's just the heat, and these stupid tears."

"It must be hard to live among us," he said.

Her back stiffened and she looked away. She was upset with herself for letting her temper get the better of her tongue and revealing private animosities that would only deepen her estrangement from the family; she was also brought up short by the concern in Grandfather Erickson's voice. Her mind grasped at diversions. "No . . . it's not that. It's . . . it's just that I miss my home." She retied her apron. "You have all been wonderful to me." Grandfather's keen eyes were on her. "Really," she finished, looking down.

"Vell, I tink it is hard for you. Everyting so different. And I tink maybe someone say someting. Maybe Elias say someting to hurt your feelings."

She opened her mouth to answer, but the lie she was about to tell stuck in her throat.

"Yah, I vas tinking so. Elias is much like his father. Dey live de gospel fiercely, and often dey offend."

For some reason this straightforward evaluation by Grandfather Erickson made Alaina feel better, but she still did not want the rest of the family, especially Nephi, to know about the incident. "I don't want anyone else to know," she said firmly.

The patriarch nodded, taking her hat off her head and fanning her with it. "Yah, I understand." He handed her the hat. "I do dis only if you promise me one ting."

"What?" she asked.

"You tell me everyting Elias say to you."

She studied the man a moment. "You won't say anything to him?"

"No, little sparrow, it vill be our secret."

She debated for a time, shame and frustration battling for and against silence. Finally she nodded.

"Goot. Now ve get back to de house for our lemonade."

She smiled weakly, a bit of color returning to her cheeks.

As they walked, Alaina pondered if she really should tell him everything or edit the conversation. Knowing Grandfather's ability to discern falsehoods, she figured she'd lay it all down—wheat and chaff together—and let him do the winnowing.

Chapter Seventeen

It was still raining. Philomene Johnson stood at the salon windows of her aunt's elegant apartments looking down onto the rue de la Montagne. The thunder had woken her around five in the morning, and she'd lain for hours drifting in and out of sleep, listening to the heavy drops splash onto the stone balcony outside her glass-paneled doors. It was a hot rain that did nothing to ease the stifling summer oppression. Philomene paced in front of the windows, trying to slow her thoughts as she worried about steamship tickets. Europe was bracing for war, and many steamship companies had canceled sailings, leaving American travelers to scramble for remaining bookings. Philomene, who had not set an actual date for her departure, had been thwarted at every turn. One agent at the port of Calais said ships were booked until September.

Tensions in Europe had escalated since the assassination of the archduke and his wife. It was no longer only an incident between Austria and Serbia, as other countries joined the fray, resurrecting old conflicts. Indeed, Germany showed no aversion to a European war, hoping it would be the means of achieving geopolitical power.

Philomene shook her head. *Am I actually organizing the facts of this frightening conflict into lessons for my students?* She pulled her dressing gown more tightly about her, staring at the rain-smudged windows and wondering if it were raining on the roses and hollyhocks in her quiet garden back home. When she thought of William Trenton, her heart saddened, and she said a prayer that his worry for her would not be too great.

Belgium and Holland had confirmed their neutrality in the conflict as surrounding countries mobilized, but Germany, who had joined on the side of Austria, actually had aspirations against Russia and France. The latest news was that the Reichstag was demanding that Belgium allow German troops to march across her soil to take France. If Belgium promised no resistance, Germany would not occupy the small country when the conflict was over. Belgium had refused, and now it was rumored that German troops were pushing into Belgium at Verviers, near Aix-la-Chapelle.

August fourth. How much has happened in one week, Philomene thought. July thirty-first had begun the mobilization of Belgian troops, and though the main Brussels newspaper, *Le Soir,* was urging calm, the tension on the streets was palpable. Merchants were refusing paper money, which sent hordes of citizens rushing to the banks. Philomene had seen one slight woman emerge from the Banque Nationale dragging a suitcase obviously loaded with coins. Late in the night of the thirty-first, church bells and trumpets calling the reservists to duty had jolted Philomene awake, and in the morning a young customs agent came to the house asking for any Belgian flags in their possession.

"We are putting them along the border and on churches and public buildings," the agent told them. "The black, yellow, and red will be seen everywhere!" There was a fierce pride in his voice, and when Aunt Hannah placed four beautiful flags in his arms, he laid his head on them and wept.

Over the next several days the stifling heat drove Philomene and her aunt out of doors, and Philomene was amazed at the change in the atmosphere and activity in the city. People in the streets wore tricolored hats and rosettes, women carried armloads of flowers to give to the soldiers, and friends crowded outdoor cafes to vent pent-up anxiety. As Philomene walked with her aunt under a brilliant blue sky in the Parc du Cinquantenaire, it was odd to see the grounds filled with organized troops, cars, horses, cannons, and caissons. They had stopped once to join a gathering of citizens singing, "La Brabançonne" for a group of recruits. It was after this spontaneous event that Aunt Hannah had encountered an American friend. The sturdy, middle-aged gentleman had rushed up to greet them as the crowd dispersed.

"Hello! Hello, Madame Finn!" he called warmly as he grasped her hands.

Aunt Hannah was obviously pleased. "Richard! How are you? I haven't seen you in an age. And look, you've grown a handsome mustache since last we spoke."

The man's lips curved into a rakish grin. "So, you like it?"

"I do," Aunt Hannah replied. It was then she noticed Philomene standing quietly to the side, watching the exchange with amusement. "Oh, dear! Where are my manners? Richard, this is my great-niece, Miss Philomene Johnson. Philomene, this is a dear friend of mine and Conner's, Mr. Richard Harding Davis."

Philomene held out her hand. "How do you do, Mr. Davis?"

"A pleasure, Miss Johnson."

Philomene liked the look of him. His face had a sincere expression, and his handshake was friendly without being insinuating. And his mustache was indeed handsome. Aunt Hannah was speaking again, and Philomene had to turn her head to bring her concentration back to the words.

"Mr. Davis is an American journalist. He's been in the foreign office for how many years now, Richard?"

"Off and on for ten or so," Mr. Davis replied.

"And his articles are picked up by every major paper in the country. My niece is an educator, Mr. Davis. She lives and teaches in Sutter Creek, California."

"I'd better mind my grammar then," Mr. Davis said, smiling.

Aunt Hannah nodded. "Indeed. Her English is impeccable, and her French isn't bad either."

"Auntie," Philomene broke in, "I'm sure Mr. Davis has more to do than listen to your praise of me."

"Actually, I find it charming, Miss Johnson." He turned to Hannah. "I have just come from the palace and was on my way to dine. I would be honored if you ladies would join me."

"We'd love to!" Aunt Hannah answered without hesitation. "I miss a man's voice at the table. And you can tell us all the news."

Mr. Davis chuckled and offered each lady an arm. "Oh, so you want a scoop, do you?"

"Such awful American slang," Aunt Hannah said, smiling. "Of course we want a scoop."

As they walked, he told them of a letter sent from King Albert to his royal relative Kaiser Wilhelm II in Germany.

"The letter is to remind him of the bonds of kinship and friend-ship between the two monarchs. It also begs that Belgium's neutrality will be respected." Mr. Davis leaned toward Philomene. "The foreign minister told me that Albert's wife, Queen Elisabeth, actually had much to do with putting the letter together."

"Of that I have no doubt," Aunt Hannah commented. "She's a brilliant woman."

Richard nodded. "Indeed. A frail, little woman with the heart of a lion. I admire her greatly."

Philomene noted his sincerity.

"And is war truly upon us, Richard?" Aunt Hannah asked fearlessly.

Mr. Davis's look was grim. "Unless Germany changes its stance . . . because we both know, Hannah, that Belgium will not bend to tyranny."

The three walked in silence the rest of the way to the café.

A distant growl of thunder brought Philomene's thoughts back from her mental wanderings. She had assured her student, Mr. Trenton, that the powder keg of European conflicts did not sit in Belgium, yet here she was directly in the path of an invading army with no means of escape. She would much have preferred her prophecies of safety to be true, but the course of human history was a fickle business, and now the tenets of history were not in a book for philosophical discussion, but on her doorstep. She shivered.

A servant came quietly into the salon. "Bonjour, mademoiselle. Would you like coffee?"

Philomene turned to smile at the girl. "I think tea this morning, Claudine. Merci." The servant curtsied. "Is my aunt awake?" Philomene asked.

"Oui, mademoiselle. She is in bed with the head cold."

"Oh, dear," Philomene said, moving to leave the room.

"I will bring her some tea?"

"Oui, s'il vous plaît. With honey and lemon."

The girl looked puzzled. "Honey?"

Philomene searched for the French word. "Le' miel," she said finally. Claudine's face brightened. "Ah! Oui, mademoiselle. Le' miel."

Philomene hurried down the hallway to her aunt's room. An illness would complicate her plans, especially if a simple head cold advanced to something more serious, like pneumonia. Philomene knew it was important for her to leave the country, but even more critical that her aunt accompany her. She had been formulating a plan to travel by train into France and then by boat to England. The decision had taken on more urgency with the unavailability of steamship tickets and the threat of German soldiers pushing across the border. If she found transport they would have to leave within days. She was praying that her strong-willed aunt would see the wisdom of flight and abandon her life in Brussels, if only for a few months.

Philomene knocked softly on her aunt's door.

"Entrez," came the muffled reply.

Philomene opened the door and moved into her aunt's bedroom. The side lamp was on, casting a rosy pool of light around her aunt's person. She was sitting up, propped against several large pillows, and writing letters on a lap table. She smiled when Philomene entered, and motioned her closer.

"Good morning, dear niece! Have you been awake long?"

"Several hours," Philomene confessed. "The thunder woke me early."

"How inhospitable. Here," she said patting the bed, "climb in with me."

Philomene gratefully did as she was told. All morning a stubborn melancholy had weighed on her, and she was glad to act like a child and clamber under the covers and into the warmth and security of her aunt's bed. She trusted Aunt Hannah's intelligence and abilities and knew she had connections in high government offices—connections that could help them out of their predicament. Steamship tickets were not to be had at the moment, but other options would surely present themselves.

"Claudine tells me you have a cold," Philomene said as she settled herself.

Aunt Hannah scoffed. "Oh, that girl is a grandmother. Two sneezes and a sniffle and she has me at death's door."

Philomene laughed. She loved her aunt's cheery optimism. "So, it's not that bad?"

"Heavens no. I've taken an elixir and will be up and dressed within the hour."

"Claudine is bringing honey-lemon tea. I asked for it," Philomene said.

Her aunt looked at her sideways. "You're not turning into a grandmother, are you?"

Philomene smiled and shook her head. "No. I'm just someone who loves you."

"That I can accept." Aunt Hannah folded a letter and placed it into an envelope. "Hmm. I hope she brings scones and black currant jam."

"And a rasher of bacon," Philomene added.

Her aunt's eyes widened. "Not a very European breakfast, my dear. You must be longing for home."

"I am, actually," Philomene said simply, "and I think leaving is something we need to discuss."

Aunt Hannah held up the letter she'd just prepared. "I am working on every possibility. A servant will hand deliver these to my friends in the government this afternoon, and I believe we will have you out of here in days."

"I want us both to go," Philomene said, taking her aunt's hand.

Aunt Hannah squeezed her fingers. "I knew you would bring this up."

"It's only reasonable," Philomene pressed. "War is coming into this lovely, peaceful place, Auntie, and you will be right in the middle of it."

Aunt Hannah folded another note and placed it in an envelope. "My life is here, Philomene—my friends, my work . . . and my Conner is buried here."

"It may only be for a short time, Auntie," Philomene interrupted, "then you could return."

Her aunt smiled. "A short time is a long time for a woman of my age."

A rush of panic filled Philomene's chest, and she turned to look at her aunt straight on. "You've already decided, haven't you?"

"I am not a fool, Philomene."

"I know that."

"I have looked at each possibility and weighed every decision. I am very aware of the canker that is pushing in at our borders, but I also know that France, not Belgium, is their goal."

"But if Belgium stands in their way . . ." Philomene interrupted.

"Then the brave Belgian army will fight, all hundred and twenty thousand of them. But, I promise you one thing," she chuckled. "I will not join the forces."

"Auntie, this is no laughing matter."

Aunt Hannah took her hand. "No, my dear, of course not, but at times like these one must look at things a bit philosophically. This is my place. I need to be with my friends and with Conner. Whether I live or die, this is my place."

"Then I'm staying with you," Philomene said stoically.

"But this is not your place," Aunt Hannah answered. "Your place is in Sutter Creek with your students."

Philomene's heart wrenched at the thought of home. "I . . ."

"I know you love me and wish to keep me out of harm's way," her aunt continued, "but I am very resourceful, and I have a circle of wise and crafty friends who will keep an eye on me. You know my Conner taught me much about courage and diplomacy, Philomene, and I am fairly sure I can handle whatever comes."

Philomene sat listening to her aunt's words, wishing she could believe them, wishing that the knot of foreboding would allow her to see a more optimistic outcome. She sighed. "I admire your courage, dear one, but I cannot see the wisdom."

There was a knock on the door, and Claudine entered with the tray.

"Bonjour, madame," she said brightly, dispelling some of the gloom that had settled into the room. "Your meal is here."

"Oui, Claudine, merci," Aunt Hannah answered. She cleared away her writing things, and Claudine took the table, replacing it with the tray filled with tea, pastries, and scones with black currant jam.

"Ah, Claudine, this looks marvelous! As Conner would say, 'I'm as hungry as a grizzly at a trout stream.'"

Claudine giggled at her mistress's enthusiasm, not understanding all the words, but liking the brash American accent. "I think you are not so sick, madame."

"Never sick enough to pass up a good meal, Claudine."

"Oui, madame. Ah, your tea is there, Mademoiselle Philomene," she said pointing to the cup.

"Merci, Claudine."

"Shall I open the curtains?" Claudine asked.

"Oui, Claudine, merci," Aunt Hannah answered, cutting open a scone and covering it in jam.

Claudine moved to the windows, pushing back the heavy draperies and opening the glass-paneled doors onto the balcony.

"Oh, look!" Aunt Hannah said happily. "The storm is breaking. Now we can go out this afternoon for our surprise rendezvous!"

"A rendezvous? With whom?" Philomene asked.

"If I told you it would not be a surprise." She turned to Claudine and held out the three envelopes. "Dear Claudine, would you please see that Monsieur Pajeurnet delivers these personally this afternoon?"

Philomene could see the girl's mind working on all the English words. Then she curtsied and took the letters.

"Oui, madame. Tout de suite." She hesitated. "I will arrive back for the tray."

Aunt Hannah smiled. "Your English improves every day, Claudine."

The girl beamed. "Thank you for helping me." She curtsied again and left the room.

Philomene got out of bed and took her cup to the window. She stood quietly, looking out at the breaking clouds and patches of blue sky, praying for a peace that now seemed impossible.

"The Lord is my Shepherd; I shall not want . . ."

Philomene turned to see her aunt reading from her bedside Bible.

"He maketh me to lie down in green pastures: he leadeth me beside the still waters. He restoreth my soul: he leadeth me in the paths of righteousness for his name's sake. Yea, though I walk through the valley of the shadow of death, I will fear no evil: for thou art with me; thy rod and thy staff they comfort me. Thou preparest a table before me in the presence of mine enemies: thou anointest my head with oil; my cup runneth over. Surely goodness and mercy shall follow me all the days of my life: and I will dwell in the house of the Lord for ever."

Hannah finished the reading and slowly closed the book. "I have found that it is at the times of darkest trial that we have the chance to grow closer to God. Faith is not powerful, Philomene, until it is tested."

A ray of sunlight broke through the clouds, and a flock of small birds soared among the chimneys.

Philomene nodded.

* * *

Aunt Hannah was chattering away like a schoolgirl. The afternoon sun was shining in a bright blue sky, and crowds of people filled the promenade of the St. Hubert Gallery. Philomene looked up to admire the domed ceiling of glass that covered the long hallway. The ground level of the gallery was filled with shops and restaurants, while the first and second floors were reserved for habitation.

"I have books to purchase," Aunt Hannah was saying. "Photo cards and a new watch. What time is it?"

Philomene smiled and took out her pocket watch. "Nearly two."

"Oh, good. Let's stop at the art shop first." Her aunt headed off down the promenade, making Philomene play catch-up.

"I believe you've outrun your head cold, Aunt Hannah," Philomene teased.

"Of course, that was my intention," the statuesque woman answered with a nod, increasing her pace. "Oh, look! Look! There she is!" Aunt Hannah waved her handkerchief at a woman in front of the art shop. "Hello! Hello, Edith!"

"Is it Miss Cavell?" Philomene asked eagerly.

"It is! It is indeed!" her aunt answered.

"But I thought she was in England."

"She was. But she cut her stay short."

They reached Edith's side, and she smiled calmly at them. Aunt Hannah was far less reserved. She grasped both of Edith's hands and drew her close.

"You're back! You're back, my dear friend." Edith smiled as Aunt Hannah continued, "I am glad to see you, but I truly would wish you safely back in England."

"Here is where I'm needed," Edith answered. "Britain has declared war on Germany, and I'm afraid it's only a matter of time before my nursing skills will be needed here." She extended her hand to Philomene. "It is good to see you again, Miss Johnson. I was hoping you had made it out."

"We are working on it," Aunt Hannah commented. "We are working on it."

"I will send out some inquiries now that I am back," Edith said. "I have contacts."

"That would be welcomed," Aunt Hannah nodded.

"And I suppose I know the answer as to whether you're leaving or staying," Edith stated, looking with admiration on Hannah Finn's determined demeanor.

Philomene shook her head. "She refuses to see reason."

"Reason and passion hardly ever walk hand in hand, Miss Johnson."

"Then sometimes passion must be set aside," Philomene answered, narrowing her eyes at her aunt.

"Well, who wants to escort me to the jewelers so I can buy a new watch?" Aunt Hannah cut in.

"I will," Edith said heartily. "I have missed walking this gallery. Indeed, I have missed this city. Oh! I almost forgot. I bought you each a gift while I was waiting." She reached into her bag and brought out three tricolored rosettes. "For strength and valor," she declared, handing her friends their badges.

They pinned the rosettes to their hats, and Philomene sighed. "Le vent soufflera òu il veut," she said, walking beside her aunt.

"Beautiful French," Edith commented.

"And an apt sentiment, my dear niece. Yes . . . the wind will indeed blow where it will . . . and who are we to know the outcome?" She took Philomene's hand. "Now enough of dreary thoughts. I say we finish our shopping and move on to sightseeing and exploration. Perhaps a jaunt to the Chinese Pavilion."

"Splendid idea," Edith said. "One must glory in every day of life."

The women moved off down the promenade, trying to believe that the normalcy of the day could push back the tenuous future.

While Aunt Hannah was making her decision in the jewelry shop, Edith took the opportunity to speak to Philomene in private. "I know you are troubled by your aunt's decision to stay."

"She will not consider any other option," Philomene said desperately.

Edith looked earnestly into Philomene's face and nodded her understanding. "Did you expect anything else?"

"No," Philomene admitted, "but how can I leave her in such danger? She is the only family left to me."

"She has many powerful and important friends, Philomene."

Philomene nodded reluctantly. "I know."

"And I promise you that I will do everything in my power to keep her safe."

Philomene was stunned by the passion in Edith's vow, and she felt a modicum of fear drain away. She knew she could trust Edith Cavell's calm declaration.

"Thank you," was all she had time to say as her aunt returned at that moment to show off her purchase.

"Now I won't need to constantly ask you for the time, dear niece."

Philomene laughed. "I will actually miss your dependence on me."

As she noted the cryptic meaning of Miss Johnson's reply, Edith Cavell cursed the oncoming tragedy created by power-hungry men—a tragedy that would shatter the lives of these women she so admired, a tragedy that would change the world forever. As they walked, she took the arm of Hannah Finn, silently recommitting to her protection.

Chapter Eighteen

Snip. Snip. The dead flowers lay in scattered heaps from one end of the garden to the other, and William Trenton showed no sign of slacking in his ministrations. The August sun was fierce, and William's face was red with heat and hard work. He moved to the rain barrel, secured the dipper, and poured a few cups onto his head. He spluttered with the dousing, wiped his face on his sleeve, and returned to work. His thoughts were as oppressive as the temperature, and he attacked a stubborn, old rosebush with the intent of pouring out his worry and anger. He watched a blue jay take flight from the plum tree and yelled at its departure.

He knew it was a dumb idea for her to go off to Europe, but would she listen to him? Oh, no. Had to go off to eat strange food and speak a strange language, and now the papers held nothing but bad news about the possibility of war. The gossip around town figured that Miss Johnson might not make it back for the start of term. William snipped off a living flower and cussed at himself. He was afraid she might not make it back at all. He'd received a letter from her the first of July, but that was really before all the trouble started.

July 12, 1914

Dear Mr. Trenton,

By now I'm sure you've heard about the assassination of the arch-duke and his wife, and I wanted to write and assure you that all is well and that life in Brussels continues on at a measured pace.

*I just returned from the Sablon church where my aunt and I said
a prayer for the peace of the world, and even though it is not the
church I normally attend, I'm sure that God hears all heartfelt
prayers.*

*You will never guess what I had yesterday for noon meal . . .
snails! Yes, snails. They are a great delicacy here. Perhaps when I
get home we can gather up all those in my yard and sell them at
Mr. Carrillo's market.*

*I must confess that I am a bit homesick and may cut my trip
short, returning home the end of July. I think often of my lovely
garden and thank you for your diligent tending.*

Please give my regards to your mother.

I remain very faithfully your friend and teacher,

Miss Philomene Johnson

William stopped work again and went back to the rain barrel for a
drink. His stomach felt sick and his head hurt. He wanted to kick
something, or punch something, but instead he sat down on the garden
bench and put his head in his hands. He was so angry with that fellow
who had shot the archduke and his pretty wife; he'd seen a picture of
them in the paper, and they seemed real nice—the lady especially. *How
could that man just shoot them?* he thought spitefully. *Didn't he think
about their kids and that they'd be orphaned? Didn't he think about them
crying at night with no mother and no father? Now, because of his
murderous act, the powder keg in Europe is about to blow and Miss
Johnson is smack-dab in the middle of things. I've always believed what
Miss Johnson told me: times tables, the right way to talk, even the stuff
about Mr. Shakespeare, but now she's told a whopper of a lie. She said she'd
be safe if she went to stupid Belgium, and she isn't safe! She isn't!*

"William, are you all right?"

The low, male voice brought William's head up with a jerk, and
he wiped angrily at the moisture on his face. The dirt from his hands

caused ugly streaks, which only added to the portrait of grief imprinted there.

"What's up, William?" James Lund asked kindly, opening the gate and walking reverently into the sanctuary of the garden. He sat down on the bench next to the suffering boy. "The world's a mess, and that's a fact."

William nodded, slowly swiping at his cheek again. "That's a fact, Mr. Lund."

The two sat quietly for a time, then James took out his handkerchief and poured water onto it from William's cup. "Here. Wash your face. It'll make you feel better."

William took the cloth and wiped it over his face. He handed it back to James with a sigh. "Thanks. Sorry it's so dirty."

James scoffed. "That? Huh. You ought to see it after I've been training a horse hard in the paddock. Sometimes Mr. Regosi makes me go out to the trough and take a dunk."

A smile twitched the corner of William's mouth. "I sure did like ridin' your Appaloosa horse the other day. Thanks for that."

"You're welcome. You were good with her."

Dr. McIntyre's automobile went by, and William jumped up to watch it. "That automobile sure is something!" William said, his eyes following the shiny machine as it moved up Main Street. He sighed and turned back to James with a boyish grin. "Still, I'd take a horse any day."

"Me too," James agreed.

William came back to the bench and sat down. "You figure there's gonna be fightin' in the place Miss Johnson's at, Mr. Lund?"

James shook his head. "I don't know, William. It's a complicated mess over there."

"That's what my brother Joe says. And now Germany's trying to plow through Belgium to get to France?"

James took off his hat. "That's what I read in the paper." He picked up the water dipper from the bench and went to get a drink.

"But that's just where Miss Johnson is!" William said in a panic. "Right there in the path. I looked at a map, and Brussels is smack-dab in the middle of the country!"

"You know what, William?" James said slowly. "I think Miss Johnson is about one of the smartest people I know. What do you think?"

"Yes, sir," William answered, shading his eyes and looking over at him. "Yes, sir, that's a fact."

"And I think she has a plan." William hung on his every word. "Yes, sir," James continued, "I think she's already figured a way out of that country, and I bet she's bringing that aunt of hers with her."

"Really?"

"I'm sure of it. Did you ever know Miss Johnson to sit around moping when things got tough?"

William brightened. "No, sir! That wouldn't be like her at all."

"Of course not. So, see . . . we just have to put more faith in her. She's probably on a boat right now heading across the Atlantic at top speed."

"That's surely possible, ain't it?" William said hopefully.

"And you know what?"

"What?"

"I'll bet she's makin' up a whale of a history test on all that's been happening over there."

William chuckled. "That'd be like her."

James stood in the shade of the plum tree, looking around at the charming garden. "You're doing a good job with the tending, Mr. Trenton. Miss Johnson will be pleased when she gets home."

"Thank you, sir."

James smiled at being called sir. He was only seventeen, but supposed he seemed older to William because he was out on his own and making his way in the world. James put on his hat, and William flicked a beetle off the bench.

"Ah . . . if ya don't mind my askin', Mr. Lund, what was it brought you to Miss Johnson's house?"

James gave him a crooked smile. "Actually I was stopping by to see if she was home yet."

William nodded.

James looked back to Miss Johnson's cottage, abandoned in the summer heat. "I never was an expert student, Mr. Trenton, but Miss Johnson always gave me the feeling that I had great work to do in the world."

William stared at the house too, his voice rough with emotion. "Yes, sir."

Solomon whinnied from the street, bringing James back to the present. "Mind if I take a bucket of water to my horse, William?"

William jumped to his feet. "No, of course not! Help yourself. I'll get some carrots from the garden, if you'd like."

"That would be fine, William. I'm sure Solomon won't refuse." James chuckled as William raced to the back quarter of the yard where the garden sat. As he filled a bucket with water, James thought realistically about Miss Johnson's situation in Brussels; a terrifying storm was on the horizon, and he prayed he hadn't given William false hope about their teacher's chances for escape.

Chapter Nineteen

Elizabeth Knight Lund's voice was barbed and harsh. Kathryn stood outside her mother's bedroom door with her ear pressed to the wood. "Oh boy! Oh boy!" she whispered to herself. "Eleanor is sure getting scolded."

"Miss Kathryn!" a Scottish voice came sharp behind her. "What are ya doin' there?"

Kathryn turned to glare at the dark-haired servant. "None of your business."

Miss McKee came close, her hands on her hips. "Don't ya be sassin' me, Miss Kathryn, for I'll have none of it." She took Kathryn's arm and led her away down the hall. The belligerent girl began to tug and protest, but Kerri shushed her. "You be quiet or I swear I'll be marchin' right into your mother's room and tellin' her you've been spyin'. And haven't ya done enough damage for one morning?"

Kathryn wrenched her arm away. "You're just mad because I told Mama what you and Ina Bell were saying." She gave Kerri a mean face.

"Oh, now that's a lovely face for such a sweet little girl," Kerri said, giving her a mocking smile. "Your mother must be awfully proud to have such a daughter."

Kathryn narrowed her eyes. "Well, she likes me lots better than Eleanor. Eleanor's in big trouble for sneaking off to that devil church and for helping with those heathen Chinese girls."

"Where . . . where'd she hear about that?" Kerri stammered.

"My Auntie Ida. She'd been keeping it secret outta fear, but when Mother asked her about it, she spilled the beans. Poor old thing looked like she was gonna faint." Kathryn broke into a fit of giggles.

Kerri was stunned by Kathryn's churlish temperament, and she longed for the rug switch and the authority to use it. Since neither was available to her, she calmed her rising anger, took Kathryn by the arm, and headed for Miss Clawson's quarters.

"Where are you taking me?" Kathryn whined.

"To your nanny," Kerri said crisply.

"But she's sleeping. She's not feeling well," Kathryn protested.

Kerri stopped. "Is she now? Well, I guess there's nothin' for it but ta take ya down to the kitchen and let ya scrub pots."

"You can't make me do that!" Kathryn said hotly.

"Well, maybe *I* can't," Kerri agreed, walking towards the back servants' stairwell, "but Mr. Palmer can, and as I understand it, he's not too fond of your sweet little self."

Kathryn put on her teary face. "He's mean."

"Aye, 'tis true," Kerri said simply. "He's very strict, and this is one time I'm grateful for it."

"I won't do pots!" Kathryn squealed as they reached the stairs.

"Ah, ya most assuredly will, Miss Kathryn, and from now on maybe ya won't be spyin' on people."

"I'm telling my mother and Auntie Ida!" Kathryn growled.

Kerri sniffed. "Tell away, little miss. Neither would go against a punishment set down by Mr. Palmer." It was a bluff, but she said it with such conviction that Kathryn believed her. She stopped fighting and started blubbering.

"I'm a guest here! I don't have to do anything!"

Her complaining faded from the upper floors as the unsympathetic servant hauled her understair. Kerri surely hoped Mr. Palmer was in the mood for addressing the little *problem* and backing her up about the scullery work. As it turned out, Mr. Palmer was in complete agreement and thought it a very good idea that Kathryn be taught to make better use of her free time.

Kerri smiled as she sat at the table snapping beans and watching Kathryn work. Every time Cook dropped a ladle or saucepan into the soapy water, Kathryn would whimper in frustration and stamp her foot.

Kerri's thoughts drifted back to Eleanor in her mother's bedroom, and she wondered how her friend was holding up under her mother's tirade. During the past several weeks those understair (excluding Mr. Palmer) were aware of Eleanor Lund's secret escapades to Chinatown and to The Church of Jesus Christ of Latter-day Saints on McAllister Street. There was no way for them not to know, as they were cohorts in the duplicity. Come Sunday morning, Mr. Palmer would drive Aunt Ida, Mrs. Lund, and Kathryn to the Methodist Church on Green Street, while Eleanor would head off with Bib Randall and Mrs. Todd to the Presbyterian Church on Asher. Aunt Ida only acquiesced, as she trusted that Mrs. Todd, being an older, settled woman, would keep a close eye on her niece. Little did she know that halfway to Asher Street, Eleanor and Mr. Randall would split off and catch a trolley to join themselves with the Mormon congregation. And as for the work with Mrs. Antonia, Aunt Ida had been an unwitting accomplice. Too afraid to divulge Mrs. Fitzpatrick's gruesome description of the work Eleanor would be doing, she had simply described it to her sister as charity work—a little fundraising for the poor children in Chinatown.

The ruse had gone extremely well until that morning when Kathryn had overheard Kerri and Ina Bell talking about the risk Eleanor was taking every Sunday. Of course the little tattler had run immediately to tell her mother, delighted to catch her sister in a lie. Mrs. Lund had called Eleanor to her bedroom straightaway.

Why can't the Dragon just leave her alone? Kerri thought sullenly. Over the months she'd tried to view Mrs. Lund's circumstance with tolerance and compassion, but failed miserably at every attempt. She felt sorry that Elizabeth Lund had lost her husband, but her children had lost their father, and the woman didn't seem at all concerned about that. Kerri also knew that Mrs. Lund's mind had slipped into grief, but didn't she herself know that feeling of desolation after her parents died? Didn't she understand how painful it was to crawl back into reality? But she had found that the sunlight of truth was so much warmer than cold despair, and she knew if Mrs. Lund would turn her feelings outwards towards others she could find the same relief. Kerri wanted to go and give Mrs. Lund a good shake and a piece of her mind, but of course that was impossible.

"Here she has a wonderful daughter who's only tryin' to do good," Kerri mumbled to herself, "and the Dragon sees it only as rebellion."

Mr. Palmer entered the kitchen. "Your nanny is awake now, Miss Kathryn, and you may go up to her."

Kathryn dropped the pan she'd been washing and jumped down from the step stool. She turned with a scowl, wiped her hands on the dishcloth, and dropped it purposefully onto the floor.

Kerri came up out of her seat.

"It's all right, Miss McKee," Mr. Palmer said calmly. "Kathryn was just about to pick up the cloth and put it into the laundry bucket, weren't you, Miss Kathryn?"

Kathryn folded her arms across her chest and gave him a defiant stare.

"Ah, no, I was wrong." He turned to Mrs. Todd. "Mrs. Todd, would you bring over more of those dirty pots? Miss Kathryn has decided she wants to remain to help us in the kitchen."

Kathryn stooped down quickly, picked up the dishcloth, and threw it into the bucket. Then she lurched for the stairwell and was gone before Mrs. Todd had picked up as much as a teaspoon.

Bib Randall came in from outside, catching the last flounce of Kathryn's dress as she darted up the stairs. "What was that?" he asked.

"I believe it was an unwilling servant," Mr. Palmer said dryly, and Kerri and Mrs. Todd laughed. Mr. Palmer gave Mrs. Todd a slight smile then went back to business. "Mr. Randall, you have just finished polishing the automobile?"

"I have, Mr. Palmer, and it looks magnificent!"

"Boasting, Mr. Randall, is for the weak of character," Mr. Palmer returned. "Please bring the auto out as you will be driving Mrs. Lund and Mrs. Westfield to the Cliff House for tea."

"Yes, sir!" Bib said brightly, winking at Kerri. Usually the automobile came out of the garage one day a week—Sunday, and then it was Mr. Palmer who did the driving.

"And since it is Miss Latham's day off, Miss McKee, you will be called upon to serve the others."

"Yes, Mr. Palmer," Kerri answered calmly, masking the eagerness she felt. It would be a grand opportunity to talk with Eleanor and discover her situation.

A bell rang on the call-board, and Mr. Palmer turned to assess the source of the summons. "Mr. Randall, the automobile to the front.

Miss McKee, if you will see where Miss Lund wishes to take tea. We will serve Miss Clawson and Miss Kathryn in the study."

"Yes, sir," the two younger servants answered, turning immediately to their individual tasks.

Kerri McKee quietly navigated the back stairwell to the dim upper hallway. She made sure she heard the front door close and the automobile drive off before she went to Eleanor's room. She knocked softly. There was no answer. She debated whether to knock again. Perhaps poor Eleanor had gone down for a nap or did not want to see anyone after the reprimand. Kerri had just decided to leave when the door opened. Eleanor Lund appeared in the opening looking pale and defiant.

Kerri curtsied. "Sorry ta bother, miss, but Mr. Palmer's wondering where ya want yer tea?"

Eleanor reached out, grabbed Kerri by the wrist, and pulled her into her bedroom. "Has my mother gone?" she asked as soon as the door was shut.

"She has, miss," Kerri answered.

"And Kathryn?"

"With her nanny."

Eleanor paced the room, clearly agitated by the proceedings of the last hour. "Spoiled, peevish child," she muttered.

"Aye, 'tis true," Kerri interjected, "but I'm afraid Miss Latham and myself must swallow most of the blame for talkin' together about your Sunday outings, Miss Eleanor."

"It was Kathryn who did the spying," Eleanor returned flatly.

"Aye, but if we'd kept our tongues from waggin', no one would be the wiser."

Eleanor shook her head. "It was only a matter of time." She moved to the window and opened it onto the hot August day. "As soon as Mother brought in Aunt Ida to see if she knew anything about the Sunday disgrace, Auntie had a fit of nerves and blathered everything about the actual job I'm doing with Mrs. Antonia in Chinatown."

"She didn't!" Kerri exclaimed, moving to stand by Eleanor at the window.

"She did." Eleanor sighed. "I don't know which deception Mother was most angry about, but it's interesting how clear her mind seemed when she was reprimanding me."

"I'm sure we're all in for it now for helping you," Kerri said, accepting her fate.

"I hope not," Eleanor said quickly. "I told them it was all my own headstrong, willful idea."

Kerri scoffed. "Miss Eleanor, you don't have a willful bone in your body."

"Huh! You think not? Then why am I still going to sneak away and work with Mrs. Antonia even after Mother forbade it? I may not be able to manage getting to church, but I am going to continue my work in Chinatown.

Kerri stared at her. "Are ya now?"

"I most certainly am. We've only found three families who are continuing the abominable practice, but I'm sure there are others. Besides, we somehow have to educate everyone in the area about the cruel long-term effects."

Kerri smiled at the slight girl standing so straight and defiant. "Ah, I see. Now that you're sixteen the world better mind itself."

"Indeed," Eleanor said, smiling back. Then her face took on a serious expression. "I will not abandon those little girls, Kerri. They are too young to speak up for themselves and protest the torture." Anguish washed her face. "You can't imagine those crippled little feet."

Kerri shivered. "I still don't understand why their parents would do such a thing. When ya told me about the poor wee ones cryin' fer the pain, and their mothers not carin' . . . it made me sick."

Eleanor bit her lip and shook her head. "Culture . . . tradition," she said with spite. "Better marriage possibilities. One mother was so angry at our interference, she kept pointing to our feet and yelling, 'Clown feet! Clown feet! You will never have respected husband. No good man will love you with feet like that!'"

Kerri looked down at her own feet. "Oh, gracious St. Michael, I guess I'll not be expectin' better than a bank robber."

Eleanor chuckled in spite of her heavy heart. "Mrs. Antonia says the men see women only as pretty objects. Also, the disfigured foot weakens them, making it easier for the man to dominate."

Kerri growled. "Ya best stop tellin' me these tales, Miss Eleanor, or I'll be joinin' you in Chinatown with my rug switch."

"Oh, I wish you *could* help," Eleanor said, taking Kerri's hand. "So you understand why I must keep working?"

"I do, Miss Eleanor. I do. It's just that I'm worried for ya gettin' caught again. I don't like thinkin' what your mother or auntie might do."

"What can they do, Kerri, chain me to my bedpost?"

"Well, that would never work; you'd just drag the bed with you."

Eleanor brightened. "I believe I would! And you could come with me. Together we'd be mighty warriors against evil and injustice!"

Kerri's laugh was cut short by a stiff rap at the door.

"Come in," Eleanor said in a strong voice.

Mr. Palmer opened the door and stepped into the room. His critical gaze went directly to Miss McKee, who had moved quickly to straighten the bed linens. He looked back to Eleanor's stoic face. "We're ready to serve tea, Miss Eleanor."

"Yes, Mr. Palmer, thank you. I will have mine in the library."

"Very good, miss." He looked over at Kerri, who had just finished plumping the final pillow. "Will you be needing Miss McKee for anything else, Miss Eleanor?"

"I don't believe so, Mr. Palmer." She turned to Kerri. "Thank you so much for all your help, Miss McKee."

Kerri curtsied. "My pleasure, miss."

They shared a secret smile as Kerri followed Mr. Palmer out of the room.

As Kerri walked to the servants' hall, she said a prayer for the pitiful Chinese girls with their bound feet and cruel parents, and for dear Eleanor Lund who also deserved better than she was getting.

Chapter Twenty

The house was dark, and everyone was sleeping, but Alaina was sure she'd heard footsteps outside the bedroom window. She looked over at Nephi, his chest gently rising and falling with each breath. He obviously hadn't heard anything. She climbed slowly out of bed, drew on her dressing gown, and headed for the kitchen. She stopped as she reached its doorway, staring with alarm into the dim interior. There were dirty dishes in the sink and covering the kitchen table—dirty dishes and scraps of food. *That's odd. We never leave the kitchen like this. Has someone been in here in the dark?* She turned quickly. There it was again! The sound of someone walking outside. Her heart was pounding, and fear clamped itself around her throat as she edged for the back door. *I should go back. Go back and get Nephi. Wake up Mother Erickson. Light the lamp.* Alaina felt dizzy as her fingers gripped the door handle. She turned the knob and silently opened the door.

Moonlight flooded the side yard as she moved down the dark steps onto the garden path. Everything was in silhouette except for the irises at the edge of the yard. She blinked. The pearly light was playing tricks on her eyes. The flowers were not purple but a shimmer of blue. How was that possible? Had Mother Erickson replanted? She was so lost in wonder at the sight of the miscolored plants that the clammy touch on her hand made her shriek in terror. Small, cold fingers grasped her hand, and she spun around to see who was clutching her. A young boy with curly silver hair stared into her face with eyes that reflected the moon. She tried to pull away but his grip was tight. He opened his mouth to speak, and a dark sound poured out like blood from a wounded bird. "Did your father love you? Did he protect you from evil?" The boy's eyes narrowed. "You shame him. Now he's down in the rotting dirt. His soul lost in the wormy earth." She felt her sanity draining out of her body fast and cold. She tried to scream, but no sound came from her. She couldn't move, and the child's voice stabbed again into her ear. "There is no resurrection or grace for an apple grower. The apples are down in the dirt, lost in the rotting earth."

Alaina stopped whimpering. She stood silent, the wind playing about her robe and hair. She looked at the flowers that stood like sentinels around the yard—little blue soldiers standing against the wind. The boy squeezed her fingers.

"No," she said, pulling her hand away. "I know you."

The child scowled as the bright moonlight washed his face to ivory.

"I know you," she said again. "You're evil, and I won't listen to you."

The child took a step back, anger twisting his features.

"Go away."

He growled, but she dismissed him completely. "No. Go away."

In bed, Alaina reached over and laid her hand on her husband's warm chest. After a moment his hand came up and covered hers.

"You all right?" His voice came thick with sleep.

"No," came the honest reply.

Immediately, though he did not open his eyes, Nephi moved closer to her and gathered her tightly against him. She felt the bare skin of his arms and the muscles through his thin cotton union suit. "Bad dreams?" he asked, kissing her forehead.

She nodded.

He rubbed her arm. "Don't worry. I'm right here, Laina . . . right here beside you."

Alaina kissed his mouth and snuggled comfortably against him. Her heart ached for the love she had for him. He was always patient with her nightmares and restless sleep, always understanding of her grief, always tender in their intimacy.

"You know what I was thinking about?" he asked, rubbing some of the sleep out of his eyes and yawning.

"That I'm a brat for waking you?"

He chuckled. "No. Remember when we went to the circus?"

She smiled at the innocent change of subject. "Yes, I remember when we went to the circus."

"Did you ever figure out how they got all those clowns into that little covered wagon?"

She broke into a fit of giggles, grabbed her pillow, and beat him with it.

He took the blows for a time, but soon the menacing object was thrown onto the floor, and her laughter stopped with passionate kisses.

The dream faded to nothing.

* * *

Chickens! Alaina couldn't stand chickens. She knew they were important to any household, but after so many years mucking out their pens she figured she could do without scrambled eggs or Sunday chicken and dumplings. Her stomach lurched as she glanced over at Mother Erickson, who was throwing grain to the squabbling flock. Miss Titus lowered her head and snorted, prompting Alaina to start working again. She looked quickly back to the unmoving currycomb in her hand.

"Sorry. Sorry, Miss Titus," she said bringing the comb smoothly over the yearling's rump. Her other hand followed after the comb as she looked for any sign of bumps or scrapes. "Move over," Alaina commanded the filly, which flicked its ears and stepped to the side. Alaina checked the horse's legs and exchanged the comb for a stiff brush. As she bent down to clean the legs, a wave of sickness rolled through her stomach. She stood quickly, and the stall blurred. *Don't be such a ninny,* Alaina scolded herself. She reached out and grabbed one of the cross ties that secured Miss Titus, fighting to steady herself. The young horse pulled back, causing Alaina to release her grip and fall to her knees. She closed her eyes against the sight of the swaying ground and sat back. She thought she heard Miss Titus whinny and someone calling.

"Alaina?" Mother Erickson's voice sounded far away. "Alaina?" The voice was closer. She felt Mother Erickson's warm hands on her arms.

Where am I? Alaina opened her eyes onto daylight and hay. "What happened?" she mumbled.

"You fainted," came the reply from an unseen person.

"Mother Erickson?"

"I'm right here, little missy."

"I fainted?"

"You did. How are you feeling now?"

"Foolish."

"Well, other than that."

"Hot. Did I faint from the heat?"

"Partly. Here, let's get you up onto the milking stool. Can you manage?" Mother Erickson asked.

"I think so," Alaina answered, attempting to stand and wavering from side to side.

"Whoops! Take your time," her solicitous mother-in-law warned. "I wish I wasn't so short so I could give you some help."

Alaina giggled.

"Concentrate, you silly woman!" Mother Erickson said, laughing. She did her best to steady Alaina and move her to the stool.

Alaina sat down and was immediately sick. "I'm going to vomit!" she said in a panic.

"Well, let it come," Mother Erickson answered calmly, holding back her daughter-in-law's hair.

Alaina obeyed.

When she was finished, Mother Erickson handed her a handkerchief and helped her to her feet. "Let's get you to the house and get some water into you."

"Good idea," Alaina said, standing weakly. "I'm probably dehydrated."

Patience Erickson smiled. "That's a mighty big word." She put her arm around Alaina's waist and guided her towards the house.

"From my sister Eleanor," Alaina said. "She always used big words."

"You said she was a smart one."

"So smart," Alaina answered. She thought of Elly using her professor words, and she longed for her sister's companionship. It seemed like forever ago when they sat in their secret bower they called Niagara Falls, talking of school and their farm and making up stories of faraway places. The last time she had been to the bower was on the day of her father's baptism. Her head began to hurt, and she pulled her thoughts away from the heartrending images.

"Alaina," Mother Erickson said gently, "how long have you been sick?"

"About a month," she confessed. She had tried to keep it a secret, not wanting to worry anyone. "It's just once in a while," she added quickly. "Nothing to fret over."

"Oh, I'm not fretting," Mother Erickson said with a smile. She opened the back porch door. "But I think we'd better give Dr. Lucien a call just the same."

* * *

When Nephi came home from work that evening, his mother met him at the front door.

"Now son," she said in a serious tone, "I don't want you to be alarmed."

"What is it?" he asked, the smile leaving his face.

"Dr. Lucien was here earlier to take a look at Alaina."

"Dr. Lucien? What's the matter? Is she sick?" He was in a panic now.

"Well, you'd better ask her that." He headed for their bedroom. "She's not in there," his mother called after him.

He stopped. "Where is she?"

"In the kitchen peeling potatoes."

He looked at his mother as if she'd gone mad. "The kitchen?" He raced into the kitchen and found Alaina at the sink. She turned to him, and he stopped cold. He had never seen her look more beautiful, and his heart wrenched. If she was sick, if something was the matter with her, he knew he couldn't stand it. "What? What is it? Mama says Dr. Lucien was here."

Suddenly tears were streaming down her face, and she moved to him and cupped his face in her hands. "I'm fine. Everything's fine."

"But, Dr. Lucien . . ."

"He said I'm fine and healthy and that I should be able to carry our baby without any trouble."

It took a moment for her words to percolate past his worry, then his eyes widened. "Our baby?" he said in a whisper.

Alaina beamed at him. "Our baby."

He let out a whoop and grabbed her off her feet. He set her down straightaway, a look of worry on his face. "Oh, I'm sorry! Did I hurt you?"

"Of course not, silly. I'm just as sturdy as I always was."

He grabbed her again. "Oh, I love you so much! I love you!"

Alaina and Mother Erickson laughed at his elated antics, glad he wasn't upset over the trick they'd played on him.

"Here, you two," Mother Erickson said, coming to give both of them a hug of congratulation. "Go take a walk on up to Grandfather Erickson's to tell him the good news, and I'll finish supper."

"You won't mind?" Alaina asked, slipping off her apron.

"Of course not. Get on out of here." She shooed them off with a smile and a tear. When she heard the front door slam, she went to the window to watch as they walked down the road hand in hand. "Thank you, Father. Thank you for the summer rain we've had, and for the garden. Please watch over Father Erickson as he's had a rough spell lately. And thank you for the new life that is coming into the world. There was a sadness come upon our girl over the past weeks, but I think this joy has lifted her up. I thank you for the happiness I see walking hand in hand out there, and I pray that Miss Sarah stays well so that soon we'll have two little grandbabies to chase around." She finished her prayer and heaved a sigh of contentment. "Back to work, woman. Do you think those potatoes are going to cook themselves?"

She turned back to the kitchen, deciding to make a celebration angel food cake with fresh peaches and whipped cream.

Chapter Twenty-One

There was a pounding on the door. Loud, desperate pounding, and Philomene, dismissing etiquette, rushed from the study to open it.

Claudine came running down the hall screaming at her. "No! No, mademoiselle! Don't open the door!"

Philomene froze with her hand on the doorknob. She turned to look at Claudine, whose face was white with terror. One hundred thousand German troops had sliced through Belgium's underbelly, and with the advance came alarming reports of burning, torture, and rape in the towns of Vise, Herve, and Battice. These reports filled the residents of Brussels with fear, especially since King Albert and the main contingent of the army had been forced to withdraw to Antwerp, leaving Brussels open to occupation.

The pounding came again, causing both women to jump. Philomene turned back to the door.

Claudine shrieked, "Non! Non, mademoiselle!"

A voice on the other side of the entry called loudly, "Madame Finn! Mademoiselle Johnson! Open the door! It's Richard Davis."

Philomene's fingers flew to the lock, and within moments she'd flung open the door for the American journalist. "Mr. Davis, come in! Come in!"

Over the past weeks of invasion, Richard Harding Davis had been a rich source of information and reassurance. He'd stop by when time allowed, telling them of the progress of the enemy and the atrocities. One of his reckless adventures had caused Aunt Hannah great distress, as he told of actually marching along with some of the German troops, and at one point, being accused of espionage activity.

"You take far too many risks, Richard," Aunt Hannah had scolded. "If you were my son I'd lock you in a cage."

"If I were your son," he had replied, a cocky smile on his lips, "I'd probably be in the thick of the political chaos, and truly, I don't know which would be more dangerous."

Philomene had handed him a drink and sat across from him. "Are they advancing quickly, Mr. Davis?"

He nodded his head. "I've never seen anything like it—thousands of gray uniforms, row on row of soldiers keeping up a steady trot mile after mile. When I was with them they kept up that pace for five hours, and they didn't bend their knees."

Aunt Hannah narrowed her eyes. "Didn't bend their knees for five hours?"

"No. It was unnatural. They kept the knees straight which shot them forward with a quick, sliding movement like they were skating. When they did stop, the men would fall down like they'd been clubbed."

Hannah Finn shuddered. "And we hear rumors that they have burnt entire villages?"

The husky man took a shot of his drink. "I was in Battice after they'd gone through. It was like moving through hell—nothing left of the houses but empty window frames. Inside, the iron bedsteads and furnishings were still smoldering—everything soot black."

"And murdered civilians?" Philomene asked, her voice rough with emotion.

The journalist slumped back into his chair. "Numbering in the hundreds, or so I've heard. I didn't see evidence, but we were moving through fast. I did see two peasants dead by a wall. My driver said they were probably suspected of being francs-tireurs."

"Francs-tireurs?" Philomene asked, trying to get her mind off the images.

"Civilian snipers."

Philomene pulled her mind back to the entryway and the present, remembering how that conversation had brought a sick feeling to her stomach. She focused her attention on Mr. Davis as he attempted to brush travel dust from his clothing.

"Please don't worry about a bit of dirt," she said kindly. "Come, let's get you comfortable."

Mr. Davis gave her a half smile. "Not too comfortable, Miss Johnson, or I may fall sound asleep."

"That's exactly what you need, my dear," Aunt Hannah's voice echoed down the hallway, making Mr. Davis smile sheepishly, like a son who'd been caught coming in late from a party. Hannah Finn reached the group and took Mr. Davis by the arm. "Heavens, Richard! You look like a team of eight ran you down." She turned to her servant. "Claudine, coffee, eggs, and croissants, in the salon, s'il vous plaît."

"Oui, madame." Claudine curtsied and was gone.

"Come along, Richard. We have to keep you awake long enough to get the 'scoop.' Then you can sleep for a couple of hours."

"Actually, I have to be back to . . ."

Aunt Hannah shook her head. "Wiser heads are in charge, my dear. I am the boss, and I say sleep."

The tough reporter succumbed to Hannah Finn's stoic insistence and allowed himself to be dragged off to the comfort of her lavish salon. Philomene followed the pair, glad for her auntie's commanding diplomacy.

Over coffee and eggs, Mr. Davis filled them in on the status of the war, and they told him of what they'd seen. Just the day before, refugees had poured into Brussels from the besieged province, and Mrs. Finn and her niece had gone out into the square to see if they could help. They'd taken food, but that was gone in an instant.

"Edith Cavell was there with her nurses," Aunt Hannah said proudly. "They were taking care of minor injuries, and they were caring for the old people who had suffered with the walking. Then the Red Cross brought in a hundred wounded fighting men from Liege. You should have seen her, Richard. She organized her nurses and the Catholic sisters like she was a general on the front lines."

Richard nodded. "I've met Miss Cavell a few times. She is remarkable." He finished his coffee. "And the refugees?"

"It was a heartbreaking sight," Philomene said softly. "There were a few cars, but most of the refugees were in wagons or on foot. There were some bicycles. Everyone carried a bundle, or household item, or a baby. The old people looked broken." She stood and moved to the window. "The good people of Brussels took them in—every last person."

"We had a family staying with us last night," Hannah said simply. "They left early this morning, saying they had relatives in Antwerp."

"I hope they make it," Richard said, rubbing his eyes with the palms of his hands. Philomene saw him steel himself for the next announcement. "I'm afraid German troops will push into Brussels in the next couple of hours, my friends."

Aunt Hannah dropped her cup. It rolled away, staining the carpet with its dark contents.

Philomene was shaken. "Then Belgium has fallen."

"I wouldn't bet on that, Miss Johnson," Mr. Davis said with assurance. "King Albert and his small army are fiercely determined. Monsieur de Broqueville, the minister of defense, has four sons in the war, and I have heard him say that they are all prepared to defend their country to the final cost."

Philomene shook her head. "What a fearful cost, Mr. Davis. It makes me angry."

"War always makes the logical and kindhearted angry, Philomene."

She was surprised to hear him use her given name. Somehow it soothed her agitation. "What should we do, Mr. Davis?"

"Your aunt shouldn't have to take steps immediately. I have a feeling the great bulk of the force will push through towards Antwerp. They'd rather not let Albert get a stronghold there so close to his French and English allies. I've heard that the German contingent coming through Louvain met with resistance. That may slow them down a bit."

"Louvain?" Aunt Hannah sat forward. "Conner and I have a dear friend in Louvain. Monsignor Jules de Becker."

"I've heard of him. Connected with the university there."

Aunt Hannah only nodded, then turned her head to gaze out the window.

"And now, the question is," Mr. Davis said, looking pointedly at Philomene, "what are we going to do with you?"

"Me?" Philomene responded quickly. She was surprised to be the center of attention.

"Yes. Somehow we need to get you back to your students in Sutter Creek."

"It's so like you, Richard, to see things clearly," Aunt Hannah broke in. "I wanted to send her last week when many of my friends in government left the city for Antwerp, but she refused."

"Doesn't surprise me," Richard said with a grin. "Seems stubbornness runs in the Johnson women."

"Leaving now would be impossible," Philomene answered, torn between her desire to go and the need to stay.

"Well, difficult," Richard countered, "but not impossible. If we can get you to Antwerp, I have contacts who will help you the rest of the way."

"And what do you suggest I do, Mr. Davis, march along with the German troops?" she asked, her tone disbelieving.

"You will go with me as my assistant," Richard answered immediately. "I have a pass to cover the war, and if we can keep ahead of things we may be able to make it."

Aunt Hannah stood. "Richard, that would be wonderful."

"Wait! Wait now!" Philomene said in a panic. "It seems like you've worked all this out without input from either of us."

"I have," the journalist stated flatly. "There is no time left for debate or counsel, Miss Johnson. Things are changing too quickly."

Aunt Hannah moved to him. "When do we need to have her ready, Richard?"

"Tomorrow morning," he answered.

"What?" Philomene choked.

Mr. Davis ignored her anger. "I figure if the German troops arrive in the city this afternoon they will stop for at least a day or two to secure the position before pushing on towards Antwerp. It gives us a very small window, but . . ."

"Wait," Philomene said again, putting up her hand as she would to an unruly school child. "Wait. It would be impossible for me to be ready by tomorrow morning."

"You won't be taking much, Miss Johnson. It must seem as though you're only traveling in country," Mr. Davis replied.

Though it was a warm morning, Philomene felt ice in her veins. She turned to her aunt in desperation. "Auntie, tell him it's impossible. Tell him."

"No, Philomene, I will not tell him. Mr. Davis has given us the only means of escape for you before this country is overrun. To argue would be to offend his generosity. I will not do that."

Philomene measured the note of finality in her aunt's voice and knew her mind would not change. "Then you must come with me."

"No."

"Aunt Hannah, I won't leave you here."

The elegant matriarch, so full of life and wisdom, came to her niece and took her hands. "This is my place, dear one. This is where I am needed. Miss Cavell and I have been discussing the possibility of turning rooms of the apartment into a nursing facility; so you see, this is my place."

Seeing unwavering finality in her aunt's eyes, Philomene gave her a hug, then wordlessly turned to the salon door.

Mr. Davis stood quickly. "Where are you going, Miss Johnson?"

Philomene turned to look at him. "I am a pragmatist, Mr. Davis. I am going to pack my bag."

Chapter Twenty-Two

The German soldiers sang as they poured into the beautiful city of Brussels like a landslide. They took three steps between each line of song, the stamp of their iron-shod boots sounding like giant pile drivers on the cobblestone streets. For hours they came like an aberrant force of nature: no halts, no open spaces, not a strap out of place. Philomene stood near the bakery shop with Edith Cavell, watching the procession, fascinated against her will. The look on each soldier's face spoke of arrogance and superiority as if to say, "Now, little Belgium, do you realize what you went up against when you tried to block us?"

Edith leaned over and whispered to her, "Do you see, Philomene, that they are trying to show us that they are entirely at home—that they own this place?"

Philomene nodded. "Look at the face of that Garde Civique," she said, pointing to the old policeman standing a few doors down from them.

Edith looked over. "Such humiliation for such a proud people."

The two friends were silent for a time as the gray flood moved like a tidal wave in front of them. Suddenly Miss Cavell picked up her bag and took Philomene by the arm. "Come on. I've seen enough."

Philomene nodded. The immediacy of events weighed on her like grief, and she tried to scour her mind of images that would take historians decades to diffuse and decipher. *Where is your philosophy now?* she thought to herself.

"Your students will be amazed with the stories you have to tell them," Miss Cavell said as the two women walked back to the apartment on rue de la Montagne.

"Or terrified," Philomene answered. "It will be difficult if not impossible for them to believe such nightmarish events."

"You're right, of course." Edith nodded. "They are far removed from our tragedy."

They passed an ornate iron fence covered in heavily scented red roses, and Philomene stopped to touch the petals and breathe in the perfume. Her mind flew instantly to her quaint little cottage in Sutter Creek, and she closed her eyes to bring it nearer. Her heart ached with the thought that in less than twenty-four hours she would be leaving her aunt. She set her logic against emotion, knowing there was nothing she could do or say to change Hannah Finn's mind, and knowing also that the doorway of escape was about to slam shut in her face.

"Are you feeling well?" Edith asked.

Philomene opened her eyes, staring straight ahead into the mass of roses. "Physically, I'm well. Mentally, I am torn between what I must do and what my heart tells me to do."

"It must be dreadful," came the caring reply.

Philomene turned to look at Edith Cavell. The tall, austere woman with the thin lips and pale brown hair amazed her with her candor and compassion. *My life will never be the same,* Philomene thought pensively, realizing that she had been transformed by the honesty and goodness of this British nurse. It saddened her that the war would rob them of more time for friendship. Philomene straightened her back and gave Edith a sly look. "Well, I will just have to return," she stated. "Auntie had a long list of attractions we were unable to see, and you have not as yet taught me how to play tennis."

Edith brightened, a smile touching the corners of her mouth. "Come back when this mess is over, and tennis lessons will be the first order of business."

The sound of the German troops, which for a blessed moment had receded from their attention, now came crushing down the side streets to haunt them.

"Come," Edith said, turning. "There is a matter I wish to discuss with you and your aunt."

* * *

A voice in the darkness was calling her.

"Philomene, it's time."

She opened her eyes onto candlelight. "Aunt Hannah?"

"Yes, dear, it's time."

Philomene sat up. "It's morning already?"

"Early morning. Edith will be here any moment with your outfit. Claudine has brought a tray; eat something." Hannah Finn turned to leave the room.

"Where are you going?"

"To gather a few things for your bag."

Philomene got out of bed and went to her dressing table. She brushed through her hair and pinned it into a simple bun at the nape of her neck. She looked over at the breakfast tray and smiled to see toast and bacon. *Dear Aunt Hannah.* Without warning, a cold fear dropped into Philomene's chest, and she found it hard to breathe. *Soon I'll be leaving the warmth and safety of this precious place.* She stood abruptly, moving to the tray and shoving a piece of bacon into her mouth. *Reason, Philomene. Reason and logic will take you through to the other side of this nightmare.* The night before, plans had been finalized for her escape to Antwerp. She would meet Mr. Davis and his driver at the Square du Petit Sablon at 7 AM. She would dress in a disguise, wear a sturdy pair of walking shoes, and carry no more than two satchels. They would drive on back roads to Malines then on to Antwerp. The journey should take half a day if all went well.

Her door opened, and Philomene looked up to see Edith Cavell entering with her aunt.

"I've brought it," Edith said, dropping the bag she was carrying onto the bed. "Is that bacon?"

Philomene smiled. "It is—have some."

"When we're done here," Edith said, opening the bag. She brought out a nurse's uniform like the ones Philomene had seen on the girls from Edith's school.

"Here, let me shake it out," Aunt Hannah said, taking the white dress overlay and smoothing out the wrinkles.

"You need not wear the cap," Edith instructed, "but you must have it with you."

Philomene took the stiff, white-banded cap and carefully placed it in her satchel. As Edith continued talking, Philomene put on her slip, stockings, and sturdy shoes. Edith then helped her put on a dark blue dress and the starched white pinafore, which was belted. To the dress was added a stand-up white collar and white cuffs.

Philomene's heart was pounding. "Edith, I don't think I can do this." She turned to her friend. "I know we decided this is a good disguise, but . . ."

Edith interrupted. "It is the perfect disguise for a woman . . . other than a nun's habit, and I couldn't get my hands on one of those."

Philomene knew her friend was trying to cajole her away from worry, but her logical mind saw flaws in the plan, and she meant to point them out. "But what if someone stops us and asks me to perform some nursing skill?"

Aunt Hannah raised her eyebrows. "It's not likely, my dear."

"But what about credentials?"

"Ah!" Edith jumped. She went to her bag and brought out a leather document case. She opened it and presented Philomene with two pieces of paper. She opened them and discovered they were official documents of the Berkendael Medical Institute with her name on them. One certified her as a nurse, and the other was a pass for her travel.

"How did you manage this?" Philomene asked.

"I am extremely resourceful," Edith answered, without the smallest degree of conceit. "Now, let me look at you."

"She looks official," Aunt Hannah said bluntly as the two women checked the disguise.

Philomene moved to the window, opening a narrow slit in the draperies and peering out into the pale morning. "What time is it?"

"Ah, now who's relying on whom?" Aunt Hannah laughed as she brought out her watch. "Six thirty. We must be on our way."

Philomene turned. "Are you walking with us to the park?"

"I am," Aunt Hannah answered without hesitation. She went to the bed, where unseen, she placed money and a small box into the side pocket of Philomene's satchel. "Eat a bit more, Philomene," she said, picking up her hat. "The day will be long."

Philomene stoically did as she was told, entreating Edith to join her. The two women snatched a few bits of toast and bacon off the porcelain plates as they made final preparations to leave.

Edith put a Red Cross band on her arm, affixing another to Philomene's, then the two placed medical supplies into the satchels. Philomene put on her light travel duster and took one last look around the room.

"Time to go," Aunt Hannah announced. Philomene picked up one of the satchels and Edith the other as Aunt Hannah blew out the candles, and the three women moved into the silent hallway. When they reached the back door, Claudine was waiting with a small package. She held it out to Philomene as she approached.

"Fromage de Camembert," she said in a whisper. "I know you like it."

"Merci, Claudine. Merci," Philomene said, taking the offering and holding onto Claudine's hand. "Keep working on your English, and I promise to work on my French."

A tremulous smile brushed Claudine's lips. "Oui, mademoiselle." She opened the door for the women, and they walked out into the courtyard. "Come back to us someday, Mademoiselle Johnson!"

Philomene nodded, and then raised her hand in good-bye. She turned and followed her aunt out onto the rue de la Montagne.

Philomene found it odd that everything seemed normal when they emerged twenty minutes later into the Petit Sablon. The women moved soundlessly to the rendezvous point, which was the large statue and reflecting pool at the back of the square. Philomene sighed. She thought of the hours she and her auntie had spent here reading contentedly in the shade of the massive trees. She looked around to see snatches of morning sunlight gilding many of the forty-eight statues that surrounded the square. These were not grand statues of mythic heroes or men of military might, but stylized bronze master-pieces of common folk—representations of bakers, wheelwrights, and fowlers—individuals from the different crafts of Brussels. Each stood proudly on its own Gothic column, and as Philomene thought of her work as a teacher, she felt a kinship to them. Philomene smoothed the white pinafore of her nurse's disguise. A nurse was also a notable profession. A clatter nearby made her jump. She looked over to see a street cleaner placing his brooms onto his cart. A tawny cat slinked past on its way home, and a carriage rumbled along the side street carrying a couple to an unknown destination. In an hour or so, shopkeepers would be opening their shops for the day's business. *Perhaps everything is normal,* Philomene thought. *Perhaps Auntie and I will go sightseeing this afternoon and buy chocolates at Madame du Roi's.* She looked down at the satchel in her hand and rebuked the innocent wishing. She looked steadily outside the square for the sight of Mr. Davis and his automobile.

"Are we early?" Edith asked.

Edith's voice, so close at hand, made Philomene jump again, and she took a deep breath to calm herself.

"No. We're right on time," Aunt Hannah answered. "They may have had difficulties. I suggest we stroll."

They set the satchels next to the pool and walked casually around the square, chatting openly about frivolous things of no consequence. After ten minutes they heard footsteps from a side street and turned to see Richard Harding Davis walking quickly towards them.

"Bonjour!" he called loudly, raising his arm in a wave. "How grand to see you, how very grand to see you!" He came up and took each woman in turn into an embrace. As he held them close he whispered, "Being followed, don't worry." He looked into the eyes of Edith Cavell. "Honored to see you again, Miss Cavell. Your idea of the nurse's disguise is brilliant. Let's hope it holds."

"Richard, where is the car?" Aunt Hannah asked, her voice sounding tense and frail.

"Side street," came the clipped reply. "My driver let me off. I'm hoping the soldiers have followed me. Ah, seems I'm right," he said as he looked over Edith's head to the eastern edge of the square.

A pair of German soldiers, each carrying a military rifle, moved purposefully into the square. They spotted the tall American immediately and headed to him, calling out menacing words and gesturing that he should stop and not move.

"Does anyone speak German?" Mr. Davis asked out of the corner of his mouth as the soldiers approached.

"Of course," Hannah Finn answered, imperiously straightening herself as though she were about to meet royalty.

"That's my girl," Mr. Davis chuckled, catching some of her spirit.

Philomene's body was trembling—trembling against every logical message she was sending it. She looked at her companions and found their faces placid, their expressions masking any sign of panic. *Philomene Johnson, get ahold of yourself,* she scolded.

Suddenly her hand was taken by Mr. Davis as he stepped closer to her, giving her a quick smile. "Speak only French," he managed before the soldiers broke into their ring of friendship.

Philomene was taken aback by the soldiers' appearance; though each wore all the trappings of an earnest enemy, their faces betrayed them. They were those of schoolboys, and she had seen their duplication hundreds of times passing through her classroom. Her heart rate slowed.

One of the soldiers was motioning with his gun and barking orders to Mr. Davis when Aunt Hannah stepped forward. "Entschuldigen Sie mir bitte," she said in perfect German. "Ich kann Deutsche. Vielleicht könnte ich helfen." She leaned towards Richard. "I told them I speak their language and might be able to help."

The Germans looked at her approvingly, and the senior of the two nodded. "Wir möchten seine Papiere sehen."

"They want to see your papers, Richard," Hannah Finn translated.

Mr. Davis nodded and brought out the leather case from his coat pocket. He handed it to the soldier.

As the young man looked it over, his eyebrows raised. "Ist er Amerikaner?" Richard nodded, figuring he wanted to know if he were American.

"Was macht er beruflich?" the soldier asked, shoving the papers at Hannah and pointing.

"Er ist Journalist. Seine Papiere ermächtigen ihn uneingeschränkt durch das Land zu fahren." She spoke to Mr. Davis without turning. "I told him your occupation and that the papers give you the freedom to move about the country." She smiled back at the soldiers, still speaking to Richard. "He is too inexperienced to know these papers will probably have to be reauthorized by his occupational government."

"As long as he's impressed for now," Richard answered, also smiling at the pair.

The soldier handed back the papers. "Und die Anderen?"

Hannah nodded. "He wants to know about the rest of us." She gave each of their names. "Sie sind alle Krankenschwestern. Sie machen eine wichtige Arbeit." She nodded at Edith and Philomene. "I told them you were nurses with important business."

This information seemed to interest one of the soldiers greatly. "Haben sie Tabletten gegen Kopfschmerzen?" he asked.

"He wants to know if you have something to relieve a headache," Hannah interpreted, a gentleness ebbing into her voice.

Much of the soldiers' stern demeanor had dropped away, making Philomene's heart ache with maternal concern.

"Of course," Edith said quickly. "Of course. Tell him to follow me."

Hannah Finn relayed the message, and the soldier lowered his gun, following Edith obediently to the satchels at the edge of the fountain. Edith went through the first-aid bag until she found several tins of aspirin. She stood and turned to him. Like a child he held out his hand to her, and Edith opened the tin, dropping several white pills into his palm.

"Vielen Dank," he said throwing the pills into his mouth and swallowing them dry. "Vielen Dank."

She handed him both of the tins, and he grasped them in his hand for a moment before shoving them into his pocket. He looked into Edith's caring face, and Philomene knew he was seeing the manifestation of pure charity.

Edith turned to Hannah. "Tell him that Mr. Davis and Miss Johnson are on assignment to take this medicine to some of their troops."

Her aunt relayed the message, and Philomene watched soberly as the soldiers turned to gaze at her. She smiled at them, and, to her amazement, they smiled back. The younger soldier nodded and said it was a good thing they were taking care of the brave German wounded. They then, through Aunt Hannah, lectured the group on proper behavior, giving them a warning to submit their wills to the superiority of the German forces. It was obviously the spiel decided upon by the upper military echelons and was to be parroted by all troops in the field whenever they came in contact with civilians.

The soldiers returned swiftly to their patrol, but as Philomene watched them move out of the square, she could see them only as schoolboys. She couldn't help but admit that war was a hideous thief of youth and innocence.

Mr. Davis blew out air in a sigh of relief. "Guess we needed a dress rehearsal."

"I think we did rather well," Aunt Hannah said, repinning her hat.

"You were marvelous!" Richard said, giving her a hug. "Conner could not have done better himself."

Hannah Finn smiled.

Edith was watching the retreating soldiers—a wistful look on her face. "Where does one draw the line? Those young men would rather have been playing sports or going to university. Could you see it?" She sighed and shook her head. "I'm glad I'm a nurse and not a general."

A man rode past them on his bicycle—the basket full of food for breakfast. The smell of fresh bread lingered for a moment in the air, suspending the group's need to face the inevitable.

Mr. Davis bent over and picked up the satchels. "It's time, Miss Johnson." He gave Hannah Finn an uncompromising smile. "We'll be fine, my dear. I'll try to get word to you as soon as we're safe in Antwerp."

"Thank you, Richard."

To give the women privacy for their good-byes, the journalist walked over to the central statue to bid farewell to the Earl of Egmont and the Earl of Horn, whose personages adorned the column.

Edith noted that both Hannah Finn and her niece were remaining true to their clear-headed thinking and their rejection of maudlin sentiment.

"I have put a little extra money and a surprise for you in the side pocket of your bag."

"Aunt Hannah, I don't need . . ."

Hannah Finn held up her hand. "My dear niece, it is purely practical. Many a poor soldier can be paid to turn a blind eye."

Philomene nodded and brushed a bit of dirt from her white cuff as she turned to Edith. "Thank you for everything, Miss Cavell. I will never forget your kindness." She looked at her straight on. "You are a remarkable woman, and my life has been enhanced by knowing you."

"I take that as a sincere compliment, Miss Johnson, for I know you are not one to flatter. And I must tell you I feel the same. The children of Sutter Creek have a treasure in their midst."

The two women grasped each other's hands, and, for a fleeting moment, Philomene felt a shiver of foreboding move through her body. She looked into Edith's calm face and rebuked the feeling with a smile.

"Remember to come back for your tennis lesson," Edith said simply.

Philomene nodded and went to her aunt. She steeled herself against the anguish and fear that knotted her stomach. "Be well, Auntie," she whispered as she held her dear one close.

"Be careful now, don't break me," her aunt cautioned.

It was their old banter, and Philomene smiled as she stepped back to gaze at her aunt's regal deportment. "Why, Aunt Hannah," she said softly, "you're one of the strongest women I know."

The matriarch nodded. "Remember that."

Mr. Davis came respectfully to the group. "Miss Johnson, if you are ready?"

Philomene held her aunt close again. "I don't want to leave you," she whispered fiercely.

"I know, but you must . . . the Lord is my Shepherd, I shall not want. Be strong." She held Philomene at arm's length. "People are counting on us—on all of us. Richard and Edith and I will look after each other."

Richard and Edith both nodded, and Philomene saw again the commitment in Miss Cavell's face.

Philomene straightened her shoulders and took her auntie's hand. "I love you."

"And I you, dear niece. Now go."

Richard Davis took his traveling companion by the arm and walked her away from the square to the waiting automobile.

Philomene Johnson walked with strength and determination, never turning back or faltering in her step. She knew it was exactly what Mrs. William Conner Finn would have done.

Chapter Twenty-Three

She had stolen a child! What was she thinking? Eleanor Lund raced down an alleyway, holding the whimpering child tightly and trying to figure out a solution to her impulsive act. She had stood passively in the home of Mr. and Mrs. Chun as Mrs. Antonia tried to explain the evil of the act they were imposing on their daughter. The little four-year-old had had her toes broken and her feet bound for two weeks now, and Mrs. Antonia was hoping to stop the process before the damage was irreparable. The grandmother of the child had been the one to contact the Civic League. The older woman's feet had been bound in China, and when gangrene had set in, part of one foot had been amputated, leaving her crippled. She was intent on saving her granddaughter from such a fate. Mr. and Mrs. Chun had been yelling at the grandmother since the Civic League women had arrived, and when the little girl began screaming hysterically at the chaos, she'd been carried to the back room and set on a chair.

In the strife that continued, Eleanor had inched her way unseen to the child's side, picked her up to quiet her fears, and, unthinking, had walked away from the noise. A few blocks from the house, she'd heard the shouts and panic of discovery and knew that people were being sent out in all directions to apprehend her. A doorway in one of the dark brick buildings opened, and a man emerged carrying a steaming bowl of noodles and a pair of chopsticks. He eyed Eleanor suspiciously, spoke a few sullen words to her in Chinese, and disappeared back into the building.

Eleanor stopped, shifting the child from one hip to the other. "It's all right, little one. I'll take you home. Soon I'll take you home." She put her hand on one of the tightly bound feet. "I just can't stand that you're suffering." Emotions of disgust, anger, and helplessness welled up inside her. She laid her cheek on the dark, coarse hair and wept. "I can't stand it!" She sat down on a stoop, placed the child on her lap, and stripped off the tight-fitting shoes. "Your mother and father are wicked to put you through such pain." Quickly she undid the ties at the top of the bands of cloth and began unwrapping the child's feet. The little girl whimpered, and Eleanor wondered if it was from pain or fear of new tortures. "I'm sorry. Sorry, little one," she cried. "You are perfect. Why would anyone think this is a good thing?"

Eleanor nearly retched at the putrid smell that escaped as the cloth fell away. She looked down in revulsion at the small bruised and grotesque toes—broken and bent under the pad of the foot. The little one buried her head in Eleanor's neck and howled.

A group of men appeared at the end of the alleyway, and a shout went up. Eleanor could not understand the words, but the intent was obvious. They rushed to her, and the child was plucked from her arms. The largest man in the group grabbed Eleanor's wrist and pulled her roughly down the lane. As they reached the main street they were met by the child's parents and Mrs. Antonia.

"Eleanor!" Mrs. Antonia gasped. "Are you all right? Is the child well?"

"Yes. Yes, ma'am, we're fine. I just . . ."

Mrs. Antonia was staring at the child's feet. "You . . . you took off the bindings?" She held up her hand before Eleanor could reply. "Don't say anything right now," she said softly. "We'll sort it out."

Mrs. Chun had taken her child from the rescuer, covering the disfigured feet with a blanket. She rounded on Eleanor with fury, snapping off a diatribe in Chinese that made the others, privy to the content, flinch.

Eleanor had had enough. She knew Mr. and Mrs. Chun understood English, because earlier they'd delivered the unmistakable message to her and Mrs. Antonia to keep out of their lives.

With courage and conviction beyond her years, Eleanor stepped towards the shrieking woman, glaring at her. Her voice was low and hard-edged. "How dare you yell at me for trying to comfort her! I was taking her away from the noise, away from your shrieking, away from your cruel stupidity."

Mrs. Chun stopped yelling, her mouth working like a fish out of water, while her husband took a step back

Mrs. Antonia put a gentle hand on Eleanor's arm. "Eleanor, now is not . . ."

Eleanor stepped forward again. "Your precious little girl has no voice to stop the torture, so I'm going to speak for her."

"You have no say in this!" Mrs. Chun spat. "You do not know our culture!"

Eleanor was relentless. "I know torture when I see it, and I know that the Chinese government has forbidden the practice. Forbidden! So you are breaking the law of your government!"

The men in the rescue group shifted uneasily. It was a shameful thing to be a lawbreaker.

"Your feet are not bound!" Eleanor spit the words at the glaring woman. "Your mother loved you enough to save you the pain!"

"My feet are small!" Mrs. Chun yelled. "Always small."

"And your daughter's feet may be small too."

"Eleanor, she won't understand your logic," Mrs. Antonia stated sadly.

"Well, maybe she'll understand it when the police come and take her off to jail!" Eleanor answered fiercely.

Mrs. Chun shook her fist at Eleanor. "You are young nobody! Young nobody with clown feet!"

"And you are a mean mother whom Buddha will punish someday!"

Mrs. Antonia went white. "Eleanor!"

Mr. Chun put his hand over his face in shame. The ferocity in Mrs. Chun's eyes flickered momentarily, and then she stepped forward and slapped Eleanor across the face.

Biting words and grumbling came immediately from the group of men, and the largest moved to Mrs. Chun's side, leveling a string of words against her action.

Eleanor did not know what the man actually said, but the effect was instantaneous. Mrs. Chun lowered her head and stepped back, bowing several times.

Mr. Chun bowed also. "Please accept apology. So sorry."

Eleanor stood straight and tall, the sting of the slap still smarting her face. Mrs. Antonia came to stand next to her, praying the girl could maintain her composure in such a tense situation. Eleanor's eventual response was unexpected and remarkable.

Eleanor took a deep breath and focused her attention on Mr. Chun. When she spoke, her voice was taut but full of compassion. "Mr. Chun, we know you love your daughter. We know you want the best for her, but some of the old ways must die. Some of the old ways are evil and bring only suffering." She pulled the blanket off the child's legs, and a strangled cry of anguish rose out of Mr. Chun's throat. Eleanor was relentless. "Even your government says it is not a good thing to bind your daughter's feet. You must be a strong father and protect your child."

Mr. Chun did not lift his eyes to look at her, but Eleanor saw his head nod several times. There was a moment of silence, and then Mrs. Chun grabbed the blanket from Eleanor, turned without a word, and walked away. The rest of the group, which cast furtive glances at Eleanor as they passed, followed Mrs. Chun.

The man who had dragged Eleanor by the wrist stopped for a moment to face her. He put his hands together in the attitude of prayer and bowed deeply, then, without waiting for any response, walked away to join his fellows.

When the men disappeared around the side of the building, Eleanor turned to Mrs. Antonia. "I'm sorry," she said contritely. "Taking the child was a stupid thing to do, and now we probably won't be allowed back."

"Actually, I think this may be a turning point," Mrs. Antonia said, smiling. Eleanor gave her an incredulous look, but Mrs. Antonia nodded. "I mean it. The large man is a leader in their local Chinese council. He has been reluctant to get involved in this matter, but I think your concern and the obvious passion for the Chun's little girl has touched him."

Somewhere nearby, a couple of cats began snarling and spitting, reminding the women that they were alone in a not-so-nice part of Chinatown. Mrs. Antonia led the way out onto the street where they found her automobile and driver waiting. On the drive back to the Westfield mansion, Eleanor kept imagining the pitiful feet of the Chun's daughter. She tried to see them without the bandages—healthy and whole again. Was it possible that something she had said might have made a difference? And where had those words and the courage to speak them come from? She had never spoken like that to a grown-up, yet somehow the thoughts came with force and great love. That was what truly amazed her; even though she was upset over the abuse inflicted by Mr. and Mrs. Chun, she had compassion for them. They were trapped in their narrow thinking, and all she wanted was for them to see what was best for their daughter. *Maybe they will.* Eleanor sighed and watched the passing buildings, forcing her mind to put aside its occupation of the last several hours.

"Headache?" Mrs. Antonia asked.

Eleanor looked at her blankly. "Hmm? Oh, no. Not a headache, just too much thinking."

Mrs. Antonia smiled. "I suppose you have that problem often, Miss Lund."

Eleanor smiled back. "My teacher, Miss Johnson, used to call it the curse of a fertile mind."

"Well, we will just have to use that fertile mind to great effect."

Eleanor shifted in her seat. "I wasn't very effective today."

"On the contrary," Mrs. Antonia corrected. "I think we will have the council to back us up now, and that happened because of you, my dear."

"Blundering luck," Eleanor said, grinning. "Absolutely nothing to do with using my brain."

"Sometimes using one's heart is just as powerful."

Eleanor studied Mrs. Antonia's striking features and thought about the apparent disparity she saw there. She'd always figured a person with such physical beauty and economic status would be self-centered and shallow, but Francine Antonia was outreaching and generous of spirit. "Have you always wanted to help people?" Eleanor ventured.

Mrs. Antonia paused, and Eleanor could tell she was measuring her reply.

"Yes and no," she said finally.

Eleanor waited.

"When I was young, I was the one being cared for. I was the middle of eight children abandoned by our father. My mother was a laundress who worked very hard to make ends meet."

Eleanor looked at Mrs. Antonia's elegant clothing and tried to picture her in poverty.

"The women of the Civic League made sure we had shoes, food, and education."

"Miss Johnson says education is the key," Eleanor offered.

"And she is absolutely right. I went to secretarial school, obtained a job with a large import company, and fell in love with the son of the president."

"You did?" Eleanor asked, her eyes wide with amazement.

"I did indeed. And he, in turn, fell in love with me."

"Is that Mr. Antonia?"

Mrs. Antonia winked. "And since I was educated, the family accepted me into their lofty realm."

"My grandparents never accepted my father. He was a plain, hard-working farmer whom they saw as poor and uncultured. In fact, my mother was disowned when she defied their wishes and married him." Eleanor's cheeks reddened, and she glanced at Mrs. Antonia. "I'm sorry. I shouldn't have said those things about my family."

"Not to worry, Eleanor. Through your Aunt Ida, I am informed of much of your mother's background."

Eleanor nodded and tried to think of a question that would turn the conversation away from her disloyal statement. "And how long have you been with the Civic League?"

"At least ten years," Mrs. Antonia stated. "Before the '06 earthquake. That's when the Civic League came into its own, I can tell you."

"It must have been a dreadful time," Eleanor said.

"Terrifying," Mrs. Antonia answered immediately. "Life is filled with enough suffering without adding a catastrophe like that one."

Eleanor thought about the countless causes that must have occupied Mrs. Antonia's heart and hands over the years.

"Mr. Antonia must be very proud of your service," she said quietly.

"Many times he works right along with me," Mrs. Antonia returned.

"Really?" Eleanor found this odd, as women normally attended to volunteer civic work.

Mrs. Antonia smiled, knowing the bent of Eleanor's thinking.

The automobile pulled to a stop at the side of the road, and the driver turned to the occupants. "William's Street, madam," he announced.

"Are you sure we can't drive you to the house, Eleanor?" Mrs. Antonia questioned her young assistant.

"Oh, no ma'am. Thank you anyway. I truly do like to walk the last few blocks. Good exercise." Eleanor exited the automobile quickly to avoid any more insistence on being driven to the house.

Mrs. Antonia rolled down the window. "You are a remarkable young woman, Miss Lund. I have enjoyed our association."

"Thank you, ma'am. I've learned much from you," Eleanor replied.

"I will pick you up next week at the same time. Dr. Burnett will accompany us."

Eleanor nodded. "Yes, ma'am. I'll be ready."

"Your aunt and mother must be very proud of you, Eleanor."

Eleanor knew the exact opposite was true, but she smiled and nodded.

Mrs. Antonia turned to her driver and gave him the order to drive on. She waved to Eleanor, and the automobile pulled away.

Proud of me? Huh! Eleanor thought as she turned for the walk back to the opulence of Aunt Ida's house. *Neither my mother nor auntie understand one whit about what I'm trying to do, nor what I want.*

Eleanor scolded herself for such rebellious thoughts. She had to show more tolerance, as she knew both women were limited in their thinking because of their entrenchment in the old century and their affluent upbringing. She had been lucky enough to be raised on a farm and to know the value of work. She also knew the joy of education and the opportunities learning offered—especially to women. She lived in an era when choice and possibility for women were expanding. *Now if we could just get the vote,* Eleanor thought hopefully.

The brightly painted Victorian house came into view, and Eleanor scowled at it. Her heart was heavy as she trudged up the last hill to Beacon Street, and she knew she would rather be living anywhere else on the planet.

Chapter Twenty-Four

"Occipital. Mastoid. Mandible." Eleanor sat in the library with her feet up under her and a huge book on her lap. It was the standard book of anatomy, and she was memorizing the bones in the head. "Supraorbital notch."

There was a knock on the door.

She removed her hand from the picture to check her answer. "Come in," she said with only partial attention.

The door opened, and Mr. Palmer entered carrying a silver tray.

Eleanor sat up and put her feet on the floor, trying to hide their unshod condition under her skirt. "Good morning, Mr. Palmer!" she said in an overbright voice.

"Good morning, Miss Lund. There is a letter for you." He lowered the tray, and she took the letter.

A thrill ran through her as she recognized the penmanship. "Oh! It's from my sister Alaina!"

Mr. Palmer smiled. "All the way from Salt Lake City?"

Eleanor looked up at him. "Yes. Isn't it grand? Oh, I just love to get letters."

"Would you like me to open it for you?"

"Yes, Palmer, thank you."

She handed him the letter. He took it to the mahogany desk, set down his tray, and secured the silver letter opener.

Eleanor padded over to him in her stocking feet. "I don't mean to be nosey, Mr. Palmer, but do you ever get mail?"

Mr. Palmer smiled and handed her the opened letter. "I do, miss, yes. I have an aunt in Portland and a brother in Sacramento with whom I correspond."

"My grandparents on my father's side were from Sacramento. They're gone now, though. My uncle too." She needed to change the subject. It was almost a year since her father's death, and for the past several weeks, painful memories had pressed in on her with more frequency. She found herself thinking and talking about death more often, and she didn't like it. She had found solace in the Mormon teachings of eternity and eternal families, but even that Sabbath enlightenment had been forbidden by her mother.

"Is there anything else you require, Miss Eleanor?" Mr. Palmer asked.

She brought her mind back from its wanderings. "Oh, no thank you, Mr. Palmer. I'm fine."

"I will call you for the midday meal, miss." He turned to move out of the room, pausing by the armchair to pick up the book from which Eleanor had been studying.

"A bit of light reading, Miss Eleanor?"

She was surprised by his friendliness. "It's just anatomy. I find it very interesting."

Mr. Palmer nodded. "Remarkable." He put down the book and moved out of the room, closing the door behind him.

Now what did he mean by that? Eleanor wondered. *Remarkable that I would like such a subject? Or that, as a girl, I would understand such a subject?* She looked at the open envelope in her hand and forgot all about anatomy and Mr. Palmer. September sunshine was pouring through the library window, and she went to stand in its glory and read her letter.

August 26, 1914

Dear, dear Eleanor,

I am going to have a baby! I had been sick for weeks and was fearful that I had some dreaded illness, but Dr. Lucien came to examine me and all is well. In fact, all is wonderful! I know that I'd written you about finally being Nephi's true wife, and so I should have imagined this could have happened, but I'm such an innocent goose that I didn't figure it. Mother never talked to us about such things, so I didn't know what to expect. Oh, how I

wish you were here to share this with me. Nephi is so kind and
excited to be a father, and Mother Erickson is a dear, but they are
not you. If you were here I'd take you to see Grandfather
Erickson's magical little cottage, and you and Sarah and I could
go shopping at Zion's Mercantile, and you could help train Miss
Titus! Oh, I miss you so much. Are you able to attend school yet?
Your last letter said you were helping the women at the Civic
League. Are you still involved? I wish we could go up to Niagara
Falls and talk for hours. I wonder how Mother will feel about a
grandchild coming into her life. I know Father would have been
happy. I'm having a hard time right now with his death date so
near at hand. I wish we could be together so the sorrow would be
lighter. Well, I'm just going on and on. It's strange how I can be
happy and sad at the same time. I miss you. I hope you had a
happy birthday. Mother Erickson and I made an angel food cake
in your honor. Write me soon.

Your loving sister,
Laina

P.S. Soon we can call you Aunt Elly.

Eleanor looked out the window. She too had gone through
elation and pain in the last few minutes while reading Alaina's letter,
but she had also experienced another emotion—envy.

Alaina seemed to be surrounded by people who loved her, and
although Eleanor had found dear friendships with Bib, Kerri, and
Ina Bell, it was not the depth of feeling that sustained itself through
deep sadness. There was a light tapping on the door, and Eleanor
turned. "Yes?"

The door opened, and Bib Randall entered. "Excuse me, Miss
Eleanor, but you're wanted in the parlor."

"Bib! Good morning, how are you?"

Bib entered quickly and shut the door behind him. "Shh. Not so
loud, Miss Eleanor. Mr. Palmer is somewhere about this morning."

Eleanor smiled. "I know. He was here not long ago bringing me a
letter."

"From your sister, Mrs. Nephi Erickson."

"Bib Randall! How dare you nose into my business!"

"Nose into your business? Well, I like that. I'll have you know that Ina Bell, Kerri, and myself check all the post when it arrives."

Eleanor laughed. "Of course, I should have known. There are no secrets understair, are there?"

Bib smiled conspiratorially. "Well, not among the younger servants anyway." He stood straight. "But you've made me forget my errand, which is to escort you to the parlor."

"Why am I needed?" Eleanor asked, going to put on her shoes.

Bib looked aloof. "I assure you, I have no idea."

"Of course you do. Now who called for me?"

Bib dropped the pretense of a servant. "Your Aunt Ida, but I think your mother has joined her."

Eleanor jerked the lace on her shoe. "Wonderful. Just what I need—another lecture on appropriate behavior."

Bib did not reply to this, but his expression showed pity, and just before he opened the parlor door he gave her an encouraging smile. "You'll be fine," he whispered.

"Into the lions' den," she whispered back.

Her mother and aunt were sitting opposite each other, Aunt Ida on the green sofa and Mother in the brocaded armchair; neither woman was speaking, but each had a look of cold anger on her face. It did not bode well for a slight reprimand.

"Sit down," Aunt Ida commanded, her frail voice sounding frightened instead of stern. "There is something we wish to discuss with you."

Eleanor sat down quietly in the other armchair.

Aunt Ida adjusted her pearls and took a deep breath before speaking. "Mrs. Langford from the Women's Civic League called on me this morning."

Eleanor's stomach churned.

"It seems that there is a rumor circulating among the membership concerning an incident yesterday in Chinatown."

Eleanor worked to calm her breathing.

"An incident where a young woman stole a child out of the parents' home."

Eleanor could feel her mother watching her.

Aunt Ida stood and walked to the fireplace. "And it seems Mrs. Langford and the other women of the league have this strange notion that the young woman was you." Ida's voice rose in intensity and pitch. "But of course that is impossible, as you were forbidden to continue your association with the league." She stopped talking, but her accusation hung in the air. "Well, niece, what have you to say for yourself?"

When Eleanor spoke, her voice was low and steady. "I'd do it again tomorrow if I thought it would save that little girl's feet."

A shocked silence followed this unrepentant pronouncement.

"Well . . . well, really!" Aunt Ida spluttered. "I . . . I never . . . such deceit, and after your first scolding I thought you had learned your lesson." She took out her handkerchief and waved it in front of her face.

"She obviously has not," Elizabeth Lund said flatly.

Mother's sudden entrance into the conversation prompted Eleanor to turn and look at her. Her face was beautiful but gaunt and pale, the skin under her eyes was shadowed, and her hair was brittle and drab. During the nine months they'd been at Aunt Ida's, mother had not eaten well, and her hands were boney, and her dresses hung on her frame like a child playing dress-up.

Eleanor's heart twisted with regret. How selfish of her to worry about her boredom and neglected education when her mother needed her concern and ministrations. The melancholia, which at one point seemed to be retreating, had come back to haunt Elizabeth Lund with greater spite. Eleanor figured her deterioration was due to the imminence of Father's death date.

"Headstrong just like her sister," Elizabeth Lund said coldly.

Eleanor focused again on her mother's face. What had happened to make her so bitter and unforgiving? Eleanor knew her mother had always been stern and distant with her children, but here was coldness and sorrow Eleanor could not understand. She must have been so different when Father first met her. Samuel Lund was a man of optimism and warmth, always ready with a kind word or a bit of common sense. Had Elizabeth Knight seen in him a chance for emotional salvation from her austere upbringing and bouts with melancholy? Had Father, the naive farm boy, been so overwhelmed by Miss Knight's beauty and sophistication that he forgot to be practical in his choice for a bride?

Attraction and love were mysterious things, Eleanor concluded. Look at Alaina and Nephi: they had married for convenience, and now love filled their lives, and a baby was on the way. The baby! Her mother didn't know about the baby. Eleanor knew it was a completely different subject, but she decided it was important to share the news; perhaps it would bring some joy into her mother's life. She was stopped short by Aunt Ida's next words.

"I regret this, Eleanor, but if you cannot be sorry for your disobedience, your mother and I have no choice but to find a different place for you."

Eleanor was stunned. "What?" She looked from her mother to Aunt Ida, who was wringing her handkerchief and shaking her head.

"Isn't that right, Elizabeth? Isn't that what we've decided?"

Elizabeth Lund nodded, a look of sadness on her face. "Eleanor, Ida feels your dishonest behavior disrupts the peace of her home and brings shame onto her good name. We are guests here, and I must respect her feelings."

Eleanor sat stiff and quiet in her chair. She was trying to figure out the exact meaning of her aunt's pronouncement. *Find a different place for me? Am I actually being sent away?* Her mother was still talking.

"We have looked into a boarding school in Virginia. The Crowshaw School for Girls. It is where our mother attended."

The words forced Eleanor out of her seat. "Virginia? You're thinking of sending me to Virginia?" The vehemence in her voice made Aunt Ida step back.

"It is a very good school, Eleanor—a very good school."

"That's not the point!" Eleanor snapped. "Do you know how far that is from my family?"

"It doesn't seem like you've cared much for family these last months," her mother said pointedly.

"That's not true," Eleanor answered, stung by the disappointed tone in her mother's voice. "I do care for my family. It's just that those little girls needed me. If you could only see . . ."

"Yes, yes. We are sure it is a terrible situation," Aunt Ida interrupted, "but there are other people to take care of it. It is not for you."

Eleanor was indignant. "It is for me! I was helping."

Her mother spoke quickly. "Eleanor Lund! Do not speak back to your aunt. This is exactly the behavior we detest. What has happened to your sweet nature?"

Eleanor's throat tightened as she tried to swallow the hurtful question. She felt like the same person, but perhaps she hadn't seen the change, perhaps she was becoming willful and disrespectful. "I won't go to Virginia," she said quietly.

Aunt Ida gasped. "You will go where we tell you, young lady."

"No, I won't. If you want me to leave your house, I will, but I must be close to my family."

"So . . . where would you go?" Aunt Ida asked, trying hard to keep the tremor out of her voice.

Eleanor decided in an instant. "Salt Lake City. Alaina is going to have a baby, and I will go there and help her." She evaluated the stunned look on her mother's face. "Yes, a baby. I just received the letter this morning."

Elizabeth Lund sat down. "But she didn't love that man."

"Well, things change, Mother. Things change all the time. And his name is Nephi, and he's a good Mormon man who loves my sister, despite your hating him."

"Eleanor!" Aunt Ida reprimanded.

Eleanor rounded on her. "No, Aunt Ida! If I'm leaving your house anyway, I'm going to speak my mind." She turned back to her mother. "Our lives could have been so much better if you'd just let Alaina and Nephi run the farm. I know you were suffering with Father's death, but so were all of us."

"Eleanor, don't," Aunt Ida whimpered, covering her ears.

"Your decision to sell the farm tore our lives into bits. I've tried to care for you since coming here. I love you and I've tried, but I don't think you want to get better. You don't want to face this life; you just want to go back to that old, safe place where you didn't have responsibilities, where you were protected and your every need was met." She stopped for a moment to slow her breathing. "Well, you can just hide here if you want while your children go on without you. You gave

Alaina and James a hundred dollars when they left home. That's all I ask. I'll make my own arrangements from there." The tears were pressing hard behind her eyes, but she refused to let her aunt or her mother see her heartbreak. She looked into her aunt's distraught face. "I'm sorry that I've caused problems for you, Auntie, especially so soon after Uncle Cedrick's death." Her aunt's eyes welled with tears, but Eleanor refused to give in to sympathy. "Is there anything else you require of me?"

Her aunt shook her head.

"Then I will go to my room." Eleanor turned and walked to the door. Her feet felt like they were made of lead. She paused with her hand on the doorknob. "I will write Alaina immediately to see if the Erickson family can accommodate me." She opened the door and moved out into the entry foyer, leaving her mother and aunt to deal with the chaotic aftermath of their edict.

Ina Bell, Kerri, and Bib met her at her bedroom doorway. Kerri was ashen faced, and Ina Bell looked as though she'd been crying.

"Yer not really goin', are ya miss?" Kerri blurted out as soon as she saw her.

Eleanor stared at the trio. "How did you . . . ?"

"Ina Bell and me were hidin' down the hallway listenin'. So, are ya?"

Eleanor felt awkward and displaced. The emotions that she'd kept so tightly contained in the parlor now brimmed over, spilling tears down her cheeks. Ina Bell started crying again, and Kerri began muttering choice words she'd like to deliver to Mrs. Lund and Mrs. Westfield.

Bib opened Eleanor's door. "Oh, for heaven's sake. Inside, you three." He maneuvered the girls into the bedroom and shut the door behind them. "Now, everybody just calm down," he pleaded, "or Mr. Palmer will be onto us in no time."

"Sorry. Sorry, Bib," Eleanor responded. "Of course, you're right. Stupid tears aren't going to change anything." She went to her dresser and brought out a handkerchief for Ina Bell. "See, that's what you get for spying on me."

Ina Bell shook her head. "Truly, miss, we were just coming to clean the room. We didn't mean to overhear."

"I know, Ina Bell," Eleanor said. "I was just teasing."

Ina Bell took her hand. "I can't believe you're really going."

Kerri snorted, "How can you leave us alone with the Dragon and the pampered Miss Kathryn?"

"Kerri McKee!" Bib reprimanded.

"Oh, now I'm going to speak me mind," Kerri said in a defiant whisper. "And didn't we all admire Eleanor when she stood up to her mother?"

Eleanor shook her head. "It was very disrespectful."

"That it was," Kerri agreed, "but it was plain truth."

"That doesn't make it right. I suppose they have good cause for sending me away."

Kerri started to say something harsh, but Bib interceded. "Miss Eleanor, we're only servants, and it's not our place to disagree with the mistress of the house, but in this case we have to say that Mrs. Westfield and your mother are one hundred percent wrong."

"Absolutely wrong," Ina Bell added.

Kerri nodded. "Wrong as square eggs."

Eleanor smiled at them through her tears. "What would I have done without you three?"

Ina Bell put her arms around Eleanor's neck and hugged her. "We think you are brilliant."

The door opened, and everyone stiffened. Mr. Palmer entered and stopped, staring at the group. His body was straight, his hands behind his back, and his face an unreadable mask. "Mr. Randall," he said solemnly, "I have just been speaking to Mrs. Westfield and her sister, and they have informed me of the situation."

Eleanor hung her head, but Bib reached over and patted her arm.

"It would also seem," Mr. Palmer continued, "that nothing can be kept from you three."

"No sir, I suppose not," Bib replied.

"Well, then, have you assessed Miss Lund's needs, Mr. Randall?"

Bib took a moment to answer. "Ah—yes, Mr. Palmer. Yes, we have. For the next couple of days Miss Lund will need our companionship and as much laughter as possible."

The girls stared at him as though he'd gone mad.

Mr. Palmer's expression did not change. "Anything else, Mr. Randall?"

"Yes, sir. Her favorite foods and special outings every day."

Mr. Palmer nodded. "You three are dismissed to get started on those plans."

"Yes, sir," Bib answered, winking at Eleanor as he moved toward the door.

Mr. Palmer stepped aside as the three servants exited. Ina Bell and Kerri each gave a quick curtsy and looked at the butler as if the world had just turned upside down.

When they were gone, Mr. Palmer looked at Eleanor. "Are you all right, Miss Lund?"

She took a breath. "I . . . I don't know, Mr. Palmer."

"An honest answer." He brought his hands in front of him, and Eleanor saw he was holding the anatomy book. "It seems you left this downstairs, Miss Lund."

"Oh! Thank you, Palmer, but I rarely take the books out of the library."

"I am aware of that, but I think this one should go with you on your travels," he said, handing her the book.

"Take it with me?"

"Yes. I'm sure Mr. Westfield would be glad someone is reading it." She ran her hand along the cover. "Thank you, Mr. Palmer."

He cleared his throat. "Why don't you have your noon meal in the kitchen today, Miss Lund?"

She looked up at him, her eyes shining with tears. "Yes, Palmer. Thank you."

"I will inform Miss McKee to set another place at our table." He paused at the door and looked back at her. "Be brave, Miss Eleanor. Life has a way of turning out." He shut the door quickly behind him.

Chapter Twenty-Five

Philomene could hear the men's voices in the hallway—Mr. Davis's voice and that of Mr. Henry Carton de Wiart. She strained to decipher the words, but it was only low rumbling. The sound should have been comforting, for it meant they had made it to Antwerp and made contact with Aunt Hannah's friend. Mr. de Wiart was a member of the diplomatic group being sent by Prince Albert to America with whom Philomene was to travel. She should have been relieved, but instead, here she stood in her hotel room, staring vacantly into the mirror and fearing to take off the nurse's uniform.

A sharp rap came to the door, and Philomene started. "Yes?"

"May I come in?"

Philomene calmed her breathing. "Of course, Mr. Davis. Come in."

Richard Davis entered and gave her a quizzical look. "Not changed yet?"

"No . . . I . . ."

"No. No, I understand," he teased. "I suppose it's hard going back to being just a schoolteacher."

Philomene gave him an Aunt Hannah look. "Just a schoolteacher?"

He laughed and handed over her leather document case. "And now you get to travel home with a bunch of high government muckety-mucks. You know . . . it might be a good idea to disguise you as minister of finance or something."

"No. No more disguises," Philomene said softly, taking the case from his hand and trying not to look at the gash on his forehead. "I want no more to do with intrigue."

Mr. Davis sobered as he took her hand. "You've been wonderful from start to finish, Philomene Johnson. You saved my life and . . ."

She pulled her hand away. "We helped each other, Richard."

He smiled at her. "Well, I don't agree, but at least you've stopped calling me Mr. Davis."

"Seems silly not to call you by your given name after what we've been through."

"Smart woman," he said approvingly. "Now, I'm going out to find a telegraph office. Hopefully they haven't locked things down yet in Brussels, and I can get a message through to your aunt."

Philomene stiffened. "You are not to mention our encounter, Mr. Davis."

"Excuse me?"

"I do not want Aunt Hannah to know anything about it. Merely tell her that we are safe in Antwerp and all is proceeding as planned. You must give me your word."

He sat staring at her for several moments, and then the line of his mouth broke into a grin. "You don't want me to say anything about our adventure?"

"No."

"You want me to keep a secret from Mrs. William Conner Finn, one of the brightest women I know?"

What was he up to? "Yes, that's exactly what I want," she said solemnly.

His smile broadened. "Well, only under one condition."

"What is that, Mr. Davis?" she asked suspiciously.

"That you will never again call me Mr. Davis."

She nodded. "A small price to pay for my aunt's peace of mind."

He shook her hand. "It's a deal then, but there'll be the devil to pay if she finds out."

"We will take that chance. Now, off you go to the telegraph office," she said, removing the white collar and cuffs of the nurse's uniform, "and I will change back into a lowly schoolteacher."

Richard gave her a nod and tipped his hat. "I'll pick up some food on my way back."

"Wonderful. Bread and cheese if you can find it."

"If I can find it?" he replied, offended. "I'm a newspaper man; I can find anything." He stopped with his hand on the doorknob. "You know what?"

"What?" Philomene asked with mock impatience.

"I think your room's bigger than mine."

"And rightly so. Now, hurry along before the shops run out of food."

He laughed and went out.

As Philomene moved to lock the door she could hear him whistling down the hallway. *He's glad to be alive*, she thought. She turned back into the room, overwhelmed by exhaustion. *Perhaps I'll just lie down for a minute or two. I'll change my clothes as soon as I've had a little rest.* She lay down on the cool coverlet and brought the white feather pillow under her head. *My document case . . . Did Richard give me my document case? I hope he can find Camembert cheese . . . I wonder if Claudine is taking tea to my aunt . . .*

* * *

"Amerikaner?" the German officer barked at Mr. Davis as he scrutinized his papers. Richard nodded. "And you are in newspaper work?" he asked now in English. Richard nodded again. "So where are you going?"

"Louvain," Richard lied. "Big story there."

"Big victory for us," the officer said arrogantly.

"Yes," Richard agreed. "That's what I've been told."

They had been pulled over to the side of the road an hour out of Brussels by a German scouting unit. There were only ten soldiers in the group, but they all looked like seasoned fighters, especially their leader.

Philomene flinched as the officer now turned to stare at her. "Ausweis sehen."

She froze.

"Papers, s'il vous plaît," Richard whispered under his breath.

The officer thrust his opened hand at her, and she gave him her leather document case. "I think she is afraid of me," he said, smiling. He looked over her papers. "And you are French?"

Philomene pretended not to understand. "French? Ah, oui. Je suis française."

His eyes narrowed as he scrutinized her nurse's uniform. "And you are . . ."

Richard realized he was searching for the English word. "Nurse," he offered.

"Yes. Nurse?"

"Je ne comprends pas," Philomene said meekly. She was trembling, and tears pressed against the back of her throat.

"Krankenschwester. Nurse," he said gruffly. He grabbed the satchel out of her hand and dumped its contents onto the road. Without thinking, Philomene stepped forward to stop him and found a field pistol aimed at her face.

Richard Davis grabbed Philomene's arm and yanked her behind him. The German officer yelled and brought the butt of the pistol down on the newspaperman's head. Philomene cried out as Richard crumpled to the ground. The other members of the scouting party came running from their resting place, but the officer ordered them to stop. It was obvious he wanted to save face and take care of the situation himself. The soldiers obeyed, but Philomene could see their rifles at the ready.

Please, God. Please help me through this, Philomene pled silently. *I know this man does not really want to kill us.* "Pardon, monsieur. Pardon," she heard herself saying. She held both hands in front of her with the palms out. "Je regrette! Je regrette!" She kneeled down in the dirt and put her hand over her heart. With the other hand she reached for the satchel. Immediately the gun was in her face. "Non! Non, monsieur!" She pointed at the bag, indicating there was something in it she wanted to give him. He seemed to understand her hand signals as he seized the bag and shook it again. Nothing came out. Philomene indicated the side pocket. The officer, not willing to put away his pistol, threw the bag to her and ordered her to open it. Philomene carefully unbuttoned the side pocket and withdrew the beautiful ivory box Aunt Hannah had hidden there. Trembling, she handed the gift to the officer, who quickly knocked off the lid with the muzzle of the gun and with the same instrument lifted out a long string of pearls. A smile twisted his lips as he slid the necklace into his hand and secured it in his pocket. Richard moaned and rolled onto his back, alerting the officer to his sense of duty. He walked threateningly towards the injured man, and just as he pulled back his booted foot to kick him, the sound of gunfire erupted to the north. The German officer swung around to face the small village approximately a quarter of a mile away, and Philomene noted that several of his soldiers were moving in that direction. The officer called to them, and they all began running together—the two civilians, the automobile, and the possibility of more treasure forgotten for the mistress of battle.

Philomene sat down beside her friend, unnerved by the events of the last few minutes. Richard moaned again. "Mr. Davis," she said in a whisper, still thinking the soldiers might hear her and return. "Mr. Davis, can you sit up?"

The journalist opened his eyes and winced at the brightness of the sun. He sat up quickly and moaned again. "Germans?" he asked feebly.

"They've gone to that village. There was gunfire."

Blood trickled down the side of his face. He squeezed his eyelids shut and then opened them to stare at her. "Are you all right? How did you . . . ?"

"I begged him in French and gave him Aunt Hannah's secret weapon."

"What was that?" he asked, mystified by their miraculous escape.

"A string of pearls."

"Amazing." Richard started to laugh, but grimaced instead at the pain in his head.

"I wish I could do something for you," Philomene sympathized.

"Well, you are a nurse. Fix me up."

"Very funny."

A volley of gunfire was heard to the north, and both former captives stood up together.

"Let's get out of here," Mr. Davis said, slumping against the vehicle.

"Are you able to drive?" Philomene asked anxiously as she gathered up the dropped articles and shoved them back into the satchel.

More gunfire came from the village. "Able enough," Mr. Davis said, quickly helping Philomene into the automobile and jumping behind the wheel. "What luck they didn't take the auto."

Philomene felt the fresh air on her face as Mr. Davis sped off towards Antwerp and safety. She heard shouting and turned her head to see if the soldiers were chasing after them . . .

* * *

Philomene felt the smooth fabric of her pillow and smiled. She *was* in Antwerp—safe in Antwerp having a pleasant little nap before Richard returned with something to eat. She slowly opened her eyes, becoming aware of her surroundings. She saw the white nurse's collar and cuffs on the vanity, she smelled lavender soap, and heard the sound of someone calling at a distance . . . or were they shouting?

She stood and walked to the window, pushing back the gauze curtain and looking out at the world. Her attention was caught by a group of children who stood gazing into the sky. Suddenly a woman came running down the street screaming at the children. Philomene could not understand the words, but the intent was obvious. She wanted them to run. A few turned to watch her frantic approach, but most continued their scan of the heavens, mesmerized by some unusual sight. Philomene followed their gaze and saw a huge, gray, oblong aircraft moving over the tops of the buildings. It was an image from a nightmare. She glanced down to see the terrified woman pushing children in all directions, scattering them like a fox among chickens. Philomene heard high-pitched screams coming from the sky, and suddenly the room in which she was standing flew apart.

Something was cutting into her leg and side—burning. She reached out to shove it away and felt the fur of an animal. She jerked her hand back and heard wood splintering, whistles, and human voices screaming. She opened her eyes onto chaos. There was rubble and fire and foul smoke. The animal she'd felt was a dead dog, the scruffy carcass covered in blood from a gash in its neck. She struggled to crawl away from the madness, but she could not feel her legs. Her side burned again, and she looked down to see her outer clothing shredded and red splotches on her underskirt and corset. *Richard? Where is Richard? Didn't he leave me in my room at the hotel in Antwerp? He was going to find a telegraph office and bring back something to eat. Bread and cheese. Isn't that what he said?*

She saw the face of a nun, and felt pain. Someone was tearing at the flesh on her leg. She tried to pull away, but strong arms held her. The nun spoke to her, the voice muffled and far away. "No, no, madame. The doctor must work." Philomene felt a jarring stab under her lower rib and passed out.

Chapter Twenty-Six

William Trenton had harvested three bushels of plums from Miss Johnson's plum tree and was now scraping the last of the fallen fruit from her walkway. The September wind was blowing dust and grit into his eyes, making it nearly impossible to finish the task to his liking.

"Dang wind," he grumbled to himself, "get on out of here and let me be. Bad enough you have to blast every plant. Just look at them rosebushes." The garden had lost the pale freshness of spring and the full blossom of summer. The plants wore a flat color as if the persistent dry wind had sapped them of their incentive to be beautiful.

The wind stopped blowing for a moment, and William grunted. "Well, it's about time." He finished with the walkway and moved on to the garden. There were beans, peppers, and squash to harvest now, and the pumpkins would be ready in another month.

Even though school had started, William came to Miss Johnson's every afternoon—and for a few hours on Saturday—to keep up the place for her return. He'd been in a fight yesterday with Hugh Markum. The older boy had stated flatly that he didn't think Miss Johnson was coming back. He figured she was trapped in Belgium, since it was being overrun with German soldiers. William had punched Hugh in the stomach and had been sent to Principal Barlow's for punishment. He didn't care. Nobody was going to get away with saying she wasn't coming home. There had been no word from his teacher for a long time, but that didn't mean anything. He figured it had to be hard to get mail out of the country under the circumstances.

William picked the ripe produce and put it into baskets to take to Mr. Carrillo's store. Whatever the grocer didn't want, William took home to his mother. Miss Johnson had given him strict orders to use up everything the garden provided while she was away.

"Waste is a great evil, Mr. Trenton," she had said. "Be sure to show God your gratitude for the bounty by making good use of everything." William was sure she'd never planned on being away this long.

Every day he went to the post office to talk to Mr. Greggs and find out the latest news about the war and where Mr. Greggs thought Miss Johnson might be. Mr. Greggs had put up a big map of Europe on the post office wall, and every day he'd reposition some little colored flags depending on the troop movement. William knew that King Albert and his fierce Belgian army still held Antwerp and the surrounding territory. They'd even opened the sluice gates and flooded several square miles of lowland to stop the German advance. William liked the thought of the German soldiers mucking through mud up to their knees.

He turned his head at the sound of a wagon pulling up at the front of the property. He heard a low, male voice, but couldn't make out the words. As he peered through all the bushes and vegetation of the garden, he thought he caught a glimpse of James Lund jumping down from the buckboard. William smiled. *He's probably come to see if Miss Johnson's home yet.*

William brushed the dirt from his hands onto his pants and walked toward the front gate to greet Mr. Lund. The wind had picked up again, and he squinted his eyes against the grit. He could hear James speaking to someone, and as he neared the front of the yard he saw him help a lady down from the wagon. William's heart jumped. *Miss Johnson?* He threw open the gate. "Miss Johnson?" he yelled. He raced around the side of the wagon just as Miss Johnson slumped against James, who held her close.

"William! Come help me!" James called.

"What's wrong with her?" William yelled in a panic, coming to grab Miss Johnson around the waist and putting her arm around his shoulder.

"I'm . . . I'm all right, Mr. Trenton," Miss Johnson said in a hoarse voice, but William knew that was a plain lie.

They reached the porch and William kicked over the flowerpot, reached down quickly, and brought up the ornate front-door key.

Miss Johnson was weeping and muttering, "My house. My dear little house."

William felt sick. Miss Johnson never showed weakness, and he'd certainly never seen her look so unhealthy. She was always strong, and her clothes were always neat. William noticed that at the moment her skin was sallow and clammy, and she wasn't even wearing a hat.

He shoved the key into the lock and opened the door. The musty smell of disuse escaped as the threesome pushed noisily inside.

"Let's get her to the bed," James ordered.

When they entered the bedroom, William hastily pulled the protective white sheet off the bed and pulled back the quilt. Miss Johnson crawled into bed shivering, although the room was quite warm. William found another quilt in a cedar chest and laid it over her, while James took off her shoes.

"Thank you. Thank you, boys," she kept repeating.

"William, take the wagon into town and find Dr. McIntyre," James said. "Tell him to get down here quick. Also, find Mr. Gregg's sister and bring her back. Miss Johnson will need a woman to tend her."

William ran for the wagon and within twenty minutes was back, pacing in Miss Johnson's front room. James sat pensively while Dr. McIntyre took care of things. When Mrs. Brown, Mr. Gregg's widowed sister, came out of the room to fetch more hot water, William blocked her path.

"What? What's wrong with her?" he snapped.

"Don't worry, son. I think she's going to be all right," Mrs. Brown answered. She said the words, but the look on her face did not carry the same confidence. "Dr. McIntyre will tell you more when he comes out."

William sat down in a heap and put his head in his hands. James let him be.

After another twenty minutes the doctor came out carrying his bag and giving last-minute instructions to Mrs. Brown.

"One dose of that powder every six hours, and use the astringent on those wounds. She's not going to like it because it stings like crazy, but it should do the trick."

Both James and William had stood when the doctor emerged, eager for news on Miss Johnson's condition.

"Wounds? What wounds?" William blurted.

Dr. McIntyre came over and put his hand on William's shoulder. "You're one of Ernestine Trenton's boys, aren't you?"

"Yes, sir. I'm William."

"And you've been tending Miss Johnson's property?"

"Yes, sir," William said impatiently. "How is she?"

"Well, she's going to be most grateful in a few weeks when she can walk around out there and admire your handiwork."

A look of relief flooded William's face. "So she's gonna be all right?"

"Given a little time she'll be right as rain."

"What happened to her?" William questioned.

Dr. McIntyre evaluated the maturity of the boy. "Shrapnel wounds up one leg and into her side."

"Shrapnel wounds?" he asked anxiously when he saw James's face go pale. "What are those? Are they like bullet wounds?"

Dr. McIntyre shook his head. "No, son, they're small pieces of metal from an exploded bomb."

William's mouth hung open, and his eyes glazed with tears. James came over and put his arm around the boy's shoulder.

"It's all right, Mr. Trenton," the doctor reassured. "Most of the wounds were not deep. The problem was they'd gotten infected on her trip across the Atlantic, so she's running a pretty bad fever, but she is a strong woman. She'll recover." Dr. McIntyre gave William a nod and picked up his bag. "What I don't understand is how in the world she got home from the train station in Martell."

"I picked her up," James said. "She'd telegraphed yesterday from Sacramento telling me which train to meet. She told me not to tell anyone." He shook his head. "She said she was feeling a mite poorly and wanted some time to herself."

Dr. McIntyre snorted. "A mite poorly? Anyone else would have headed for a hospital."

"How did she get shrapnel wounds?" William asked, his mind still fixed on the frightening image of Miss Johnson being anywhere near a bomb.

"I don't know, Mr. Trenton. She was not coherent enough to tell me much about it."

"What's *coherent* mean?" William asked.

"Clearheaded. In a few days I'm sure she'll tell you all about it." He motioned to the door. "For right now, let's leave her to rest in the capable hands of Mrs. Brown."

William looked reluctantly towards the bedroom.

"Come on, Mr. Trenton," James said. "I'll drive you home in the wagon."

"I promise to take good care of her," Mrs. Brown reassured, "and you can come back day after tomorrow for a visit."

William put on his hat and headed for the door. "Actually I'll be back tomorrow to finish picking the squash."

* * *

In her fevered dreams Philomene Johnson could not tell if she had actually come home, or if she were still in the hospital in Antwerp, or on a ship crossing the ocean. At times Mr. Davis would come and stand by her bedside and put cool towels on her head, but she knew that was impossible, as she had left him in Antwerp. Her mind drifted again as it had in the hospital—drifted relentlessly. The face of the doctor . . . the gray window of her hospital room coming in and out of focus . . . the sound of Mr. Davis's voice. *I'm so sorry you were hurt, Philomene. The Germans dropped bombs from a zeppelin. They were targeting the royal family, but my sources tell me they're fine, and you're going to be fine. You are. Please rest and get well.* The anxious voice floated away through a cold autumn mist, and she found herself walking in the beauty of the Petit Sablon. Tendrils of fog swirled about, distorting the images of the many bronze statues, turning them into menacing ghosts. No other person intruded on her solitude, yet she felt as though she were being watched. She turned her head slowly from right to left, peering through the haze for the slightest movement. The water from the fountain pounded in her ears, blocking every other sound. She looked down into the pool and was horrified as scarlet plumes of blood reached out into the water. A body was floating in the pool—floating languidly to where she was standing! She wanted to run, to close her eyes, but she was para-lyzed—captivated by the hideous sight. The corpse kept moving towards her as if pushed by an invisible hand. Bile rushed into Philomene's throat and pressed against her clamped teeth as she stared down into the cadaverous face. *No! No! It can't be. It can't.* She strug-gled to wrench her eyes from the long, pale fingers suspended in the bloody water, and the light brown hair floating like seaweed around the face of Edith Cavell.

Philomene Johnson flung out her hand and felt someone grab it.

"Miss Johnson," a young voice called to her, "Miss Johnson, it's all right. Me and Mrs. Brown are right here with ya."

Philomene opened her eyes onto the face of innocence. "Where . . . where am I?"

"You're home. Miss Johnson," William Trenton assured her. "Right as rain, you're home."

Chapter Twenty-Seven

It was the twenty-fifth of September, and Eleanor was coming to stay! Her last letter had said the train would be arriving in Salt Lake City at 4:50 in the afternoon. This very afternoon! Alaina pinned on her brown felt hat and took a final look into the mirror. Though she was only three months pregnant her skirts were all becoming too tight for comfort. Soon she would have to hand them all over to Mother Erickson and let her do the maternity alterations. Maternity alterations! She couldn't believe how happy she was even with the illness and swollen ankles. And now Elly was coming to stay!

When Eleanor's letter had arrived several weeks earlier, Alaina had been heartbroken by the injustice her sister was facing.

September 10, 1914

Dear Alaina,

I have sad news to relate. Please don't be alarmed, as the health of everyone here is fine and the house on Beacon Street still stands as a monument to opulence.

At that point Alaina had put down the letter to chuckle at Elly's "professor" words. How she missed her sister's optimism and intelligence. She returned quickly to the letter to find out what sad news Eleanor had to relate.

Actually the turmoil in the home is my doing. For the last month I have been leading a secret life and am now discovered. On the

*sly I was attending the Mormon Church services and also
helping the Civic League with charitable work. Both of these
activities I knew Mother would not approve, but I went against
the obedience required of me and must now bear the conse-
quences. Please do not think ill of me, dear sister. I am normally
considerate of rules, but these two events were of such importance
that I took the risk.*

*Upon discovering my treachery, Mother and Aunt Ida concluded
my behavior was causing sufficient upheaval in the home to
necessitate my being sent away.*

Sent away? Alaina read the sentence again to be sure she hadn't
confused the words.

*. . . to necessitate my being sent away. They want to send me to a
boarding school in Virginia, but that would be torture for me. I
must be around family. I must. As it is unlikely there would be
room or occupation for me on Mr. Regosi's ranch, I am writing to
inquire if there might be a place for me in Salt Lake City.*

At these words Alaina had come out of her seat and yelled for
Nephi. She ran through the kitchen and out the back door to the
pasture, waving the letter as she went. Mother Erickson came from
her sewing machine and followed her to the yard. Nephi bolted from
the barn and ran to her, fearing something was wrong.

"What? What is it?" he shouted as he neared her.

She smiled joyfully and waved the papers. "It's a letter! A letter
from Eleanor!"

He stopped dead in his tracks. "A letter? You scare the wits out of
me over a letter?"

She laughed as she threw her arms around his neck and kissed
him several times on his face. "I'm sorry. I didn't mean to frighten
you." She was giggling at him when Mother Erickson joined them.

"Are you all right, little pumpkin?" she asked with concern.

Nephi grunted and Alaina laughed. "Yes! Yes, I'm fine." She put
an arm around Mother Erickson's shoulder and gave her a squeeze.

"It's a letter from my sister Eleanor, and I need to read it to you." She related the first part and began reading with the section about being sent away and Mr. Regosi's ranch. Alaina slowed as she read the next lines knowing this would be the part to involve them all.

> *. . . I am writing to inquire if there might be a place for me in Salt Lake City. I would not want to inconvenience anyone, and would be grateful to be set to work at any task to earn my keep. I know I am asking a great deal, Laina, but I cannot imagine being sent so far away from those I love.*

Alaina struggled to keep herself from tears as she read the final lines.

> *I promise I would work hard and not be a burden.*
>
> *I love you,*
> *Elly*

Nephi gathered Alaina into his arms while Mother Erickson patted her back.

"She sounds like the dearest thing on the face of the earth," her mother-in-law said quietly.

Alaina nodded and stepped back from her husband's embrace. "Dear and kind and smart. How could they send her away? I don't understand."

"That's not for us to question or judge," Mother Erickson said, taking her hand. "No indeed. It's our job to find a place for her."

Alaina's face lit up. "Is that possible?"

Mother Erickson smiled. "Well, it's interesting how the Lord works. I was just in the temple the other day praying about what we were supposed to do about Grandfather Erickson."

Alaina turned to look at Nephi for enlightenment, but he just shrugged.

Mother Erickson winked at the pair and continued. "Well, you know he hasn't been feeling very well of late, and with Miss Sarah being so far along in her time, it's been hard for her to care for him properly. I was praying for inspiration to figure out this problem, and here comes the answer. Here it comes to us right through the postal service."

"You mean Eleanor could care for Grandfather Erickson?" Alaina asked.

"Perfect solution as far as I can see," her mother-in-law answered. "He has that small extra bedroom, and you said she was thinking of becoming a nurse."

Alaina's look of joy deepened. "It would be perfect!" she said, giving Mother Erickson a hug. She stepped back, and her mood sobered. "Perhaps we should wait and see what Grandfather has to say first," Alaina conjectured, her voice taking on a measured tone.

Patience Erickson tapped her fingers to her lips and narrowed her eyes. "Well, that's a thought. Yes, ma'am, that's truly a thought, but you know what I'm thinking?"

"What?" Alaina asked, watching her intently.

"I'm thinking you should write to your sister and tell her to come straightaway. There will be plenty of time for Grandfather Erickson to give his approval before her arrival."

Alaina laughed at the mischievous look on Mother Erickson's face. She turned to Nephi, who nodded his acceptance.

Alaina gave a big whoop and hugged Nephi tightly. "Oh! I love you!" Then she hugged Mother Erickson. "Thank you. Thank you so much!" She turned and ran for the house.

Nephi laughed. "Where are you off to?" he called after her.

"To write a letter!"

* * *

Alaina's thoughts were brought to the present as she heard the truck pull up in front of the house. She looked out their bedroom window and saw Nephi jumping out of the driver's seat. It was strange to see him there, as Elias usually did the driving while everyone else in the family went along as passengers. Today, though, it would just be her and Nephi, and in a few hours—Eleanor! Alaina was so excited she was making herself sick. She made a conscious effort to calm her breathing and finish getting ready. *It won't do for me to faint on the station platform.* She heard the back door open and

Nephi come into the kitchen. He hurried through the front room to their bedroom.

"Are you ready?' he asked when he saw her.

"I am," she answered, picking up her coat from the bed.

He helped her on with it. "Are you all right?" he asked, wrapping his arms around her from the back. "You're trembling."

"I'm just excited," she said laying her hands over his. "You and your mother are so dear to me. How can I ever thank you for this kindness?"

He kissed her neck. "I think blessing our lives with a baby is more than enough."

She giggled and turned to kiss him.

He held her shoulders and gently pushed her back. "Don't do that," he said with a grin, "or you might make us late for the train."

She went to kiss him again, and there was a knock on the door frame.

Mother Erickson stood there chuckling. "I wasn't trying to intrude, but you make that difficult with the door wide open." She held out a piece of dark blue fabric. "I was wondering if you might want to take this along."

Alaina knew immediately what it was, and the poignant memory of her sweet mother-in-law standing on the station platform holding the handmade California flag came vividly back to her. She stepped forward and took the material. Several moments passed as she struggled to get her emotions under control. "I can't tell you what this means to me. Not just the flag, but taking me in, and having such a fine son, and now opening your heart to include my sister." She hesitated, but no one intruded on the silence. "There was so much pain when our father died and the farm was sold, I thought I'd never be happy again . . . never find anything to . . . to hope for." Nephi moved forward and put his arm around her waist. Alaina reached out and took Mother Erickson's hand, managing a trembling smile. "You are a wonderful person."

Mother Erickson looked uncomfortable with the praise. "Well . . . well, that's kind of you, little sweet pea, but in truth I think Nephi got four aces when he married you."

Nephi chuckled. "Mama, you make it sound like I won her in a poker match." He took Alaina by the arm and moved to the door. "Now if you women are done sniveling, we have a train to meet."

* * *

A cold wind was blowing across the train station platform, causing greeters to huddle together by the ticket house. Some were actually inside the lobby keeping warm by the stove. Nephi had asked Alaina numerous times if she wanted to wait indoors, but she always declined, saying she wanted to see the train coming from its very farthest point.

She stood with the California State flag draped over one shoulder and a flush of color on her cheeks. "Look!" she said excitedly, as she pointed to train personnel emerging onto the platform with dollies and carts ready to help the arriving passengers.

Nephi nodded. "Yep, anytime now."

Within minutes a distant rumble could be heard, and the people in the ticket office spilled out onto the platform.

"There it is!" a young boy yelled, and everyone turned to peer down the tracks. Details on the heavy metal locomotive could soon be seen, and Alaina took the flag off her shoulder and began waving it in front of her, being careful to keep it low enough to not block her view.

"Do you see her? Do you see her?" she asked Nephi as the train slowed in front of them, and people's faces could be seen in the windows.

"Not yet," he answered, trying to catch a glimpse of Eleanor for his wife's sake.

Alaina was fairly jumping up and down now—her expression a mixture of delight and worry. "What if she missed the train in Ogden?"

The whistle blew and the train hissed to a stop. The workers moved forward, bringing down the metal steps, affixing loading planks, and unlatching baggage doors. Passengers began disembarking almost immediately, and Alaina moved to the side of a group of people to get a better view. She looked from one portal to the next without satisfaction. "Do you see her?" she called to Nephi.

He shook his head.

The next moment a hand shot out of a clump of people clustered around the bottom of a step unit. "Alaina!" a voice called, "Alaina!"

Alaina turned to look as Eleanor politely pushed her way past a burly man and his wife. Alaina was stunned for a moment by the sight of her younger sister and knew why she hadn't recognized her straight-away. She had been searching for a thin slip of a girl with country clothing and a straw hat, but here was a polished young woman, still tall and lithe of form but exhibiting a more womanly figure and clothes of style and sophistication. Then she saw Eleanor's sunshine smile and she was back home racing to be queen of the county fair. "Elly!" she shouted, rushing forward and grabbing her sister in a joyful embrace. "I told you! I told you it wouldn't be forever!" She wept. "I told you."

Eleanor was laughing and crying at the same time, both young women oblivious of everything around them.

Nephi came up shaking his head and laughing. "Somebody'd think you were glad to see each other."

Eleanor broke from Alaina's embrace and without hesitation hugged Nephi tightly.

He stepped back, a rush of color in his cheeks. "Excuse me, young woman, but do I know you?"

Eleanor laughed. "Am I that changed?"

Nephi's eyebrows rose, and he looked at Alaina. "What would you say, dear wife?"

Alaina nodded. "Elly, I hardly recognized you."

"It's just the fancy clothes," Eleanor said dismissively. "Aunt Ida insisted I bring my new wardrobe." She looked at them both with tenderness. "I can't believe I'm really here. I've missed you so much."

"We've missed you too," Alaina said, taking her hand, "and I can't wait for you to meet Mother Erickson, and Grandpa Erickson, and Sarah."

Eleanor was aware of the obvious exclusion of Elias's name, but she didn't mention it; she only squeezed Alaina's hand and smiled. "And a baby," she said, a look of wonder on her face. "What an infinitely fine thing."

Alaina's thoughts flew back to the day in the pear grove when Eleanor had first used that "professor" word—a day when she had worked side by side with her father. Alaina steeled herself against the rush of emotion. She knew Eleanor's arrival would bring memories of the farm and their life there, but she was determined not to wallow in pity or bitter reproach, but cherish all the joy with which her soul had been endowed by her time in that beautiful place. She smiled at her sister. "It is an infinitely fine thing, even when I'm sick."

Eleanor locked her arm in her sister's. "Well, aren't you lucky that I'm here to take care of you then?"

"So lucky," Alaina answered.

Over the next hour as they gathered Eleanor's belongings, stored them in the truck, and drove to Grandfather Erickson's, the girls shared a myriad of experiences. Alaina talked about Miss Titus, learning to cook, and going to the circus, while Eleanor told her about Bib, Ina Bell, and Kerri, Uncle Cedrick's library, and working with Mrs. Antonia. Once in a while Nephi would get a word or two into the conversation, but mostly he just drove and smiled at the happy chatter.

As he turned into Grandfather Erickson's drive the talking ceased, and Eleanor sat forward in her seat.

"Oh, Alaina," she gasped. "It is magical. It's the most magical little house I've ever seen."

"And wait until you see it in the spring with the trees and flowers in blossom."

Nephi ran around to open the truck door for them as Mother Erickson came out onto the porch. "Oh, look! Mother's walked over to greet us!" Nephi said helping Eleanor out.

"She's a very cute woman," Eleanor whispered to Alaina when she joined her.

"And kindness itself," Alaina whispered back, waving to Mother Erickson.

"Hello, Mother!" Nephi called.

"Hello, son," she answered brightly. "I see you brought home a truckload of sunshine."

Eleanor giggled.

"Yes, ma'am, I did," Nephi said, taking Eleanor by the arm and bringing her to the house.

Mother Erickson smiled warmly as they drew near. "We can't tell you how nice it is that you've come to stay with us, Miss Eleanor."

Eleanor blinked at the honesty of the sentiment, enjoying the total lack of guile she felt in this woman's presence. "Oh, no, Mrs. Erickson, it is so nice that you would take me in," she answered running her hand over one of the enchanting carved posts.

Mother Erickson winked at her. "Well. I don't know. We felt mighty lucky to have one of the Lund girls, and now we have two. Seems to me we're double blessed."

"Just don't wish for three Lund girls," Alaina said, bringing Eleanor's satchel to the porch, "or you might get more than you bargained for."

"We'll just have to pray that Miss Kathryn grows into her potential," Eleanor said kindly.

"See, I told you," Alaina said. "Eleanor's the good one."

"And you're the industrious one," Eleanor answered.

"And you're the intelligent one," Alaina countered.

Mother Erickson was enjoying the sisterly exchange when a cold gust of wind blew down from the canyon. "Oh my! I hope winter's not coming early this year," she growled, drawing her shawl close. She nodded at Eleanor. "So are you ready to get in out of the cold and meet Grandfather Erickson, Miss Eleanor?"

"Yes, ma'am," Eleanor answered sedately.

"Then in we go." Mother Erickson turned to open the front door and hurry them all inside.

Eleanor was just as pleased with the inside of the house as the outside. The walls were plain white, and the wood floors were covered in simple braided rugs. The furniture looked comfortable but unadorned. She could feel that the rooms were filled with good memories and companionship.

"This way," Mother Erickson was saying. Eleanor brought her mind back to the moment and followed Alaina's mother-in-law to the back of the house. "He's sitting in his bedroom. It's warmer back there."

Eleanor tried not to be nervous, tried to remember all the wonderful things Alaina had told her about the august Danish man; tried telling herself that he was a believer just like her father. It was this last thought on which she'd hung her confidence. This man had listened to the words of the gospel, had read the writings of Nephi and Moroni, and in a country far away had embraced the truth he'd found there. Eleanor took a deep breath and prayed for her knees to stop shaking.

They walked into the room and found Lars Erickson sitting in a rocking chair of his own design and carving. He looked up from the book he was reading to assess the young woman in front of him, his face an unreadable mask.

"Lars," Patience Erickson said, "this is Eleanor Lund."

Eleanor moved to him and without pause took the hand he offered in greeting.

Alaina was surprised at this gesture from Grandfather Erickson. When they had first met he'd kept his gnarled hands hidden away under his blanket.

Eleanor didn't flinch at the bent and swollen fingers, but cupped the large hand in the two of hers. "Ah, a reader," she said eyeing the book on his lap. "I like you already."

A slight smile played about the patriarch's mouth as he looked intently into his caretaker's face. She looked back at him without reservation.

"You're not afraid of the big, gruff Danish man?" he barked.

Eleanor leaned over and whispered something in his ear, upon which he immediately broke into rumbling laughter. Eleanor stood straight and waited for him to look at her. "So, do I get to stay?" she asked.

"Yah. Yah, you can stay," he chuckled. "You're not very sturdy, but you make up for it in character."

"And I can cook, too."

Alaina looked at her sister as though she'd never seen her before. She had gained so much confidence over the past months, and Alaina wondered if she herself had changed as drastically.

"Well, now that's decided," Mother Erickson said, "let's get you settled. Nephi, you and Alaina take Eleanor and her things and get her moved into the spare bedroom."

"Yes, ma'am," Nephi answered. "This way, Miss Lund."

Eleanor laid her hand on Grandfather Erickson's. "Thank you for letting me live in your beautiful cottage," she said softly. "I feel as though I've stepped into a fairy tale."

Grandfather nodded, and Eleanor left with Nephi and Alaina to set up her room.

When they'd gone, Lars looked at his daughter-in-law and smiled. "I like her, Patience."

"I like her too."

"Yah, she is funny little ting."

"What on earth did she whisper to you?" Mother Erickson asked.

The big man chuckled and picked up the book from his lap. "She said how could she be afraid of anyone who read Shakespeare."

Chapter
Twenty-Eight

Harvest time was over, and half the fruit from the diligent trees on the Lund farm lay rotting on the frosted October ground.

Frederick Robinson, his son Daniel, and James Lund had left their own labor many an afternoon to salvage a quarter of the crop for shipment out of Martell. The money garnered from the sale was deposited in the First Federal Bank in Sutter Creek and used for the upkeep of Moccasin, Titus, and Friar Tuck.

Folks from neighboring farms had also taken fruit to bolster their winter storage and diminish the unnatural sin of waste. It wasn't as if they were stealing—Mr. Blackhurst was uncaring of the bounty as he sat in his office in Sacramento figuring numbers and purchases. He'd sold the property to a family from Grass Valley who wouldn't be moving onto the place before spring, and, to minimize any further outlay on his side of the bargain, he'd authorized Mr. Clayborn, the caretaker, to sell all the livestock and clear off the place by September. The cantankerous overseer had done just that, leaving the home and outbuildings in disrepair.

James walked around the deserted place with an anger itching in his fingers. He was angry with Mr. Clayborn, angry with his father for dying, angry with himself that he hadn't seen the glory of Eden when he'd walked its ground every day. He looked across the faded meadow as a cold wind picked at the withered vegetation, knowing that soon a blessing of snow would cover the unkempt fields and disregarded orchard in a blanket of dormancy.

Friar Tuck snorted and pawed the ground, and James ran a comforting hand down his shoulder. "I know. You don't like the state of things either." He kicked a stone that then tumbled across the ground, striking the wood of the porch steps. "Whatta ya say we get out of here?" He pulled himself onto the saddle and turned Tuck toward the main gate.

"Let's stop by the Robinsons," James said to the horse. "They'll want to know the state of things."

Twenty minutes later James rode onto the Robinson property at a full gallop, using the fast pace and the sting of the wind as an escape from his harsh feelings. Fifty yards from the house he saw Daniel on the high point of the roof fixing shakes, and he lifted his hat and called a greeting, to which Daniel turned carefully and waved. James liked Daniel Chart and found it interesting how he'd come to respect the caliber of his friend even more since establishing himself on the Regosi ranch. James supposed it was because the demanding work he'd taken on with the horses made him feel more like a man and diminished the span of years between them.

James suspected that at one time Daniel had been partial to his sister Alaina, but their relationship had changed abruptly with Alaina's engagement and marriage to Nephi Erickson. James shook his head. Life could surely throw out some sore trials.

At least Alaina seemed to be happier in Salt Lake City. Her last letter said that she and Nephi were expecting a baby sometime in March. *My sister expecting a baby?* He couldn't imagine it. He wondered if he should tell Daniel the news, then thought better of it. Alaina had also written that Eleanor was leaving Aunt Ida's home and moving to Salt Lake City. Some sort of rift had occurred for which Eleanor bore the punishment. James thought of his reserved younger sister, and found it hard to imagine a serious misdeed of which she would be capable.

James tied Friar Tuck's lead rope to the corral railing and moved over to the tall ladder propped against the side of the house. Daniel was halfway down as James approached. "Hey! Don't stop working on my account," he called to the descending figure.

"It's just about dinnertime," Daniel shot back. "I suspect that's why you came by."

James smiled. "Yep, I have to admit, the smell of your mama's cooking yanked me right off the Carson Track."

Daniel stepped onto the ground and set down his toolbox. "Well, we're always glad for company. Put Mr. Tuck in the paddock and come on in."

James obliged without any argument. Edna Chart Robinson's cooking was becoming renowned in the area, and James found it interesting how many of the prudish ladies who had once snubbed Edna Robinson for being a divorced woman now spoke of her cooking with high regard and even asked for a recipe occasionally.

As James and Daniel were washing up at the sink, Frederick Robinson came in from his chores, stamping and muttering under his breath. The man was six feet four inches tall and weighed well over two hundred pounds, so it wasn't surprising that his muttering took on the tone of a menacing growl.

James gave Daniel a mock look of fright, because even though he knew Daniel's stepfather to be the soul of goodness, he wouldn't want to be on the wrong side of him in an argument.

"Edna!" the big man barked as he walked to her. "Do you know what that John Drakerman wants to pay me for one of my prize sows?"

Mrs. Robinson turned from the stove. "I can't imagine, Mr. Robinson, but right now it is of no consequence."

"No consequence!" he sputtered.

"No," she answered, staring him in the face, "considering we have company."

"Company?" Mr. Robinson looked over and spotted James. The anger on his face dropped away immediately, replaced by a good-natured smile. "James Lund! How are you, lad? You look good. Yes, indeed. Look at the muscle on you."

James grinned. "Don't be expecting an arm-wrestling match, Mr. Robinson. I'm no fool."

Frederick Robinson laughed as he went to wash up. "Ah, come on now, a young fellow like you? This old man would be no match, no match at all." He moved to the sink to wash as his wife tutted at him.

"Now, leave the boy alone, Frederick. He won't want to be staying for dinner if you keep challenging him."

"Oh, there's no chance of that, Mrs. Robinson," James said quickly. "I'd take on a bear for a bowl of that soup."

Mr. Robinson laughed. "See there, Edna! Your beef barley soup wins out again."

They all sat down around the big kitchen table, James next to Daniel with Daniel's half sister Grace on his other side. The group fell into easy conversation as the meal progressed, the younger Robinson children listening but not talking, as was their place. Daniel's full sister, Anne, was sixteen and of an age to join in the talk, but kept quiet out of shyness. It always amazed James how different Anne was from Daniel. Where Daniel was outgoing and headstrong, Anne rarely looked a person in the eye and spoke only when spoken to. Their coloring was the same: rich brown hair and soft brown eyes, and they both possessed well-defined high cheekbones and full lips. Anne obviously followed her mother's petite body frame and height, being only five feet three inches or so, while Daniel was of average height.

"Is Miss Johnson's health improving?" Mr. Robinson was asking as James's attention came back to the table.

"Yes, sir. I believe so," James answered, taking the plate of rolls Daniel was passing him. "I haven't seen her for about five days."

"Heard it's been a struggle," Mrs. Robinson added.

James nodded. "Yes, ma'am. The infection was bad."

"She's been home, what, about a month now?" Daniel asked him.

"About." James shook his head. "I don't know how she made it all the way from Belgium in that condition."

"She's a brave woman," Anne said quietly. Everyone turned to look at her, waiting for more words from the timid girl, but she kept her head down and stared at her soup bowl.

"Yes, Miss Chart," James said after another few moments of silence, "a very brave woman."

Anne's eyes flicked up to James's face then back down to her bread, which she picked up to butter.

"Such a tragedy, what's happening over there in Europe," Mr. Robinson said. "So many countries getting involved. The Brits are in the fray now, from what Mr. Greggs tells me."

"Well, I'm just glad it has nothing to do with us," Mrs. Robinson said, ladling soup into their youngest son's bowl.

Daniel hurriedly swallowed a mouthful of food. "I don't think it's right for President Wilson to take such a strong stand about not getting involved. Aggression can't be tolerated, Mother. I mean, how can he sit safe over here and lecture both sides about morality when people are dying?"

"Glad to see you have an opinion, son," Frederick Robinson chuckled as he thumped Daniel on the back, "but I think I agree with your mother. Let them tend to their own affairs over there. I would hate to see you and James sent to fight another man's war."

"Well, at least the president should offer to send armaments," Daniel scowled, unwilling to abandon his entire argument.

"Or food shipments," his mother said, nodding. "Food shipments would be appropriate."

The conversation shifted to concerns over the price of pigs and whether the roof repair would be completed before the first big storm. As James sat eating soup, his thoughts returned to the farm and troubles closer to home. Mrs. Robinson was right. Why worry about a conflict that had nothing to do with them? He glanced up to see Anne Chart watching him, but before his smile got halfway across the table her eyes were again on her soup bowl.

* * *

Steps were the hardest thing to navigate with her stiff leg and her cane, but Philomene Johnson was determined to honor the invitation of Mrs. Tullis to speak to her class concerning her experiences in Belgium. She was also determined to walk the distance to the intermediate school under her own steam. Now, as she struggled up the last of the entrance steps, she wondered if pride was not indeed one of man's greatest follies.

Many of the students she would address today were hers from the previous year: Mr. Flynn, Miss Carrillo, and Mr. Trenton. During her weeks of recovery, Philomene had been notified by Mrs. Brown that several of the youngsters had stopped by to leave notes and wish her well, but other than Mr. Trenton, Philomene had not wanted any of her students to see her incapacitated. In this instance, it was regard for their sensibilities, not pride, which prompted her decision. She hoped now in speaking to them that some of their worries would be eliminated.

Afternoon classes had already begun as Philomene entered the building, so she had the hallway to herself. As she hobbled to the appropriate classroom, she evaluated her mixed feelings about being back in school. She was sorry to have missed the beginning of the academic year with its bustle and expectations; on the other hand, she was grateful to be alive and looking forward to the possibility of taking over her class after the Christmas holidays. Her mind flew back several years to decorating the one-room schoolhouse in Pine Grove for Christmas: pine boughs and cones bordering the windows and chalkboard, silver sleigh bells on the door, and even a small Christmas tree in the corner decorated with stars and snowflakes cut out by the children.

"Miss Johnson?" A sweet voice brought her from her reverie, and she turned to see Mrs. Tullis standing at her classroom door. "I saw you walk past," Mrs. Tullis continued kindly. "I thought you might have forgotten which room was mine."

Philomene smiled. "No, I was just lost in a daydream. I'm glad you caught me—I might have walked clear to Amador City."

Miriam Tullis laughed. Philomene liked her laugh. In fact she had liked the young teacher since her first day of teaching several years ago. One would never imagine that behind that shock of blond curly hair, which she always wore tied back with brightly colored ribbons, was a mind of brilliance and discipline. Philomene had had the opportunity, as senior instructor, to observe Miriam's teaching prowess on several occasions that first year, and marked her able without reservation. Philomene reached the door that Mrs. Tullis swung wide to receive her. The venerated educator moved into the sanctuary of the classroom and was met by faces filled with smiles and trepidation. Then to Miss Johnson's amazement, the students stood as one and applauded. William Trenton held his arms above his head and clapped enthusiastically, while some of the boys called out, "Bravo! Bravo!" and several of the girls cried. Philomene Johnson turned to look at Mrs. Tullis, who had joined her students in their heartfelt admiration. Miriam leaned close and whispered, "No higher praise can thus be given than from the souls we've turned toward heaven."

As Mr. Vanderveur, the head schoolmaster, drove her home later that afternoon, Philomene kept her emotions in check by avoiding thoughts of that touching display, turning them instead to an evaluation of her presentation. She had started with a travelogue, passing around pictures she'd taken with her own Kodak camera, and, if she did say so herself, she'd captured much of the wonder of Brussels. The young ladies were thrilled with the grand buildings and plazas, while the boys were delighted by the comical statue of Mannekin Pis. As the subject matter turned to the beginning of the war, a somber feeling settled on the group. Martin Flynn was interested in how the German soldiers marched, while Mary Carrillo was skeptical that homes and towns were actually burned.

"I know, Miss Carrillo," Miss Johnson agreed. "It is difficult to comprehend. May I read to you from the one and only letter I've received from my aunt since returning home?" When all the heads nodded assent, Philomene reached into the pocket of her skirt and brought out the missive. She glanced over several pages before finding the passage she wished to read.

> *While Brussels has escaped the torch, dear niece, the same cannot be said of other places. Do you remember my friend Monsignor Jules de Becker—silver hair, always such a striking figure in his black soutane and red sash? He was the rector of the college in Louvain.*

Here Miss Johnson stopped reading and moved to the chalkboard. She drew a rough outline of the country of Belgium and put a star to indicate the location of several cities—Brussels, Antwerp, and Louvain—writing their names in bold letters.

"Louvain, students, is a charming town established in the eleventh century and filled with beautiful Gothic architecture. They have an exceptional university built in 1425."

"That's before Columbus!" William Trenton blurted out.

The class laughed.

Miss Johnson turned back to the chalkboard to hide her smile. "Yes, Mr. Trenton, before Columbus. There is a magnificent library connected to the university, the Halles de l'Université." She wrote the name on the board. "There were about two hundred and thirty thousand volumes in its collection, including eight hundred ancient manuscripts and books." She wrote these numbers on the board and turned back to the class. Mary's hand was in the air. "Yes, Miss Carrillo?"

"Two hundred and thirty thousand books?" she asked in amazement.

"Yes, Miss Carrillo. Louvain was a great center of learning." Miss Johnson found her place again in the letter. "Remember, we were reading of my aunt's friend, Monsignor Jules de Becker."

> *He barely escaped with several colleagues from the university, bringing us word of great destruction in the city. Thousands of houses burned to the ground, including his brother's and his father's house. He saw friends tortured, and old men and women were shot as they ran. As he hid on the outskirts of the city, he watched as a fire ascended above the rooftops with a thick column of black smoke and a whirlwind of sparks glowing in every direction. He said he looked up into the sky and saw fire-rimmed bits of paper. As they blew down around his feet he picked one up and realized he was looking at a piece of ancient manuscript. Oh, dear niece, the look on his face as he told us this story was utter desolation. "The library . . . the library," he choked. "They burned our glorious library."*

Miss Johnson stopped reading. There was no movement or sound in the room. As the eyes of her audience stared at her blankly, Philomene knew their minds were in Louvain watching priceless bits of parchment falling out of a soot-choked sky. When she spoke to them again, her voice was low and gentle. "You may wonder why I tell you these sad and bitter occurrences." A few students coughed, and Mary Carrillo laid her head down on her arms. "I know it is difficult to hear of pain and death and destruction . . . truly difficult, but my question is, what has it to do with us?" Mary's head came up, her eyes red rimmed and her lips trembling. Miss Johnson persisted. "It isn't our conflict. We did not start it or encourage it. The bullets and the fire do not reach us here."

"But . . ."

Miss Johnson stopped. "Yes, Miss Carrillo?"

"But those people are suffering," she said, her voice quavering with tears.

No one in the class laughed or disagreed with her, and Philomene looked into their faces. "And what are we to do about that?"

"Help them," the young girl said softly. There was muttered agreement from several of her classmates.

"What would you propose?" Miss Johnson asked, pulling down the atlas map of the world. "We are here," she said pointing to America, "and the war is way over there." She traced a line across the ocean to Belgium.

"We have boats!" Mr. Flynn called out.

"And money," someone called from the back.

"And guns," William Trenton said fiercely.

Miss Johnson held up her hand, and the room grew still. "We are passionate about this war because I have made it personal for you. I have brought the words and feelings of people who are actually in the battle."

"Yeah, and they almost killed you," William growled, his jaw set in anger.

Miss Johnson took a deep breath. "Yes, Mr. Trenton, and it was a terrifying ordeal, and if America was to get involved in this European war it may mean sending our young men over to fight and be killed by bullets and bombs and shrapnel."

No one spoke. "It is just this issue that our president and others in government are debating. And for now they say we will remain neutral."

A tear slid down Miss Carrillo's face. "But those people are suffering."

Miss Johnson walked to her and took her hand. "Yes, Mary, I agree with you. The human heart sees injustice and longs to reach out and remedy the pain. That is why I honored Mrs. Tullis's request to come and share these things with you. We are of one mind on this issue and felt you were old enough to think beyond your own self-interests. It is time for you to think of the welfare of others—to cultivate compassion for people far away who do not speak the same language or live as you do."

"But aren't we all God's children?" Mr. Flynn asked, not bothering to raise his hand.

"Yes. All God's children, Mr. Flynn, on all sides of the conflict—*all* God's children."

The students sat, unspeaking, pondering this difficult concept.

Philomene's thoughts were brought to the present as the wagon jolted to a stop and she felt a stab of pain in her side.

"Sorry, Miss Johnson," Mr. Vandeveur was saying. "I should have warned you. You were so deep in thought I didn't want to bother you."

"Not to worry, Mr. Vandeveur," Philomene assured him, as he came around to her side of the wagon to help her down. "It only troubles me once in a while now."

Her feet touched the ground, and she supported herself with her cane. In truth she was tired beyond measure. Perhaps her first venture out had been too ambitious. All she wanted to do was crawl into bed and sleep for three days.

"It was so good to see you at the school today," Mr. Vandeveur said brightly as he walked her to her house. "Can we expect you full-time next year?"

"I hope so," Philomene answered, stopping at the door. "We shall see what Dr. McIntyre has to say. Thank you for bringing me home, Mr. Vandeveur."

"My pleasure, Miss Johnson," the schoolmaster said, tipping his hat. "My pleasure."

Philomene stood for a moment on her porch watching Mr. Vandeveur's wagon pull away and listening to the rumble of thunder announcing an approaching storm. It sounded too much like distant cannon fire, and she moved quickly into her little cottage, shutting the door against fear and memory.

Chapter Twenty-Nine

"You drew the short stick, Ina Bell Latham. Don't be denyin' it," Kerri said, fixing a stern eye on her friend.

"Yes, but I thought the short stick got to decide what they wanted to do," Ina Bell whimpered.

"Nice try," Bib chuckled, checking again the length of sticks before throwing them into the trash bin.

"Ah, no," Kerri said, smiling. "Sure enough, the short stick gets to take care of the Dragon for the day. Besides, I did it yesterday."

Kerri returned to organizing china on the breakfast trays, and Ina Bell followed like a puppy. "But she scares me."

Kerri scoffed. "Scares ya? What, that poor sufferin' woman?"

"She always glares at me when I'm cleaning, and sometimes she says the strangest things."

Kerri McKee drew a deep breath. "I know," she said sincerely. "I sort of feel sad for her."

"You do?"

"Aye. She's not doin' well without Eleanor to calm her. And it's right near the time her husband died, now isn't it?"

Ina Bell nodded and crossed herself. "I guess we need to show her some compassion."

Kerri patted her friend's hand. "And you're the one to do it. You can be gentle with her when all I want to do is tell her off for makin' such a mess of things."

Ina Bell said a silent prayer, then resolutely picked up the tray and headed for the upstairs bedroom. When she reached the landing she stood for a moment assessing the quiet. *Perhaps she isn't awake yet,* Ina

Bell thought hopefully. *Perhaps I can just sneak in, leave the tray on the side table, and sneak out.* She tapped ever so lightly on Mrs. Lund's door, expecting no response. When she heard the muffled reply to enter, her heart sank. She offset the tray on her hip and opened the door. She moved efficiently into the room, avoiding any misstep that might bring a reprimand.

"Good morning, Mrs. Lund," she said with a curtsy as she set the tray on the table.

Elizabeth Lund was sitting up in bed with her knees hugged tightly to her chest, her hair falling long and tousled onto her shoulders. Ina Bell tried not to stare at her, but she looked painfully like a little girl who had just been scolded.

"Would you like me to pour you a cup?" the servant girl asked softly.

Mrs. Lund nodded, but did not speak.

Ina Bell poured the tea and carefully handed it over. She then moved to the window and slowly drew back the brocaded outer curtains. Pale morning light poured into the room, illuminating edges and details. When Ina Bell turned back to Mrs. Lund, she had to bite her lip to keep from crying out. On the left side of the woman's face and neck was a dried smear of blood. Ina Bell moved to her quickly and saw the same evidence of blood on the ivory linen of her pillow.

Ina Bell forced her voice into calmness. "Mrs. Lund, you have blood on your face and pillow. Do you know what happened? Are you cut?"

Elizabeth Lund looked at her blankly, the cup of tea forgotten in her hand.

Ina Bell took the cup, set it back on the tray, and moved to the washbasin. She thoroughly soaked a cloth and brought it to the bed. "Now, I'm just going to wash this a bit." Her hand trembled. "Should I get Mr. Palmer?"

Elizabeth Lund stiffened. "No."

"All right. All right then . . . just . . . just turn your head a little my way."

Elizabeth Lund complied, and Ina Bell could see a quantity of crusted blood around Mrs. Lund's nose. Her breathing slowed. "Oh . . . oh, it's just a nosebleed, ma'am. It's not serious." She began carefully wiping Elizabeth's nose and face. "I've had plenty of these in my time. My mother used to say it was because I was so high-strung."

Mrs. Lund whimpered and closed her eyes.

Ina Bell was suddenly back at home in memory, with her mother gently washing her face and holding back her hair, and she found herself mimicking the gestures and using the same words of comfort. "Though your sins be as scarlet they can be as white as snow. Don't you worry now; we'll have your face shining in no time. There . . . see there . . . almost done."

Elizabeth Lund put her head down on her knees as Ina Bell returned to the washbasin to rinse out the cloth. "Put your head up now," Ina Bell instructed upon her return, and Mrs. Lund followed the command obediently. There was a streak of blood in the grand woman's hair, and Ina Bell took the piece, massaging it gently between the folds of the cloth. "There now . . . see . . . that's looking better." She ran her fingers through the strands and hooked the hair behind Mrs. Lund's ear. "All clean now." She was amazed at how calm she felt. Normally just being in the presence of the Dragon, as Kerri called her, brought a sick feeling to the pit of her stomach, but this morning as she looked at the chalky face and red-rimmed eyes she felt only charity.

Mrs. Lund's hand came up and grasped Ina Bell by the wrist. The mouth opened to speak, but before any words escaped, a wash of tears coursed down her face. "My Samuel died."

Ina Bell was quiet, waiting for more. Finally she sat down on the edge of the bed. "Yes, ma'am, I know. Last year about this time."

Mrs. Lund nodded.

"I'm sorry, ma'am. It's such a hard cross to bear." Ina Bell wiped away some of the tears with the cloth.

Mrs. Lund stared at her. "What's your name?"

"Ina Bell Latham, ma'am."

"Latham? Did your mother and father serve our family?"

"Yes, ma'am, and my grandparents. Three generations of Lathams have served the Knight family," Ina Bell said proudly.

Elizabeth Lund sat taller. "You must find it totally inappropriate for me to be crying in front of you."

Ina Bell took a chance. "No ma'am, not at all. You've had a terrible time of it."

Elizabeth Lund sat back against the headboard. "Are your grandparents still alive, Miss Latham?"

Ina Bell nodded. "Yes, ma'am." She was amazed at Mrs. Lund's proper deportment and found it strange that the unbending root of privileged upbringing influenced a life so strongly that its tendrils could snake through grief, pain, and even madness.

Mrs. Lund turned her head to the window, and tears started anew. "Still working for my father? And are your parents still married and in love?"

"Yes, ma'am."

"I remember all of them. They were always good to me, even when I was . . . my Samuel was a good man. We met in this very house, in the parlor downstairs. At first I was offended by him . . . his clothing was plain, his manner unsophisticated . . . how stupid . . . how shallow and stupid."

Ina Bell wasn't sure she should be listening to such personal expressions, but she was held by the story and Mrs. Lund's emotion.

"After that first night, my brother-in-law Cedrick invited Samuel back." A faint smile brushed her mouth. "He became a regular visitor . . . so different from the other young men who courted me . . . always kind and genuine. Always . . . funny." She went to laugh but it came out as a strangled sob. "He . . . he could always make me feel better." She threw back the coverlet and struggled out of bed.

Ina Bell stood up.

Elizabeth Lund went to the window and shoved aside the lace undercurtains. "He saved me . . . he saved me . . . he came one day when I was in one of my dark moods." She wrapped her arms around herself. "And instead of leaving me like all the others did . . . instead of being repulsed at the sight of me, he held me tight and sang hymns. I could feel his heart . . . he smelled like sunlight." Ina Bell moved to her as she went down on her knees. ". . . Like sunlight, and he stayed with me until I could see the world again. He was sunlight, and I had to be with him so I could stand the world." She crawled to the window and laid her head against the cool glass. "Father and Mother didn't see . . . they saw only a farmer . . . not worthy of me. They . . . they said . . . not to marry him . . . not a proper choice. But I had to marry him . . . he could save me." Her hand beat on the glass. "They said no. No! I wouldn't be their daughter anymore. Not their daughter! They never wanted to see me again. Papa, please!"

Her nose started bleeding, splattering crimson blood onto the white nightgown. Ina Bell jumped up and ran for the cloth. "It's started again, Mrs. Lund!"

Elizabeth Lund absently wiped her hand across her face, smearing the blood into her tears. "I didn't want children . . . it was too difficult . . ." Ina Bell went to put the cloth to Mrs. Lund's face, and she batted it away. "Too difficult. But I knew Samuel wanted children . . . I needed to give something back because he saved me." She laid her bloody hand on the glass. "And now I've killed them."

Ina Bell whimpered in fright. "Mrs. Lund, stop now. Stop."

"Samuel went away, and I killed them."

Ina Bell took her arm. "Listen to me! You did no such thing! No such thing." Elizabeth Lund turned her head, and Ina Bell had to force herself not to cry. "Ma'am, your children are well. They're well."

A knock came at the door, and Ina Bell could hear Kerri McKee's muffled voice calling her name.

"Kerri!" Ina Bell yelled loudly. "Come in!"

The door opened immediately, and Miss McKee entered. She rushed forward when she saw the two women kneeling and the blood on the window. "Holy Saint Peter! What's happened?"

"Get Mr. Palmer!" Ina Bell snapped. "Have him get the doctor!"

"No!" Mrs. Lund said forcefully, grasping Ina Bell with a bloody hand. "They give me laudanum, and I don't want it. Please, please, don't . . . I promise to be good . . . I promise to be quiet."

The servant girls were stunned by her response.

"I promise," she said weakly, sitting back against the window.

"Here then," Ina Bell said, gently wiping blood from her face. "Let Miss McKee and myself get you cleaned up and back into bed."

Kerri looked quizzically at her friend, unbelieving of the tender tone in her voice.

"Come on, Kerri. Help me get her up," Ina Bell said, standing and handing Mrs. Lund the cloth. "Here, ma'am, hold that to your nose."

The two servants proceeded to lift Elizabeth Lund and walk her to the bed. They brought her a new nightdress and changed the soiled bed linen. Ina Bell made sure the bleeding had stopped and tied Mrs. Lund's hair back with a ribbon. The older woman complied with the servant girls' quiet efficiency like a tired child. Ina

Bell put her into bed while Kerri gathered the bloodied articles and the washbasin.

"Oh! Your tea's probably cool by now," Ina Bell said, touching her hand to the side of the pot. "Shall I bring you up a fresh pot?"

Mrs. Lund shook her head "No, thank you. I want to sleep."

Ina Bell curtsied. "Yes, ma'am. We'll inform Mr. Palmer that you're not to be disturbed before noon meal."

Mrs. Lund shut her eyes and lay back against her pillows. "Miss Latham," she said quietly, "I'm sorry to have burdened you."

"Nonsense, ma'am," Ina Bell said softly, picking up the tea tray. She looked over at the smear of blood on the window. "You rest now. I'll come back later to clean the room."

Mrs. Lund pulled the covers around her and curled herself into a ball as the girls moved silently out into the hallway. Ina Bell again set the tray on her hip and closed the door. She stood staring at the tea items, lost in thoughts and feelings—feelings of pity, compassion, and anger. The anger was directed at herself for all the times she had joined in the gossip about poor Mrs. Lund's condition, or laughed behind her back when she'd dressed inappropriately or forgotten to wear shoes. Ina Bell knew she had failed in her faith, and her heart ached with recrimination.

"Ina Bell Latham," Kerri said in a harsh whisper, "are you all right? Tell me what happened."

Ina Bell looked at her friend. "No, Kerri, I won't do that. I'll only say that Mrs. Lund has demons to fight that we cannot imagine, so we need to be kinder to her."

Kerri smiled. "Kinder to the Dragon?"

Ina Bell fixed her with a reprimanding stare. "You're not to call her that anymore."

Kerri looked shocked, and then saw the determination on Ina Bell's face. "Aye, all right. I was only kiddin'."

Ina Bell steadied herself and moved off down the hallway.

Kerri stared after her for a moment then back to the closed bedroom door. Her curiosity itched to know what had gone on in there, but the tone in Ina Bell's voice had indicated absolute discretion. Kerri figured Ina Bell would tell her eventually, as they had never kept secrets from each other, so she would just bide her time. She hefted the dirty laundry and followed after her companion's departing footsteps.

Chapter Thirty

"Whose truck is that?" Alaina asked Nephi as they came in sight of Sarah and Elias's house.

Nephi looked up, and his walking slowed. "My father's."

Alaina looked over at him, watching the tension in his jaw. "Oh," was all she could find to say.

"I should have known he'd come to the blessing." He stopped and retied the scarf around Alaina's neck. "Are you warm enough?"

She nodded. "We can go back if you'd like."

"Ha! And give my father more ammunition against me? No, thank you." He took her arm, and they started walking again. "Besides, I think it's time they met you."

"They?"

"Hmm. My father and his first wife. I'm sure she's come with him."

The warmth Alaina had felt moments before drained out of her like ice water, leaving her chilled from the top of her head to her toes. She had become comfortable with Mother and Grandfather Erickson's style of Mormonism and their total acceptance of her in her unperfected state. She didn't know if she was ready to meet Alma Erickson, who she imagined was simply an older version of Elias. She was sure Nephi's father would see her only as the selfish nonmember who had stolen away his son's chances for salvation. She pulled her coat tightly across her belly and forced herself to keep up with Nephi's pace. She also knew she was not looking forward to being scrutinized by Eunice Erickson, the first wife. From the few things Nephi had said of her, the woman was stoic and self-serving. Out of sheer curiosity Alaina had tried to extract further bits of information from Mother Erickson, but the kind soul would merely shake her head and say things like, "Well, Eunice has a great mind for business. She has certainly helped Alma make a success of that hardware store," or, "She keeps those children in line, yes indeed." Alaina thought she remembered being told that one of the girls from the first marriage was Nephi's age, Fran . . . Fern . . . something like that. There were actually six half brothers and sisters, but she couldn't remember their names because she and Nephi never talked about them. She wondered if Nephi had ever had a relationship with them or if bitter feelings had precluded any association. Alaina had nearly forgotten about the tenets of polygamy that defined the lives of her husband's family. Nephi had corrected several misconceptions she'd had about the practice, explaining that a man couldn't just decide to take another wife, but had to be called by the prophet to do so. And then only about two percent were ever called. Since its abolishment in 1890, the role plural marriage played in the lives of the Mormon Saints and their society had diminished in significance and impact.

Alaina tried to divert her worrying by thinking about Sarah and sweet little Zachary. Zachary Alma Erickson had been born early and was only now, at six weeks old, filling out his wrinkled skin. Alaina and Eleanor had secretly gone to see him long before the sequestering period was over, and Sarah had been a willing participant in the artifice. As she had lost two babies before Zachary's birth, Sarah was fretful about his constitution and eager for female companionship and reassurance. Eleanor had proven to be a soothing balm for Sarah's often-irrational concerns, evaluating coughs and stomach bubbles and skin rashes with a gentle efficiency. Alaina always smiled at the serious attention Eleanor gave to Sarah's questions, no matter how mundane, and she knew that if symptoms moved to anything of consequence Eleanor would alert Dr. Lucien immediately.

Zachary was actually a very good baby and beautiful besides. He had grown into his large brown eyes and now sported a shock of curly brown hair. Alaina admitted freely that she was captivated by the little man and tended to dominate his attention during their visits. Once Mother Erickson had joined the girls when her workload was light, and Eleanor had teased her sister that she would now have to share him since a grandmother relationship took precedence over that of an auntie-in-law.

Alaina couldn't wait for her baby to be born. She was anxious to discover if it was a boy or a girl, whom it would look like, and most especially to confirm that he or she was healthy. She couldn't imagine losing two babies as Sarah had done. It was a tragedy she pushed far from her mind, but which fostered a deep compassion for her sister-in-law.

Alaina looked up. Somehow they had arrived at Sarah and Elias's cottage, and she laid her hand on the carved door frame while Nephi reached for the handle. She tried to inhale peace from the beautifully carved flowers and vines that imbued the wood, trying to think of Grandfather Erickson's weathered hands as they lovingly fashioned the creations, trying to convince herself that some of his noncritical blood must run in his son's veins.

Nephi opened the door, and Elias turned from his wife to look at them as they entered. He smiled at his brother and ushered them into the crowded front room. "Nephi! Glad you're here. Hope you brought along your priesthood."

Nephi smiled. "I did."

Alma Erickson had stood when they entered, but Nephi looked only at Elias and Sarah. Alaina felt adrift when Nephi moved to take his sister-in-law's hand.

"Congratulations, Sarah. From what Mother reports, your son is a delight."

Sarah blushed. "Thank you, Nephi. He seems to be healthy."

Alaina came to Nephi's side and took his arm. "He's absolutely magnificent!" She hesitated. "From what I hear."

Sarah grinned at her.

"Hello, son." Alma Erickson's deep voice intruded on the congratulations, forcing Alaina and Nephi to turn in unison to greet the people who were both now standing in stiff politeness. Alma Erickson had indeed passed down much of himself to his son Elias, not in coloring, but in feature and form. His wife, Eunice Erickson, of course, did not resemble any member of the family grouping with whom she shared only a surname. In fact, Alaina could not believe the contrast between Alma Erickson's two wives. Eleanor Patience Erickson was short and round with a welcoming face and eager blue eyes, while Eunice Erickson was average height but thin and boney.

Her eyes were dark, close set, and judgmental. Alaina supposed she might be pretty if she ever softened her face into a smile.

Nephi put his arm around Alaina's waist, and they stepped forward towards the imposing couple. "Hello, Father, Eunice," he said without looking at her. "I'd like you to meet my wife, Alaina Kaye Erickson."

Alaina felt her throat constrict as she looked up into Alma Erickson's face.

Nephi continued. "Alaina, this is my father, Alma, and his wife Eunice."

Alaina smiled at both of them with as much charity as she could muster and extended her hand. The gesture was unexpected, and it took several moments for Alma Erickson to respond to the offering. He took the hand and shook it once.

"How do you do," he stated, a smile coming to his lips but not his eyes.

"Very well, thank you," Alaina answered. She felt a giddy rush of emotion as the baby moved inside her, and she shook Father Erickson's hand enthusiastically several times. "Very, very well. I'm glad we finally get the chance to meet." Her hand went to her locket. "Fathers are such important people, and I know Nephi has missed having you as part of his life." She felt Nephi's body stiffen, but the strong emotion she was feeling threw aside any caution or decorum as the words tumbled out of her mouth. "In a couple of days it will be a year since my father died, and if there was any way I could have him back for one minute . . ." Her voice caught and her eyes filled with tears. ". . . One minute . . . but I can't . . . and here you are . . . here you are well and healthy and not a part of your son's life." She brushed tears away with the back of her hand. "Anyway, if it hadn't been for the kindness and caring of your son . . . well, I don't know what I would have done. I know I'm not a member of your church, but I'm trying to be a good person and a good wife to your son, and hopefully a good mother when the baby comes." She turned to look straight into Eunice Erickson's beetle eyes. "And I hope we can lay aside differences and forgive and forget, because from what Mother Erickson's taught me, the Mormon doctrine truly does include forgiveness."

"Well said, little chicken. Well said."

Everyone had been stunned into silence and inaction by Alaina's speech, so the sound of Patience Erickson's voice at the hallway door made them start and turn in her direction. She stood there smiling and holding baby Zachary. "So, I see you have all met our lovely girl."

Alaina felt sick. The emotion that had supported her outburst was now ebbing, leaving her woozy and humiliated. *They must think me the oddest creature on the planet,* she thought woefully. *I'm sure my tirade is not going to help the relationship between Nephi and his father. What made me do that?*

Mother Erickson was standing by her now, looking up at Alma and Eunice with a bright smile. "Best close your mouth, Eunice. There's no response to that kind of honesty. Here, hold your grandson." She handed the sweet little baby over to the first wife and turned to Nephi. "Son, why don't you and Alaina take off your coats and stay awhile?" They did as they were told. "Elias," she commanded, holding out the coats to him, "take these to the bedroom." Elias, looking almost as appalled as Eunice, took the coats and exited to the bedroom. "Now," Mother Erickson said happily, "don't we have a baby to bless?"

* * *

As the cold October sun slid behind the Oquirrh Mountains, Alaina and Mother Erickson walked home together arm in arm. Nephi had stayed behind to help his father and brother carry in and assemble Elias and Sarah's new bed.

"I don't know what came over me!" Alaina groaned, pulling her hat down over her ears with her free hand. "The words just kept coming out of my mouth."

Mother Erickson chuckled. "Having a baby does a lot of things to your emotions."

"Like turning you into a fool!" Alaina growled. Then she shook her head. "I don't know, I think it's just me, because I never see Sarah behaving oddly."

"Well, Sarah is Sarah," Mother Erickson said with a wink. "Calm and shy."

"And I'm the odd, bad-tempered heathen from California. Oh, and I'm loud, too—don't forget that flaw."

Patience Erickson chuckled again and squeezed Alaina's arm. "You are a dear, and I love you."

Alaina's berating thoughts stopped immediately, and she took a deep breath of cold evening air. "I love you too." She marveled at the depth of feeling she had for this gentle woman. In their months together Alaina had discovered a mother's warmth and tenderness. But now Mother Erickson was talking, so Alaina pulled her attention to the words.

"And don't you fret about one thing that flew out of your mouth. You did a lot of housecleaning tonight—said things that needed saying for near on two years. You got Nephi and his daddy talking again, and that is no small wonder." A laugh overtook her, and she stopped to catch her breath. "Whew . . . I wish I knew how to work one of those new camera things. I would have loved to get a picture of Eunice's face."

"Mother Erickson!" Alaina choked.

But Patience Erickson's infectious laugh pulled Alaina in, and it was some time before the two women could temper their behavior.

"Oh, that's terrible of me," Mother Erickson said finally, wiping tears from her eyes. "Eunice is a . . . very efficient woman."

Now it was Alaina's turn to burst out laughing. "You were going to say 'good woman,' but you couldn't stand to tell a lie, could you?" she teased.

Mother Erickson clucked at herself. "I am not going to the good place, and that's a fact."

Alaina took her arm, and they started walking. "If there was someplace better than the good place, that's where you'd be, Patience Erickson."

Mother Erickson patted her hand. "Well, I need to try and make it where my sweet little Evelyn is so I can raise her up."

Alaina fell silent. Whenever Mother Erickson spoke of her departed child it was always with the confidence of reunion. It was a confidence Alaina envied, but could not understand. This was a piece of what Nephi called "the doctrines of eternalism," and these Mormon canons of eternity so outreached the spiritual teachings of her youth that her mind faltered in comprehension. It was easier to set the words aside and not dwell on the meaning or majesty of the concept.

"Wasn't Zachary a sweetheart today?" Alaina said to change the subject.

"Oh my, what a cute little boy," Mother Erickson agreed. "And so good during his blessing."

Alaina nodded. "I wish Eleanor could have been there, and Grandfather Erickson." She thought back to the moment of the priesthood blessing, and even though it was plain truth that she could not abide Elias Erickson, she had to admit that the blessing he'd given his son was powerful and genuine. Alaina found the man impossible to understand. How could he be secretly disdainful of her, while being openly demonstrative to the rest of his family, especially his wife and baby? Alaina had to remind herself that Elias did not consider her family, which made her fair game for his enmity—especially since he believed she eliminated his brother's chances for heaven. She shook the hurtful thoughts out of her mind and pondered again the blessing. She had to say that it was touching to watch Nephi, Elias, and their father standing together in a circle and holding little Zachary for the prayer. Alaina wondered if the men would do the same for the blessing of their baby.

Mother Erickson sighed. "I am so relieved to have your sister watching over him."

"Excuse me?" Alaina said, bringing her mind back to her mother-in-law's comment.

"I just think Eleanor is the ray of sunshine Grandfather Erickson needed. And she's very efficient. I don't worry about him for a second while he's in her care."

"I'm so glad to hear you say that," Alaina answered. "They do seem to be getting along, don't they?"

"They do indeed," Mother Erickson said with a chuckle.

There was a slight incline in the road, and Mother Erickson stopped talking to save her breath and energy. Alaina gave her more support and slowed her pace. As the road leveled, Mother Erickson again found her voice.

"Good thing I didn't have to walk here from Nauvoo," she said with a snort. "'Course I was a bit thinner as a girl."

The two women walked along in mutual affability, and Alaina felt a peace enfold her as she thought about her life with these good people. Somehow she and Eleanor would get past the anniversary of their father's death; somehow they would settle into the occupations offered them; and then perhaps somehow the vivid and painful images of meadowland and apple trees would blur and fade from memory.

Just as Alaina and Mother Erickson reached the house, they heard the hardware truck pulling up behind them. They turned to look as Alma Erickson's truck stopped and Nephi jumped out. He leaned over and said something to his father and Eunice before shutting the door.

Mother Erickson waved as the truck pulled away.

"I told you, you should have waited for a ride," Nephi laughed as he came up to them. He took Alaina's hand. "You're half frozen."

"Your father gave you a ride home?" Alaina asked, turning to watch the departing truck.

Nephi noted the look of wonder on her face. "Yep. Seems he's talking to me again. Now, Eunice is still a piece of ice, but I think it would take the Spirit in person to thaw that woman."

"Nephi," Mother Erickson said in a warning tone.

"Sorry, Mother," Nephi said, hugging her. He put his arm around Alaina. "It seems that someone's tirade gave my father quite a shock."

Alaina looked at the ground. "I'm sorry for that."

"Well, I'm not!" he barked at her. "In fact, I'm thinking that the Spirit might have given you a little inspiration. Yep. I think it's just the kick in the pants we all needed."

"That's just what I've been telling her," Mother Erickson chimed in.

Alaina tried to smile at them, but a cold gust of wind nipped at her uncovered skin, making her shiver instead.

"Here now," Nephi said, moving them to the house. "Let's get you two inside. We can talk about wonders and miracles when we're out of the cold."

"I'm for hot cocoa!" Mother Erickson announced as they reached the porch.

The vote was unanimous.

Chapter Thirty-One

"Pardonnez-moi, Madame Finn," Claudine said quietly as she entered the dim salon. "Monsieur Davis has come to see you."

Hannah Finn turned from the window to smile at the girl. "Thank you, Claudine. Please show him in."

Claudine curtsied. "Oui, madame."

"Your English is coming along," Mrs. Finn complimented.

"Thank you, madame. I work much at it."

Mrs. Finn nodded. "You do indeed."

Claudine left the room to escort Mr. Davis, while Mrs. Finn turned back to the windows and the slate gray sky lowering over the roofs of the buildings. It was the last day of 1914, and the weather seemed to echo the mood of the beleaguered country on welcoming a new year with little hope.

It was cold, and sleet had been falling off and on since early morning, making the cobbled streets slick and treacherous. There would be no going out for her today. Of course, she rarely went out these days; it was too painful to see the German soldiers everywhere, to watch them slap some poor shop owner for a suspected sneer, or hear them call out lurid words to passing girls.

She reached up to the two articles that hung by a delicate chain around her neck: one was a medallion imprinted with the images of King Albert and Queen Elisabeth; the other was the timepiece she had purchased the day she, Philomene, and Edith Cavell walked together on the promenade of the St. Hubert Gallery. She looked down to check the time and smiled. She, like every other truehearted Belgian, kept her watch set to local time in defiance of the inane edict set down by the occupiers that all clocks be set on German time. Her chest tightened as she thought again about the lovely adventures she had shared with Philomene and of all the plans now ruined. Tears pressed behind her eyes, and she fought to keep them under control. She hated that the constant strain of the occupation and the lack of food had diminished her capacity to keep her emotions in check. Worry seemed to be her constant companion, and the face of her dear niece was the image that most often floated into that mist of concern. Hannah Finn missed her kinswoman terribly and wondered how she was faring. There had been no letter since the departure, and Hannah wondered if any of her letters were getting through to Sutter Creek. Mr. Davis had made solemn assurances that he had seen Philomene safely onto the ship, and since no word had come to them of disasters at sea, Hannah figured the lack of correspondence was due to a breakdown of the postal service. Indeed many institutions in the little country were refusing to work under the Law of Siege, and Hannah Finn smiled as she thought of the stubborn resistance of the Belgian citizenry.

Claudine entered the room, followed closely by a gaunt and haggard Mr. Davis. "Monsieur Davis," she announced.

"Richard!" Hannah Finn exclaimed, moving toward him. "Oh, Richard, you look like death."

He smiled slightly. "It's nice to see you too," he answered, taking her hand.

"Here, sit down," she said, her voice a mixture of command and concern. "Claudine, some coffee please."

Claudine whimpered, "I'm sorry, madame, but we have no coffee."

"Tea then."

"And something to go with the tea," Mr. Davis said, extending a box to Claudine.

"What is it?" Hannah asked.

Claudine untied the ribbon and opened the box. "Oh!" was all she could say before tears sprang into her eyes. She handed the box to Mrs. Finn, who stared down in disbelief at the dozen hard rolls and three tins of salmon.

"How? How did you manage this, Richard?" she asked, her fingers trembling on the box.

"I have a friend."

She smiled to block the tears. "Of course. Of course you do. Claudine, please take this to the kitchen and share it equally with the staff."

"And I will bring you both some with your tea," the girl said, taking the box.

"Oh, none for me, thanks," Richard said firmly.

"You must," Hannah answered in a tone that matched his, "or I will refuse to eat any in your presence."

Richard Davis sighed. "Stubborn. All you Johnson women are stubborn."

"Yes, indeed we are," Hannah Johnson Finn returned.

"All right then," Richard relented. "Half a roll with some salmon."

Claudine curtsied. "Ah . . . madame," she said hesitantly, "may I keep this for my hair?" She held out the black, yellow, and red ribbon that had been tied around the bakery box.

Hannah Finn smiled. "Of course, my dear. Wear it proudly."

Claudine curtsied again and left the room.

"The Belgian people amaze me," Hannah announced after Claudine's departure. "The Germans ban the flag, so the merchants tie up their parcels and boxes with tricolored ribbon, which the people then make into rosettes, or the young girls tie into their hair."

Richard pressed his palms against his eyes and laid his head back. "A remarkable people." He folded his arms across his chest and stared at the ceiling. "Where is Belgium now? That is my question. Thousands of people fleeing to Holland or France, the majority of the country occupied and run by German generals, and Albert and his mighty little army holding onto one last sliver of ground in West Flanders."

His voice was rough with fatigue and sorrow, and Hannah wished she had something stiffer than tea to offer him. Perhaps quiet and sleep was what he needed most. She hadn't seen him for months, and though she was curious to find out his occupations, she sat silently looking out the window, waiting for him to continue.

Finally he looked over at her and leaned forward. "If I tell you this, you must promise to tell no one else."

"Of course, Richard," Hannah answered without offense.

"I have seen them."

"Who?"

"King Albert and Queen Elisabeth. In fact, since the fall of Antwerp and their retreat, I have met with them several times."

Aunt Hannah's face drained of what little color remained in it. "Are they well?"

"Physically they are well," he answered. "Of course they are heart-sick over the suffering of their people. King Albert is . . ." He broke off midsentence and shook his head as if memories of the monarch's anguish were too painful. "They have lodged themselves in a small villa in La Panne."

"I know the town," Aunt Hannah said. "It's on the coast."

"Yes, and only twelve miles from the front line at Nieuport."

"Front line?"

Richard stood and paced to the window. "Albert and his army have dug in along a line that reaches from Nieuport on the coast down past Ypres to the French border, and they vow not to give up one more clod of Belgian ground, but . . ." He stopped to watch the continual fall of sleet.

"But?" Hannah prompted, moving to him. "You don't think it possible."

Richard hesitated, rubbing his lower back and evaluating his response. "Ah, I don't know, Hannah . . . maybe now that the French and the Brits are with them, they might be able to hold on. One chance in a million, but I'm a betting man."

Hannah loved his American expressions and smiled in spite of her misgivings. She rubbed the monarch medallion between her fingers and thought of the beauty of the Belgian countryside now mangled by conflict, the streets of Brussels besmirched by a hostile visitor. "But, is victory possible, Richard?" she asked sincerely.

He shrugged. "As you said, Hannah, the Belgians are an amazing people."

"And you are an amazing man," she answered, looking over at him with a penetrating gaze, "who I suppose has been in the thick of things since last we spoke. Actually, from the look of you, you have been in the thick of things and then some."

He nodded. "I have, Hannah, and most of it I can tell you nothing about."

She laid her hand on his arm. "Running messages for Albert and others in the cabinet would be my guess."

Richard blew out an exasperated blast of air. "Well! You take the cake, I must say."

"Don't I wish," she said in earnest. "A cake would be lovely."

He looked at her straight on. "What made you think of me as a messenger, Hannah Finn?"

"I have been privy to government shenanigans too long not to know the way of things, Mr. Davis. You are a perfect candidate with your travel pass and credentials."

His look of consternation turned into a smile, and he took her hand and held it against his heart. "Can't keep secrets from you."

She shook her head, returning to her place on the sofa. "I wouldn't be too sure about that, Richard. I have a feeling our Edith Cavell is hiding something from me, and from everyone else."

Richard gave her a fearful look. "Really? Hiding what?"

"I don't know . . . don't know for sure. She has just been very distant of late. We were supposed to set up some of the rooms here as a clinic, but that hasn't happened."

"Well, she's been busy, Hannah. I'm sure that's why."

"Maybe, Richard, but you know I have an intuition about things, and something is not quite right."

Claudine entered with the tray filled with cups, saucers, hot tea, and the marvel of food. Hannah Finn's emotions bubbled again to the surface, and she chided herself for weakness. *Don't be a fool, Hannah Finn . . . weeping over a bit of salmon.* She set her mind to the task of hostess and pouring tea. The activity helped push back thoughts of the war and Miss Cavell, thoughts that always ended in dark foreboding.

Sometime after eleven o'clock that night when Claudine returned to the salon to clear away the tea service, she found the two friends asleep—Mrs. Finn on the sofa and Mr. Davis slumped in the over-stuffed armchair. Quietly Claudine gathered the cups, saucers, and silverware, picking up the tray and creeping silently to the door. Suddenly a loud boom made her jump, causing the dishes to rattle on the tray. Both sleepers were up instantly as Claudine tried to calm herself and keep from dropping her burden. The booming continued.

"Madame! Je regrette! Je regrette!"

"Never mind. Never mind, Claudine," Mrs. Finn said, trying to steady herself on her feet. She turned toward the window. "What in the world is that sound?"

"It is bombs!" Claudine cried.

Richard Davis moved quickly to the window and looked out onto the dark street below. The booming sound was indeed coming closer, but to his experienced ear it did not sound like cannon fire.

"It's all right, Claudine. I don't think there are bombs."

Claudine hesitantly went to stand beside him. "No bombs?"

He shook his head. "No. No bombs."

Hannah Finn joined them. "What is it then?"

Just as she reached them at the window, a rowdy group of German soldiers came marching from the side street onto the rue de la Montagne. They were banging several big bass drums and singing "Die Wacht am Rhein" at the top of their lungs.

Mr. Davis put an arm around each woman and gave each a reassuring squeeze. "Welcome to 1915," he said grimly.

* * *

Mr. Palmer raised his glass and tapped on the side of it with a spoon from the household silver. "This year has seen many changes come to the Westfield mansion, and I proudly toast the staff who has taken on every challenge with skill and aplomb."

"Whatever that means," Bib said out of the corner of his mouth, and the women laughed.

Mr. Palmer cleared his throat and gave Bib a narrow look. "It means, Mr. Randall, a job well done."

"Ah, well ya just should have said so then," Kerri put in, lifting her glass.

"I have not finished, Miss McKee," Mr. Palmer said, motioning for her to lower her glass.

Ina Bell giggled.

Mr. Palmer straightened his vest. "I would also like to toast Miss Eleanor Lund—a young woman of remarkable ability. She is not with us as the year closes, but we wish her well in 1915."

"Here! Here!" Bib responded, lifting his glass high.

"Here! Here!" the women called out strongly.

"And I would like to make a toast," Ina Bell blurted out before anyone could get the glass to his or her lips.

Mr. Palmer looked at her with interest. "Well, by all means, Miss Latham. Let's have it."

Ina Bell looked down at her shoes and cleared her throat. "To Mrs. Lund," she said, raising her glass.

Kerri McKee frowned at her. "You're toastin' the Dragon?" Ina Bell shot her a fierce look, and Kerri choked back the remainder of her critical words. "Aye . . . of course, to Mrs. Lund!" She raised her glass high. "And now for the music box and a bit of dancin'," Kerri said, setting down her empty glass. "What d'ya say, Mr. Randall? Shall I teach ya a bit of highland jig?"

The tall lad smiled and offered his hand.

As 1914 slid out of existence, the staff understair at 238 Beacon Street in San Francisco did their best to undo regrets, forgive mistakes, and cherish the good of the previous year, while welcoming the New Year with hope.

* * *

Philomene sat in the dark waiting for the New Year that seemed reluctant to come. Her mind was a hopeless tangle of thoughts as images of the previous months overlapped themselves in unending succession: the Grand' Place, Aunt Hannah's silver hair, the bakery shop, the pounding of German boots on the cobblestones, the bombs dropping. She growled at herself and forced her mind to think of William Trenton harvesting big orange Hubbard squash from her garden. The picture stayed briefly and then flickered back to smoke and fire and the thud of bombs and the blast of explosion. Her fingers clenched and unclenched on the arms of the rocking chair. She knew the town fathers would fire the cannon at midnight and that a cheer would go up from the men and women at the saloon, but she also knew the rest of Sutter Creek would be asleep or at least dozing by their coal stoves, and she envied them.

She pushed herself out of the rocker and paced the floor, pulling her shawl tightly around her and mumbling words of frustration. She was afraid, and she hated it. She turned quickly to her desk and hauled out her ink pen and stationery. She would write a letter to Aunt Hannah. She didn't know if any of her letters were getting through, but she'd write anyway. She would make up a nice, newsy letter about how well she was doing and how lovely her Christmas had been. She would fib and say she was being put immediately back to work at the school. She would ignore the cannon blast when it came. She would write and write and write until the fear retreated.

* * *

Eleanor knocked softly on Grandfather Erickson's door. She hesitated, pressing her ear against the wood, and hearing distinctly the low moaning which had brought her from her bed. She knocked again a bit louder. "Brother Erickson? May I come in?"

The moaning stopped, and finally she heard a "yah" come from inside the room. She opened the door and stepped inside, bringing the oil lamp with her. The light showed an empty room and an empty bed. Eleanor's heart jumped.

"Brother Erickson?"

"I'm here," came the feeble reply.

Eleanor moved quickly to the other side of the bed and found Grandfather Erickson on the floor, his eyes closed, and his face chalky with pain.

She set down the lamp and moved quickly to his side, kneeling down and placing her hand on his chest. "Is it your heart? Are you in pain here?" she asked, trying to keep the panic out of her question.

"No. No, my back, little one," Lars answered. He kept his eyes closed, and though his voice was a harsh whisper, Eleanor heard the words with relief. She looked over at the clock—11:15. *What was he doing out of bed at this hour?* she thought. She took a deep breath, and an assured calmness filtered into her brain and body.

"Did you get up because of the pain?"

"Yah, yah. I vas going to sit in my chair." He started to move, and a spasm of pain shot across his face.

"Lie still," she commanded gently. "Let me check for breaks, then I'll go out and get Nephi, and he can get the doctor."

All the bones she had memorized out of Uncle Cedrick's anatomy book came clearly to her mind, and deftly she moved from bones in his hands and feet to the vertebrae in his back, asking every now and then for Grandfather Erickson to acknowledge any increase of pain. She worked calmly and efficiently, speaking in soothing tones and massaging strained back muscles as she went. She watched the body relax and the pain drain out of his face. After twenty minutes of ministration Eleanor sat back, breathing deeply.

"I don't think anything is broken, so I'll go and get Nephi now." She started to stand.

"No. No. Don't leave me alone. I tink I vill be fine. Anyway it is late . . . almost midnight."

"That doesn't matter."

"No, I mean et. I feel much better. I tink I can sit up."

Eleanor was reluctant to have him do any drastic moving. She was fairly sure of her assessment, but she had no formal training or even years of experience to back up her evaluation.

"Yah, help me up. Remember I am tough pioneer."

Since he was already maneuvering onto his knees, Eleanor figured she'd better at least make sure he didn't fall again. After several minutes of struggle she was amazed to see him kneeling by his bed.

"Are you in any pain?" Eleanor asked him anxiously.

"No more dan usual," he grunted. "Look at dis!" he said, finding himself in a kneeling position. "Now dat I'm here maybe ve should have prayer."

Eleanor laughed. "You'd better pray for the strength to stand up because there's no way I can lift you."

He chuckled and used the bed as a wedge to shove himself onto his feet. "Dear Lord," he prayed as he pushed, "here I am an old Danish voodcarver, who yust needs a little of your strength to stand up."

Eleanor stood by like a mother hen watching for any sign of trembling or weakness. "How are you?" she asked, gazing at him in wonder.

"Good," he declared, standing without support. "Yah, you are good nurse."

"And you are a mountain!" she said with admiration.

He laughed as she helped him to his chair. "Yah, dat is yust vat your sister say."

Eleanor laid the plaid blanket over his lap when he was seated and gave him a withering look. "Are you sure you don't want the doctor?"

"No, little one. I am fine."

"And your pain, what about the pain that got you out ot bed?"

"Ah, vell my hands are still aching. Must be a storm coming," he said with a wink.

"Well, we know what to do for that," she said, winking back.

"Is too much trouble," Grandfather Erickson protested. "And it's too late . . . almost a new year."

"And what else have we to do?" she answered, smiling. "I can't think of a better person to celebrate with."

Grandfather Erickson looked into Eleanor's face for a long time and then nodded. She turned to the kitchen and the job of stoking the wood stove and putting on the melting pan.

Lars Erickson laid his head back and listened to the young woman's humming as she prepared the concoction for his hands. She was back in what seemed like only minutes with the metal pan of melted paraffin wax infused with slippery elm. She put a flat, stiff pillow on the plaid blanket and set the pan on top.

"So, one hand at a time or both together?" she asked.

"One at a time. My big hands fit better."

Eleanor helped lift his arm and carefully dipped one hand and then the other into the hot wax. Afterwards she wrapped each hand with a warm towel. She removed the pan from his lap and took it back to the stove to keep it warm for the next soaking. She came back with a hot water bottle to ease the stiffness in the patriarch's back.

He looked up at her gratefully as she readjusted his blanket. "I tink it is easier to cross country by vagon dan to get old," he said, closing his eyes and pressing his back against the hot water bottle.

"Would you like me to read to you?" Eleanor asked. "Maybe Shakespeare?"

A slight smile played at the corner of Grandfather Erickson's mouth. "No. Too tired for so many words. Maybe a song."

Eleanor wondered if he were serious. "You want me to sing?"

"Don't you sing?"

"In church."

"Vell, pretend dis is church." He smiled but kept his eyes closed.

Eleanor sat for a moment trying to think of a song. She knew many, but for the life of her could not think of one.

"Perhaps 'A Mighty Fortress,'" Grandfather Erickson suggested. "You know dis hymn?"

"I do," she said with a sigh.

When she began singing, her sweet, clear voice sounded to Lars Erickson like the sea spray off the ocean by his boyhood home, of sparrow song in the forest where he chopped fir trees, of his mother's prayers. Tears ran over his scruffy face as he listened to the angel voice, and he knew that without celebration or fanfare the year changed over on the sweet notes of her simple song.

Chapter Thirty-Two

Mr. Greggs looked up from readjusting the pins on his war map to acknowledge the entrance of James Lund into the post office. "Good morning, James," he said cheerily. "Grateful that the sun is finally showing its face?"

James nodded. "Yes, sir. Maybe we can start to put winter behind us."

"I'm hoping, James. I'm hoping," Mr. Greggs agreed as he moved a couple of the brown-flagged pins representing German troops slightly closer to France.

"Not much movement this winter," James remarked, watching the postmaster's careful placement.

"No, James, you're exactly right. Both sides are holed up in their trenches . . . have been all winter."

"Can't imagine that misery," James said.

Mr. Greggs slapped the morning paper on his leg. "Neither can I, son, true enough. Some of the soldier stories they put in the news-paper are grim . . . mighty grim." James followed the man as he moved back to the counter. "Those trenches have to be earth's own hell; I'll tell you that," Mr. Greggs continued. "Here we are complaining about the rain, but can you imagine standing in cold mud up to your knees?"

"Or water covering your feet for days on end?" James added. "It's a strange war to my way of thinking."

"Well, there's not much good about war of any kind," Elijah Greggs stated, looking over his map and shaking his head.

"That's true, sir—I agree. Good thing it has nothing to do with us."

"Well, I don't know if I agree with you there," Mr. Greggs said in a patient voice. "I think what happens anywhere in the world affects us all."

James was aware that a few other people, his friend Daniel for one, shared Mr. Greggs's outlook, but he couldn't understand it. To his mind it was clearly a European conflict that needed to be sorted through without the United States' interference. To be sure, James thought the Belgian people were suffering a great injustice, but since Miss Johnson's safe return from the war zone, his thoughts rarely strayed to the miseries on the other side of a very wide ocean.

"So, what can I do for you, Mr. Lund?" Mr. Greggs asked in an official tone.

"I need a stamp for this letter to Salt Lake City," James answered, placing the envelope on the counter. "I'm writing to my sisters."

"That's right! I heard tell from Miss Johnson that Eleanor is living in Salt Lake City now," Mr. Greggs said, reaching for a two-cent stamp.

"Yes, sir. She's caring for Nephi Erickson's grandfather."

"Quite brilliant, that sister of yours."

"Yes, sir."

"And Alaina?"

"She's doing well. She's due to have a baby any day."

"Is that so? Well, I'll be. I remember when you three were babies yourselves," Mr. Greggs said, shaking his head. "You know, March is the very best time for a birth."

"Why's that?" James asked.

"Because it's *my* birth month." Mr. Greggs laughed.

"Mine too," James responded. "March eighth."

"See, I told ya. Well, how about that?" Mr. Greggs chuckled. "March eighth. You know, you could have a niece or nephew born on your birthday."

"I hadn't thought about that," James said smiling.

The door to the post office opened, and Philomene Johnson stepped inside. She smiled broadly at the two men, but James could see a hesitation in her expression and dark circles under her eyes. He hated to see her with that cane and the slight limp in her step.

"Good morning, Miss Johnson!" Mr. Greggs said openly. His face showed nothing but genuine welcome, and James checked his own expression of concern.

"Good morning, Mr. Greggs," Philomene answered, moving to the counter. "Good morning, James."

"Good morning, Miss Johnson," he returned. "The sunshine bring you out?"

"That and my mail," she answered.

James watched as she consciously avoided looking at Mr. Greggs's war map. He figured it must be painful for her to think back on her frightening experiences and to know that her aunt was still surrounded by danger and degradation.

Mr. Greggs returned to the counter carrying a single piece of mail, and Miss Johnson's face lit up with hopefulness.

"I think you'll be glad to get this one," Mr. Greggs said, holding out the envelope to her.

Philomene took the letter, looked at the handwriting, and pressed the missive to her heart. "Thank you, Mr. Greggs," she said softly. She turned immediately and left the post office.

The two men watched Miss Johnson's departure through the post office window, each too stunned by the change in her person to comment.

Finally James licked the stamp, affixed it to his letter, and handed it to Mr. Greggs. "I can't imagine what she went through," he said.

Mr. Greggs shook his head. "No, son, we can't."

* * *

Philomene walked to the Methodist church cemetery, eager to share her letter with Samuel Lund. She realized it was an odd senti-ment, for she had only been a friend to him through his children. Perhaps it was because she'd always admired him as a genuine man of common sense, a man who always treated others with a great deal of respect. She glanced at the letter crushed in her hand and decided not to question her reasons for seeking solace among the dead. She would gather peacefulness at Samuel's graveside and then move on to visit with Mother and Father. She knew it was a sad comment on her condition that she was unwilling to share her emotions with anyone who could give words of comfort or offer her looks filled with pity.

She walked into the graveyard and felt quietude surround her. Leaves that littered the ground from autumn now made a carpet of soft decay that swallowed every footstep as if to help in her desire not to disturb any of the sleeping souls. The low rock wall at the edge of the cemetery had shed its coat of water in the warm March sunshine, and Philomene sat down, laying the letter on her lap and gently smoothing out the wrinkles. *Precious epistles that keep us tied together.* She stared at the ivory envelope for a long time, trying to picture Hannah Finn as she penned the words at her cherry writing desk, a cup of tea and buttered scone set to the side and the sunlight pouring in through the salon windows.

She looked up and saw that light was falling on Samuel's tombstone, bringing out the carvings in sharp relief. She rubbed her fingers along the rough stone.

"Hello, my friend," she said tiredly." I've come to bring you a bit of news and to read you a letter from my Aunt Hannah. I haven't heard from her in months, so I suppose very little mail is getting in or out of the country. I pray that to be the case and not that she is ill." Philomene tapped her cane on the stone wall and took a deep breath. "Oh, I'm tired, Samuel . . . so tired. I don't know if I'll ever be able to go back to teaching." A knot of pain tightened in her chest, and she forced her mind to another topic. "Eleanor has moved to Salt Lake City, but I'm sure I read you her last letter. Also the one from Alaina about the baby." Emotion caught in her throat. "You would have made a fine grandpa, Samuel." Tears filled her eyes. "Foolishness!" she scolded, shifting her mind again. "James is doing well. You would be proud of him. Emilio Regosi keeps him in line, and Rosa feeds him so much that it seems he's grown a foot taller in the last year."

Birdsong trilled from the nearby leafless oak, and Philomene shaded her eyes, looking up to find the singer. "So much has changed in the past year, Samuel. Things used to move slowly, but now . . ." A twinge of pain from her side made her readjust her position. She took Aunt Hannah's letter and unsealed the flap, noting the obvious reapplication of glue, which indicated the letter had been previously checked.

"Don't expect much," she said with derision. "Aunt Hannah does not write anything of substance because of the censors, but at least it means there is still paper and ink and a modicum of decency in the world. Besides which, I have learned to read between the lines for the unwritten information." She looked down at the date, February 6, 1915. *Written over a month ago,* she thought with trepidation. *So much could happen in a month.* She bent out the fold in the stationery and began reading out loud.

February 6, 1915

My dearest Philomene,

Our dear newspaper man has had a difficult time delivering the news of late, but I have every confidence in him and expect a paper on the doorstep tomorrow.

Philomene smiled. So, Mr. Richard Harding Davis was still in the country and watching over her aunt. That information brought her such great comfort that she actually felt a lifting of her spirit.

I wish I could say the same for my nurse. She has only brought my medicine twice. Of course, she is very busy taking care of so many sick people. I fear she is not watching out for her own well-being.

The worry came back into Philomene's heart as she thought of the struggles Edith Cavell must be experiencing trying to care for the sick and injured under such restrictive circumstances with limited supplies and medicines. And was there more hidden information and worry that her aunt was trying to convey? Philomene reread the paragraph but could glean nothing more except that Miss Cavell was probably sacrificing her health in her service to others.

That book of stories from Sutter Creek never arrived, so I worry that the postal clerks have mislaid it. Not to fret. I have much to occupy my time until it comes.

Philomene now knew that her aunt had not been receiving any of her letters. That knowledge would not deter her; she would just keep writing until one communiqué made its way into her auntie's hand.

Claudine sends her best wishes and says hello. And I assure you she says it very well.

Philomene set the letter down and spoke directly to Samuel. "She speaks of dear Claudine. She is the sweet servant girl who was learning to speak English." Images of her time in Brussels began to flood in, and Philomene tapped her cane roughly on the stone wall to distract her emotions. She cleared her throat and went back to reading.

Manneken Pis also says hello. He cannot wait for the day you come back to visit. Remember Psalms 23.

I love you.
Your Auntie H

Philomene folded the letter, placed it in the envelope, and put it back into her pocket. As she twisted her body to perform this final task, the deepest wound on her side sent a shock of pain through her that made her gasp. She sat panting as the pain slowly diminished. She was a strong woman, and yet the explosion in Antwerp had robbed her not only of health, but of serenity. She gritted her teeth as anguish rose like bile in her throat.

"Oh, Samuel," she whispered, laying her hand on the tombstone, "will I ever be myself again? Will my dark dreams ever go away?" She laid her head on her hand and wept. "Will the world find its way back to peace?"

Read the book.

Philomene looked up. Who had spoken to her? She glanced around the cemetery, but could see no other person. She brushed angrily at her tears, trying to make sense of the words that had come so clearly into her mind, so clearly in fact that Philomene asked out loud, "Which book?" There was no outward answer to this inquiry, but Philomene stood and put her hand on Samuel's marker, knowing exactly what book it was.

At that moment Joanna Wilton, the pastor's daughter, came around the side of the church carrying bread for the birds. She noticed Miss Johnson standing near Samuel Lund's grave and waved to her. "Hello, Miss Johnson!" Joanna called.

"Hello, Joanna!" Philomene returned. "I wonder if you would do me a favor?"

Joanna walked immediately to her former teacher. Miss Johnson rarely asked favors of anyone, and she was curious to find out the request as well as anxious to be of service.

"Yes, Miss Johnson?" she said upon reaching her. "How may I help you?"

Philomene swallowed her pride. "I would like to get home quickly, my dear, and my cane does not accommodate that wish." Joanna tried not to look uncomfortable. "I was wondering," Philomene continued, "if I could borrow the use of your arm and your company to get me home."

Joanna smiled brightly, laying down the bread and holding out her elbow. "Of course, Miss Johnson. I would love a stroll with you."

Philomene was grateful that Joanna had placed the task in the realm of companionship. She took the young woman's arm, and they began their promenade.

Joanna began talking straightaway. "I've been wanting to talk with you about Alaina and Eleanor, and what details you might know about their lives . . . I mean, I get letters from Alaina all the time, but it's nice to be able to talk to someone else about mutual acquaintances, isn't it?" Philomene smiled as her former student chattered on about this and that, grateful that the innocent conversation kept her mind from weightier subjects and darker feelings. They soon reached her precious cottage, and Philomene thanked Joanna sincerely. Her former student departed without any comment concerning her teacher's injuries or physical limitations, and Philomene concluded that Miss Wilton was quite a bit more sensitive than her flibbertigibbet behavior indicated.

Philomene moved into the sanctity of her little house and shut the door. She went to the old trunk in her bedroom and, kneeling precariously in front of it, unlocked the lock and opened the lid. The musty smell of books assailed her senses, and she smiled down at the collection of old friends. She rummaged in the trunk for several minutes before finding the book she wanted. She knew this was the book the voice in her head wanted her to read—the book her friend from the Mormon congregation in Placerville had sent her over fifteen years ago. She had read it once with purely academic interest; now she would read it for enlightenment.

She shoved herself painfully to her feet and moved into the kitchen to put on the teakettle. She felt weariness seep into her bones and apprehension into her heart. *First a cup of tea,* she thought. *A cup of tea, a nap, and then enlightenment.*

Chapter Thirty-Three

"Go! Run! Run, you silly girl!" Mother Erickson flapped her apron and laughed at Eleanor's startled face.

"Now? She's having the baby now?" she gasped.

Patience Erickson looked over at her father-in-law, who stood chuckling at her side. "Isn't that what I've been saying?" she quipped.

Lars Erickson nodded. "Yah, dat's vat I hear. Baby. Now."

Eleanor turned and bolted for the door.

"Wait!" Mother Erickson called after her as Eleanor flew out onto the porch. "Get your coat. It's cold out."

Eleanor scrambled back inside, grabbed her coat off the hook, and ran out again, stopping on the porch to throw it on. She noticed the hardware truck parked in front with Elias at the wheel. *Is he going to drive me over to the house?* Eleanor wondered. A cold anger coiled into her head, and she bit her bottom lip in frustration. She wanted to get quickly to her sister, but riding alone with Elias was not a pleasant prospect. She didn't trust herself not to confront him about the mean words to her sister. In one of the many conversations she and Alaina had shared since her arrival, her sister had finally confided the full story of what Elias had said to her, and Eleanor had found it difficult ever since to abide his presence.

"Is he driving me?" Eleanor asked quickly.

"Well, of course. You don't think I ran up here, do ya?" Mother Erickson laughed, joining her outside. "Now go! Alaina wants you by her side."

"And the doctor?" Eleanor asked, running to the truck.

"He's already there," Mother Erickson called after her.

Eleanor pulled open the door and jumped into the truck as Elias put the vehicle in gear and took off.

"Whew!" Patience Erickson sighed as she waved good-bye. "Did we ever move that quickly?"

Lars Erickson chuckled. "Yah, ven ve ver sixteen."

Patience turned quickly. "What are you doing out here?" she scolded, shooing him back into the house. "It is much too cold out here for you."

"Wait now. I am tough pioneer man," Lars grumbled.

"Yah, yah," Mother Erickson returned, "ven you ver sixteen."

* * *

Eleanor ran up onto Mother Erickson's porch taking the steps two at a time. She tamped down her exuberance as she opened the front door, being sensitive to the serious medical happenings taking place inside. She took a deep breath and moved into the front room. Hearing voices from the back bedroom she went in that direction. "Nephi?" she called. "Nephi, it's Eleanor."

The bedroom door opened, and Nephi came out to meet her. Eleanor had to stifle her reaction when she saw him, for he looked just like a little boy being asked to ride a horse for the first time, his face a mixture of wonder, delight, and fear.

Eleanor hugged him. "How is she?"

"Fine. She's fine." He nodded. "Well, I mean she's not always fine, she's in pain, but . . . oh, she'll be so glad to see you. Dr. Lucien's in there with her."

Eleanor had never seen Nephi in such a nervous condition, and she found it charming and a mark of the love he had for her sister. "Should I go in now?" she asked.

Elias came in through the front door, and Nephi's face brightened. "I'm glad you're here, brother." He turned to Eleanor. "Go on in, Eleanor. I'll be there in a minute."

Before opening the door, Eleanor glanced at the brothers as they embraced, trying to understand why Alaina had never told Nephi about Elias's harsh words.

"Elly!" Alaina exclaimed as her sister entered the room. She reached out her hand, and Eleanor went to take it. "Your competent assistant is here now," Alaina said, smiling over at Dr. Lucien.

Eleanor turned and was surprised to find the healer sitting nonchalantly in a chair, reading a newspaper. He stood for a brief moment, nodding at her. "Very nice to meet you, Miss Lund. Your sister has been going on and on about your brilliance."

"I have," Alaina confessed. "She is brilliant and humble and a very good cook."

Suddenly Alaina's grip tightened, and Eleanor winced. "Ow!"

"Oh, sorry. Sorry, Elly."

Alaina tried to break the grasp, but Eleanor held on. "It's all right, Laina. That's what I'm here for." She looked over at Dr. Lucien calmly reading his newspaper. "Is she doing well, doctor?" Eleanor asked, deliberately bringing calm into her voice.

"Excellent," Dr. Lucien answered, turning the paper to the next page. "Normal as can be. If you like, you can wipe her face with that cool cloth when the contraction subsides."

Eleanor felt a thrill of excitement. This man, this learned professional, trusted her competency. He wasn't seeing her as a young know-nothing, but as someone on whom he could rely. When Alaina's grip slackened and her breathing returned to normal, Eleanor went smartly to the basin and brought back the towel.

"You are wonderful," she complimented as she wiped Alaina's face. "I think you're queen of the county fair ten times over."

Alaina smiled. "Thanks, Elly. I'm so glad you're here."

Nephi came into the room, glancing quickly at his wife and then at Dr. Lucien. "Is it all right if I come in?"

"Of course!" Dr. Lucien said brusquely. "I'm not one of those fool doctors or midwives who think the husband should be out having a nap while their wives are in labor. They don't call it labor for nothing." Alaina and Eleanor laughed as Nephi came over and kissed Alaina on the forehead. "Besides, just look at her face—lit up like one of those lightbulbs when you came in."

Eleanor stepped away, busying herself at the washbasin and sneaking looks at the twosome. Images came to her mind of precious times together on their farm in California: of harvesting pears and apples, of Nephi playing first base in the Fourth of July baseball game, of the locket he'd given Alaina for her birthday.

"Eleanor!" Dr. Lucien's voice brought her back from her mental wanderings.

"Yes? Yes," she stammered.

"I would like you to take your sister's pulse."

"How do I do that?" she asked with interest.

Nephi stepped back as Dr. Lucien instructed Eleanor in the process. When the next contraction came she was to monitor the fluctuation. Eleanor concentrated when the time came, taking the count and relaying the information to Dr. Lucien, who marked the number on a chart.

"Good," he said. "Very good."

Eleanor didn't know if he was commenting on Alaina's condition or on her performance as a nurse, but she felt exhilarated about being involved.

"Now," Dr. Lucien said, picking up his paper, "I want Nephi to stay, and Eleanor, you go out into the front room and rest."

Eleanor was hurt. "But I'm not . . ."

Dr. Lucien cut her off. "It is a while yet before the time, and I need you rested. I will be counting on you, Miss Lund."

Eleanor brightened. "Yes, doctor." She waved to Alaina, who waved back. "I'll see you soon," she whispered, and Alaina nodded.

"Oh, and eat something!" Dr. Lucien barked.

Eleanor smiled. "Yes, doctor."

She moved out into the hallway, shutting the door behind her. When she went into the front room she found Elias asleep, his legs outstretched and his head against the back of the divan. She crept past him and into the kitchen where she looked around for something to eat. She felt funny getting into Mother Erickson's cupboards and icebox, but Dr. Lucien had given her a direct order, and she figured he must have his reasons. She finally settled on an apple, some cheese, and a piece of chocolate cake. It was only nine o'clock in the morning, but Eleanor didn't care; besides, Mother Erickson's chocolate cake was just too much temptation. She had just shoved an unladylike bite into her mouth when Elias came into the kitchen, yawning and running his fingers through his hair. He gave her a quizzical look as she tried to close her lips over the bite and chew down its volume.

"Any more apples?" he asked, going to the icebox.

She nodded.

He brought out two apples and sat down at the table across from her.

Eleanor swallowed hard and wiped her mouth with her napkin.

"Cake for breakfast?" Elias asked, a rakish smile on his lips.

"Cake anytime," Eleanor answered, looking him straight on. "Don't you think it would be tragic to die not having eaten enough cake—especially your mother's cake?" She took another bite.

Elias was quiet for a moment. "Mother says you're taking very good care of Grandfather Erickson."

Eleanor was surprised by his statement. "Well, he's an amazing man, isn't he?" she said sincerely.

Elias nodded. "He is." He watched her take another bite of cake. "Mother also tells me you two read the Book of Mormon together."

Eleanor swallowed. "Yes, and Shakespeare, and Jane Austen. What's your point?" She didn't like where this conversation was headed.

"Just a simple statement," he said. "No need to get upset."

"I'm not upset."

"I just think it's commendable that you're studying the gospel, that's all. It just shows you have respect for my grandfather, and for your own father, for that matter." Eleanor went to speak, but Elias interrupted her. "You have a bit of frosting, there." He motioned to a place on his own lip to indicate, and Eleanor quickly wiped her mouth with her napkin.

"Am I acceptable now?" she questioned.

Elias frowned. "What does that mean?"

"Well," Eleanor forged ahead, "I wouldn't want to bring any sort of embarrassment or disrespect to the family."

"We're not talking about cake here, are we?" Elias shot back.

"No," Eleanor answered, laying down her fork. "You see, Elias, Grandfather Erickson and I not only read together, but we talk about life, and the way people choose to live the gospel, and how they choose to treat one another. He's very perceptive, especially when it comes to his family. Do you think he's not aware of your feelings of contempt for Alaina?"

Elias looked shaken. "It's not contempt."

"No? Well, it certainly isn't tolerance or respect."

"Grandfather's never said anything to me," Elias replied gruffly, trying to get the upper hand.

"Because Alaina has asked him not to," Eleanor returned. "And Nephi's never caught on because, in front of the family, you're careful to mask your ill will."

"I care about my brother," he said, a bitter edge to his voice.

"And you show that by wounding his wife with cruel words and ostracism?"

"Cruel words?"

"Yes, Elias, she shared with me some of what you said to her at the ball field." Elias opened his mouth to respond, but Eleanor cut him off. "And, you know, I find it interesting that my sister respects her husband so much that she's never told him one word about that day—never mentioned a thing about what you said to her. In fact, she respects her husband so much that she's never complained about your mistreatment, or said anything that might jeopardize your brotherly relationship. She understands the bond you share."

Elias glared at her. "She has no concept of the bond we share, of the eternal bond a family should share. You say she respects my brother? How is that possible when she turns her back on his faith— the most important part of his life?" Elias's voice was filled with pathos. "He's given up salvation for her."

Eleanor stared at him, dismayed by the finality of his words. "You can't actually believe that."

"Of course I do."

"And that's why you're trying to shame my sister into joining the Church?"

Elias gave her a cold look. "You don't understand."

"Oh, yes, I do. You've taken it upon yourself to be my sister's judge, but it's not your job, Elias. It's not your job to shame my sister into joining the Church, or condemn her for her shortcomings. My sister is a wonderful person. You'd appreciate that fact if you took half a moment to get to know her instead of judging her. If we're reading the same scriptures, and I think we are, then isn't our job charity? Fear and trembling in working out our own salvation, and charity when it comes to others?" She reached out and laid her hand on his arm. It was an unexpected gesture, and Elias flinched. "You say you have so much faith in Heavenly Father. Then why not step back and let Him take care of things? Isn't that what Grandfather Erickson would counsel you?" The cold look in Elias's eyes wavered, and Eleanor felt the tightness in her chest relax. A warm feeling of compassion flowed into her. "Have faith, Elias," she said in a low voice. "Have faith that Heavenly Father knows how to soften hearts."

There was a yell of pain from the bedroom, and Eleanor was on her feet. Nephi opened the door and called out to her. "Eleanor! Dr. Lucien wants you in here, and bring the kettle from the stove."

She did as she was told, leaving Elias alone in the kitchen staring at the apple in his hand.

* * *

Hours later, Dr. Lucien laid a perfect little girl into Alaina's arms. Under the doctor's supervision, Eleanor had cut the cord and cleaned the baby, and was now staring in wonder at her older sister, unable to comprehend how she could have lived through the pain of the last two hours.

Alaina had told her once, at the train station in Martell, that they were strong women, but this was strength beyond anything she could imagine. Several times during the process Nephi had sat down on the floor in exhaustion. Eleanor smiled at him now as he kneeled by the bedside gently touching his little girl's head. He looked up and winked at her.

"You were wonderful, Eleanor," he said with a husky catch in his throat. "Thank you. Wasn't she wonderful, Dr. Lucien?"

"Indeed," the doctor answered. "Both sisters did very well in their respective roles."

Alaina smiled and kissed her baby's fingers. "Look at that perfect little hand."

"Oh, no!" Nephi said, jumping up. "I forgot to tell Elias!" He moved to the door. "He can come in, can't he?"

Alaina hesitated. "Of course, Nephi. Of course he can come in."

Eleanor shared a look with her sister, and then went back to washing her hands and cleaning up the towels.

Within moments, Elias stood at the doorway looking in at his sister-in-law and the fussing baby in her arms. "How are you?" he asked.

Alaina was surprised by the question and the lack of criticism in his voice. "I'm fine, Elias, thank you. Come in. I'm very tired, but I'm fine. Would you like to hold her?"

"Is it all right, Dr. Lucien?" Elias asked as he moved to the bed.

Dr. Lucien grunted. "Why of course, Elias. I'm sure little Zachary has taught you a thing or two about holding babies."

Alaina handed the baby up, and Elias took her carefully. Eleanor was amazed by the feeling in the room, and wondered if new babies brought a special love and peace with them. The Mormon dogma of spirits coming from the realms of heaven was manifest in that moment.

"Have you given her a name yet?" Elias asked, watching every jerky movement of his niece's arms and face.

Eleanor was surprised at herself for not thinking of this.

Nephi looked at Alaina and smiled. Then he looked at Eleanor. "In honor of my mother and other good women by the same name, we've decided to call her Katie Eleanor Erickson."

Eleanor's pent-up emotions cascaded in a torrent of tears. The sound made the baby cry, and Elias immediately handed her back to Alaina.

"Sorry. I'm sorry, Alaina," Eleanor spluttered. "You should have told me ahead of time."

"Then it wouldn't have been a surprise," Nephi chuckled, giving her a one-armed hug.

"Well," Dr. Lucien said, packing the last of his instruments, "I will stop by your grandfather's and send Patience back to you."

"Oh, I'd better go with you then," Eleanor said with regret. "I can't leave Grandfather Erickson alone."

"You stay," Elias interjected. "I'll sit with Grandfather for a time." His eyes flickered to Alaina then back to Eleanor. "I have some things to talk over with him." He turned to the doctor. "I'll send my mother back, Dr. Lucien."

"Fair enough, son," the healer said, stretching his back. "I was up last night with Irma Craig's sick girl. A good sleep would be welcomed."

Eleanor looked at Elias and wiped the tears off her face. "Thank you, Elias."

He nodded and patted Nephi on the back. "Congratulations, brother."

Nephi gave him a strong hug. "God is good to us, isn't He?"

"He is," Elias answered.

Eleanor followed the two men out onto the porch. Dr. Lucien turned to Eleanor and took her hand. "Now, young woman, I think you ought to consider the job of a healer."

Eleanor blushed. "I have thought about nursing," she answered shyly.

"All well and good," he said, dropping her hand and buttoning his coat. "But actually I think you'd make a mighty fine doctor."

Eleanor was stunned by this pronouncement. "A doctor? Is . . . is that possible?"

Dr. Lucien laughed. "We're into a new century, Miss Lund. Anything is possible!" He tipped his hat to her and continued on to his automobile.

She was so astonished by Dr. Lucien's words that she stood on the porch like a statue. Elias chuckled, and she jumped. "Oh, Elias . . . sorry . . . I was . . . it's just that . . ." She shook her head. "A doctor? Well, that was odd."

"Not really," Elias countered. "You are smart enough, you know."

She turned to look at him. "Too smart for my own good . . . and sometimes too direct with my opinions."

Elias shook his head. "No. What you said to me was necessary." He shifted his weight, trying to contain his emotion. "It's just because I love my brother."

"I know," Eleanor answered.

"I'll . . . try to make it right with her," he said in a low voice.

"I think you've already started," Eleanor said, measuring the sincerity in his eyes.

Elias nodded and walked down to his truck. He stopped halfway there and turned back with a slight grin at the corners of his mouth. "Are you sure you're only sixteen?"

"Sixteen and a half," Eleanor answered with an air of confidence.

"Ah . . . well, that accounts for it." He shook his head and moved to the truck.

Eleanor would have stayed to watch him go, but from inside the house she heard the raspy cries of baby Katie, and she turned immediately to attend to her little charge. *Dr. Lund,* she thought as she passed into the house. *Dr. Eleanor Lund.* It sounded completely impossible and completely astounding.

Chapter Thirty-Four

James Lund stood on the porch of his old home, his heart aching as he evaluated the changes: the beautiful rose-of-Sharon bush by the front porch was gone and one of the windows was still broken, but at least the glass was clean, and there were curtains in the windows.

He had knocked on the door moments before, but really did not expect an answer, as he could hear no sound of voice or movement from within. He turned to look up on the hillside of apple trees and thought he caught the flash of a red shirt. He pulled himself into Solomon's saddle and urged the horse in that direction. Daniel had informed him that a family by the name of Rosemount had moved onto the property the week before. James tried to remember if he'd seen any new faces the last time he was in town, but couldn't recall. Of course, he hadn't been to town much in the last few weeks as the coming of April brought on a flurry of activity at the ranch: several of the mares had foaled, and a buyer from Arizona was spending days evaluating breed stock.

As he neared the swath of trees on the eastern hillside, James began to hear the babble of voices—male and female, young and old. Suddenly a little sandy-haired boy emerged onto the path, causing Solomon to shy sideways.

"Hey, Papa! It is a horse. Horse and rider!" he yelled. "I told ya it was a horse. Hi! What's your name?" he asked confidently, smiling up at James.

"James Lund," James answered, smiling back. "And yours?"

"I'm Samuel Rosemund," he answered, maneuvering himself so the sun wasn't in his eyes.

James checked his emotions. "My father's name was Samuel."

The youngster nodded. "I'm four and a half, but my father says I'm a little man."

"And your last name is Rosemund?" James checked. "Not Rosemount?"

Samuel swung his arms at his side. "Nope, Rosemund. With a *d.*"

James was surprised at the brightness of the boy. He did not remember learning the alphabet until he was eight.

"Well, a visitor!" came a man's voice from behind them, and James turned in his saddle to watch his approach. The man had sandy hair like his son, but sported a mustache and a well-trimmed beard. He seemed to be in his early forties and was about James's height but more solidly built, especially in the chest and shoulders. He wore wire-rimmed glasses and an open expression. "Hello, sir!" he said happily, coming to James and extending his hand. "Name's Rosemund, Edward Rosemund. Are we neighbors?"

James took his hand. "I'm James Lund, sir. My family used to own this farm."

Mr. Rosemund shook his head and grunted. "Must have made you angry how they let the place go last year."

"Yes, sir, it did," James answered, grateful for the man's competent assessment.

Several others of the Rosemund brood were now filtering out of the orchard, causing Mr. Rosemund to turn and smile. "Ah, I figured it wouldn't be long before curiosity overcame their work ethic. Come on!" he encouraged. "It's just the former owner come to keep us on our toes."

A fair woman with braided blond hair stepped up next to Mr. Rosemund, and though she looked young, James figured she must be his wife. Next came a girl of eleven or twelve carrying a toddler, and two boys. One boy looked to be the same age as his sister Kathryn and the other only a year or two behind that. They were all dressed in simple, sturdy clothing, and James admired the sense of industry about them. The three older children all bore a strong resemblance to their mother, but James noticed they did not carry the same open, expectant expression of their brother Samuel.

"So, introductions," Mr. Rosemund said, laughing as the youngest let out with a squeal. "That is Elizabeth." James stiffened, but Mr. Rosemund went on, unaware of the painful memories the name engendered. "And you've met Samuel."

"Hey, his dad had my name!" Samuel announced.

"I know, son," Mr. Rosemund returned. He looked up at James. "We've heard from several folks in town about your father and his work on this farm. He was obviously a wonderful man, and we're sorry for your loss."

"Thank you, sir," James said, swallowing the lump in his throat.

"This is my wife, Victoria. Victoria was first married to my brother, Jonas. He died eight years ago."

James looked into the upturned face of Mrs. Rosemund. "I'm sorry for your loss, ma'am."

She nodded. "But God works in mysterious ways, Mr. Lund. As you see I've found a second Mr. Rosemund to help me on through life."

"Indeed. Her prayers turned me from a stodgy Harvard professor to farmer, husband, and father, in one short season," Mr. Rosemund responded good-naturedly.

Samuel hooted. "And nobody even needed to change their name!"

Edward Rosemund ruffled his son's hair and turned to smile at the three older children as he continued the introductions. "June, William, and Jacob are my brother and Victoria's children." He smiled at them. "And now they are mine."

James tipped his hat. "Glad to meet you," he said, knowing that he'd already forgotten half their names.

"Don't worry about keeping everyone straight," Mr. Rosemund said as though reading his mind. "I had to put name tags on the three boys until I got them figured out."

Little Samuel guffawed and slapped his hand on his knee.

The fair-haired Mrs. Rosemund looked up at James and smiled. "We want you to know how much we love this place, Mr. Lund. We had property in Grass Valley, but this place . . . well, it's a little piece of heaven, isn't it?"

"It is, ma'am," James said, looking up to the stand of pines on the hilltop.

"So where are you living now, James?" Mr. Rosemund asked.

"I work on the Regosi ranch," James said with pride.

"Ah," Edward nodded. "I've heard his name about town also. He's supposed to be the best horse handler in six counties."

"Probably the entire state," James answered.

"You must be the best too," Samuel said, dancing around in front of Solomon. "Just look at your horse."

James laughed at the boy's antics, and Solomon snorted and bobbed his head. "Seems he likes your dance, Samuel," James complimented.

Samuel's brothers teased him, and the four-year-old ran behind his mother to hide his shame. Mrs. Rosemund laughed and turned to put her arm around her son. "Would you like to stay for noon meal, Mr. Lund?" she inquired.

"Oh, no ma'am, thank you anyway. I need to get back to the ranch. I just wanted to stop by and meet you."

Edward gave him a knowing look. "I haven't been a farmer long, James, but I promise that we'll be good stewards over this land. We can tell how much you cared for it."

James nodded. "Thank you, Mr. Rosemund. My father would be pleased to hear you say that."

"And my dad's word is his bond," Samuel blurted out from behind his mother's skirts.

"A good trait, Samuel," James answered. "My father believed the same thing." He looked again at each member of the family and felt peaceful about them taking over the place. It was difficult to turn it over, and he knew he would always consider it his home, but if Mr. Blackhurst had to sell the farm to someone, James was glad it was to Edward Rosemund and his family.

As James rode back to the ranch in the warmth of the April sunshine, he was surprised to find himself thinking about his mother. He had worked hard to eliminate her from his life, yet here he was thinking about sending her a letter—sending her word about the home she had so callously thrown away. He shook his head. He would write to his sisters. He would tell them of the sale and about the Rosemunds. He would even attempt to put in all those silly details of which women were so fond. He'd include a sentence or two about the Robinson family and Miss Johnson, and sneak in a sentence of congratulations to Alaina and Nephi on their new baby,

Katie. He hadn't done that as yet, and as his niece was about a month old now, he figured it was time. As he looked around at the emerald hillsides, James wished his sisters back to Eden. Then he sighed and patted his horse's neck. "Well, Solomon, maybe Eden can be found in many places."

* * *

Elizabeth Lund sat in the parlor attempting to read a book entitled *Silas Marner,* but she was having a difficult time concentrating on the meaning; she stood up and moved to the window as a knock came to the door.

"Yes?"

The door opened and Mr. Palmer entered with a small silver tray. "The post has arrived, and there is a letter for you, Mrs. Lund."

She turned to him with a frown. "A letter? No one ever writes to me."

"Well," he said, looking down at the letter on the tray, "there seems to be a letter for you today from a family member."

She glared at him. "A family member? Who?" she demanded.

"Your daughter," he said gently.

Her hand went to her throat. "Eleanor?"

Mr. Palmer took the envelope off the tray and held it out to her. "The name on it says Mrs. Nephi Erickson."

Elizabeth Lund stood frozen in place, her voice suspended in disbelief.

After several moments, Mr. Palmer realized that she was not going to take the correspondence from him, so he walked slowly to the marble-topped side table and laid the letter down. "I'll just leave it there for you, ma'am. Is there anything else you desire?"

Mrs. Lund shook her head, and Mr. Palmer left the room. Long after he'd gone, Elizabeth Lund stood at the window distracting herself with the comings and goings of people and automobiles on Beacon Street. Finally she turned, walked to the table, and picked up the letter. She stared down at her daughter's penmanship, wondering if she'd ever seen it before. She thought back to Alaina's school reports and notes to Eleanor, but those were in a child's hand . . . a child's hand. Elizabeth clenched her teeth against the demons of anguish that thumped inside her mind. She ripped open the envelope, causing a jagged tear, and drew out the letter.

There were two pages of paper, but the message on the first page was very short. Elizabeth sat down and forced herself to concentrate on the words.

April 2, 1915

Dear Mother,

Eleanor and I are well. My husband is a good man whose heart is filled with kindness and whose hands are calloused with labor. With heart and hand he drew this picture of our daughter, Katie, and asked me to send it to you. She is now a month.

Alaina

Elizabeth Lund kept reading the words over and over, unwilling to succumb to the temptation of moving to the next page. She knew she was afraid, afraid beyond reason of being confronted with a picture of her granddaughter.

She dropped the first page and looked down on the simple ink drawing. At first she thought her mind was playing tricks on her, for she was seeing the face of her own baby, seeing Alaina's angelic face, but that was impossible. Beneath the simple ink drawing the artist had written *Katie Eleanor Erickson.*

Elizabeth Lund ran her finger along each lovingly drawn letter, then up to the lines that created the chin, nose, and ear of the charming child. She stood abruptly and walked the length of the room. She picked up the mantel clock and threw it against the wall. She grabbed a crystal candlestick and threw it onto the fireplace hearth. As the parlor door opened, she threw a heavy bronze figurine into the gilt-edged mirror, shattering it into slivers.

"Elizabeth!" Ida's high, shrill voice pierced the mayhem. "Sister! What are you doing?"

A glass parrot crashed against the wall.

Mrs. Westfield turned and fled down the hallway. "Help! Help, Palmer! Help!"

Kerri McKee and Ina Bell Latham ran past her and into the parlor. They stopped abruptly as they saw Mrs. Lund pick up the fireplace iron and smash the flower vase to pieces. The girls stared as yellow mums and water cascaded to the floor.

Ina Bell crossed herself and raced forward to grab Mrs. Lund's arm.

"Ina Bell, no!" Kerri cried. "She's gone mad! She'll crown ya for sure!"

"Help me!" Ina Bell yelled to her friend. "Get the iron!"

Kerri obeyed without thinking, grasping the thrashing weapon and wrenching it out of Mrs. Lund's hand. The woman went limp in Ina Bell's arms and fell weeping to the floor.

The servant girls heard Mrs. Westfield's hysterical voice coming down the hall. "She's smashing everything . . . everything, Palmer!"

Mrs. Westfield and Mr. Palmer appeared simultaneously at the parlor door, gazing in shock at the scene of destruction.

"Oh . . . oh," Mrs. Westfield whimpered. "I think I'm going to be ill, Palmer."

Mr. Palmer shot his mistress a scornful look, but immediately put an arm around to support her. "Here, madam, I'll take you to your room and call for the doctor. Is Miss Kathryn still out with her nanny?"

Kerri nodded. "She is, sir."

"Good. Miss McKee, Miss Latham, can you handle things here for a time?"

"Yes, Mr. Palmer," Ina Bell answered. "I think the storm has passed."

Mr. Palmer moved Mrs. Westfield toward the stairway as Kerri closed the door. She turned back into the room and shook her head at the mess. She noticed the pages of Alaina's letter scattered among the wreckage and moved to pick them up. She began silently reading.

"Don't read that!" Ina Bell hissed. "That's personal."

"How are we going to handle things if we don't know what set her off?" Kerri shot back. She finished reading the short note and looked at the picture. She handed the papers down to Ina Bell, who sat protectively by Mrs. Lund. The woman had her head in her hands and was rocking back and forth. Ina Bell put her hand on her arm, and the rocking stopped.

"It's all right, Mrs. Lund, there's someone here with you," Ina Bell assured. As she read the note and studied the picture, Mrs. Lund's hands came away from her face, and she stared at the girls. "I'm sorry, ma'am," Ina Bell said immediately, holding out the letter to her. "These are yours. I shouldn't be looking at them."

Mrs. Lund laughed a dreadful laugh which sent a chill down Ina Bell's spine. "Shouldn't?" the woman growled. "Shouldn't? Who am I to say shouldn't?"

Ina Bell and Kerri exchanged a look.

"Please don't talk like that," Ina Bell pleaded. "You've just had a rough time of it."

Mrs. Lund shook her head and glared at the girl. "You don't understand. I've brought myself low."

"No, ma'am," Ina Bell disagreed. "You have a sickness . . . a sickness that makes it difficult for you to do certain things."

Elizabeth Lund laughed again. "Like loving my children?"

"Perhaps so," Ina Bell stated flatly.

"Land of Perdition!" Kerri gasped. "Don't be tellin' her that."

"No, I mean it," Ina Bell persisted, looking at Mrs. Lund straight on. "I mean it. I think it's harder for you. You've dealt with it the best you could." She hesitated and then continued, "And you loved your husband."

Mrs. Lund's face was ashen. "Yes . . . I did. He was my salvation." Tears rolled from her eyes. "And he told me to love them more . . . to love my children more . . . and I didn't . . . couldn't."

Ina Bell held out the picture of the angelic little baby. "There's still time," she whispered. "Why do you think they sent this to you? They're telling you there's still time."

Elizabeth Lund reached out and took the picture, but did not look at it.

Mr. Palmer opened the door and was relieved to find Mrs. Lund calm. He moved to the threesome and offered his hand to her. "May I help you, madam?"

"Yes, Palmer, thank you." She took his hand, and he lifted her up. Not a word was spoken about the tirade or the destruction, and though Kerri well understood the etiquette, she found it odd. The proper distance between mistress and servant had been reestablished, yet Kerri was sure that given a choice, Mrs. Lund would have preferred to stay and talk with Ina Bell, attempting to vanquish or at least subdue some of her demons with the help of the young girl's innocent encouragement.

"Ina Bell," Mr. Palmer said briskly, "please go down and tell Mrs. Todd, strong hot tea."

Ina Bell stood. "Yes, Mr. Palmer."

"And Kerri," he added as he guided Mrs. Lund to the doorway, "you will begin cleaning."

They moved out into the foyer and Kerri grumbled, "Start cleaning, is it? Well now, why doesn't that surprise me?"

"Kerri McKee!" Ina Bell whispered, crossing herself.

"Don't ya be prayin' for me, Ina Bell Latham, for I'll have none of it."

"You're just lucky to have a friend like me, Miss McKee, who will keep trying, no matter what a heathen you are." She turned to leave the room.

"Heathen am I? And where are you goin'?" Kerri asked, following her to the door.

"To the kitchen," Ina Bell answered haughtily, "to do as I've been told."

"Well, I have to go to the kitchen too," Kerri said, following Ina Bell into the hallway.

"What for?" Ina Bell snipped.

"To gather all the things for cleanin' up," Kerri snipped back. "And don't be takin' that tone with me, Miss Latham."

The sound of the girls' harmless banter faded as they moved understair, allowing the house on Beacon Street to regain the facade of peace and propriety.

Chapter Thirty-Five

Mr. Palmer walked into the servants' hall carrying the morning post. For a time, he watched Mrs. Todd dressing the crown roast in preparation for the oven, savoring the quiet momentary respite in his workday. "Where are the others?" he asked at last.

Mrs. Todd looked up in surprise, never having had this question posed to her before. "Well, sir, I . . . I believe the girls are in the drawing room hanging draperies, and Mr. Randall is . . ." She chuckled. "Is coming in the back door!"

Mr. Palmer turned to him. "Mr. Randall, I'm shocked at your appearance."

Bib gave him a crooked smile and held up his grease-covered hands. "I've done a jim-dandy job on that gasket, Mr. Palmer. The auto should run like a clock now."

"Ah!" Mrs. Todd warned as he moved towards the dish sink for a washing up. "The utility sink if you please, Mr. Randall."

Bib grinned at her. "Only teasing, Mrs. Todd."

Mr. Palmer laid the post on the table. "You two stay here," he said. "I'm going to get the girls." He left the two servants watching after him with wonder.

"Stay here?" Bib said, giving Mrs. Todd a questioning look. "Where did he think we were going?"

Mrs. Todd chuckled.

"Any idea what he's up to?" Bib continued, drying his hands on the hand cloth.

"I don't," Mrs. Todd said, going back to her food preparation. "Perhaps someone needs a good talking to." She narrowed her eyes at the younger servant. "So what have you done, Mr. Randall, to warrant a scolding?"

Bib's eyes widened. "I'm innocent, Mrs. Todd! Trust me!"

"Enough of that," she said, picking up a wooden spoon. "Just because you're the son of a preacher doesn't mean I have to fall for all your malarkey."

"I'd never give you malarkey!" Bib answered, looking shocked.

They quieted their banter as they heard footfalls on the stairs. Mr. Palmer returned with Ina Bell and Kerri in tow. As they entered the kitchen, he directed them all to take seats at the table. Kerri gave Bib a questioning look, but he just shrugged his shoulders. On this occasion he was not privy to any inside information.

Mr. Palmer cleared his throat and picked up one of the letters from the post. "There is a strange envelope here which conveniently has this address, but inconveniently is addressed to all of us." Kerri broke into a smile and started to speak, but Mr. Palmer held up a warning finger. "Ah, so you think you've solved the mystery, Miss McKee?"

"Aye, Mr. Palmer, to be sure. I'm thinkin' it's a letter from Eleanor Lund in Salt Lake City."

Mr. Palmer looked down to the envelope as if discovering the return address for the first time. "Well, what do you know? I believe you're correct, Miss McKee." He handed the letter to Bib. "Mr. Randall, would you do the honors?"

Bib smiled. "Love to, Mr. Palmer! I washed my hands and everything." He took the envelope and opened it, noting the eager looks on the faces of Kerri and Ina Bell. He unfolded the paper slowly.

"Bib Randall!" Kerri barked. "If you're not about openin' that letter in two seconds, I'll be usin' the broom on ya."

Bib laughed. "All right, calm down. You're such an impatient lot." He cleared his throat in imitation of Mr. Palmer.

May 9, 1915

Dear Mr. Palmer, Mrs. Todd, Mr. Randall, Miss McKee, and Miss Latham,

I write to all of you together because I miss you as one. So often during my days here my mind will recall images of Kerri and Ina

Bell in their caps, or Mrs. Todd stirring something on the stove, or Bib reading us Spark the Wonder Dog.

Mr. Palmer furrowed his brow at this announcement and cast a doubtful look at Miss McKee. She glanced over at him, gave a crooked little smile, and returned to listening to Mr. Randall.

I miss Mr. Palmer's calm efficiency and the sounds of voices from understair. I know you were not aware of how comforting that sound was to me. When we first arrived at 238 Beacon Street my heart was ice. It held so much grief over the death of my father and loss of my brother and sister that it was painful even to breathe. One night I could not sleep, and I crept down and sat at the top of the stair landing and listened to the babble of voices. It was the voice of family, and though it might seem strange to you, it gave me hope.

Ina Bell sniffed, and Mrs. Todd handed her a handkerchief.

I don't wish to be maudlin, but . . .

"What's *maudlin?*" Kerri interrupted.
"It means overly sentimental," Mr. Palmer said, casting a buck-up look to Ina Bell.
"Sorry, Mr. Palmer," the girl sniffed. "I can't help it."
"*Maudlin.* Now there's a word!" Kerri said with admiration. "She's brilliant, that Eleanor Lund, isn't she, Mr. Palmer?"
"Indeed," Mr. Palmer said, nodding.
Bib rattled the papers. "Would anyone mind if I continued?"
"Not at all," Mr. Palmer said officiously. "Carry on, Mr. Randall."

I don't wish to be maudlin, but you were my family for the months I was in my aunt's home . . .

Bib's voice became thick with emotion.

. . . and I will forever be grateful for your kindness.

The room was silent except for Ina Bell's sniffing.

"Here now!" Kerri chided. "Don't everyone go gettin' maudlin. Come on, Mr. Randall, buck up, or we'll be havin' to put bloomers on ya." Bib straightened his shoulders, and Kerri gave him a brisk nod of approval. "On we go then!"

Bib shook his head at the girl and continued reading.

Please say hello to Mr. Glassey and Roxann for me, and let them know I'm reading from my father's Book of Mormon and attending church with Mother Erickson and Nephi. Remind Mr. Glassey to be guided by the eighty-ninth section of the Doctrine and Covenants. He'll know what I mean.

My sister Alaina has had her baby, a sweet little girl whom they have named Katie Eleanor Erickson. She was born on March sixth, just two days before my brother James's birthday. I feel so honored that she shares my name, and I pray I can be a good aunt to her. Katie is a very good baby, and Alaina and Nephi adore their little one as do the rest of us!

Ina Bell and Kerri shared looks of sorrow as they remembered Mrs. Lund's adverse reaction to the letter about her granddaughter.

Dr. Lucien actually let me help with the birth! He thinks I would do well as a doctor. Not as a nurse, but a doctor! I find it a far-fetched notion, but it has made me consider the people I could help if I were to pursue that occupation. Indeed my heart returns often to those innocent little girls in Chinatown and the help I could have given them had I been skilled. I would love to know how they're doing. If there's any way to get word to me of their condition, it would be greatly appreciated.

Mr. Palmer held up his hand for Mr. Randall to stop reading, and turned to Kerri. "Miss McKee, I believe that would be an appropriate assignment for you, would it not?"

"Wot? Sneak down to the Civic League to dig up information? 'Twould be grand. I'd love it."

Mr. Palmer nodded and motioned for Mr. Randall to continue.

I'm sure the news of the sinking of the Lusitania *has reached you.*

Bib stopped reading, gritting his teeth against the anguish that invaded his body whenever he thought about the gruesome loss of innocent lives. He looked over at Mr. Palmer, who gave him a look of understanding and encouragement. Bib lowered his head and went on.

The Mormon people know well the tenets of injustice and brutality, but knowing only intensifies the empathy. There is a great mourning here, and we wonder what the world is coming to. The Mormon prophet called for love and brotherhood in April Church conference, but he also spoke of an ancient general from the Book of Mormon named Moroni. He was a holy man who served God, but who also honored the call to defend his people when war was forced on him. It is difficult when men of peace must become men of righteous indignation. I often wonder where the years will take us, and if the world will ever know anything but strife and sorrow.

But enough of that. I will leave it alone for brighter topics. I love taking care of Grandfather Erickson. I love cooking for him and cleaning his beautiful little home and helping ease his discomfort. He is the most amazing person I've ever met, leaving behind Denmark and coming across an ocean and a country for his faith. I will have to share with you some of his wagon-train adventures.

We still have bouts of cold rain in the valley and snow flurries in the mountains, but winter has lost its bite. The weather grows warmer every day, melting the snow off the foothills and greening the grass. Soon I will be out in the dirt planting a vegetable garden.

Kerri and Ina Bell both laughed. "Well, she finally has her heart's desire to work," Ina Bell said fondly.

Bib nodded. "Ah, here's a bit for you Mr. Palmer."

Dear Mr. Palmer, thank you for keeping watchful care of my mother and Aunt Ida. Would you please alert me if there are worrisome changes in their situations, and please tell Kathryn that her sisters are well and we wish the best for her prudent upbringing.

Kerri snorted. "Aye, that's a way of sayin' we hope you're not being pampered to death."

A bell clanged on the call-board, causing all the servants to come to attention. Mr. Palmer stood and motioned everyone to sit down. "I will see to it," he said calmly, "but first we will finish the letter. Mr. Randall, if you please."

Life goes on well here and I am truly happy. I miss all of you and imagine fondly a time when I will stand on the front porch of that elegant Victorian house and ring the doorbell for a visit. (Actually I think it would be heaven to march in through the back door and right into your lives again.)

Until that time we will stay tied to one another through letters. Stay well. I think of you with great . . .

The bell rang again.

. . . fondness,
Eleanor

"That was a nice letter," Bib said, placing it back into the envelope. Kerri nodded, and Ina Bell wiped a tear from her cheek.

Mr. Palmer took a deep breath and let it out slowly. "So, she's doing well in Salt Lake City. Good. That's good." He turned to the girls. "Miss McKee, Miss Latham, back to your draperies; Mr. Randall, the coal buckets; and Mrs. Todd, you may return to that superb sauce." He took the letter from Mr. Randall, placed it in his pocket, and went to answer Mrs. Westfield's persistent demands.

Chapter Thirty-Six

Philomene Johnson was counting on her fingers how long she'd been home from Belgium. *September to October, October to November, November to . . .*

"What ya doin', Miss Johnson?" William Trenton asked, looking up from tilling the garden. His teacher's recent odd behavior unnerved him, so he always tried to intrude on it quickly. This time she had stopped working and was standing with her foot on the shovel, poking out her fingers one by one and mumbling to herself.

Philomene looked over at the boy and changed her expression. "What? Oh, nothing." She began digging again. "Just calculating how long I've been home."

"Eight months," William answered without hesitation.

"Eight months? Truly?" Miss Johnson tried to relax her face, but her heart was beating rapidly and her mind was racing. *Eight months? How is that possible? What have I been doing with my life?* "What day is it?" she asked sharply.

The boy took a breath. "It's Saturday, Miss Johnson."

"What date?" she corrected.

"The fifteenth. May fifteenth."

"May fifteenth," she repeated.

"Ah, Miss Johnson . . ."

"Yes?"

William bit his lip. "You're not tilling, you're digging a hole."

Philomene stopped working and glared down at the dirt mound at her feet. "Sorry, William. Sorry. Since I don't have teaching and I don't read the paper anymore, it's hard to keep track of time."

William Trenton flinched at this pronouncement.

"Good morning!" someone called from the front gate.

Philomene straightened. "Good morning, Mr. Greggs. We're in the vegetable garden."

The lanky postmaster ambled his way to them, and William was glad for the company.

"Hello, Mr. Trenton," Mr. Greggs said as he spied the boy. "You two are getting a late start on planting."

"Yes, sir," William answered, "but not too late. Miss Johnson's gonna have a great garden this year."

Mr. Greggs winked at him. "Right you are, Mr. Trenton. Always look on the bright side." He turned to Philomene. "Good morning, Miss Johnson. Quite a day."

"Quite a day, Mr. Greggs, to bring you out of the post office."

"Post office is closed today." He smiled and reached in his pocket. "But I'm still here on official business. You haven't been to the post office for almost a week, and there's been a letter for you." He handed it to her.

She reached out to take it, then stopped. "Is it from my aunt?"

"I believe it is," Mr. Greggs said cautiously, noting the look of apprehension on her face. "Are you all right, Philomene?"

She took the letter. "Yes. Yes, of course. Why don't you join us for the noon meal, Mr. Greggs? I'll just read my letter, then I'll fix the three of us a picnic out here in the garden."

"I'd be delighted to break bread with you!" Mr. Greggs answered, taking the shovel from her. "I'll even work for my food."

As the two men tilled, Philomene went to her bench under the blossoming plum tree and opened her letter from Aunt Hannah. Before reading a word, she frowned at the frail penmanship and the lack of a date. Not like her aunt at all.

Dearest,

I know not whether this letter will reach you. Our dear Richard says he will use every means to sneak it out to you. If you are reading these words then he has been successful. One part of me wishes the message to get through so you will not have to discover the news in a paper. The other part wishes desperately that you could be spared such sorrow.

Philomene could hear her own ragged breathing.

Edith Cavell is dead. She was taken prisoner by the Germans and shot.

Philomene's hands went numb, and she wondered how she was holding onto the paper or why she was still reading.

For many months our dear friend had been protecting and smuggling out allied soldiers trapped behind enemy lines. Richard said she has helped over two hundred men escape to Holland. None of us knew, not even her nurses. Please, please be brave, dear one. Please hold on to hope during this time of insanity. The Great War may rage for reasons of greed and evil, but there is still goodness in the world. There is still beauty and goodness. Edith was good.

Philomene clamped her teeth together to keep herself from screaming.

An English chaplain by the name of Stirling Gahan was given permission to visit her the night before she died. Richard spoke with him immediately after the execution and brought me word.

Philomene wondered how her aunt found the strength to transfer this scene of grief onto paper.

Together, she and Stirling said the words to "Abide with Me," and Edith received the sacrament. Richard wrote down the last thing she said to the chaplain—"I expected my sentence and I believe it was just. Standing as I do in view of God and eternity, I realize that patriotism is not enough. I must have no hatred or bitterness towards anyone."

Here the penmanship failed, and Philomene had to squint to read the words.

*Richard said when they took her out into the yard . . . she forgave
her executioners.*

Philomene gripped the pages so tightly her knuckles went white.

*When I went with Dr. Depage to clean out her rooms, I found
something with your name on it. I send it along to you.*

*Remember her with joy, dear niece. She would not
want us to grieve her life. Remember where she turned for
strength at the last.*

I do the same.

Your loving aunt

Philomene unfolded the second piece of paper and opened it to
find one of Edith's watercolor paintings. It showed two young blue-
birds sitting on a blossoming branch, ruffling their feathers.

Philomene went down on her knees, crushing morning glories
and hyacinth, dropping Aunt Hannah's letter into the dirt. Her mind
searched frantically for reason and relief. *Trust in the Lord with all
thine heart . . . I, Nephi, having been born of goodly parents . . . yea,
though I walk through the valley of the shadow of death, I will fear no
evil: for thou art with me . . . thou art with me . . .*

Mr. Greggs was speaking into her ear, and someone was holding
her hand. "There now. There now. We're right here. We're right here
beside you."

Someone patted her arm. "Don't cry. Don't cry, Miss Johnson,"
came William Trenton's voice.

Her mind clamped itself around the innocent appeal. Here was
sanity and redemption—the tender voice calling her back to herself
and to a semblance of peace. She breathed air into her lungs and
opened her eyes onto the ruined flowerbed. She willed herself to stop
crying. Gently she pulled her hand away from Mr. Greggs and wiped
her eyes on the sleeve of her blouse.

"Are you better now, Miss Johnson?" William asked quietly.

She turned to him. "I am, William." Then she said honestly, "I will try to be."

"It must have been awful bad news," he ventured.

"William, that's not our business," Mr. Greggs said kindly.

"No, it's all right, Elijah. I want to talk about it. I've been keeping my pain to myself for too long." She went to stand, and the men helped her. She brushed the dirt from her skirt and picked up her letter. "Sit here in the sunshine with me, and I will tell you about my remarkable friend and about her death."

As she poured out the words and images of Belgium, sharing the anguish and terror, she felt her spirit shed darkness. She felt her heart brave the possibility of hope and her mind the possibility of occupation. The world was truly an unhallowed place at the moment, but God was still manifest in the life of her garden and in the wonder that blossomed on every branch of her plum tree.

Chapter Thirty-Seven

July 24, 1913

Today was my birthday and I turned 49. There wasn't much fuss made and that suited me fine. The day was bright and fair with enough work for six men. Thank heavens for Nephi Erickson. He can do the work of four men, which means I only have to do the work of two. Now if Fancy were out here with us I'd only have to do my work.

Alaina looked up from her father's journal and pressed her lips together to stop the emotion. *Fancy.* It was hard to see her father's pet name for her written down in letters. She set the rocking chair moving back and forth, back and forth, and kissed the top of her daughter's head. "I wonder if your father is going to give you a nick-name, Miss Katie." The sleeping baby gave an angelic smile, and Alaina chuckled at the coincidence. She looked around the quiet living room, feeling guilty that she wasn't in the kitchen helping Mother Erickson and Nephi with supper, but they both insisted she spend time with her daughter, and she wasn't prone to argue with them. She looked back to the green book in her hand. She loved this book. Nephi had been right when he said she should read it. Every page was precious correspondence, and over the months of gleaning Father's words she had drawn him near, gaining insight into his strength and character while examining traits within herself that were similar and singular. She made a slight shift in Katie's placement, lifted the book closer to her face, and read on.

*Mr. Erickson is a remarkable man—quiet yet self-confident.
Since his arrival he hasn't talked much about his past, but I
figure each man is entitled to his privacy. Even without knowing
much about him, I have been intrigued with his peaceful character. Today I received an inkling about that. He'd sent off to Salt
Lake City for a Book of Mormon, and he gave it to me this afternoon for my birthday.*

Alaina remembered that day well. She had been angry with their
farmhand for giving Father the devil book, and angry with Father for
accepting it. She focused back on the words to block her remorse.

*More than that, he told me how he felt about the book and about
the "gospel," as he calls it. He said it was a message of hope in a
dark world.*

Alaina closed her eyes and laid her head against the back of the
chair. Every day the newspapers reported a dark world brewing on a
distant shore, and Alaina shuddered to think that the tendrils of
gloom might spread to engulf the ones she loved. She thought of her
friend Joanna Wilton, of Miss Johnson, of her brother, James, of
Eleanor, of Katie, and of her dear Nephi. An intense ache pressed at
the back of her throat. Where *did* one find peace in a turbulent
world? Was it any wonder that her gentle father would have been
intrigued by Nephi's testimony?

*He said it was a message of hope in a dark world. It was a simple
powerful declaration, and I can still sense that power stirring up my
feelings. Could this be the answer I've been searching for all my life?*

Her father's words spoke to her beyond the separation of death. Tears
welled up in Alaina's eyes, and she whimpered in self-recrimination. Katie
snuggled into a new position as Alaina closed the journal and wiped the
tears away with the back of her hand. She was angry with herself. How
long was her stubborn pride going to keep her from investigating the
Mormon Church? How often had she heard her father say, "There's no
harm in listening, Fancy, only in a closed mind." Even sweet Eleanor

had reprimanded her for her stubborn spitefulness. Alaina looked down at her sleeping baby. She owed her at least a mother who knew something about her father's religion. Couldn't she moderate her anger and pride for the people she loved? She set the journal on the side table, leaned forward, and opened the table drawer.

Mother Erickson stepped to the doorway of the kitchen to see if the baby had fallen asleep and if Alaina could come to supper. Instead of interrupting the scene before her, she turned and whispered quietly to Nephi, "Have your been praying every day, son?"

Nephi lifted the lamb roast out of the oven and set it down on top of the stove. "Yes," he answered, giving his mother a skeptical look. "Is this one of your Primary questions?"

She ignored his teasing. "Praying for your glorious little baby and your good wife?"

Nephi transferred the roast to the platter. "What are you up to?"

"Answer your mother," Patience Erickson said with a grin.

"Yes, Mother," he said, coming to stand beside her. "I pray for my family every day."

The jolly woman put her finger to her lips and pointed towards the front room. "Well, then, isn't that sight a bit of answered prayer?" she whispered, giving a nod in Alaina's direction.

Nephi saw the wife he cherished and the child he adored. "It is indeed, heaven on earth."

Mother Erickson waited for him to comprehend the full picture. She smiled as she watched puzzlement come into her son's face.

"Is that the Book of Mormon she's reading?" he whispered.

"It is, son. It surely is."

Nephi backed into the kitchen, his eyes filling with tears. Suddenly he grabbed his mother's hand and spun her around. She let out a whoop, which caused Katie to squawk.

"Stop that now!" Mother Erickson scolded in a whisper. "You're gonna wake that baby!" She shoved him towards the back door.

The revelers stumbled out into the evening twilight filled with the delight of expectation and rewarded faith. The setting sun lingered over the Oquirrh Mountains, sending shafts of light across the valley and illuminating Nephi Erickson and his mother as they danced a joyous dance in the spring-drenched pasture.

HISTORICAL NOTE

Richard Harding Davis and Edith Cavell were actual figures of the Great War Era, as represented. I utilized many journalistic essays of Mr. Davis and other newsmen of the day to flesh out the historical references.

For the story's timeline, I wrote the execution of Edith Cavell occurring in the spring of 1915, whereas the actual incident took place October 12, 1915.